The drip of rain water from the tree branches could be heard as utter silence reigned. Somewhere in the hills a man coughed and a horse whinnied and stamped. Then a trigger lock clicked, and more than five hundred men took firmer grasps on their weapons.

C-c-r-a-a-a-c-k! A rifle spoke out in the silence, and there was immediate bedlam. No one could tell which side had fired, and no one waited to find out. Deadly pellets of lead began to fly between the two forces.

Dry, pungent puffs of burned powder rose in the air, then settled back on the leaves of the sycamores. The battle was on in earnest, and further parley was impossible. A series of heavy flashes burst from a position near the creek, and four small Carolina cannon barked in unison. Major Elholm needed no added invitation to fight, and his three-inch gun sent a red-hot ball crashing through the stout timbers of the Tipton house.

Other titles in the Ace Hall of Fame series:

A HALL OF FAME *Historical* Novel ™

THE CUMBERLAND RIFLES

by
Noel B. Gerson

ace books
A Division of Charter Communications Inc.
A GROSSET & DUNLAP COMPANY
360 Park Avenue South
New York, New York 10010

THE CUMBERLAND RIFLES

An ACE Book

Produced by Lyle Engel

Published by arrangement with
Hall of Fame Romantic-Historical Novels, Inc.

2 4 6 8 0 9 7 5 3 1
Manufactured in the United States of America

For Cynthia

Foreword

While Tennesseans are familiar with the unique history of their state in its earliest days, during the years following the Revolutionary War and prior to the adoption of the Constitution, the majority of us have never known the curious background and development of what was once the self-styled fourteenth state of the Union, a state unrecognized by her sisters, the "lost state" known as Franklin.

Franklin possessed a governor and executive department, a two-house legislature, courts, law-enforcement agencies, a private army, and even boasted a special department that spasmodically minted money. Twenty thousand marriages were solemnized within her borders and were given her official blessings, and tens of thousands of citizens received land grants within her domain. Opposition to her membership in the Confederation of the United States of America was sparked by North Carolina, which had long claimed the region as her own. Under the weak and ineffectual Articles of Confederation, North Carolina was able, time after time, to veto the status of full statehood that the Franks so earnestly sought. Only the adoption of the Constitution and the pressure on her neighbor caused by mutual dangers and disturbances at last permitted the state to receive her proper due, and then she took a different name.

FOREWORD

The men of Franklin were a turbulent, restless people living in an age of upheaval and never-ending conflict. John Sevier, sole governor of the state, went on to become the first citizen of Tennessee. Andrew Jackson, Tennessee's foremost statesman-President-soldier, came into his maturity in Franklin.

That revered elder statesman, Benjamin Franklin, who inspired the state's first name, played a strange role in her history. With all his heart he wished the Franks well but cannily and carefully withheld his approval of what they were doing for fear of offending the North Carolinians. Men on both sides of the mountain border were grieved that he did not live to see the hatchet buried when, some thirteen years after the inception of Franklin, North Carolina enthusiastically sponsored the admission of Tennessee into the Union.

I have found it next to impossible to include in a single volume of fiction more than the sketchiest outline of the complications that plagued the existence of Franklin. I have tried, however, to give some idea of living conditions there, of the character and temper and casual, incredible courage of the young men and women who blazed trails and created a civilization where only a few short years before there had been nothing but an opulent wilderness.

So many novels could be written about Franklin: the heroic efforts of Colonel James Robertson, who hacked a path through the forests and founded Nashville, would make one; the work of the men who built the city of Memphis on the site of the Indian village of Chickasaw Bluffs might become the core for another; and the activities of the contradictory Kentuckian, Colonel James Wilkinson, Revolutionary War hero who went on to become one of America's most diabolical secret traitors, could certainly inspire a third. Wilkinson, who was scheming against his native land during the lifetime of the state of Franklin, became a principal in the so-called Aaron Burr conspiracy a generation later, but was so devious in his techniques that even

8

his most intimate friends continued to regard him with the deepest respect. I regret that I have been unable to devote more time and attention to the brazenly, magnificently two-faced colonel.

Factual accounts and embroidered tales of almost continuous Indian wars abound in Franklin's history, yet the part played by the empire-hungry, land-greedy Spaniards in this never-ceasing conflict has been all but forgotten. It has been my intended purpose to scatter a little of the dust from the pages which relate this fascinating phase of our nation's growth.

Aside from such obvious historical figures as John Sevier, Andrew Jackson, George Elholm, the Reverend Sam Houston, the Robertsons, and John Tipton among the Americans, and the Conde de Bolea Aranda, Don Diego Gardoqui, the Conde de Florida Blanca, Baron Hector de Carondelet, and Don Esteban Miró among the Spaniards, all characters in this novel are products of my own imagination, and any relation they may bear to real persons is coincidental.

I should like to express my thanks to the staffs of the library of Vanderbilt University at Nashville and of the Library of Congress for their generous help and for opening their records to me. I am especially grateful to my editor, LeBaron R. Barker of Doubleday and Company, for his extraordinarily valuable suggestions, his sound advice, and above all for his patience. My thanks, too, to my agents, Paul R. Reynolds and Oliver G. Swan, who worked with me paragraph by paragraph, comma by comma, to bring this book to fruition.

N. B. G.

St. Andrew, Jamaica, B.W.I.

THE
CUMBERLAND
RIFLES

Chapter I

Three swordsmen advanced cautiously toward the Dane.

Janus Elholm threw back his head and laughed; it was a sound of complete merriment, utterly lacking in fear. His own sword, of a length seldom seen in Madrid, remained in its scabbard, and he made no attempt to draw either of the short-muzzled, silver-handled pistols which hung from his belt. He ran his fingers through his close-cropped blond hair and pushed away the nearest of the blades.

"Do not provoke me," he said with easy good nature. "Put away your toys and announce my presence to the Marquesa de Guzman."

The three stalwarts in the Guzman house livery of scarlet and sky blue looked uneasily around the reception hall of the great mansion, then at each other, seeking reassurance. Then they looked again at the towering intruder, and what comfort they found was small and cold.

Standing well over six feet in height, the Dane had the build of an athlete who has never permitted his body to grow soft. His muscles, showing through his thin linen shirt and tight-fitting breeches, were sinewy, and he carried no excess flesh. It was plain that he was a military man, for he not only scorned a wig but wore his hair short, after the manner of the mercenary soldiers. Despite the heavy cut of his thick, high boots he was quick and agile on his feet, and careless of the odds against him, he seemed in no way concerned.

His eyes, unexpectedly, were black, and so piercing that the guards shivered and transferred their gaze to his strong, cleft chin, to his clean, hard mouth and his thin, sharply defined mustaches which showed surprising glints of red.

At last one of the men found his voice. "Her Excellency is not at home to guests at this hour, señor," he quavered.

Janus settled his weather-beaten hat on his head as though it were both new and costly. "You will announce me to Her Excellency," he repeated, and though he spoke softly, his tones carried to the farthest corner of the great hall. "You will inform her that Janus Elholm, recently colonel of infantry to the Tuscan dukes, honors her with a visit."

The men gaped, then recovered. This was too much. That a threadbare adventurer should force his way into the little palace was in itself an insult; that he should speak of honoring one of the great ladies of Spain with his presence was insufferable. The tallest of the three took a firmer grip on his sword, but Janus noticed the gesture.

"I wish no ill to you, monsieur," the Dane murmured. "I am an old friend to the *marquesa* and have come a long distance to see her. Perhaps if you tell her that Monsieur Elholm has come to renew his acquaintance with Francisca Espartero, the door to Her Ladyship's boudoir will be more rapidly opened."

Not even a uniformed servant could tolerate such a slap in the face; at no time was any mention made under the Guzman roof of the *marquesa's* maiden name or her past. The tall guard lunged forward abruptly.

But Janus Elholm was no longer within reach of the man's sword. Leaping backward, he had whipped his own blade from its sheath, and in his eyes was the sheen of impending battle.

"So be it," he said. "If I must carve my way into the presence of the beautiful Francisca, I shall."

He jerked free the dust-stained cape that hung from his neck and wrapped it around his left arm. Then, after saluting the guards ironically with his sword, he advanced several paces, as light and sure on his feet as a panther.

A set of massive, carved oak doors were flung open, and a high-pitched, surly voice snarled, "What is the meaning of this disturbance?"

In the open doorframe stood one of the ugliest creatures ever seen in Madrid. A dwarf, he was partly bald, and his skin shone with a damp yellow pallor. His nose was long and crooked to the left, and his lips were so pale and thin as to seem nonexistent. His eyes were deep-set and partially concealed by thick, overhanging brows. But if the malevolent posture he struck was ludicrous, the guards apparently did not consider the newcomer to be an insignificant figure. At his first word they cringed, and they backed away now, their swords dangling helplessly.

But the effect of the dwarf on Janus Elholm was equally remarkable. "Ramiro!" he shouted, crossing the room in giant strides. "Ramiro Sanchez, by all that's holy!"

With his left hand the Dane lifted the small creature high into the air, unmindful of the gasps of horror from the men in scarlet and blue. The dwarf struggled to free himself from his tormentor's grasp, and his tiny, hairy fingers crept toward a jeweled dagger at his belt. But Janus anticipated the move, thumped him hard on the floor, plucked the dagger free, and threw it with a careless gesture across the room.

"Ramiro, you rascal!" Janus cried happily. "I should have known you were here."

"Señor Captain Elholm," the dwarf piped sourly. "I might have known that only you would so disrupt the morning peace of this house."

"My last commission was a colonel, *mon ami*," Janus re-

15

sponded. "But we will discuss such matters later, at our leisure. Tell me you are delighted to see me after so many years, then lead me to your mistress. I burn for a glimpse of her."

"I am not glad to see you, señor." Ramiro was making no compromise. "And Her Excellency will not be happy to hear of your presence either. It is best that the past remain dead. Leave at once, Señor Elholm."

Once again Janus laughed, but the sound was cold and mirthless now, and the guards wished themselves elsewhere. "Perhaps you have changed, Ramiro," he said. "Perhaps the lovely Francisca has changed too. But Janus Elholm does not change. I am unaccustomed to taking orders from a gibbering, humped gnome. You will take me at once to the *marquesa*, or I shall have the pleasure of wringing your head free from your body, a service I should have performed for mankind long ago. My patience grows thin, Ramiro. Lead the way—at once!"

Their eyes bulging, the scarlet-and-blue-clad minions watched the dreaded major-domo of the mansion turn meekly on his heel and lead the brash Dane toward the grand staircase and the private apartments of Francisca Espartero, Marquesa de Guzman. . . .

In the center of the chamber stood a mammoth four-poster bed topped by a thin silk canopy of exquisite workmanship. Over the sheets was laid a coverlet of the same fine-spun material, and in the center was worked the crest of the Guzmans in gold thread. Against the far wall stood a large dressing table, its top filled with creams, ointments, and perfumes, and the profusion of jars and bottles seemed endless, as their likenesses were reflected in an enormous mirror of magnificent Venetian craftsmanship. Beyond stood a closet, the door of which was ajar, revealing row after row of dresses, evening gowns, formal court attire, and negligees. There were high, arched windows on three sides of the room, and air circulated freely, but the hot May sun was kept out by ingeniously devised blinds. Janus sprawled in a padded chair near the bed, his legs stuck out indolently before him, and surveyed the splendor of the room, missing nothing.

He conquered a desire to yawn and damned Madrid and its climate. The last time he had been here was seven years ago, in 1780, and he had sworn never to return to this land where his blood thinned and his brain dulled. With an effort he pulled himself together. The next few minutes would determine the course and pattern of his life. Provided, that is, that Ramiro had really gone to tell Francisca of his presence. Once, to his regret, he had underestimated the dwarf; now he loosened his pistols in their holsters. It would be typical of Ramiro to appear with a full company of royal troops and have him carted off to the foul prison near the Puente de Segovia and lodged there on some trumped-up charge that would keep him in a cell until his bones rotted.

Footsteps approached, and Janus tensed. But no one watching him would have guessed that he was prepared now for any emergency; his heels still rested on the richly woven rug three feet from his body, and his head lolled back against the thick velvet cushion of the chair. The door opened slowly, and Ramiro entered, then stood aside to permit his mistress to enter.

The gentlemen of the court were fond of recalling the gallant words of His Majesty Charles III at a state dinner only two years past. Looking down the long table from his raised position on the twin thrones of Castile and Aragon, the King had said, "The greatest of our assets are our army, our empire over the seas, our splendid navy—and the beauty of our Marquesa de Guzman." No lady would admit the truth of His Majesty's words—and no man could deny them.

Looking at her now for the first time in five years, Janus felt an old yet ever-new excitement stirring within him. Time had blunted the edge of his memory, and he had forgotten how breath-takingly beautiful Francisca really was. Tall and with a regal bearing, she had a slim waist and neck, but her high, pointed breasts and her rounded thighs were models of feminine perfection. Her arms and legs were slender, and her hands, he noted, were still youthful. Francisca was his own age—twenty-nine years—but she looked considerably younger. Her skin, with its dusty, faint olive tint, was warm and fresh; her delicately chiseled nose and chin had not spread or sagged; and there were no lines around her large, violet eyes or her patrician forehead. Her hair, a luxuriously thick and shining blue-black, was still braided and wound around her small head after her morning toilet, revealing her small, pink ears.

Her eyes bored into Janus, and he remembered other things about her that had slipped his mind. There was no expression in the pupils now, and he recalled that no woman he had ever known was as ruthless, as calculating, as demanding as the Marquesa Francisca de Guzman. Still staring hard at Janus, she spoke to her major-domo. "You may go, Ramiro," she said, her deep-throated voice soft and musical even when she was annoyed.

The door closed softly, and Janus was on his feet instantly. He swept forward to take her in his arms, but she evaded him, and the train of her clinging satin dressing gown brushed against him. He stopped and stood very still.

"You offer a poor greeting to an old friend, Francisca, my love," he said lightly.

"I bade you farewell in Paris five years ago, Janus. I did not expect to see you again." If there was any emotion behind her cool mask of a face, she did not betray it.

"Farewells were said between a captain of mercenary troops and a dancer named Francisca Espartero," he bantered. "The captain was accepting a commission to serve with the Poles against the Swedes—or with the Swedes against the Poles. I cannot remember, and it does not matter. The dancer had scored a triumph in Paris and had become a favorite at Versailles. It was rumored that she had become the mistress of the Duc d'Orléans, and it was also said that the Princess de Polignac found her charms irresistible. The captain demanded constancy in his bed companions and departed. Idiot that he was.

"Not long afterward he heard that a countryman of the dancer, the aged Marqués de Guzman, had no foolish scruples and had married the lady. So be it. Now, my dear Francisca, a colonel of infantry pays his respects to the widow who is the sole living member of the ancient house of Guzman. You will be flattered to learn that I heard only lately of the sad death of your beloved Marqués. I resigned my commission, gave up my part in the siege of Florence, and rode immediately for Madrid."

Not a muscle of Francisca's lovely face moved during Janus's recital. But he noticed that her breathing was more rapid and her breasts quivered beneath the silk of her low-cut robe. "What do you want?" she asked bluntly, a harshness appearing suddenly in her voice.

He studied her in silence for a moment. "You," he said.

She threw back her head haughtily. "It is not the custom of the Marquesa de Guzman to invite itinerant soldiers into her bed," she said coldly.

Janus sat himself in the padded chair and reclined, smiling amiably. Without haste he poured himself a goblet of white wine from a carafe on the table at his side, and sipped it appreciatively. "I commend your taste, my love," he said. "But I should have known. You have always liked good things. So have I. . . . And I have not come all the way to Madrid merely to exchange petty insults with you. I have gone to considerable trouble on your account, dear Francisca. I have learned that half of the noble families of Spain are looking with covetous eyes on the estates of the heirless Guzman. But your wise King wants no disputes in these uneasy times, and if you remarry, your husband will be granted title to the lands jointly with you. It was the great misfortune of the late marquis that neither his first wife nor you bore him a child. But that is my good luck!"

Francisca's dark red lips parted incredulously, and she sat down slowly on the bed, unmindful of the fact that her gown had parted at the bottom, revealing a long, smooth expanse of bare leg. "Do I understand you correctly, Janus? You have come here to—to offer yourself in marriage to me?"

"Precisely. It will be no easy matter to protect your claims against the avaricious nobles, who certainly resent the unpleasant but unmistakable fact that one of Spain's oldest titles has fallen into the hands of a beautiful but nevertheless common woman who only a few years ago was forced to earn her bread by dancing and by—ah—other means. Your new marquis must needs be a man both strong and clever. I am both. Further, it is not necessary for me to recommend myself to you as a lover. I will only say that I have become even more polished, if that is possible, since our last encounter."

Francisca de Guzman's feigned indifference was gone, but there was no softening of her features. Here was a man of her own kind, and she could be frank, without artifice. "There is much to commend your little plan," she said. "And you well realize that, although I have known many men, only one has ever held my love. He was indeed stupid when he failed to understand that I was ambitious and that my activities at Versailles bore no relation to my regard for him. But he is older now, and so am I."

"Not you," Janus interrupted. "I am sure you have discovered that fountain of life-giving youth which so many of your countrymen have sought." He started to rise and would have gone to her, but she motioned him back into his chair.

"From your appearance, my Janus, I assume that although you have progressed to the rank of colonel your purse is not weighed down with gold. Your breeches and shirt are scarely those of a man of great wealth, and the soles of your boots are perilously thin."

"True enough," he agreed without rancor. "I am, as always, very poor. A colonel who resigns before the conclusion of a siege receives but little pay. However, I have already sent word to the First Minister of Spain that I will gladly accept a commission from him. The good Conde de Bolea Aranda knows a soldier when he sees one, so I shall soon have employment again. Perhaps I will even be given command of one of the household regiments, so it will not seem too poor a bargain when you make the announcement that we are to be married."

Without warning, Francisca began to laugh. She rocked back and forth on the bed, and tears came to her eyes, but she seemed unable to control her mirth. Only when Janus jumped to his feet, a slow, dull flush creeping up his cheeks, did she attempt to explain. He towered over her, his powerful fists clenched menacingly, and Francisca, still giggling, slid down out of reach.

"This is so droll," she finally gasped. "You will see the humor of it, too, sweet Janus. Here. Look at these earrings and tell me what you think of them." She removed a dangling diamond pendant from each ear and threw them to him.

Janus examined them carefully. "These," he said in some awe, "would ransom a duke of the realm."

"The originals would have done so. These trifling baubles are no more than paste. They are imitations of jewels I have been forced to sell. The same is true of my ruby necklace, my sapphires, and most of the other pieces of the once-famous Guzman collection."

Janus's black eyes narrowed dangerously. "Is this the truth?" he demanded.

"It is. You may take any of my jewels to the moneylenders, if you wish, and have them valued. On condition, of course, that you tell no one they are mine. I do not lie, Janus—not to you. We parted because I told you the truth about the attentions of the Duc d'Orléans."

He sat on the bed beside her. "But the Marqués de Guzman was one of the richest nobles in Spain. How could you squander his fortune in the brief year since his death? How——"

"It was Juan himself who squandered the money," she cut in, and her voice was venomous. "He was a decrepit old donkey. When he discovered he was no longer capable of siring children and that his line would end with him, he began to drink heavily. And to gamble. In the names of St. Teresa and of St. Martin, how he gambled! When he died he left me nothing save this house, the mansion in Toledo, and the estates in Aragon. Houses and fine clothes and staffs of servants are a great expense. The olives and grapes were ruined by frost, and though I have bled my peasants, they can give me no more than what they have. It is not enough. And so—I have been forced to sell my priceless trinkets one by one."

Janus slipped an arm around her supple waist, and this time she offered no resistance. "Then you are almost as poor as I," he said sympathetically. "Very well. Let us sell what remains of your diamonds. Let us rid ourselves of these millstones, your houses and lands. We will still realize enough to keep us warm for years to come."

Violently she wrenched herself away. "No!" she cried, her eyes turning a deeper shade. "What remains is my only hope for the future. Dolt! Donkey! Satan-befuddled carrion! Why do you think I make such an effort to keep up appearances, eh? There are many highborn here who are not insensitive to my beauty. I will yet entice an offer of marriage from one of them. He will have my title to add to his—and he will have *me*. Yes, I will have what I want—wealth. Never again will I risk poverty, Janus—never! I have known what it means to go without food, without a roof over my head, and I swear by all the saints that it will not happen to me again!"

He took Francisca's hand and stroked it tenderly and expertly. "Then all that remains," he said softly, "is for me to find a fortune somewhere. I also seek wealth, but even more I want a title. And through you I intend to achieve my goal."

"You are mad," she replied scornfully. "Never can you amass a fortune even a small fraction as vast as those of our great grandees. Not even if His Majesty were to give you one of the tracts from which gold is mined in Peru. And that is not very likely."

"It is even less likely," said Janus imperturbably, "that one of the great grandees would marry you. They will bed you if they can, to be sure. Any man who does not try to do so is no man. But marriage? No, Francisca, my love. Your reputation precedes you. Your title will mean little to a man who already has one of his own. I tell you, my conniving little dove, you will wait a lifetime before you again find one as senile, as blind, as stupid as Juan de Guzman."

A sharp knock sounded at the door, and before Francisca had an opportunity to speak, it was thrown open. Ramiro sidled into the room, his beady eyes taking note of the two occupants seated side by side on the bed.

"You have a visitor, Your Excellency," he said with a triumphant glance at Janus. "His Excellency Philip, Marqués de Florida Blanca, nephew of the Conde de Florida Blanca, begs your indulgence for calling at such an early hour, but expresses the hope you will receive him."

Janus chuckled, and his grip on Francisca's hand tightened. "You may show the marquis in," he said blandly. Then, as Ramiro hesitated, he added more roughly, "Now, you misshapen imp of hell, or I'll speed you with a boot on your rump!"

Ramiro looked at his mistress for corroboration, but she said nothing. Indeed, she was unable to do so, for Janus was squeezing her fingers together so painfully that it required every effort to keep from screaming. At last the dwarf shrugged, and after throwing a murderous glance at Janus, he stalked out into the corridor with as much dignity as he could muster.

Janus released Francisca's hand, then took it again and rubbed the fingers to restore circulation. "So that popinjay of a Florida Blanca is one of your suitors, my love," he whispered. "If your dreams are centered on his ilk, I advise you to wake up and face the reality of dawn. The little fop's uncle is Minister of Finance and is second in the government only to the Conde de Bolea Aranda, whom he hopes to displace. And I can hardly see the Conde de Florida Blanca permitting his nephew and heir to marry a lady who gained fame in a score of cities by her unique presentation of an old nautch dance of the East. The count aims high, you know. He will never be satisfied with less than a dukedom, and he will scarcely allow his hotheaded nephew to spoil his ambitions."

"Please go!" Francisca commanded. "I—I neither know nor care how you have learned so much of affairs here. But I do not wish you to interfere with my plans. I will lead my own life, without help from you. And I don't want you here when Don Philip comes in. You may slip out by that door—over there."

"I have made it my business to learn of high affairs of state in this charming country," Janus replied casually, leaning back on his elbows. "I neglected to tell you that I have already spent three days in Madrid. Ah! Our guest approaches," he added, hearing footsteps on the landing. "I shall remain with you throughout your interview with Philip de Florida Blanca. It is the duty of your husband-to-be to sit at your side when you receive guests in your bedroom. We want no scandal to soil our good names, do we, my love?"

The approaching footsteps stopped, and Don Philip Moñino y Redondo, Marqués de Florida Blanca, bowed low to his hostess. A thin man, he was dressed in the height of current fashion, and virtually every color of the rainbow was represented on his person. Despite the heat, he wore a coat of brocaded, padded silk, and on his head was a magnificently combed and powdered wig. His build was slight but wiry, and on his swarthy face sprouted a pointed beard, worn by the traditionalists who wanted to return to the customs of their world-conquering ancestors. Of principal interest to Janus was the marquis's sword. It was a military model, as long as Janus's, and on the hilt were mounted two rows of emeralds, each the size of a woman's thumbnail, set apart by smaller stones, most of them diamonds.

Don Philip bowed low. "I abase myself before the most gracious, the most beautiful woman in Christendom," he lisped in pure Castilian.

Francisca de Guzman sank to the floor in a full, graceful curtsy. "Your Excellency honors my humble home with your exalted presence," she said, her accent as much that of the aristocracy as his own.

Janus shot a glance at her out of the corners of his eyes and marveled. He still had many things to remember about Francisca. Not the least of her assets was her ability to adapt herself to any group of people by faithfully mimicking their manners. In a cheap café behind the Tuileries she could be as common as the Parisian trollops who sat at every table; yet she could meet a blue-blooded grandee on his own ground and could speak to him in his own language.

For the first time Don Philip noticed the presence of Janus, and his dark face grew even blacker. Straightening, he tugged at his beard and stared fiercely at the shabbily dressed soldier. Janus's lips parted slightly in a humorless smile, and Francisca intervened quickly.

"Your Excellency," she said, "may I present an old acquaintance, Colonel Elholm of Copenhagen. He is passing through Madrid on his way home from Milan and has stopped to deliver a message to me from my dear friend, the Princess Anna Maria."

Somewhat mollified, Don Philip condescended to acknowledge the Dane's presence by an infinitesimal inclination of his

25

head. Then, as though he and Francisca were alone in the room, he turned back to her. "Most adorable of women," he said, "I was desolate last night when I arrived at the salon of the Duchess of Alcudia, only to learn that you had already departed. My heart was broken, and I could not sleep all night, so deeply did I pine for you. I beg you, if you have any mercy in your heart, permit me to escort you this evening to the assembly of the Conde de Luna!"

Janus seemingly ignored the slight and sauntered slowly toward the door. Don Philip, if he was aware of what the other man was doing, probably thought he was leaving to give his betters an opportunity for intimate conversation. But Francisca, who knew Janus better, watched him nervously as she tried to smile at the marquis.

Leaning casually against the doorframe, Janus stared at Don Philip's backside, frowning intently. "Ah yes!" he exclaimed to no one in particular in a penetrating voice. "Don Philip de Florida Blanca. I knew there was something familiar about the name and the body, but I did not recognize him from the front."

Don Philip whirled around, and color drained from his face. "You will explain yourself, señor."

"Gladly." Janus's manner was innocence itself. "I had the great honor to meet Your Excellency—in a manner of speaking —a year ago, in the battle before Naples. You were a member of the contingent sent by King Charles to support the King of the Neapolitans."

"That is correct." Don Philip was rigid, his tone glacial.

"You see, *Marquesa?*" Janus sounded positively joyous. "I knew I had not forgotten. Permit me to further refresh Your Excellency's memory. I was fighting that day against you, Your Excellency—on the side of the Tuscans. Ah, I remember the battle so well. A troop of Spanish cavalry led the attack against our lines, with Don Philip de Florida Blanca in the lead. Our riflemen fired a single volley, and Don Philip's horse was hit.

Yes, it all comes back to me now; the gentleman ran back to the safety of the Neapolitan lines as fast as his trembling legs could carry him. . . . Now you know why I recognized you from the rear, Your Excellency. I had such a fine opportunity to study you as you retreated that day."

The young marquis was shaking with rage. "I—I demand satisfaction!" he screamed.

Francisca felt a desire to laugh, but was sobered by the realization that a duel begun in her home would certainly result in repercussions that would bring her increased notoriety.

"I forbid you to fight here," she said, her overripe lips forming the semblance of a pout. "And I must apologize to you, Your Excellency, for this foreigner's abominable manners. You understand, I trust, that he is no friend of mine. He is merely one who has carried letters and documents for certain highborn persons. And I assure you, he will never again be welcome here."

"I attach no portion of the blame to you, most adorable Excellency," choked the mortified nobleman. "Nor do I intend to dishonor your home by brawling here. As for you, señor—I demand satisfaction at once, elsewhere."

Janus had not budged from his comfortable position. "Whatever my many faults, I am not a murderer, Your Excellency. No, Don Philip. I will not cross swords with you now—nor any other time. You would not challenge a gunsmith, for the making and perfecting of guns is his business, and he must be a superb shot in order to test his product. The proper use of the sword is my profession, Don Philip, and I do not wantonly stick little boys with it."

His eyes smoldering, the marquis studied Janus for a moment, then ostentatiously turned toward Francisca. "With your permission, Excellency, I will retire. May I anticipate the pleasure of acting as your escort tonight?"

"Of course, Your Excellency." Francisca smiled politely. "But

I beg you not to leave now, Don Philip. This—this uninvited visitor shall go, not you." She glared a challenge at Janus.

He accepted it without moving. "You forget, Madame Excellency. I have not yet delivered to you all of the messages from your dear friend, the Princess—ah—Anna Maria. The most important of these I committed to memory, as she would not write them on paper. And I must repeat them now, for my time in Madid promises to grow more complicated, and I may have no opportunity later."

Don Philip broke the deadlock. Bowing deeply to Francisca, he kissed her hand fervently, murmured a brief "Until tonight, most enchanting of goddesses," and left without another glance at Janus. As the nobleman's footsteps echoed up the stairs, Janus carefully closed the door. He turned just in time to see Francisca pick up a vase and hurl it at him with all of her force. He stepped nimbly aside, and the porcelain shattered harmlessly against the wall.

Red spots burned in Francisca's cheeks and she stamped her foot so hard in impotent fury that her high, tapering heel snapped off. "How dare you make a scandal in my home!" she blazed. "Simply because Don Philip bruised your precious vanity by refusing to address you was no excuse for jeopardizing my position, for forcing me to lie about you, for insulting a nobleman of one of the first families, for——"

Her fingers closed around a small china rouge pot, but Janus was at her side in an instant. Twisting her hand sharply, he forced her to drop the potential weapon. "Be still and listen to me, you rowdy baggage," he said calmly, continuing to hold her hand powerless at her side. "You know me well enough to realize I never do anything out of mere vanity."

"Let me go. There will be marks on my arm tonight, and I cannot afford loose gossip."

"Promise you'll sit quietly and not lose your temper again, my love?"

"I——"

"Promise, Francisca! You try me sorely!"

Wearily she dropped her head, and a ray of sunshine peeping through the blinds touched a strand of her shining hair. She looked as though she was on the verge of breaking into tears, but Janus was unimpressed. His grip tightened, and she winced. "I promise, Janus. In the name of St. Teresa, I promise! Now let me go!"

He released her, pushed her onto the bed, and then seemed to lose all interest in her as she dropped to the coverlet and buried her face in its silken folds. When he spoke he was as impersonal as though he were alone in the room, thinking aloud. "The little popinjay will be unable to keep the story of this encounter to himself," he began. "He'll repeat it to everyone he knows at court."

"Indeed he will." Francisca's voice was muffled. "And when his uncle hears of your insults, you will be rewarded by the enmity of Don José de Florida Blanca. It is not humorous to be hated by one of the most powerful men in the kingdom," she added angrily, startled by Janus's sudden laugh.

"I will speak, my love—and you will listen," he directed. "The Conde de Florida Blanca may be strong, but there is one who is stronger. The First Minister, Aranda. And their hatred for each other transcends any petty dislike that Florida Blanca may conceive for an unimportant Danish adventurer. But Aranda—aha! He will be pleased at the calculated insult to the nephew of the man who aspires to replace him. He will be more inclined to favor the request of a young gentleman from Copenhagen who aspires to the command of a household regiment—and to the hand of a great beauty and noblewoman."

Francisca lifted her head, and her eyes shone with undisguised admiration. "You thought of all this before you spoke as you did to Don Philip?"

"Of course."

29

She sighed and pulled a thick pillow under her shoulders. "Perhaps you will acquire your fortune after all, Janus. You are not the impetuous firebrand you were five years ago. There is method to your wildness now, and that is good. Yes, you may become wealthy, and if you do, I shall reconsider my refusal."

Janus chose not to hear her. "I indicated that I had a variety of reasons for acting as I did. Are you not anxious to hear another of them?"

Francisca nodded and settled herself more comfortably on the huge bed. Her dressing gown had spread open at the neckline, and the swelling of her breasts was an invitation to Janus to move closer. He did.

"It has been a long time since we were last together, Francisca, my love," he said softly, lowering himself to her side. "I was jealous of the presence of that strutting little rooster and wanted to be rid of him as rapidly as possible. I have yearned to be with you and had no wish to be deprived of the occasion."

She watched him with unblinking eyes as he moved closer. He put his right arm around her and pulled her yielding body to him. With his free hand he began to unfasten the braid that held captive her silken blue-black hair.

Chapter II

The sun was in the west and a faint but cooling breeze was
sweeping over Madrid from the Manzanares River when Janus
left the mansion on the Calle de Alcala and headed for the
Plaza de Madrid a few paces away, where he had left his horse
in the care of a hired animal watcher. He whistled a French
marching song softly through his teeth and looked at the water
spraying and bubbling through the fountain in the center of
the plaza. A marble goddess, pulled in her chariot by two stone
lions, stood in the center of the fountain, and as he looked at the
silent figure he grinned and took a deep breath.

The goddess could in no wise compare with Francisca. No
woman was her equal in the arts that men prized, and marriage
to her would be as much of a pleasure as it would be a convenience. At no time had he doubted his ability to reconquer
the dazzling *marquesa* herself; to that extent his scheme was still
intact. More troublesome was her insistence that he bring a
substantial monetary settlement into their union. She had stubbornly refused to back down from her stand through the long
and lazy hours of the day, and he was convinced at last that she
really meant what she said. He shrugged; if money in large
quantities was necessary to acquire Francisca's title, he would

have to devote himself to the problem of building a fortune. Wealth, he thought with some annoyance, was in itself unnecessary—the Marqués and Marquesa de Guzman would have unlimited opportunities to promote whatever capital they needed, no matter where they might travel in Europe. And the sale of Francisca's remaining jewels would certainly stave off the day when they would be forced to use their wits.

But no woman had ever been more obstinate than Francisca Espartero when her mind was made up. She had proved that beyond all doubt by swearing he would not again be admitted to her home unless and until he met her conditions. Perhaps he should have shown less ardor in his love-making today. Had Francisca remained unsatiated, she might have agreed to less stringent conditions.

Again he shrugged and resumed his whistling. Don Janus Elholm, Marqués de Guzman. Maybe he'd change his first name to Juan in order to make it easier for the Spaniards to pronounce. It didn't really matter. He was on the right road at last, and the title would be his. What a long climb it had been, he thought, for a boy who had never had enough to eat. For the first time in many weeks he thought of his parents. Father— there had been a weakling; a minor official in the royal post office in Copenhagen, he had eked out a plain, bare living without patronage or favor from anyone. And his mother? It was difficult to think of her without cursing. He could remember her only vaguely from his early childhood as a lovely, fair-skinned queen; then she had run off with a dashing young viscount, deserting her family. To his last day, her unfortunate husband had bemoaned his lack of a title; nothing else, he had sworn, had driven his wife into another man's arms.

Janus leaned against the stone parapet of the fountain and let the cool air play around his head. It would be good, he thought, if his mother were still alive. He might find her at one of Europe's courts, and he was positive he would know her anywhere. He would identify himself to her, would make sure that she knew he had been elevated to the peerage for which she had sacrificed honor and her family, and then he would leave without another word.

The rough stone of the wall bit into his hands, and he smiled wryly to himself. How often as a child he had dreamed that same dream about his rise in the world, about his mother's chagrin when he revealed himself to her. What had been the wistful fancy of the little boy was going to become a hard reality in fact for the man. The desire to acquire a title, to be someone to whom the world bowed low, had actually become the important factor; he no longer really cared if he ever saw his mother. No woman, he had discovered, was worthy of respect or admiration or wasted thought.

A voice sounded close to Janus's ear, and he jerked his head around. "Señor Elholm?" The speaker wore the black jacket and yellow-striped breeches of an officer attached to a household regiment of the Spanish Army, and looking over his shoulder, Janus saw six others, mounted and fully armed.

He backed away a scant foot and reckoned his chances. If he could draw his pistols, he might hold the soldiers at bay until he could reach his own horse on the other side of the plaza. He had miscalculated, he thought: Don Philip de Florida Blanca was acting quickly. But he had been in worse spots, and he hooked his thumbs into his belt and let his hands inch toward his pistols.

"I am Janus Elholm," he admitted cautiously.

"You will please come with me, señor." The officer was polite but remote.

"May I ask where you want to take me?" Janus felt the butts of his guns under his hands. And the Spanish officer had not noticed.

"Don Pedro de Bolea Aranda has expressed a desire that you appear before him. That is all I know, señor."

"Oh." Janus's hands relaxed, and he felt curiously let down. "Permit me to mount, Señor Lieutenant. I hope you will lead the way. I'm none too familiar with the streets of your city." An unaccustomed sense of elation replaced the tension and its aftermath. He had written only forty-eight hours ago to Aranda and was amazed at the early reply. Without a trace of doubt this was an eventful day, and the future was fat with promise. . . .

Moorish guards, their faces dark and impassive under white turbans, stood rigidly at attention in the corridors of the sprawling, magnificent Palacio de la Gobernación. Outside, in the Puerta del Sol, a half regiment of Moors or household troops was stationed at all times. With the peasants, merchants, and artisans of France rumbling in discontent at the ruling class across the border, Imperial Spain was nervously alert. Don Pedro Abarca, Conde de Bolea Aranda, First Minister of the Twin Kingdom, Viceroy Extraordinary of the Empire beyond the Seas, Lieutenant General of the Realm, Governor of Granada and Vice-Admiral of the Fleets on the High Seas, did not believe in leaving matters to chance.

His own suite of offices on the second floor of the *palacio* were as carefully guarded as the bedchamber of King Charles, into which, it was rumored, even the mistresses of the monarch had a difficult time gaining admittance these days. Here, once past the room of uniformed troops and the heavily armed gentlemen-at-arms, visitors who had been summoned into the presence of the First Minister were struck by the severe simplicity of his workroom. A portrait of the sovereign was hung behind a long mahogany desk; on the opposite wall was a flattering study in oils of the heir to the throne, who, if he survived the insatiable demands of his gluttonous appetite, would someday be known as Charles IV. There were no other decorations.

At first glance, Aranda himself seemed both plain and simple. But Janus, studying him closely, was not deceived. The count's coat, waistcoat, and breeches were an unadorned black, but examination revealed them to be of the finest-spun silk. The buckles on his shoes were masterpieces of quiet dignity and were wrought of pure gold. And the little square-cut emerald he wore in his stock was clear and virtually flawless.

Only five and one half feet tall, the count dominated his large office and everyone in it. His hair was white, but his dark eyes were those of a far younger man and seemed both lively and kind. But the impression was reversed by the set of his mouth. His lips were thin and compressed and were perpetually curved downward. His look of disdain was enhanced by his nose, which was long and thin, with a pronounced hook making it seem even larger than it was.

Janus drew his sword and saluted with a flourish. "Janus Elholm the Younger at your command, my lord," he said loudly.

The count concealed a dry smile as he bowed. "You are welcome, soldier," he lisped in the faultless Castilian of his kind. "But be good enough to put away that big butcher's knife. The sight of steel unnerves me. An old idiosyncrasy of mine which I'm sure you'll humor."

Janus hastily sheathed the sword and took the straight-backed chair into which his host waved him. He composed the muscles of his face in order to betray no emotion. There was little doubt that something of consequence was brewing; men of Aranda's standing seldom granted poor mercenary officers the privilege of sitting in their presence.

"So, Elholm the Younger, you seek military employment from me." Unlike his compatriots, the First Minister was a man of few words. "You aspire to the command of a household regiment. I regret that the posts are hereditary and are reserved to the nobility. And none are open now. Only if such a one as His Lordship, the good Conde de Florida Blanca, should die, would there be a vacancy. And it is to be feared that the family of the Florida Blancas are in exceedingly hardy good health."

His eyes twinkled, and Janus knew at once that Aranda, in keeping with his reputation for being well informed at all times regarding everything inside Spanish borders, had already heard about the scene at the home of the beautiful Marquesa de Guzman. However, he certainly was not wasting his time by making oblique jokes at the expense of his enemies; he must have some specific assignment in mind for Janus.

"I was unaware of the conditions pertaining to command of the household regiments, my lord," the Dane said crisply. "How, then, may I serve you?"

"A man who approaches the heart of a problem without subterfuge. I like that, Elholm. I like it very much indeed. The gentlemen of Barcelona and Madrid and Toledo with whom I spend the greater part of each day are able only to say the things they do not mean. This is a refreshing experience." He paused, examined his manicured nails, and flicked an invisible fleck of dust from the sapphire-and-diamond ring that adorned his little finger. "Elholm," he said abruptly, "have you ever desired to see the New World?"

"No, my lord," Janus answered quietly but emphatically.

"What a tragedy—for you. The riches of the world and the future of Spain lie across the seas."

Janus looked into the eyes that searched his so shrewdly. Aranda was not a man one could outguess. "I confess to an ineptitude for riddles, my lord. But if you will speak plainly, I will attend to every word."

"Very well. You disappoint me, Elholm. Your brother has achieved a position of honor and stature in that new land, the United States. Have you no desire to emulate him?"

"My brother, my lord?"

"Brother—cousin—uncle—it matters little. I know everything of consequence concerning the United States, Elholm. I have also amassed a considerable quantity of information concerning you and those close to you. It was not by accident that you learned

36

of the widowhood of a certain *marquesa*. The officer with whom you shared a hogshead of sack in Milano is in my employ. I thought the bait would be sufficiently tempting to lure you to Madrid, and it was." The count smiled and leaned back in his chair, completely at his ease.

Janus's composure was shaken, but he tried not to show it as he determined on a bold approach. "And now I'm here, willing to accept any reasonable offer."

The First Minister smiled again, but when he spoke his words cut like a lash. "You are not now dealing with some insignificant German or Italian princeling, Elholm. Spain was once the first power of the world and soon will be once again. By your mere presence here, you are committed to our cause, for you are about to learn of matters that no outsider is permitted to know. It is already too late for you to depart."

Janus nodded his assent. "So be it," he murmured.

"His Majesty's empire in the New World is not so great as it once was, Elholm, but it will before long be greater than ever before. In time to come, all of the continent of North America will be ours. You need not lift your brows. The puny new United States is helpless now that it no longer suckles at England's breast. What have the Americans accomplished in the years of their freedom? Nothing! What does their Congress of the Confederation do? Nothing! Soon, aided by us, she will fall apart, and we will be quick to pick up the pieces."

Rising stiffly, Aranda walked to a cabinet, unlocked it, and withdrew a limp, rolled map which he spread on his desk. "Attend me, Elholm. Here you see the thirteen states of America. And here are the imperial colonies of Louisiana and the Floridas. Now, I ask—what is this territory between, located on the great river?"

"A friend who fought in the West with the Americans once sent me a map of this region, my lord." Janus was relaxed once more. "This is the Kentucky district of the state of Virginia—here.

37

And this area directly south of it is the state of Franklin, of which my—ah—relative is an official. According to what my friend wrote to me a year or more ago, it is the next state which the American Congress will admit to their Union."

Aranda tapped the map with an emphatic gesture. "Neither Kentucky nor Franklin will remain American, Elholm. They are to be His Majesty's next annexations. We will pluck the fruit from the tree within the next year. In time the whole tree will be ours—but I digress. I want you to go to America, Elholm. Your brother's name and position will give you entry to Franklin and——"

Janus drew himself up proudly. "I am a soldier, my lord. I am not a spy. I cannot accept your offer, even if it means the dungeons of Barcelona."

The count bowed ironically. "I would gladly send you to prison, but we have need of you, my impetuous young hothead. But you will not serve as an espionage agent. Of these we have more than enough already in America, including many of her own prominent citizens. No, Elholm. You will remain in Franklin and Kentucky only long enough to familiarize yourself with the land. You will determine whether our friends are of sufficient strength to stage an insurrection at the time of our conclusive attack. You will confer with our agents there, of course, and determine how they may best serve you. Any whom you deem valuable you may take with you into New Spain to assist you. But you will not linger overlong in Franklin. As soon as it is convenient, you will proceed to New Orleans and the Floridas. Don Alfonso Galvez, my military director there, is a fine general, but he is old and unfit for hardships. You will serve as his deputy in the field, with the rank of brigadier general."

Searching the First Minister's face for some trace of mockery, Janus could find none. "My lord," he said slowly and distinctly, "there must be twenty or more brigadier generals on the active list of the Spanish Army. Why do you offer a commission like this to a foreign adventurer?"

"You force me to speak with candor, Elholm. Perhaps you are unaware of what transpires across the Pyrenees, but I can assure you that His Majesty is not. The scum of France have been stricken with an inflammation that threatens the Crown itself. And while King Charles is filled with solicitude for his cousin, he is even more determined that these wild notions concerning freedom for the masses will not infect the subjects of Spain. Therefore, our native-born generals remain here, and their armies stay with them."

"I see." Janus saw many things, among them the virtually insurmountable hazard of fighting a war without troops. "Suppose I accept, my lord. Am I to be a general without any army?"

"On the contrary, you will have two divisions of Castilians, one already in Louisiana and the other at Pensacola in the Floridas. You and your political agents will make every effort to induce the red-skinned savages to join you too. And doubtless many of the Americans in Franklin and Kentucky will rally to your cause."

"Mmm. I'll not count on their aid for the moment. However, certain things are becoming clear to me, my lord. You have a great need for a qualified professional officer, and I am admirably suited to your purposes. Hence your need is greater than mine. What are you willing to pay me?"

Aranda took the abrupt request in his stride. "The salary of a brigadier general is generous," he said. "In addition, you may be sure His Majesty will remember you with a handsome gift when you have won his victory."

Janus grinned unpleasantly. "I already own a large and varied collection of guns, swords, and daggers—the gifts of rulers whose hearts overflowed with gratitude. No, my lord. I will consent to join my cause with yours on a single condition. I demand a grant of one million acres of land in Franklin—a grant that will cost *you* nothing. America is an expanding land, and even after we conquer her, people from the world over will continue to come there. By selling one million acres of farmland, I can realize a very pretty profit. And I need the money these days."

The count was clenching and unclenching his fists. "I am well aware of the *marquesa's* financial difficulties," he snapped. "I have personally been the purchaser, through my representatives, of the larger quantity of her jewels. But one million acres—that is a large parcel of land, Elholm."

"Not in America. When the American leaders are dispossessed, someone must take over their property——"

"Our military conquers in the name of the Crown."

"So it shall." Janus paused, feeling his way. He was treading on spongy ground now, and the count's face was ominous. One mistaken word, and a cell was waiting. But if he could turn a phrase properly, he would truly be in a position to secure the wealth that Francisca demanded in return for her title. "The greater share will naturally be claimed for His Majesty," he said delicately. "That is understood. And you, my lord—you, too, have a right to your fair portion."

Aranda was suddenly erect, and though he made no overt sign, the tension grew and crackled. His eyes began to glisten, and he waited for Janus to continue.

Sure now that he was on the right track, Janus plunged on. "We could sign a private agreement, my lord, you and I. I can lay claim to lands in your name. For each three acres to which I gain title, two will be yours and one will be mine."

The count tugged at a bell pull behind him, and a moment later an aide stepped through a small inner door, a tablet of paper and a freshly dipped quill pen in his hand. He bobbed his head to his superior and waited submissively.

"Doro," said the First Minister, "you may bring me the commission prepared for General Janus Elholm, and I shall sign it. Then I want you quickly to prepare a private document, two copies only." He detailed the particulars and did not look at Janus as he said, "Each unit will be divided into four acres. My share shall be three, and Señor General Elholm will take one."

There was no possible protest, and Janus was able to smile broadly as the secretary left and Aranda turned back to him. Even if the terms of the agreement were unfair, Janus felt that his future was assured. The governors of colonial Spain would not be niggardly in parceling out choice property to the nation's most powerful citizen, and his Danish general could hardly come out a loser. All that was needed now to assure him a fortune—and Francisca's glittering title—was to wrest the territory from the Americans. Aranda had made such a contingency a condition of the contract.

"When do you want me to start for New Orleans, my lord?" Never had he felt so lighthearted, so assured.

"You will go first to New York, General Elholm. There you will receive specific instruction from Don Diego Gardoqui, our minister to the Confederation. You will take passage at your earliest convenience. Doro will give you one thousand gold dollars, which will be enough until you reach New York. Don Diego will keep you supplied with funds thereafter."

The sum was far more generous than Janus had hoped. As a colonel it would have taken many months for him to earn such a figure. But it was best not to show either surprise or too much gratitude. "Thank you, my lord," he said flatly. "I'll ride for the coast tonight."

"Surely you will not run off in too great haste, Elholm; I want no weeping *marquesa* wetting my shoulder. You need not hurry because of me—you will find me an easy master. My only requirement is that you complete the military conquest of Franklin and Kentucky within one year."

"I shall do so in less time, my lord." Thinking the interview at an end, Janus stood up. "As for the lady, I have no intention of seeing her again. We, too, have an—ah—agreement. I'll merely

41

write her a letter of farewell and will tell her nothing of our understanding."

"Naturally, Señor General! You are very wise. You might say to her only that you have been overcome by a desire to explore the mysterious wonders of the New World. No more. Keep in mind that I maintain relations of friendliness with the United States, and while within her borders you will conduct yourself circumspectly. I long ago learned that the greatest weapon in an attack is that of surprise. You should know that, Elholm. And you should know, too, that even a perfect woman is incapable of keeping silent. Good-by, Señor General. I wish you good hunting."

Aranda twisted in his chair and stared out into the broad Puerta del Sol, busy with early evening traffic. Janus conquered an impulse to offer his hand to the count. Only an equal was permitted to touch the skin of a great grandee of Spain, and a mere hireling officer, even if granted a temporary high rank, scarcely qualified, no matter if he was—in a manner of speaking—the nobleman's partner in a business venture. He bowed himself out of the room and went in search of the secretary, from whom he would collect his much-needed gold and his copy of the business agreement. . . .

Within the hour Janus was riding toward the eastern gate of the city. His few belongings had been speedily packed, and he had scribbled a hasty note of farewell to Francisca. When he reached a seacoast town he would buy more suitable clothes for his journey; long experience had taught him that silks and leather were invariably more expensive in a capital where nobles and courtiers were careless with their purses and merchants raised their prices accordingly.

The multicolored, sloping roofs and the broad patios of homes in the fashionable western sector of Madrid were giving way to meaner, cramped dwellings. The streets grew narrow, and the odors drifting through open windows and doorways became more pungent, more fetid. Balconies leaned crazily high over the cobblestones, and here and there those on opposite sides of a street almost touched. Food vendors pushed low-slung carts from which hung festoons of green and red peppers, onions, and thick, juicy cloves of garlic. An ancient crone and an equally aged donkey combined their efforts in tugging forward a dilapidated cart filled to overflowing with crates of fluttering, squawking chickens. The old woman advertised her wares in a monotonous, cackling singsong which sounded uncannily like the noise of the birds she peddled.

Children of all ages, dirty, raucous, and clad in rags, darted everywhere, and mongrel dogs of every possible combination of breeds yapped and frolicked at their heels. Unable to press through the careless throngs without injuring someone, Janus slowed his city-bred horse to a walk, and the animal obediently picked a dainty way through the mobs. A girl of no more than sixteen, clad in a once white peasant blouse that exposed a broad expanse of generous bosom, and in a coarse black skirt that revealed her sturdy but well-shaped legs almost to her knees, leaned against a wall in studied, sensual indolence, her hands resting carelessly on her broad hips. Her hair was as black as coal in the gathering twilight and streamed down her back. Looking at her, Janus thought of Francisca. She had started in an atmosphere much like this; how far she had come in a brief fifteen years.

Instantly aware that she had attracted his attention, the girl lowered one eyelid slowly and permitted her long, thick lashes to rest for an instant against her cheek. Then she opened both eyes wide and stared boldly at Janus, thrusting her breasts forward and smiling provocatively. He reached into the purse, found a smooth silver Ferdinand piece, and tossed it to her. The gesture was extravagant, even for a man whose belt was heavy with a thousand gold Spanish dollars. As he rode on he saw the girl bite the coin, then raise her skirts without self-consciousness and deposit it in her garter. She looked after him in wonder tinged with

43

scorn. According to her creed, anyone who gave without receiving his last penny's measure of worth was a fool who deserved to be bilked.

A violin, slightly off key, squeaked plaintively in the distance, accompanied by a rich, mellow male voice. The song was soothing and flowing, and for some reason the liquid tones made Janus a trifle sad. A phase of his life was coming to a close, and the greatest risk of his life lay ahead. Despite the calm assumption of the Conde de Bolea Aranda that the military campaign would be a success, Janus knew that the First Minister entertained serious doubts about his ambitious plans. Aranda's reputation was not that of an openhanded man, and Janus felt sure he must be seriously concerned over the venture; otherwise he would not have agreed so readily to the prospect of permitting the Dane to acquire title to one million acres of American soil. The count must have reasoned that the incentive would serve as an excellent spur to Janus in the event of trouble.

Perhaps Aranda was being cautious in his agreements because Florida Blanca threatened his own position, but Janus did not think so. As a student of military strategy and tactics he had followed the developments of the American Revolution, and he knew only too well that the Yankees would be a tougher nut to crack than the Italians, in whose benign land dukes and generals often sold out their people even before battle was joined. While it was true that the American victory had been achieved at least in part because of the help of French regiments and Polish, German, and French generals, Janus was not inclined to underrate the American fighting man. He had questioned too many English officers who had been at Saratoga and Yorktown for that.

Then he remembered Aranda's brief reference to Americans in Spanish pay, and brightened. Spurring his horse to a faster gait, he smiled cynically. People, he reasoned, were universally greedy. No matter what reasons they gave to others or themselves for their conduct, they were invariably motivated by avarice and lust. That must be as true of Americans as of every other nationality he had encountered, and he had built his own career to date by juggling and playing on the selfish instincts of others. A raw, new country inhabited by ambitious men should prove itself fertile soil for one who had learned his trade from expert teachers.

And for the next year, at any rate, he would have the right to call himself "General." Not that the rank would mean much to Europe's mercenary commanders when they learned that he had reached the top in his profession in the wild borderlands of the New World. But if all went well, this would be his last war. With money and the title of "Marquis," he could live for pleasure thereafter in any of Europe's great cities. Of course he and Francisca would be legally bound to each other then, and he frowned suddenly at the prospect of taking the one-time courtesan as his wife. No matter, though, for in time they would tire of each other, as they had done before, and would go their separate ways. When that happened, his marriage to her would be a great convenience, for he could look with favor on any attractive woman without fear of marital complications.

The Puerta de Alcala, chief eastern gate of Madrid, stood directly ahead, a high stone wall extending to the north and to the south on either side of it. A major of cavalry, resplendent in his black-and-yellow uniform surmounted by a shining silver helmet with a scarlet plume, stood leaning against one side of the open gates, elegantly picking his teeth and contriving to look very fierce. Two sentries with muskets lounged not far from him, and half a dozen or more other soldiers were eating, drinking, and talking in a small guardhouse set in the wall. The sight of the officer's gaudy costume made Janus wish he had ordered a uniform for himself from one of Madrid's better tailors, but he thrust the temptation aside. If he was to spend weeks in American territory, the risk would be too great; it would be virtually impossible to explain—to anyone who chanced to see the clothes—what he was doing with the regalia of a Spanish general in his kit. It would be wiser to wait until he reached New Orleans, which travelers said was the only half-civilized town in North America. Surely he would find a tailor worthy of the name there.

The major threw away his toothpick and gestured insolently to Janus, who obediently drew his horse to a halt. "Name, nationality, and destination, señor. Your identity papers—at once."

Janus conquered an impulse to drive a fist into the weak, smug mouth, and he wisely refrained from showing his commission from Aranda, an act that would bring momentary satisfaction but might jeopardize his mission. No matter what the provocation, he reminded himself, he must keep his assignment a secret; it would be time enough to reveal his identity when he led an army against the Americans.

"Here you are, Señor Major." Janus opened the drawstrings of his purse and pulled out his battered Spanish passport. "The name is Elholm. Danish citizen. I ride for Lisbon."

The officer barely flicked a glance at the papers but looked hard and long at Janus's long sword. "Your occupation, señor?"

"Soldier." Janus felt annoyance rising like a lump into his throat.

"Indeed?" The cavalry major professed to show amusement.

"Indeed. And my credentials for that, Señor Major—are these." He tapped his pistols significantly, then let his hand rest on the handle of his sword. Staring at the Spaniard, he withdrew the blade several inches from its scabbard.

There was nothing the major wanted less than an incident at the moment. He would soon be off duty and had a rendezvous with a ballerina from the Royal Company of Musicians and Artists before going home to dinner with a fat and stupid wife. Much as he hated the gamecocks who fought anywhere under any flag for pay, this shabby upstart who seemed so anxious to test him at swordplay was of less importance than the red-haired señorita and her smooth, creamy skin and soft curves. "You may ride on,

Señor Dane. And if you are lonely on your journey, you might pass the time by contemplating your good fortune in never having crossed the path of a Spanish regiment in your wars. Had you done so, you would not now be alive. . . . Well, why do you sit there, Señor Dane? You have leave to go!"

Janus dug his heels in his horse's flanks and spurred forward. Only complications would ensue if he informed the stupid, strutting dolt that he had three times led his men to victory against the best troops Spain could put in the field. Let the major have his moment of petty triumph. Janus's turn would come in New Orleans and Pensacola, and he hoped fervently that he would have some of these younger sons of the petty nobility in his divisions. They would give him full payment for every humiliation he had ever suffered at the hands of the aristocracy.

Gradually, as he rode on, his anger cooled. An olive grove stood on the left side of the road, and cork trees lined the right. The moist heat of the day was gone, and the air had become crisp and bracing. A sliver of a moon was rising in the sky, and the road ahead was clear. It was wrong on so perfect a night to harbor grudges against little people; he had long ago learned that one rose in the world only as he put aside unimportant men and their affairs.

Enjoy each moment for itself, he said aloud, breathing in the sweet air of the countryside, so different from the stale odors of Madrid. Save your thoughts and strength for self-advancement, and waste no time on inconsequential anger and hatred. Or, for that matter, on false pity or loyalty either. He thought of the fargone day when his father had fallen ill but had confidently expected the government to help a man who had devoted a lifetime to the postal service. But no assistance had been forthcoming, and when the family's money was gone, Janus had been forced to beg bread at the great houses of Copenhagen.

The roof of his mouth was suddenly dry, and he wanted a drink. Cursing himself for his lack of foresight, he wished he had brought a bottle of brandy with him from his lodgings and decided to stop at the next inn he passed. If he liked the place, he would sup there, too, and spend the night. The coming days of his trip to the New World would be the freest he had known in years; this was the interval before responsibility would lay a heavy hand on his shoulder, and he decided to follow his own advice. He *would* enjoy each moment for itself.

A patch of linden trees crowded close to the road, and as Janus approached, a figure in a light silk cape and a broad-brimmed hat rode from the protecting shadows into the broad path and blocked it. Janus reached immediately for his pistols and slowed his horse to a walk. Bandits were uncommon but not unknown so close to Madrid, and if the man ahead was merely a decoy for a band of robbers, there might be serious trouble.

Then as he drew closer Janus saw a familiar nose and lips under the big hat and felt like laughing. His relief was so great that he jammed his pistols back into their holsters. He had been followed from the city, it was evident, by no less a personage than Don Philip, Marqués de Florida Blanca. If a few soothing words would settle the little blueblood's ruffled feathers, Janus was prepared to utter them. Don Philip had already served his purpose, and even the thought that he might win his way beneath Francisca's silken coverlet didn't disturb Janus. He knew that later, when Francisca was alone, her thoughts would dwell on the better man.

Don Philip flourished his long sword over his head. "Prepare to die, Señor Dog!" he cried loudly, his voice trembling with emotion and excitement.

Janus drew rein and doffed his hat politely. "Your Excellency," he said mildly, "I fear that I abused you cruelly when last we met. For this, and for any other injury I may have done you, I crave your pardon. And I wish you good night."

He tried to ride past, but Don Philip sat firm and again brandished his sword. "You sought to replace me with your loathsome self in the eyes of the Marquesa de Guzman," he accused, pushing his hat back out of his eyes.

"I am sure, Your Excellency, that the lovely *marquesa* has her own opinion of—both of us. Now, if you will pardon my haste, I have a long ride ahead, and——"

"No, you—you heathen Nonconformist!" The young noble's features were contorted with rage. "There is no man who may insult me as you did—and live. You have poisoned the *marquesa* against me. You yourself heard her accept my offer to permit me to be her escort tonight. Yet late this afternoon I received word that she was suffering from the vapors and was confined to her bed. And mark you, she was in the best of health when I departed from her only a few hours before. A disease has struck at her and must be wiped out."

Janus looked at the violently upset marquis with tolerance. He didn't doubt that Francisca was too tired to go anywhere tonight. "Although I have never before been referred to as a disease, I will not take offense, Your Excellency. Now permit me to pass."

"Never!" Don Philip's voice almost squeaked, so angry was he. "I sent my seconds to call upon you only two hours ago, but you had gone. Fortunately Major Santinas y Galmirez, who was on duty at the Puerta de Alcala, remembered you. And so I have ridden in pursuit. You shall not escape me or my vengeance, son of a slit-nosed whore!"

The good humor left Janus's eyes, and he clenched and unclenched his fists several times. Then, as he felt his temper subsiding, he permitted himself to speak. "Don Philip," he said in an even, quiet voice, "no man of good sense looks into the barrel of a loaded musket and pulls the trigger. And no gentleman in his right mind challenges to mortal combat one who earns his bread with his sword. I have already tendered you my apologies. If it will give you satisfaction, I will repeat them. I have already been more patient with you than is my custom, but I have no wish to spill your blood. My journey is taking me many leagues from

Madrid, and it will be a long, long time before I return. Return to your siege of the *marquesa* with a light heart. I wish you good fortune and bid you farewell."

Don Philip's little eyes blazed, and his lips curved scornfully. "You will never return from the journey on which I shall send you, offspring of a loose-tongued sow. You have heard of my prowess within the dwelling salons and you fear me. But you will not escape my just wrath. Dismount, heathen dog—and fight."

"So be it." Janus drew his sword and dismounted, sighing. He would wound the marquis sufficiently to put him out of action— no more—and would then resume his ride. If a change of government took place in the months to come, his claim to the land he intended to win might be complicated should Don Philip's uncle choose to be meddlesome. For the first time Janus began to realize why men of property were always so cautious in their dealings.

Hoofs thundering down on him caught him unawares, and he looked up just in time to see Don Philip's horse towering over him. The young noble had raised his sword high in the air and was about to bring it down full force on the head of his enemy. Only a fraction of a second between life and death remained. If those plunging, pawing hoofs did not kill him, Don Philip's sword would surely cleave his head in two.

He leaped forward as he had seen Swedish foot soldiers do in combat with Polish cavalry and caught hold of the saddle strap around the horse's belly. As the animal crashed down on his front legs, Janus hung on with all his strength, then swung himself out from under on the opposite side, away from Don Philip's restless blade.

Prudence was swept away by a wave of rage, and Janus was consumed by the lust to kill. That the marquis had tricked him into dismounting while keeping his own seat was bad enough, but attacking an enemy unawares while pretending to prepare for a duel was beyond the pale of civilized behavior. Unmindful of his disadvantage or danger, he reached up long arms, caught

Don Philip by one leg and by his silk cape, and pulled with all his might.

The strands of the cloth began to give way, but the cape was fastened securely at the marquis's neck, and the pressure of the cord at his throat jerked his head back, and he lost his balance. The iron vise around his left leg did the rest, and he tumbled to the ground.

Janus jumped clear and picked up his own sword from where it lay in the dust of the road. His first instinct was to strike at once, but he had been an officer for too long, and no matter how grave the provocation, he could not attack a man who was unable to defend himself. Instead he slapped Don Philip's horse smartly with the flat of the blade, and the animal reared and then cantered off into the linden grove. Backing toward his own horse while he watched the marquis scramble to his feet, Janus patted the beast, muttered some clucking noises, and threw the reins over a low-hanging branch. He had no intention of being forced to walk when the business at hand was concluded.

Flushed and angrier than ever, Don Philip regained his feet. He clutched his sword in his right hand and ineffectually tried to brush dust from his elegant suit as he glared at the Dane. Janus stamped his feet to free the soles of his boots from moist grass or leaves that might cause him to slip, and raised his sword in salute.

"*En garde*, Spaniard!" he called.

Don Philip wasted no breath on words but came at Janus full tilt, his blade slashing wickedly. Surprised at the fierceness of the onslaught, Janus gave way, parrying the blow as he studied the marquis's style. Then Don Philip feinted, smiled menacingly, and renewed his drive. For a second time Janus was forced to give ground.

There was no doubt that the young noble was a superior swordsman. Questionable though his conduct may have been in the battle for Naples, he was at home with a long blade. Unlike

51

many of his countrymen, to whom finesse meant more than vigor, he apparently favored a bold and slashing attack. And there was no doubt that he was grimly determined to kill.

Janus continued to retreat and waited for an opening. It came at last as Don Philip drove a trifle too hard and too far. The Dane stopped abruptly and lunged forward, the point of his blade aimed directly at the marquis's heart. But Don Philip recovered with amazing adroitness, beat off the thrust, and danced away. Each knew now that he faced an opponent of no ordinary skill, and with increasing respect came increasing caution.

For a quarter of an hour or more they moved back and forth across the empty road, the stillness of the night broken only by their heavy breathing and by the clanging impact of steel against steel. Janus remained confident that he would ultimately win. His strength was greater than that of Don Philip, and he was sure that sooner or later the marquis would tire. Meanwhile his mind was functioning again, and he realized that he would be courting possible disaster if he killed the nephew of a count of Spain before no witnesses. Much as he longed to sink his blade into Don Philip's heart, it would be wiser to return to his original plan and merely incapacitate him.

But it was extraordinarily difficult to curb his temper, for the marquis began using every trick of the swordsman and was trying to goad him by calling curses on Janus and his ancestors in an astonishingly varied stream of epithets. Then suddenly Don Philip slipped and stumbled, and Janus raised his sword high in order to give his enemy time to recover. But again Don Philip showed himself to be a stranger to the code of an officer, for no sooner was Janus's blade out of position than he drove forward with a savage cry of triumph.

Janus jumped to one side but could not completely escape the lunge. However, the thrust that had been intended for his throat merely passed through the flesh of his upper arm. The wound bled freely, soaking his shirt, but it in no way halted him. Nevertheless, he realized that he must make short work of the fight, for the marquis was too cunning an enemy to wear down and would resort to any means, fair or unfair, to win.

Concentrating with all his might, Janus began an attack of his own and thrust again and again, bearing in relentlessly, his eyes never wavering. It was Don Philip's turn to retreat now, and he did so gracefully. Soon they were off the road and fighting on the thick, damp grass of a meadow which spread out past the linden trees. The footing of neither was as sure here, and although Janus tried to compensate for the difference with increased swordplay, the marquis seemed less certain of himself.

All at once his guard became careless and his left shoulder was exposed. Janus suspected another trick, but the opportunity for a strike was too good to miss. A thrust in the shoulder would put Don Philip out of action. Aiming for an invisible mark on the marquis's shoulder, Janus lunged. Too late he saw that the Spaniard had planned a trick of the most elaborate kind, that he had deliberately exposed himself so that Janus would strike, and now was pretending to stumble in order to maneuver his own sword inside Janus's guard. Had the strategem been successful, the Dane's sword would have ended its lunge in thin air and the marquis, recovering his stance easily, could then have delivered his *coup de grâce* at his leisure. However, he did not count on the speed and vehemence of Janus's blow, which upset the delicate timetable of the marquis's calculations and left him still vulnerable. Both men realized at the same instant what was happening. But it was too late for either to draw back, and Janus's sword passed into the marquis's body a foot below his shoulder. . . .

Wiping his sword clean on the marquis's cloak, Janus stared at the body at his feet and considered his predicament. When Don Philip failed to return to Madrid, an alarm would be sounded, and sooner or later the major of cavalry who had been on duty at the city gate would testify that the young marquis had

53

ridden out in search of a Danish soldier of fortune. Were his uncle First Minister now, that testimony alone would be Janus's death warrant, once Don Philip's body was found.

But, he reasoned, it was unlikely that Aranda would order the arrest of a man whom he had just assigned to a secret mission of importance, at least not without more conclusive proof that he had murdered the marquis. And while Janus himself could not prove that he had killed Don Philip in a duel in which he had fought with scrupulous fairness, it was equally true that there were no witnesses who could state that the two men had ever met.

It would be best, then, to cover in some way, while maintaining an air innocent of any knowledge of violence. He rejected the thought that he should ride for Paris rather than Lisbon. He had told the cavalry major he was going to the Portuguese capital, and he would. In no way would he alter his plans. But what possible scheme could he concoct, he wondered, to throw pursuers off the track and to convince possible accusers of his innocence?

He stood lost in thought for many minutes, and at last the idea came to him. Stooping quickly, he removed the rings from Don Philip's cold fingers, cut away a moneybag that hung limply from his belt, and then as an afterthought broke off the young marquis's sword at the hilt, threw away the useless blade, and kept the jeweled handle. Leaving the body where it was, Janus looked with distaste at the booty in his hands as he ran to his horse, mounted, and rode rapidly down the road in the direction of the Portuguese border.

After traveling for half an hour he found what he was looking for. A small brook ran parallel to the road for a short distance, and beside it stood a cluster of fruit trees, their roots reaching down to the stream. Janus dismounted quickly, ran to the brook, and with his bare hands dug a hole beneath a tree root near the water line, scooping out the damp earth easily. After a brief struggle with himself he pocketed the money—perhaps ten gold dollars in all—and then placed Don Philip's gems in the hole and gazed at them for an instant. But he felt no regret at leaving them here, despite their value. One diamond found on his person would guarantee his hanging. He placed the earth back over the moneybag and jewels and patted it into place. Then he washed his hands clean in the brook, checked carefully to see that he had left no footprints that would lead a curious peasant to the root, and hurriedly returned to his horse.

As he galloped off down the road, he felt well satisfied with what he had done. When searchers found Don Philip's body and saw that his money and jewelry had been taken, it would be natural for them to assume that he had been set upon by bandits. And though the Conde de Florida Blanca might suspect Janus— if he listened closely to the cavalry major's story—there was no proof whatsoever. So long as the gems remained hidden, Janus felt he was safe. Making up for his lost time, he dug his spurs into the horse's sides and rode on toward Portugal—and America.

Chapter III

David Walker slumped in the special chair that the carpenters at Pa's lumberyard had built for him and stared through the open shutters at the crowds hurrying along Beacon Street. Autumn was coming early to Boston this year, and there was a sharp tang in the air, though the sun was still hot. David stirred, sighed, and his right hand groped for the sturdy oak crutches that were propped against the chair. He caressed them with his finger tips, then shoved them violently from him and they fell to the floor with a crash.

But the accident left him unmoved, and he resumed his aimless watch of the life outside the window. A door opened somewhere at the far end of the modest frame house, and a pair of light, quick footsteps approached. David didn't turn his head.

"My watchful sister," he said reproachfully. "Hears every move I ever make and won't let any harm come to the helpless wretch."

Rosalind Walker stood over him silently, then smoothed the coverlet over what had once been a pair of sturdy legs. She tried to appear stern, but it was difficult for one so lovely to feign anger when she felt nothing but tenderness and concern. Tall and thin, with a ripeness of figure that had come with recent womanhood, she pushed back the mass of soft golden curls that encircled her head and fell to her shoulders, and at last allowed her eyes to meet his. He looked at her for a moment but was unable to meet the cool scrutiny of those enormous light blue eyes and wrenched his gaze away.

"You refused to quit the field when you lost your left leg at Ticonderoga, Dave," Rosalind said in a soft, musical voice. "You fought through three more campaigns, and when they finally carried you off you cried because you couldn't fight any more. Why do you stop fighting now?"

He tugged savagely at the blanket that hid his shattered knees. "Fight, Roz? With what will I fight?"

"You know the answer to that as well as I." She sank to the floor behind him and smoothed her simple skirt. "You'll soon be fit enough to work in Papa's office—and you know how he needs you, Dave! There's never been anyone as clever as you with account books and ledgers and——"

David laughed unpleasantly. "Pa needs someone who can get out in the yard and stir up the lads. He needs someone who'll give the other lumbermen a battle. Pa is too old to wrestle for what little business there is these days—and I'm not able to race around Boston, offering bids for work before some other yardman beats me to it. Can you see me running—anywhere, Roz?"

She took his hand in her long, cool fingers, and when she smiled a large dimple appeared in her left cheek, near her mouth. "You can do anything you set your mind to do, David Walker," she said firmly. "You told me that once. Remember the first time a horse threw me? It was old Savage, the dear. You insisted that I get right up and ride again, and when I wouldn't, and stood there crying, you lifted me up into the saddle, slapped Savage so he cantered off, and shouted after me, 'Now ride, you silly girl!' Remember?"

In spite of himself, he grinned. "Yes, I do. Prudence and Bessie Small were there too."

"And speaking of Prudence——" Rosalind paused imperceptibly, and one hand stole toward her soft, creamy white throat. "Prue said that after I leave she's coming over to spend the afternoons with you, until you're strong enough to go to Papa's office."

David stiffened. "She needn't bother. I don't want her pity."

"Pity, Dave? I don't think it's pity that Prue has felt for you, and you know it as well as I."

"She deserves a man who can stand on his own feet. And who isn't going to inherit a business so puny and weak that his sister is forced to travel out to the frontier so she won't starve."

Rosalind's clasp on his hand tightened. "I'm a very fortunate girl to have a position waiting for me in Franklin, Dave. There are many schoolmistresses in Boston better suited to operate a girl's seminary than I, and I shall never know why the committee of ministers chose me. But I'm grateful they did. Think of it— I'll be earning more than twice the salary I'd get here, even if I were made headmistress, which isn't very likely."

"I've thought of nothing else all day, Roz," her brother replied sourly. "I see you going off to a new part of the world—to an exciting, alive place. And here I sit, rotting in the same old surroundings, tied to a lumberyard that'll never make me more than a skimpy living. It's been bad enough in the years since the war, watching so many of my old friends leave Boston for Franklin and Kentucky. Roger Perry and Austin Barton and even little Newman Burns. Yes, and the letters I've had from men in my regiment. 'Sorry you won't be there with us, Lieutenant, but we'll send you a grouse or a deer or a partridge.' I'll never hunt partridge again, Roz."

She stood and faced him squarely, her hands on her hips. "Indeed you won't—when you whine. And I don't understand this, Dave. Your whole attitude was so much improved—until recently."

"Was it?" His eyes followed the pattern of the little hooked

58

rug that Ma had made that first winter she and Pa were married, up in Maine Province.

"Dave."

"Mmm?"

"Look at me, Dave. Are you upset because—because I'm going out to the new lands where your friends have gone—and where you'd like to go?"

The young army veteran tried to raise himself from his chair, then fell back, exhausted. Beads of perspiration glistened on his forehead, but he accepted his sister's challenge. "Yes, Roz. I can't say I'm jealous of you, but I keep wishing I was going out to Nashville too. Nashville—what a place that must be. A new town, a city almost, way out on the far edge of nowhere."

Rosalind laughed. "You're romantic, Dave. A romantic little boy. You see a town filled with savages and trappers and goodness alone knows what. It doesn't seem very wild or very romantic to me. How could it be, when they hire a prim and respectable girl like me to come out and teach school?"

He passed his fingers through his sandy hair and grinned. "You're the best teacher in New England, and those ministers knew it when they selected you. Yes, and it's a mighty good thing you'll get such good pay, for it'll be a help to Ma and Pa. But the real reason you're going out to Nashville is because you're too bored here."

Glints of amusement showed in Rosalind's eyes. She and Dave had always understood each other, and this was like old times. "You wouldn't expect me to stay here and marry somebody like—like Responsibility Edwards, now would you, Dave? All he ever wants to be is a deacon of the church, and he will be, too—before he's thirty."

For the first time in many days David chuckled. "It's like I thought, all right. You've got the smell of the forests in your nose, and that whole country is in your blood. But I know a bit more about that kind of country than you do. And maybe I know a mite more about men than you too. And I tell you flat that there aren't many gentlemen thereabouts."

Her chin tilted forward. "I can care for myself."

"I guess maybe you can, Roz. But it does no harm to be fore-warned, you know. It won't be easy in a town where you don't know anyone. Excepting Harold Jordan, of course. He'll look after you."

Rosalind smiled. "Why? Because his sister Anne is a friend of mine? You'd be nice to her, I'm sure, if you were in Nashville and she were coming out. But I don't expect much from Harold. I never knew him any too well, and he left Boston almost right after he came back from the war. He's been in Franklin for a long time."

"Well," he said, "it's still good to know that someone will be near at hand to look after you should you ever need looking after. . . . And, Roz—write to me sometimes, will you?"

She viewed him with affectionate exasperation. "You know I will. I'll write to all of you regularly."

"I know the kind of letters you'll send to Ma and Pa. What I mean is—I'd like you to write to me special occasionally. Let me know what it's all really like out there. What you think of the land and the people and the game in the forests and the fish churning up the Tennessee River and——"

"Yes, Dave." There was an undercurrent of infinite sadness in her voice. "I'll write you very long letters, and I'll try to make it seem for you—as though you're in Franklin yourself."

The salesman of iron products from Hartford considered himself a very lucky man. He had awakened cursing the fate that sent him from Boston to New York on a Sunday. The coach, he had told himself, would be empty, the driver would be reckless, and the trip would be both boring and bumpy.

He couldn't deny that he had enjoyed smoother journeys, and

he made a mental note to make a business call on the makers of Red Lion coaches the next time he paid a business visit to Providence. No axle should behave so outrageously on a highway as broad and well traveled as the Post Road. Then, business matters momentarily put into the background, he returned to the pleasant occupation that had absorbed all of his attention for the past two hours, that of covertly watching his sole companion in the coach, the comely blonde who sat opposite him.

She was prim enough, he concluded as he studied her through lowered, puffy eyelids, but if he was any judge, there were hidden qualities in her that held considerable promise for the right man. In the light of his previous experience and conquests, he had few doubts as to the identity of that man.

Surreptitiously cleaning his fingernails on the elk's-tooth ornament that dangled from his watch fob, he leaned forward and caught her eye. "Is this your first trip to New York, ma'am?"

"No, I've been there twice before on brief visits with my family." Rosalind smiled politely, but the fingers of her right hand continued to grip her small cedarwood traveling box that contained her few jewels, her money, her papers, and a new Bible that her mother had given her at the last minute.

"Ah, then you don't know New York. A grand little town. Nowhere like Boston or Philadelphia in size, of course, and never will be, but there's sport to be had there for those who know where to seek it. Perhaps you'll dine with me there sometime. Tomorrow night, after we arrive and have a rest, shall we say? I know a little inn called the Gamecock, where they serve the finest beefsteak pie and the best mulled rum punches——"

"You're very kind, sir, but I fear my stay in New York will be exceptionally brief." She continued to be courteous but impersonal.

"Oh? You're going on to Trenton, perhaps? My business affairs often take me into Jersey, you know, and if I might make so bold as to inquire——"

"My destination is very far from here." She was secretly amused. "I am en route to the town of Nashville, in the new state of Franklin."

"Franklin?" The salesman from Hartford pursed his thick lips and whistled softly. "That's no mean journey for a lady. You go to join your husband, perhaps?" His eyes slid toward the ring finger of her left hand.

"I am unmarried, sir." The conversation was beginning to bore Rosalind, and she looked out of the window at the rolling green hills of Connecticut. Like all those born and raised in Massachusetts, she privately considered this countryside inferior to her own.

Rudely and without warning, her contemplation of the countryside was interrupted. The iron salesman from Hartford had shifted his not inconsiderable bulk to her side of the seat, and he sat less than two feet from her, leering at her in his horrid way. He fingered his slightly dirty stock, then tugged a perfumed lace handkerchief from his sleeve and mopped his brow. He performed the gesture with a flourish that gave him a faintly ridiculous appearance.

"So you're making your way in the world alone, little lady?"

Rosalind controlled an impulse to giggle. "You might call it that, yes." He inched imperceptibly closer, and the gleam in his watery eyes was all too easy to define. She reflected that a sharp, short scream would bring the coach to an immediate halt and that the driver, an elderly man with a kindly face, would certainly come to her aid instantly. But she rejected the idea as one lacking in dignity, and without changing her expression she took a tighter hold of her wooden box.

The salesman was rapidly coming to certain conclusions, and his face was growing ruddy. "You—mmm—you intend to set yourself up in a—mmm—business of some sort out there in the wild lands, is that it, little lady?"

"You might say so, I suppose." Rosalind had mapped a course

of action and was as cool as her brother Dave had reputedly been before the start of a battle.

"Anything in particular you aim to do?" The man slid expertly toward her, and his breathing grew heavy.

"As a matter of fact, there is. I'm going to teach school. I have a warrant from the governor of Franklin and from the Reverend Mr. Houston, his adviser on education, to organize the state's first seminary for young ladies."

Chuckling heartily, the salesman vowed to himself that his good fortune was even better than he had realized. There was nothing he liked more than a sense of humor in his women, and this wench was certainly jolly. The mere notion that any girl so beautiful would waste her time and her obvious charms on a schoolroom struck him as superbly funny. He threw his right arm around the back of the panel against which Rosalind leaned, and with his left hand he patted her knee. "That's good, that is," he said. "And what will you teach your pupils, little lady?"

"I intend to teach them many things," Rosalind declared sweetly. "Among other subjects will be that of deportment, for I firmly believe that nothing is more important to any of us than the knowledge of how to behave."

Swiftly she swung her knees away from the groping fingers and brought the traveling box crashing down on the back of the salesman's hand.

He yelped with pain, drew his bruised fingers to his mouth, and sucked them with the concentration that a small child devotes to a slight injury. Rosalind favored him with another impersonal smile, then turned and again devoted herself to a contemplation of the hills and cattle of Connecticut.

The salesman took note, however, that she had not relaxed her grip on the lethal weapon with which she had struck him. He stood up in order to return to his own side of the coach, but at that moment the rear wheels struck a deep rut in the road, the vehicle bounced dangerously, and the salesman's head encountered the crossbar of the ceiling with a resounding crash. He slid back into his seat and nursed his hurts silently for a time. At last he turned again to Rosalind, and when he spoke there was a reluctant admiration in his voice.

"Little lady," he said, "when you first told me you were going to the far ends of the Western country to live, I felt sorry for you. I did indeed, ma'am. But I've come now to regard the matter in a different light. I'll say it like this to you. The one I pity is the one who crosses you. He'll look at you and he'll think he's dealing with a sweet and soft little gazelle. But he'll find out—too late—that he's crossed the path of a she-wolf."

Chapter IV

Without question the home of Don Diego Gardoqui, minister plenipotentiary of Charles III to the Confederation, was one of the sumptuous and elegant residences in New York. Visitors to New York, even members of Congress, gaped at Number 56 Wall Street in awed envy. But Janus Elholm, lighting a clay pipe from an ornate rack at his side, seemed thoroughly unimpressed. Don Diego patted his curly, well-tended black beard and thought that rarely in his long and varied career had he encountered so determined and forthright a man. But after the fashion of diplomats, his expression remained bland.

Janus leisurely lighted the bright shreds of Virginia tobacco and removed the pipe from his mouth. "It occurs to me, Your Excellency," he said quietly, "that it would serve our purpose well if we converse only in English, incomplete though my mastery of that tongue may be."

Unaccustomed to receiving orders in his own house, the minister stiffened slightly. "Your reasons for making this suggestion, Señor General Elholm?"

"I have noted that your servants are American. Hence they are a curious folk. But from those whom I had an opportunity to study on board the foul tub that carried us across the ocean, I

65

have learned a paradox. They are both trusting and gullible, and will ignore what we say if only we speak in their impossible language."

Don Diego nodded admiringly. "You are most discerning, Señor General. It is true that the natives here are a strange race, like all new people. They are naïve but shrewd, careless but brave, impetuous yet steady and faithful. Their own worst enemies are themselves. In Kentucky District, which shall soon be ours, no two leaders can agree on a proper form of government, though the rulers of Virginia State, General Washington and Governor Henry and Señor Jefferson, are willing to grant them statehood. And in the other Western stronghold, the state of Franklin, there is even more confusion. There most of the people are agreed on statehood and have proclaimed their separate status. But a minority, stirred up of course by our agents, swear fealty to North Carolina State, where I have spent many thousands of our good gold dollars to insure that a sentiment against Franklin prevails."

The mention of gold alerted Janus, but he took care to puff negligently on the pipe and sipped of the excellent dry madeira at his elbow. "Our legions will sweep across the countryside like a plague of locusts, Don Diego." He smiled contemptuously. "These gawky townsfolk and stupid peasants are fit only to squabble and scream at each other like a bevy of blowzy trollops over a tipsy gentleman who recognizes them not for what they truly are."

Don Diego smoothed the velvet cuffs of his impeccably tailored suit, and the veins stood out on his slender, patrician hands. "The English made the mistake of thinking that these bumpkins could neither band together nor fight, but today the American colonies are a free union," he drawled. "You soldiers always think you can conquer by the sword alone, but you are wrong. I tell you plainly that we must tread warily, delicately, softly, if this rich plum is to fall into our laps."

Genuinely amused, Janus laughed aloud. "You diplomats are always shortsighted, Don Diego," he said emphatically. "I have been in New York for two days, and what do I find? The capital city of a new nation is a pigsty at which even the lowliest Polish peasant would turn up his nose. I have been buffeted and elbowed aside in the streets by the poorest of scum, wearing the meanest of garb. I have been addressed as an equal by serving-folk who carry their heads as high as do the gentry. If the hinterlands be like New York, the whole country will fall apart at the first sound blow. And I intend to deliver that blow."

The minister shook his head, and his thin face grew even more pinched. "The military are a breed apart," he sighed. "Miró in New Orleans is a senile lecher who thinks of nothing save lewd women; Galvez in Pensacola is a martinet who builds stronger and yet stronger fortifications and foolishly dreams of conquering worlds with them. And now Madrid sends me——"

"The man who will conquer the New World for you." Janus was positive and flat.

"Please listen to me, Elholm. The Americans held a convention in Philadelphia through the summer months and have drawn up a new Constitution—a document that will invest real powers in a strong and balanced central government. Once their states ratify the agreement, they will never be dislodged from this continent—never. Fortunately for us, they do not realize what a strong weapon they have, and their petty leaders in each state argue and bicker over the Constitution. Two or three years will certainly pass before their new form of government is established. Two years, three at the most—that is all the time that remains to us. If we have not eaten the Western lands by then, we shall never digest them. And the seaboard states will forever remain independent of us."

"Then we must strike as rapidly as possible," Janus replied. "My regiments will make this prized Constitution into no more than a worthless scrap of soiled paper." There was less time than

Don Diego realized. The private agreement with Aranda specified a limit of one year.

Again Don Diego sighed. "There are other techniques equally effective, my bloodthirsty colleague. I have recently concluded a pact with the foremost donkey in America, who happens to be Foreign Minister here. In return for free trade in the coastal ports, Señor John Jay has agreed to permit us to close the Mississippi River to American shipping. And so I have already begun to starve the peasants of the Western lands into submission. Meanwhile my agents stir up unrest and rebellion in one hundred—in five hundred—places. Yes, Elholm—I do all these things —and only when the plum is ready to drop from the branch will I call upon you to lift your sword and cut her down. Until then —travel into the borderlands—and learn to respect and fear these men as I do."

There was no levity in the minister's tone, and Janus regarded him thoughtfully. Either Don Diego was a womanish pessimist, or else that million-acre tract and the title of marquis would be harder to achieve than Janus had believed possible. His doubts were reflected in his face, and Don Diego arose and grasped him by the arm with fingers that were still surprisingly strong.

"Come here to the window, Señor General. Do you see that great brick house across the street? It does not appear to belong to one of the rabble, do you agree?"

Janus was forced to concede that none but a man of wealth and prominence could own such an establishment.

"That, my blind colleague, is the home of one who was himself a penniless immigrant to America. Colonel Alexander Hamilton, aide-de-camp to Washington in the insurrection. And to us the most dangerous man in North America. He is archpriest of a new faith, a faith that brings pilgrims to his door by the hundreds and by the thousands. He preaches the doctrine that the United States must expand to the Western ocean, that all territory between the two great seas must and will be hers. His people hear him, and they become inspired."

Coins jingled in Janus's money pouch, and he restlessly sought to change the subject. "I grant that you are right in all that you say, Don Diego. So much more the reason, then, that we attend to business. The Conde de Bolea Aranda informed me that you would supply me with funds."

Don Diego took his time in replying. "How much did Don Pedro give to you?"

"Four hundred gold dollars." The words came out easily. Janus was sure that Aranda had not bothered to keep his minister informed of the details of their arrangement.

"And how much do you want from me?"

"I have incurred many expenses and must resign myself to many more. I must buy a horse and a suitable wardrobe. I must—— Let us say fifteen hundred gold dollars."

Taking a step backward, Don Diego contrived to look horrified. "Even Miró does not ask for such sums! Not even he who throws gold at the feet of his dancing girls dares to—— My treasury cannot stand it. I will give you one thousand. No more."

"So be it." Janus bowed his head and pretended to cough. Raising his hand to his mouth to conceal his smile of triumph, he reflected that he was doing far beter than he had anticipated.

"I will give you the money in American pounds. Our dollars would cause everyone to whom you paid them to look on you with suspicion. You will sign a receipt, of course. Also for this."

Janus found himself staring at a very large silver coin into which a small hole had been punched. He took it and examined it curiously. On one side was imprinted a Crucifix and on the other a figure of a man holding forth a regal crown surmounted by seven points. Below the image was the inscription, SVINTILLUS REX OFFERET. Disdainfully he weighed the metal in his hand. Surely Don Diego was not such a bumbling fool that he would give a Papist bauble to a Danish Protestant!

The minister smiled thinly. "It is a medallion of Svintilla of the Visigoths, whose crown rests today in the cathedral at Toledo. Wear it at all times in a visible place. All of my key men wear such a medallion while on American soil. Thus they may be recognized by my scores of lesser agents, many of whom can neither read nor write. Without the medallion you would not be received by Don Esteban Miró or Don Alfonso Galvez, nor would one of our army march at your bidding.

"Wear it in pride and dignity, Señor General Elholm, for it marks you as a conqueror of a continent. And though you be not of the One True Faith, know, too, that it has been blessed by the three cardinals of Spain and that with it upon your breast you cannot fail. Neither you nor our cause will falter, but will triumph together."

Philadelphia, Don Diego had warned, was the most suspicious town in America, conscious of her role in the formation of the new Republic and filled with citizens who made a practice of ferreting out the interests and business of strangers who failed to conform to the common mold. Having been warned to remain as inconspicuous as possible, Janus wore his oldest clothes and glanced ruefully at his frayed cuffs as he sat in the common room of the Market Street Tavern. Trying to choke down an incredibly peppery soup as though he liked the stuff, he thought that tomorrow morning he would take to the Franklin road and would bury his miserable garb as soon as possible. A general of Spain, even if traveling incognito, should not be forced to travel in a costume little better than that of a peasant.

But despite the dictates of prudence that forced him to wear such mean attire, he felt that his work was at last beginning. Don Diego had said that the tavern was a headquarters for those who planned a new life on the frontier, and true to his predictions, two men at the next table were discussing the current prices of whiskey, wool, and kitchen utensils in such far-off places as Louisville and Nashville. Past the traders, at a table close to the hearth, sat a party made up of a man, two women, and three small boys, and they were bubbling with talk of Franklin too.

One member of the group in particular caught Janus's eye and took his mind off the highly seasoned soup. Fashionably dressed, she was one of the most delicately beautiful blondes he had ever seen, and he told himself that America was truly a land of paradoxes, for she seemed to have little in common with her gross, crude companions.

The tavernkeeper, removing Janus's soup plate and placing a platter of stewed beef before him, noticed the direction of his gaze. "Pretty, eh?"

Unaccountably resenting the man's tone, Janus endeavored to remain civil. "She is lovely," he said, sure that his quiet reproof would go unheeded.

An avaricious spark lighted the innkeeper's dull eyes. Digging Janus slyly in the ribs with his elbow, he leaned closer to the table. "Rich, too. She's paid the folks with her a full five pounds in silver to escort her to Franklin. Five pounds, mind! I know for sure, 'cause I set up the deal."

The man drifted away when his remark went unanswered, leaving Janus to speculate at his leisure. So the lady was not only exceedingly pretty but wealthy. His journey to Franklin might prove less boring than he had anticipated. His chance to strike up an acquaintance came sooner than he had hoped, for the adult male member of the girl's party arose abruptly from the table and made his way toward the door and the privy beyond. Janus stood up, brushed a small chunk of potato from his breeches, and drifted toward the group.

"Mademoiselle," he began without preamble, "I am informed that, like me, you travel to the distant state of Franklin."

A startled look appeared in the girl's deep-set eyes, and without bothering to look at him she turned her back on him, shrugging her shapely shoulders in the universal disdain of a lady for one beneath her. The older woman copied the girl's behavior, and Janus found himself staring at two rigid backs.

"Mademoiselle," he said again in his most honeyed voice, "you

71

do not comprehend me correctly. I offer you no insult. I——"

He broke off abruptly as the tavernkeeper loomed at his elbow, a long, curved carving knife in his hand. Janus's eyes swept the room quickly, and he saw that the two Yankee traders had arisen from their chairs, ready to join in if a dispute threatened.

His first impulse was to challenge the three men to immediate combat. Despite the tavernkeeper's bulk and the wiry, lean appearance of the others, he had no doubt of his own ability to make short work of them. It would require no great effort on his part to force the blond heiress to recognize him, and he was sure that his charms would then soon guarantee him an interesting and exciting traveling companion.

But, once he drew his sword, he would be advertising his prowess with the blade, and there would be considerable comment—talk that might conceivably follow him to Franklin and do him harm there. Reluctantly, therefore, he forced himself to assume a bland expression and turned to the owner of the tavern.

"Yes, monsieur?"

"You talk like a foreigner, mister," the man growled, "so maybe you don't know about our womenfolk here. They don't talk to casuals on the road unless they want to. And when they don't—well, it's a blame sight healthier to let them be."

A mild autumn sun blazed almost directly overhead, and although Rosalind had been in the saddle since dawn, she felt no weariness. On the contrary, she had never been more alert or awake in her life. Ever since traveling through Cumberland Gap into the territory of Franklin State, she had been growing increasingly uneasy, for despite her eagerness to see the West she was shocked by the ruggedness and desolation of the countryside. This eastern portion of Franklin was supposedly the most heavily populated, yet she and the Dolson family, with whom she was riding, had passed only four scrubby little cabins since breakfast.

Nat Dolson, short and swarthy, drew rein beside her on the narrow, stump-laden path that was supposedly the best road in the state. "Matter, Roz? You a-gettin' scared o' this here country? Want t' go home t' your ma 'n' pa up Massychusetts way?"

Rosalind swallowed a sigh. "Not really, Nat. I just never expected Franklin to be so—so lonesome, that's all. But if you and Min and those three little ones of yours can stand it, then so can I."

Dolson shifted his rifle to a more comfortable position under his arm and amiably scratched a three-day growth of blue-black beard. "Shucks, this ain't so bad. Not after the Tidewater scrub-lands where I been tryin' t' farm. Look yonder, Roz. This pass we're a-ridin' through leads into the Holston Valley. See it down there? Soil so rich you need only drop seeds in the ground and they grow. And mild—look at the green on them trees. Gosh-a-mighty, girl, it's the middle o' October, but it's still summertime here, and the mountains yonder'll keep winter out o' here for a long spell yet. And that ain't the half'n it. My cousin Len, who writ me to come t' Franklin, says this here country ain't nothin' compared t' what it's like in that new town o' Nashville. Len ain't never been one t' lie much. He's too dull-like t' tell anythin' but the truth. And from what he says about this here section—which I've proved rightly so with my own eyes—I s'pect the rest is true too."

There was an awkward pause, and Rosalind felt a pang of shame for troubling the man who had been kind enough to give her his protection and had treated her like a member of his own family through so many days on the trail. "I'm sorry, Nat. I knew this must be wonderful farming country, and I'm sure you and Min were right to leave the flatlands to come here. But you see, there are five of you in your family, and you'll never have a chance to be lonely."

She looked back toward the rear of the little caravan, where eleven-year-old Carl, holding a rifle taller than himself, was shouting vehemently at his two younger brothers, who were squirming and bouncing in the saddle of an extraordinarily patient pack horse.

"Shucks, girl. 'Tain't lonely hereabouts. See that curl o smoke in the valley? That's a house. And less'n half a mile t' the north is another. And you see the clearin' straight ahead, pas them pines? That's a man-made clearin'. Why, there's more neighbors in less'n two hours' ride 'n you'd care t' holler at."

He grinned, patted her hard on the back as though she were one of his unruly sons, and spurred his horse to the front of the caravan. Rosalind bit her full lower lip nervously. She should have known better than to betray her fears to a man who was proving himself beyond fear. Out of the corner of her eye she caught a glimpse of Min Dolson bouncing on the hard planks of a miserable wagon loaded with bedding and household goods. Min was going to give birth to her fourth in a few months' time, but in the two weeks they had been together Rosalind had never once heard her complain.

Again Rosalind sighed, then straightened in the saddle. Without doubt this *was* beautiful country. Nowhere had she seen grass so thick, spreading like a rich blue-green carpet. Nor were the pines and maples and spruce of New England and Pennsylvania as majestic as the giants that lined this path. A wood pecker was setting up an infernal racket somewhere deep in the patch of woods to the left, and the faintly moving shadow directly ahead, where the trail rose sharply before dipping into the valley, probably betrayed the presence of a deer.

Yes, she could grow to love Franklin eventually, Rosalind told herself sternly, and she would. She was behaving like a baby when she permitted herself to lose heart; granted she hadn't expected to find neighbors so close that you could converse with them from your bedroom window as you could in Boston, and in time she would become accustomed to the vast emptiness of the region. She had to discipline herself.

Suddenly the shadow in the pines burst into the open and a masked rider pointed two long dueling pistols at Nat Dolson's head. Rosalind reacted before she had time to think and began to fumble in her saddlebag for the ornate mother-of-pearl-handled pistol which had been her brother Dave's parting gift. But a harsh voice from the woods to her left stopped her and sent a chill racing down her spine and into her legs.

"Stay like you was, blond lady, and there ain't nobody will get hurt. Clem, take that fowlin' piece from the young'un back there afore he shoots himself."

There were three in the raiding party, and Rosalind watched in a helpless rage as they methodically spilled the contents of the Dolsons' wagon onto the trail and helped themselves to items of value, which they piled beside a young pine. Rosalind's own cedarwood box was at the bottom of the cart, and she had no doubt that when they realized it contained objects of some value they would take the box intact.

"I suppose you think you're very brave, three of you robbing one man and a party of women and children." Rosalind was surprised to hear her own voice, cutting and clear. "When the authorities of Franklin catch you, they'll——"

The leader of the bandit trio threw back his head and laughed raucously. "Ain't no such thing as Franklin, ma'am. This here is part o' North Car'lina. Just like Colonel John Tipton says 'tis. And when folks get ready t' bow t' the courts 'n' the law 'n' the sov'reignty o' North Car'lina, then I recokon they ain't goin' t' be molested no more on these roads. When you report this t' Jack Sevier, tell him Tipton 'n' North Car'lina could keep order hereabouts. Tell him——"

The man's last words were drowned by the crack of a rifleshot, and the painted plate in his hand exploded into a shower of tiny pieces. A second shot sounded, and the broad-brimmed hat that covered the leader's head was blown violently to the ground. The filthy rag that served as a mask fell away from his face. Clutching it to his nose, he bolted into the saddle. His companions, who had been staring into the tree-studded hills above, fingering their long rifles, were scarcely aware of what he was doing until he bawled an order.

"Clem! Howie! We got to get to blazes out o' here. It's a Sevier trap!"

His companions needed no further invitation, and without another glance at their victims they leaped onto the backs of their horses and plunged into the thickest part of the forest. Two more rifleshots pursued them, and then all was silent again. A few seconds later the industrious woodpecker returned to his labors, and a peculiarly sibilant hissing in the underbrush hinted at the presence of a raccoon. Nat Dolson wiped his face and neck with a far from clean square of linen and waved to his sons.

"Better help pack this mess o' goods back in the cart, boys," he said quietly, only the tremor in his voice revealing his true emotion. "We've got us'ns a long haul t'day if we're a-goin' to drop Miz Roz here by the Meetin' o' the Waters Inn."

The little Dolsons immediately began throwing skillets, petticoats, a wooden chopping bowl, eating knives, and various other objects into the wagon, but Nat did not join them. Instead he hastened to Rosalind and his habitually silent wife, who had instinctively moved closer together, and the three of them stared up into the hills from which the shots had come.

After a few moments their patience was rewarded, and their benefactor rode into view. Rosalind saw that he was wearing dark and unadorned but expensive breeches and a very new fringed hunting shirt of butternut-stained buckskin. He wore a conventional three-cornered hat, but Rosalind was quick to note that it was trimmed in real gold bullion braid. There was something unusual about his appearance, and only after a moment or two did Rosalind realize what it was. His feet were shod in the most magnificent boots she had ever seen. Fashioned of a soft, dull black leather, they reached to his knees and clung to the calves of his legs as though they were a part of him. General Washington, whom Rosalind had once seen in New York, had worn beautiful boots, but even he had not sported such regal footgear.

The man's eyes were unexpectedly dark, and so piercing that she shivered and transferred her gaze to his strong, cleft chin. She heard Min Dolson gasp and quickly knew why. Never had either woman seen anyone so heavily armed. From his left side hung a sword of a length seldom seen in America, and under his right arm he carried a very short musket with a carved oak butt inlaid with crescent-shaped bits of silver. Around his neck this one-man arsenal had slung a delicate poniard which dangled from a thin chain of wrought silver. Also affixed to the chain was a large silver medallion which tinkled pleasantly as it fell against the dagger shaft.

Indifferent to the impression he was causing, he rode to within a few feet of Rosalind, and before his horse had quite stopped he jumped to the ground, swept off his hat in a flourish, and bowed low.

"I am happy to be of service to the lovely mademoiselle and her servants," he said in a resonant voice through which filtered a faint but unmistakable foreign accent.

"We thank you for saving us, sir." Rosalind wasn't quite sure why she was annoyed. The difference between her dress and that of the Dolsons was responsible for the young gentleman's natural misunderstanding. "However, Mr. and Mrs. Dolson aren't in my employ. On the contrary, I'm very much indebted to them, for they've escorted me all the way into Franklin, and they're going out of their way to take me to Jonesboro."

The young man raised an eloquent eyebrow but said nothing. Nat Dolson, who was too good-natured to take offense, especially against one who had salvaged his property, pumped the newcomer's hand vigorously.

"Stranger," he said heartily, "me and my family and Miz

77

Walker here sure be obliged to you. Two minutes later and them skulkin' timber wolves o' John Tipton's would have made off with the whole kit 'n' caboodle o' what we own. Nat Dolson is my name, and this here's my wife."

The young foreigner adjusted his stock carefully. "The thieves who were sent scampering are of the band of the so illustrious Colonel John Tipton?"

"Seems like, 'ccordin' t' what they was sayin' t' each other. I've heard tell that Tipton wants this state t' be part o' North Car'lina agin, so he keeps things in an almighty uproar. But I never reckoned he'd send his polecats a-preyin' on innocent travelers."

"I also have been informed that conditions here are far from stable." The foreigner flicked some dust from his breeches.

"Then you're new t' Franklin, too, Mr.—uh——"

"Elholm. Janus Elholm of Copenhagen, but recently arrived in the town of New York from Lisbon and journeying for the first time into Franklin."

Nat's features were working with excitement. "Did you say *Elholm?* Be you related t'——"

"He is my brother," Janus Elholm said after an imperceptible pause, a faintly mocking smile touching the corners of his mouth. It was the first time he had told the lie about his alleged relationship to John Sevier's adjutant, and he was pleased to note that the effect was immediate.

"Say, this is great. Min! This here is the brother o' the most important man in Franklin next t' Gov'nor Sevier. Yes, sir— George Elholm is sec'tary 'n' treasurer o' the state, and adjutant gen'ral o' the whole shebang o' state militia b'sides. Boys, quit that infernal ruckus or I'll switch you. Come over here 'n' shake hands with a real gentleman o' quality. Roz—you know who this feller is? Look at him!"

The advice to Rosalind was unnecessary. Indeed, she had been unable to tear her eyes from the soberly elegant young Dane.

Rarely had she seen such a handsome man. But her fascination was caused by something more subtle, more intangible. He was vaguely familiar, and she tried without success to remember where she had seen him before. In any case, he was returning her stare unblinkingly, ignoring the Dolsons, who thronged around him.

Then without warning he wheeled toward Nat. "It is true, the impression I receive, that you travel out of your path to escort Mademoiselle to the end of her journey?"

"That's about the size of it, Mr. Elholm," Nat replied, nodding his dark head. "Me and my family, we're a-headin' out t' Nashville, and were plannin' t' stop for supplies and suchlike at Greeneville. But Roz here—Miz Walker—is aimin' t' get t' the Meetin' of the Waters Inn, and t'morrow she's a-plannin' t' go on t' Jonesboro and see the gov'nor. Like you saw for yourself, it ain't safe for a purty gal t' go a-traipsin' around this here country alone, so——"

Janus smiled, and there was no denying that he was genuinely pleased. "The Inn of the Meeting of the Waters! As I will gladly prove to you from dispatches in my pouch, I myself am traveling to this same inn. So I will happily relieve you of your burden and act personally as Mademoiselle Walker's escort for the remainder of the journey."

"I'm none too sure you would be a proper escort, Mr. Elholm." Rosalind was horrified to hear her own words. What in the world had impelled her to make such a bald, ungracious statement?

The Dane's tone was grave as he responded, but there was an undeniable twinkle in his eyes. "I shall watch over you with great care, mademoiselle. Also, may I remind you that we will arrive at the Inn of the Meeting of the Waters by sundown this evening? Or so I am informed by those who have mapped for me my itinerary."

Nat concentrated on a deep rut in the road and shuffled his

feet. "Roz," he said huskily, "if's there wasn't no choice, I'd keep to my bargain with you. But I—well, I'm a-scairt and I ain't ashamed t' admit it. I got my family t' think about, and the quicker I c'n leave this here borderland b'hind, the happier I'm a-goin' t' be. This ain't a matter o' leavin' you t' travel by your lonesome. You know Nat Dolson wouldn't let nobody down that-a-way. But this gentleman is the brother o' George Elholm —and there's nobuddy in the state as big as him, 'ceptin' the gov'nor, o' course. So you'd be travelin' in good hands. And it's only for a few extry hours. O' course we'll take all your heavy boxes o' clothes 'n' things on t' Nashville for you, and they'll be a-waitin' there for you when you arrive there."

Rosalind's every instinct cried out against riding on alone with the self-assured Dane. But she could certainly sympathize with Nat's desire to put as much distance as possible between his wife and children and a turbulent area.

"I—I understand your position, Nat," she said faintly, wondering what excuse she could find to avoid being forced to travel in Janus Elholm's company.

But there was no opportunity to explore the possibilities, for Nat leaped at his chance. "I'll give you back your five pounds," he said, fishing in his pocket.

"No, Nat. You've earned the money. More than earned it." Her brother Dave had always told her that the time not to show fear was when she felt most afraid, and when Nat mumbled something further she held up her hand to stop him. Her change in escort had been decided upon, and she had to put the best face on a bad bargain.

"I've caused you good people enough delay already. If you don't hurry, someone else may lay claim to the land you want at Nashville. And you must think of yourself and your family— and your future—first. I'll be all right now. I'm sure a gentleman of Mr. Elholm's standing will see me safely to the inn." Rosalind found herself stressing the word "gentleman," and her impatience with herself increased.

"You will not regret your trust in me," Janus murmured, again bowed low, and then ignored her as he helped Nat transfer her smallest clothes box and other portable possessions from the cart to the broad back of her pack horse.

No traveler on the frontier willingly wasted the daylight hours that were so precious for cross-country movement, and the farewells were soon concluded. In a remarkably short time Rosalind found herself riding through the bounteous but desolate Holston Valley with a gaudy and handsome foreigner. During the next hour her misgivings began to dissolve, for Janus proved a most agreeable companion. He rode in the lead along the narrow trail, and whenever, after consulting his map, he had to cut across open country or through patches or woods, he was careful to slow his pace to one that was comfortable for Rosalind. He spoke but little, and when he did it was to point out an unusually colorful wild flower or to inquire the names of trees that were unfamiliar to him.

It was early afternoon when they approached a small river and paused to let the horses drink. Janus walked his animal a short distance upstream, calling over his shoulder, "It is time we stopped for a short drink, too, Mademoiselle." He jumped to the ground, threw his reins over a tree branch, and hurried to Rosalind.

She took hold of the hand he raised to help her down, and slipped from the saddle. Then, before she quite realized what was happening, both of his arms were around her, pressing her to him, and his lips were insistent against hers.

Never had she been kissed with such fiery passion. She began to struggle, but Janus's grip grew even tighter. Even as she fought she cursed herself for having been so stupidly and incredibly naïve as to travel alone with a stranger and a foreigner in the first place. It was small consolation to know that she had been a fool; this was a predicament worse than she had ever experienced. She was miles from help, and the man holding her helpless was no mealymouthed Connecticut salesman but a hard, ruthless adventurer who only too plainly took what he wanted without regard for either decency or propriety.

Something cold and hard brushed her arm, and she became aware of the nearness of Janus's pistol. Quickly she drew it from its holster and pressed it unflinchingly into his ribs. He was at first unaware of what she was doing, and she jabbed him with it menacingly. Then, and then only, did he draw away.

"You picked yourself the wrong girl for this kind of a tussle, Mr. Elholm," she said coldly. "Make one more move toward me and I'll blow your head square off your shoulders. I mean what I say."

He shrugged eloquently. "You neglect an opportunity, mademoiselle. Do you wish such exquisite perfection as yours to be wasted—thrown away—on some unresponding, unappreciative oaf in this miserable wilderness, *cara mia*? Come with me—and you will see what showers of wealth can be drawn from this impossible country. You deserve——"

"And I don't care for any more conversation." She aimed the pistol directly at his head, unwavering.

Again he shrugged. "Shall we resume our journey, then?"

"All right. But I'm keeping this gun until we reach the inn, and if you try one trick, Mr. Elholm—just one—you won't live to dig into that fancy gold mine of yours. I'm warning you now."

There was no further attempt at conversation through the long hours of the afternoon. In fact, Janus rode at least ten yards ahead of Rosalind, and by neither word nor gesture did he indicate that he was aware of her presence. He might have been traveling alone, and gone was the consideration he had shown her earlier. He seemed to take a perverse delight in increasing the pace whenever they rode through brambles, thickets, or woods, and whenever they crossed a stream he chose the spot most difficult to ford.

Rosalind looked down at the long rents in the delicate blue fabric of her skirt and at the muddy splotches on her shoes and stockings. It was only through great effort that she controlled her desire to burst into tears, and when an overhanging branch slashed an ugly tear in the back of her brocaded jacket she couldn't refrain from sniffling.

Then she began to wonder whether Janus Elholm was really leading her to the Meeting of the Waters Inn, and her worry over possible danger again drove all else from her mind. If need be, she kept repeating to herself, she *would* shoot him. . . .

By late afternoon they began to ride through more cultivated territory, and in spite of herself Rosalind's tension began to ease. Every mile now they passed a farm, and twice they caught glimpses of buildings more imposing than the typical settler's cabin of clapboards or rough logs. As long as there were dwellings to be seen and daylight remained, she felt comparatively safe, but when the sun sank behind the high hills in the west, a clammy feeling gripped her, and she determined to accuse Janus of taking her elsewhere than the inn.

She spurred toward him, then fell back again at almost the same instant. For directly ahead, through an opening in the rocks, was a waterfall which seemed to spring from nowhere, and beside it was an imposing three-story building with glass windows and curtains, the first solid evidence of civilization that Rosalind had seen in many days. Through the gathering dusk she was barely able to make out the painted board that swung from a chain over the entrance, but she saw enough to assure her that this was indeed the Meeting of the Waters Inn.

The door was open, and looking into the taproom which seemed to fill most of the first floor, Rosalind saw a surprising number of guests—apparently all of them men.

"Evenin', folks!" a hearty voice sounded from the stables, and a pair of heavy footsteps approached.

Janus slid from his saddle and crossed to Rosalind in three gigantic strides. He held out his hand:

"My pistol, please."

She stared down at the dueling weapon which had served her so well. Without thinking, she had shifted its position as he had moved, and it remained pointed directly at him. He reached up, grasped it by the muzzle, and wrenched it from her hand. Then to her mortification he laughed sardonically as he tucked it into his belt.

"This," he said, emphasizing each word, "is the pistol I used when I fired my last shot at the Tipton bandits who so wrongfully molested you. I have had no opportunity to slip another charge of powder and lead ball into it. Hence at no time since it has been in your possession, mademoiselle, has it been loaded."

He swept toward the open door of the inn without a backward glance.

Chapter V

"Shoulder your muskets, march away to war,
  Knife and pistol, powder too, bring them all and more;
  Up your arms! Drive the redcoats to the sea!
  Free our homes, our land for the Sons of Liberty!"

The words of the old war song rolled across the courtyard as Rosalind prepared to follow Janus into the inn. Perhaps there was no particular significance in the appearance of a large throng of men at the inn, but Rosalind felt instinctively that there was trouble of some sort brewing.

She tried without success to push her way through the buckskin- and linsey-woolsey-clad throng at the door. The men were heavily armed with a variety of weapons from frontier rifles and Continental Army muskets to Choctaw war axes, and the air was thick with alcohol fumes and sweat. Someone in the back of the mob shouted, "Look at the beautiful blond wench, boys!"

The cry was taken up immediately. "Take her along for luck! It'll be cold sleeping on the ground, but she'll help warm it up!"

"I saw her first, you mangy timber wolves! I'll take her!"

"Like hell you will! She's mine and I'll beat the living tar out of any man who says me nay!"

"I'll toss you for her, Hez. The best of three throws and we'll use my dice!"

The room was in an uproar. Rosalind, panic-stricken, attempted to back out, but she was hemmed in on all sides. A hairy hand pawed at her shoulder, and someone slipped an arm around her waist. She stood very still, her eyes big with terror.

Suddenly a voice rang out from the doorway: "What's going on here?"

The men turned their attention to the newcomer and saw a very fat young gentleman, who stood with hands on his hips, scowling fiercely as trickles of sweat ran down his brow. He ignored the throng as he tried with no success to push and shove his way to her side.

"It's the tavernkeeper," someone cried.

One of the tallest and roughest of the frontiersmen clapped a heavy hand on the fat man's back. "You a Frank, mister? Be you a citizen o' this here state?"

The tavernkeeper attempted to shake him off. "Yes, of course, of course," he muttered impatiently. "I built this place right after the war, and I've lived here ever since. What has that to do with this lady?"

"We got us'ns a new recruit, boys!" The ringleader's voice was lifted in triumph. "Mister, there's a militia call out for every able-bodied man. You're comin' with us on a little huntin' trip. We'll sweat a mite o' that blubber off'n you!"

He laughed raucously, and his companions joined in. The innkeeper made the error of trying to strike off the offending hand that gripped the back of his coat. What happened next was almost too quick for Rosalind to follow. The man's fist crashed against the innkeeper's jaw, and he dropped to the floor with a groan.

"Pick him up, boys! Take him outdoors and—and swear him in. But don't rough him up too much—remember, he's got t' be in shape t' march t'night!"

Three willing volunteers lifted the struggling innkeeper and hauled him through the entrance. He bellowed and screamed in protest for several seconds; then followed the sound of several dull blows in quick succession, and all became silent. The men transferred their attention back to Rosalind.

"Now, sweetheart," said the tall leader, "we'll see if you know how t' act as purty as you look."

Rosalind caught her breath. Once more the mob closed in on her, and she could see nothing but a sea of unshaven faces and glittering eyes.

Unexpectedly there was a brief scuffle at the far end of the taproom; then the crowd parted very suddenly, leaving an open path before Rosalind. Moving toward her at a lazily indolent pace was Janus Elholm. In his right hand he held his long, two-edged sword, and he flicked it negligently. The men grew very quiet, and when Janus spoke his voice carried to everyone present despite its low, casual tone.

"Gentlemen, you astonish me. Is it unknown in Franklin how properly to treat a lady? Alas. A lady, my dear friends, is the most sensitive of all creatures, far more sensitive than women who are not ladies, and she lacks appreciation for our more robust manners. She does not enjoy the caress, the kiss, the sweet hug as we do. She can be touched by no one, not even her protector. Nevertheless, I hereby proclaim myself the protector of this lovely lady."

The heavy-set ringleader started out of the mob toward Janus and found the point of the naked sword lightly touching the fringe of his buckskin shirt directly over his heart. Janus spoke again, very softly. "For your health, my dear friend, I recommend that you remain where you are. Without hesitation I will carve to tiny ribbons anyone who stands in my path. A lady often wishes to ornament her hair with ribbons." He smiled happily, and his voice was kind and gentle.

Still frozen, Rosalind could only gape at the Dane's audacity.

There were at least twenty men in the room, yet he held them at bay with his lone sword—and his lack of concern. He arrived at a spot only three feet from Rosalind before he stopped. Then he bowed profoundly.

As he raised his head she saw a sardonic gleam in his eyes, and his mouth twisted in a wry, silent laugh. "Permit me, mademoiselle," he said, offering her his free arm.

She had no choice but to take it, and walking at a maddeningly slow gait, he maneuvered her to the staircase and waved her ahead. She raised her skirts above her ankles and began to climb, repeating to herself over and over again that under no circumstances must she break into a run, for then the pack would surely be at their heels. Janus Elholm was right behind her and seemingly had forgotten the presence of the men. But he was so near that she could sense the tenseness of his body, and as she reached the top of the landing and turned, she saw that he was walking with catlike lightness on the balls of his feet, ready to spring in any direction if need be.

"I had just inquired for rooms for you, mademoiselle. You won't be bothered there." He gestured toward a door at the end of the hall.

"I—I don't know how to thank you, Mr. Elholm," she stammered.

"Thank me? For what? For helping remove you from the presence of somewhat drunken savages? It was nothing. No trouble, I assure you, mademoiselle. Men forever lust before they go into battle. It is nothing new."

"Battle, Mr. Elholm?"

"So it would seem. These men are members of the state militia."

"And—and the innkeeper—the gentleman who tried to help me?"

He grinned. "He has apparently been—shall we say?—persuaded to join the expedition. Now, if you will forgive me, please, I have business elsewhere."

He wheeled abruptly, but Rosalind laid a hand on his arm. "Wait, Mr. Elholm. If you—if you go back down there, those men—they'll kill you."

"I consider the eventuality most unlikely. However, if it will relieve your mind, know then that soon their officers will arrive and will control them."

"Oh, but there aren't any officers here now. So—until they do arrive, wouldn't it be better if you—kept out of sight?"

"I thank you for your kind invitation to join you in your apartment, but I regret that I cannot."

Embarrassed and angry at his knack of deliberately misunderstanding her, she stamped her foot. "I never intended to convey to you the impression, Mr. Elholm, that I——"

"You are, as always, discreet beyond belief. I will say only this to you, mademoiselle—I can care for myself. Never fear for me, because I never fear barbarians—only those who possess some small measure of wit and intelligence. And in this forsaken land I have encountered no one of such a caliber." He bowed again and was gone down the stairs.

Rosalind's pulse was throbbing. She raised a hand to her throat as he moved around the bend with easy grace, turned for an instant, and winked at her familiarly. Then he disappeared from sight.

A low, menacing murmur arose from the crowd in the taproom, and Rosalind caught her breath. She should run to her room and bolt the door, she knew, but she was unable to move until she learned what would happen below. The noise grew louder, then Janus's voice cut through the talk. Despite the carrying quality of his tone, she was unable to hear what he said.

There was a sharp second of silence, then someone laughed. That broke the spell, and soon the whole mob was shouting and bellowing. But there was neither hostility nor anger in the persistent rumble now, and the danger to Janus was clearly dissipated.

No doubt the Dane had mollified the men with some vulgar remark at her expense. She knew it was wrong—even childish—to resent it, for he was showing extraordinary cleverness and adroitness in winning these surly frontiersmen over to him so rapidly. She hated, though, to be in his debt; yes, that was it—she loathed the need for being grateful to him. But there was no doubt that he had saved her from a humiliating and possibly a dangerous situation.

She turned and walked firmly down the hall of the little inn to her room. She would be gone from the inn in the morning, long before Janus Elholm awakened, and she would not see him again. What was more, it was unlikely that their paths would ever cross in the future. She told herself that nothing could please her more.

It rained all morning, and by noon the streets of Jonesboro were reduced to puddles of sticky clay. Then it cleared slightly, but low, scudding clouds made the two-story frame building in the center of town appear even more dismal than it was, though at best the structure could scarcely have been called imposing. Flanked on one side by a tavern and on the other by a dilapidated stable, it was built of roughhewn boards which had long ago been whitewashed but which now showed only a few streaks of dirty gray. Oiled paper served in place of glass in most of the windows, and the shingled roof sagged dangerously.

Two filthy, nondescript Indians sat on the damp ground in front of the building, propped against the wall, their greasy black hair falling into their eyes. One was asleep, and the other scratched and searched halfheartedly for lice.

Aside from its size, the only thing that distinguished the structure from its drab neighbors was the flag which flew from a tall pole planted in the center of the shabby yard. The background of the banner was blue, and on it blazed fourteen stars which circled majestically. As every Frank knew, it was the only flag of its kind in the United States, for elsewhere a scant thirteen stars rode on the field of blue.

An unshaven youth in his early twenties lounged against the doorframe of the entrance, his left hand negligently grasping a long frontier rifle. He was dressed in drab, patched buckskins, and on his right shoulder was sewn the epaulet of a sergeant. He was chewing a wad of tobacco, and his jaws moved slowly and rhythmically, but otherwise he gave no sign of life.

Suddenly he blinked and almost swallowed his cud, for approaching the building was the prettiest girl he had ever seen. To be more accurate, she was more than pretty—she was ravishingly beautiful. She was wearing a dark green dress of some crinkly material that rustled as she walked, and over her blond curls was fastened a long bonnet with a visor to keep off the rain. Her skirts were lifted to her calves to keep them from trailing in the mud, and the young sergeant silently swore that he had never seen a neater pair of ankles or daintier feet.

The girl looked at the crumbling building, slowed her step, and glanced uncertainly at the flag. The sergeant shifted his weight. "Lookin' for somethin', mistress?"

"Yes, I am. I—I'm trying to find the state government building, and I was told——"

Lord, but she had a sweet voice. The sergeant, ordinarily the most pragmatic and unimaginative of men, was sure there was music in it. "This is Gov'ment House, mistress. Lookin' for anybuddy in partic'lar?" He grinned and tugged at his faded shirt. He'd be off duty in an hour or so, and Abel's Tavern would be glad to provide a private room for a soldier and his friend at a not too outrageous price.

"I've come to see Governor Sevier, if you please. Is this where I'll find his office?"

The excitement that had been mounting in the sergeant sub-sided abruptly. The boys were right when they said that every breath Nolichucky Jack Sevier drew was a lucky one. "Inside and down the hall," the young man said gruffly. He leaned back against the doorsill and fished with his tongue for the tobacco he had stowed in his cheek.

Rosalind stepped rapidly inside and then halted abruptly. There was virtually no light in the corridor, for rooms lined both sides, and the only illumination came from an open doorway at the far end of the gloomy hall. She made her way slowly toward the welcome shaft of light, her footsteps echoing slightly on the ancient, rotting floorboards. When she reached the open door she heard the irregular scratching of a quill pen and hesitantly peeked inside.

A man was sitting in a large, bare room at a long pine table, writing industriously and with great speed. Before him stood an inkwell and a small basket filled with quills, and beside them was an untidy mound of papers. Within easy reach on the table was an ugly horse pistol, heavy and ungainly. It was cocked, ready for instant use.

The occupant of the room seemed as plain as the walls. He was wearing simple dark broadcloth breeches and an old buck-skin shirt from which most of the fringe had been worn to stubble. His brown hair was brushed back severely from a high forehead and was clubbed in back with a bit of frayed black ribbon. He raised his head for an instant to call, "Don't just stand there, girl. Come in, please." Rosalind caught a glimpse of a long, thin nose, high cheekbones, firm lips, and a pair of strong, sharp brown eyes. He was in his early forties, the oldest person by far whom Rosalind had encountered since entering Franklin.

"How did you know I was out here? And how could you tell—without bothering to look up—that it was a girl in the corridor?" She had no right to question him, but she was curious.

The man merely smiled enigmatically and waited for her to continue.

"I'd like to see Governor Sevier, please."

He rose slowly to his feet. He had not appeared tall when slumped in his rickety chair, which groaned when relieved of its burden, but when he straightened he towered above Rosalind and the whole room seemed filled with his presence.

"Who wants to see the governor?" His voice was crisp, and although his accent was the soft, liquid slur of Virginia, his tone was authoritative.

Rosalind stiffened indignantly at his demanding air. While she knew she was just being contrary, she immediately determined to tell this rude underling nothing of the business that had brought her here. "Be good enough to tell him that Mistress Rosalind Walker of Boston desires an audience with him," she said imperiously.

"What is it you wish to see him about, Miss Walker?" He remained courteous but unyielding.

"A private matter."

He was amused by some secret joke, and sparks of humor twisted his quick eyes. "I'm afraid you'll have to tell *me* what it's all about, Miss Walker."

Angry but helpless before this stubborn boor, she plunged her hand into the commodious pocket of her dress and drew forth the warrant that had been signed by the governor himself, the warrant that charged her with the responsibility of organizing and operating a seminary for young ladies. "Perhaps this will convince you that my mission here is genuine," she replied tartly, handing him the paper.

He held it to the light, his office boasting a pane of glass in the window, and examined it carefully. For an instant he seemed startled, and his eyes darted to Rosalind. He studied her openly for a very long moment, then he leaned back and motioned her into a straight chair beside the table. Strangely, his gesture was as courtly as it was abrupt.

"I bid you welcome to Franklin on behalf of myself and of our people. I apologize for forgetting your name. But I've been somewhat preoccupied of late. Rest assured that I have been expecting your arrival, however."

Rosalind's knees gave way, and she sank to the hard wood of the chair. She had treated this gentleman like a servant, and his identity was becoming painfully obvious. "Governor Sevier?" she asked in a tiny voice.

He bowed, trying not to laugh. "I am Jack Sevier—at your service. Your obedient servant, Miss Walker."

"I—I'm dreadfully sorry, Your Excellency. I—you see, I thought——"

A deep laugh rumbled through his solid frame. "Yes, my dear. What you thought was quite apparent. But we'll say no more about it, provided you don't call me 'Your Excellency' again. We don't stand on ceremony in Franklin, Miss Walker. We're a new state, beset by troubles, and we're too poor and too sparsely settled a land to be proud. Our citizens are too busy chopping out homes for themselves in the wilderness, too busy fighting off Indians and Spaniards to build me an imposing office. And I'm damned if I'd want it or feel at home in it if they did."

He smiled, and his face was suddenly illuminated. Feeling the warmth and magnetism of his personality, Rosalind was instantly drawn to him, and her sense of embarrassment promptly vanished. Nat Dolson, who had fought under Sevier at the battle of Kings Mountain, had told her that every man who had ever known the general would gladly lay down his life for him, and she began to understand that feeling. Sevier might be an implacable enemy to those who stood in his way, but he would be equally unswerving in his friendship.

"You're very kind, Your Excel—— Governor Sevier." Her brilliant smile flashed at him for the first time.

"Shall I confess to you that I wouldn't have known you either, Miss Walker? I received a long report from the Boston gentlemen who were kind enough to select a schoolmistress for us, but they neglected—being clergymen—to say anything about your appearance."

"My appearance, Governor Sevier?" An odd feeling of uneasiness stole over her.

"Yes, my dear. Your rather spectacular appearance. As the father of a brood as old and older than you, I have the right to say it. And I am myself not so old that I fail to appreciate beauty when I see it. I'm afraid you bring a series of unexpected problems to Franklin with you, Miss Walker."

Rosalind felt both flattered and annoyed. "Under the terms of my contract with Franklin, I am to be paid for my capabilities in a classroom, Governor Sevier—and not for the shape of my nose or the curve of my eyelashes."

"Well put, my dear. Exceedingly well put." Sevier nodded and looked pleased. "But I fear I must explain in more detail. As you have no doubt been informed, the Reverend Sam Houston is the official but unpaid adviser to the state in all matters regarding education. Sam has worked wonders for us—he's set up five or six boys' schools. But he's a cantankerous old rascal, and it's no accident that there are to date no seminaries for members of your sex, Miss Walker. Sam doesn't like or trust women, and I don't care to think of his reaction when he discovers that you're young and pretty."

"I shall have to prove to him then that I am competent."

"Quite so. Provided he gives you the chance, Miss Walker."

Color drained from Rosalind's face, and her feeling that all was not well grew deeper. "Gives me the chance, Governor Sevier? Now I must confess that I don't understand you at all!"

He picked up a quill pen and toyed with it for a moment. "Surely you read the warrant of office we sent to you, Miss Walker. Here—let me study it. . . . As I thought, the language is both specific and clear. Listen to this: 'The appointment of the afore-mentioned Mistress R. Walker is binding upon both the state and upon the individual for a period of two years, under proviso of confirmation and concurrence by the governor of Franklin, prerogatives of said concurrence to be vested in the governor or his chosen representative.' That representative is Sam Houston, of course."

Thoroughly bewildered, Rosalind could only stare at him. "You sent me the money to come to Franklin, didn't you? I was under the impression that what you've read was no more than legal language like all the 'whereases' and 'afore-mentioneds.' "

"In the most liberal sense, that is true." Sevier smiled at her sympathetically. "However, more than legal language is involved. In the strictest application of the agreement, it would be possible for Sam Houston to turn you away, to send you packing right back to Boston. I don't suggest he's likely to do that, Miss Walker. And I sure don't suggest that you worry about it, either. But it's only right and fair to give you warning so you'll know how to act and talk when you see Sam. . . . Now let me turn you over to my adjutant. While I would like to prolong our discussion, I'm much occupied at the moment with an unpleasantness involving our state military." He was out of the chair and at the door before Rosalind was quite aware that he had arisen. "George!" he bellowed. "Come in here first chance!"

He bounded back and settled in his chair with a resounding crash. An instant later a pair of footsteps sounded on the sagging boards outside, and a heavy-set man of medium height entered the room. His blond hair was thin, and a layer of flesh covered what had once been lean muscles. It was difficult to see his eyes, for he wore spectacles of an unusual thickness of lens.

"Mistress Walker, may I present Major George Elholm? This is our lady schoolteacher, George." Sevier's mind was already straying back to the pile of work on his desk.

Very few men could have made a leg to a lady in the best accepted style when dressed in old, limp buckskins, without appearing ludicrous, but George Elholm accomplished the feat neatly. Rosalind studied him briefly and was somewhat surprised at the lack of similarity between him and Janus Elholm. One would hardly have imagined them to be brothers.

After a brief exchange the governor waved them from his office, half rising to his feet, then thumping back into his protesting chair as he became immersed in his work. Rosalind curtsied and a moment later found herself in the corridor with the major, who remained silent as he guided her a short distance down the hall and bowed her into his office. The room was as bare as that occupied by John Sevier, save for one significant difference. Three bearskins had been crudely sewn together and spread out over the floor, and although they were black in color they lent a surprising note of warmth to the cubbyhole.

"Pray be seated, Mistress Walker." The major did not sit but began to pace around the edges of his rug. "I shall make all the necessary arrangements for your transportation to Nashville——" he began, when Rosalind interrupted him.

"I am to see the Reverend Mr. Houston first, I believe," she said with a faint trace of bitterness. "Governor Sevier has told me that I need final confirmation from the reverend before the job of establishing the seminary is truly mine."

He chuckled. "Sam may bark at you, but he's as harmless as a coon dog, so don't you worry. However, you'll not find him here. He's either in Nashville—or will soon be there. I'm afraid I can't send you out at the moment, though."

"Oh." Rosalind waited for him to continue as the tempo of his stride around the perimeter of the rug increased.

"West of here are Cherokee lands, Mistress Walker. So folks play safe and travel together in large parties, in convoys. Unfortunately there won't be any convoys leaving Jonesboro for a time. No men to spare. You've heard of John Tipton, the idiot who insists that Franklin is still part of North Carolina, I suppose?"

"Yes, I have." This was not the time to tell him about the

bandits who had proclaimed themselves Tipton's followers.

"Well, the old rum-head led a raid on Mount Pleasant, the Sevier farm. One of the most vicious acts ever perpetrated in Franklin."

Rosalind tried to speak but could not. For the first time since leaving home she longed for the peaceful dignity and the tidiness of her family's quiet parlor on Beacon Street.

"Some puny court in North Carolina judged Sevier a rebel and ordered his lands and property confiscated. So while Jack was on his way here to Jonesboro on state business, Colonel Tipton and a company of fifty men rode to his farm in Greene County and cleaned the place out. They took his furniture, his silver, his pelts and supplies—even his slaves. The ones who didn't run off into the forests, that is, and who'll never be found. There was nobody home but Mrs. Sevier at the time—all three of the boys were here with their father—and she couldn't stop Tipton, though she threatened him with a rifle."

"Oh, the poor woman." After her comparatively insignificant brush with the men in the taproom of the Meeting of the Waters Inn, Rosalind could feel intensely for the governor's wife.

"Of course the Franks aren't going to stand for such shenanigans." The major blinked angrily behind his spectacles. "A punitive expedition to teach Tipton and his followers the meaning of law and order will start out tomorrow morning."

"It all sounds uncivilized, major. Primitive." Rosalind was shocked and made no attempt to hide her feelings.

He regarded her owlishly. "This is a raw country, Mistress Walker. It's a chaotic land, and it'll take us time to put things to rights. Are you sure you want to stay here and go to work for us?"

She rallied at once. "I'm sure Franklin is no rougher than New England was when my ancestors settled there, Major Elholm. And the women of our family all survived."

The major grinned, and the quality of his smile, something

indefinable in his expression, reminded her of Janus. She spoke quickly, on impulse.

"For the first time you remind me of your brother, Major."

He removed his spectacles, then put them on again. "My brother?" He seemed genuinely puzzled.

"Yes. Janus Elholm. I met him on the trail yesterday. He was very kind to—to the party with whom I was traveling." There was surely no need to tell the major her true opinion of Janus—that he was crude, ungentlemanly, and without doubt the most ruthless human being she had ever encountered.

"You must be mistaken, Mistress Walker. I have no brother." The major was pleasant but very firm. "I have no relatives whatsoever, save for one elderly maiden aunt who still lives in Copenhagen. Of course the Elholm name is a common one in Denmark —as common as that of Robertson is here in Franklin. So perhaps you simply presumed——"

"He told me in so many words that he was your brother." Rosalind had no idea why she was being so positive, so emphatic.

The major smiled and perched on the edge of his desk. "Lots of folks claim they're related to state officials, I reckon. Every once in a while some fast talker from the jails of Philadelphia or Charleston comes along and pretends to be Jack Sevier's father or brother or son. And after he's bilked a few honest families out of their savings we catch him. For a while we used to put people like that in our own jails, but now we save ourselves the expense and send them riding off with a nice warm coat of tar to keep them from getting a chill on the road. I hope the man who told you he was related to me didn't try to sell you something."

"Oh no. He——"

"Good. Because I'm the only Elholm in Franklin. And as far as I know, I'm the only one in the whole United States."

Rosalind felt both annoyed and embarrassed. She might have known that Janus had lied to her. The best thing to do now would be to conclude her business with the major as rapidly as possible and then return to her tiny room at the Senators' Inn, where she would try to wait patiently for the formation of the convoy that would take her to Nashville.

Rosalind had been gone from George Elholm's office less than twenty minutes when someone knocked at the door, and the young sergeant who had been stationed at the entrance of the building came in. Saluting with a vigor that made up for his lack of military polish, he blurted out his errand quickly. "Two men here t' see you, Major. One of 'em is Colonel Wilkinson, and the other——"

"Jim Wilkinson of Kentucky?" The major was on his feet at once. "Show him in, Sergeant. Don't keep someone of his standing waiting!"

"Yessir. That's what I figgered." The sergeant grinned amiably, saluted again, and ducked out.

George Elholm tightened his belt a notch, then began straightening the papers on his desk. A visit from the illustrious James Wilkinson was an occasion. Only Governor Sevier and Jim Robertson of Franklin and Wilkinson's neighbor in Kentucky, Dan Boone, were so highly regarded throughout the Western lands. Indeed, Wilkinson was looked upon by many as the first citizen of Kentucky, and it was whispered that both Mr. Jefferson and General Washington of Virginia favored him for the governorship when Kentucky achieved her statehood. But when such talk had reached Wilkinson's ears he had modestly stepped aside and had declared that the honor belonged to Boone. His fame had catapulted even higher thereafter, for it was common knowledge that by neither education nor temperament was the taciturn Boone fitted for the post.

As a military man Colonel Wilkinson had few equals, Major Elholm reflected. Brilliant commander of regiments and brigades, he had distinguished himself as both a tactician and as a fighter of unquestioned personal valor. And late in the war, when the

Lobsters were at last on the run, he had shown his versatility by performing with notable success as a member of the personal staff of the commander in chief.

Now, in the post-war era, he was showing that he was as shrewd a businessman as he had been a soldier. His home was one of the largest in Kentucky, his farms were among the most prosperous, and his trading posts were patronized by unending streams of immigrants to the new lands.

Crisp footsteps sounded in the corridor, and Major Elholm jumped to his feet. Colonel Wilkinson entered, his right hand outstretched and a broad grin creasing his rugged, tanned face. Almost six feet tall, he looked considerably younger than a man in his thirties had any right to look. He scorned a wig in favor of his own prematurely white hair, which he kept meticulously combed and clubbed. His dark woolen suit appeared on first inspection to be similar to the clothes worn by any prosperous farmer or merchant, but careful scrutiny revealed that only a top-ranking Philadelphia tailor could have made these clothes.

"George, lad, it's good to see you!" There was no denying the impact of Wilkinson's personality.

"Welcome to Jonesboro, Colonel. Does General Sevier know you're here?"

"No, and I don't want you to tell him. He has enough to keep him occupied in this new Tipton outrage. Besides, I've only dropped in for a moment. George, I'd like you to meet a namesake of yours. Comes from your part of the world too. Major George Elholm, Mr. Janus Elholm."

For the first time George looked at Wilkinson's companion and studied him sharply. This was unquestionably the impostor of whom the new schoolmistress had spoken, the man who had claimed to be his brother.

He murmured an acknowledgment to the introduction and, in spite of himself, George was impressed. Rascal or gentleman, the stranger's appearance was imposing, and there was no denying that he shook hands like a man. "Sit down, Colonel. Mr. Elholm. Let me offer you a pipe." The major was slightly wary.

Colonel Jim Wilkinson eased himself into a chair gracefully. "I'll take up only a moment of your time, George. Three or four traders are waiting for me at this minute over at Henry's store. I hate to admit it, and I don't know how you Franks do it, but your beaver pelts are better than ours." Wilkinson's tone implied that the major was in some way personally responsible for the quality of locally trapped furs.

"Not ready to admit that our women are prettier than yours, are you, Colonel?" George smiled as he remembered a necessarily inconclusive argument in an all-night drinking bout two years ago.

"We'll resume that little discussion one of these days." Wilkinson recalled the incident too. "But right now I'd like to do Franklin a favor and give a hand to Mr. Elholm here too. You need men for this little expedition of yours against Tipton, don't you, George?"

"We do, sir." The major shot a searching glance at Janus from behind his thick glasses, but the young Dane's face was bland and expressionless.

"So I thought. Well, here's an experienced soldier for you, George. You haven't forgotten Colonel Jan Sablinski, I dare say."

"The Pole who was on General Charley Lee's staff? Sure, I remember him. Used to heat his ale with a bayonet that he'd stick in red coals."

Wilkinson nodded his heavy, well-shaped head. "That's the one. He and Mr. Elholm served together last year in Bavaria——"

"No, Colonel. In Tuscany." Janus spoke for the first time. "He was my adjutant for six months."

Major Elholm's eyebrows shot up. "*Your* adjutant, Mr. Elholm? *Colonel* Sablinski was a senior officer in our army."

"As he was in ours. His rank and mine were the same, Major. But it so happened that when one of our major generals—rot his soul—went over to the enemy, I was given command of his division for a time." Janus took great care not to sound condescending.

"I see." The major was none too sure of what he did see.

Wilkinson pulled himself to his feet suddenly. "I'll leave you gentlemen to your own devices," he said. "My regards to Jack, and good luck to you both, George. I hope you drag John Tipton back here at the looped end of a rope. Good-by, Mr. Elholm. If ever you come up to Kentucky, I hope you'll drop in to see me. We have a brand of hospitality up there that turns the Franks every color of a rainbow in envy." He shook hands quickly and was gone.

Major Elholm leaned back in his chair and examined the remaining visitor more openly. There was no denying that his namesake was a fellow Dane; no one but a Scandinavian could boast such fair hair. Judging from his attire and the quality of his weapons, it seemed a fair guess that he was in no urgent need of funds, and the major veered toward the opinion that pretty little Mistress Walker of Boston had been mistaken about him. It was logical to conclude that because of the similarity of names someone else had expressed the belief that they must be brothers. Well, it was idle to speculate. "I take it you've had considerable military experience, Mr. Elholm," he said flatly.

Janus nodded soberly. "I've been a soldier all my life."

The medallion hanging across the front of his visitor's shirt caught the light, and George's attention was drawn to it. He had once seen an insignia much like it and tried to remember where. The notion persisted that a year or so ago he had observed such a medallion hanging from Colonel Jim Wilkinson's watch fob.

"I hope you realize, Mr. Elholm, that we cannot offer you a commission as an officer. The time is too short and, frankly, our troops will only follow leaders whom they know and trust."

"I understand. It is not my intention to embarrass you by requesting a commission from you, Major. But it was my hope that my experience might prove of benefit to you in some way."

The major was both relieved and grateful. "There's not much doubt that we can use your services, Mr. Elholm. But I hope you realize that we're a mighty poor state. Our colonels draw very small pay, and our enlisted ranks get almost nothing."

Janus shrugged and smiled. "I have no need of a militiaman's salary to pay for my dinner," he said lightly.

"Mind if I ask why you want to join us, then? I gather you're a stranger to Franklin."

"Both to Franklin and to America, Major. I shall be honest with you. I have two motives. First, I am a fighting man. You know what that means. I have been inactive for too long and I yearn for the excitement of battle. I am told that a physician who does not use his knife eventually loses his skill in severing limbs. A soldier without a war is in much the same predicament."

"Mmm." George waved his hand deprecatingly. "Your point makes sense, but I'm afraid you're going to be disappointed in our 'war,' as you call it. It won't amount to an anthill the day after the first frost. You say you have two reasons—what's the other?"

He was going to tell the absolute truth, Janus reflected, though the major would not know it. "I am traveling through your state in order to observe the nature of the people and of the country. I know of no better way to do this than to see your men in battle."

"Very interesting. May I inquire why you are visiting us, or is it none of my concern?"

"I may—or may not—decide to settle here. In any eventuality, I anticipate becoming the owner of considerable tracts of land in Franklin, and I intend to survey the property." Janus was inwardly pleased at his secret joke.

"Is there anything I can do to help you?"

"Indeed you can—brother."

Through slightly narrowed eyes Janus watched the effect of his use of the word "brother." The major, utterly startled, sat bolt upright, then arose to his feet and glowered. "What poor attempt at humor is this, Mr. Elholm? You and I are in no way related, and you know it as well as I."

"Perhaps I do." Janus took command of the situation instantly. "But hear me out before you judge. My real purpose in coming to this land is the same as that which motivated your migration. I have fought under many flags for many generals. I have come now to this New World to make my fortune. I have said to myself, 'If the illustrious George Elholm is enabled to become wealthy and is the partner of Governor Sevier and of William Cocke in the ownership of thousands of acres of fine lands, I can do likewise.' "

George sat down abruptly and glared. The schoolmistress from Boston had been only too right. "You seem to know much of me and my affairs," he growled.

Janus gestured disarmingly. "It is not difficult in a land where everyone sings the praises of Governor Sevier's adjutant. It is known to all that you were wounded during the American insurrection——"

"Revolution!"

"Very well, then. Revolution. It is common knowledge that you served on the staff of the American artilleryman, Henry Knox, that you commanded the cannon at the battle of Kings Mountain under Sevier, and that you later took part in the decisive battle of Yorktown. Also at one time you were a liaison officer with General Francis Marion——"

"You've gone to a heap of trouble to look me up!" George's voice began to rise, and for the first time he spoke with more than a trace of a Danish accent.

"That which serves my purpose is never a trouble to me." Janus remained unruffled.

"Plainly you have a purpose, then, in claiming me as your brother, Mr. Elholm. If that really is your name."

"I have never lied about my identity, Major. I am famous

throughout Europe as a soldier, and I have good reason to be proud of my name. As for my claim that you and I are related, my purpose should be obvious to you. Were I to come here as a total stranger, your people would be suspicious of me, would keep their doors shut to me. As a near and dear relative of one of the best-loved and most powerful personages in Franklin, I find myself welcomed everywhere. And it makes far easier for me my task of deciding where to invest the little capital I have accumulated."

George made no attempt to hide his outraged honor. "You freely admit that you are an impostor, sir?"

"Certainly not. And you, my dear Major, will gladly abet my harmless little deception. You will of your own accord tell people that we are brothers."

"You must be mad, sir!" George reached for a small bell that rested on a far corner of his desk, but Janus deftly knocked it from his hand to the bear rug.

"Hear me out before you make any rash moves, Major." In deadly earnest now, Janus no longer maintained his pose of negligent unconcern. "Fail me in this and you will regret it to the end of your life. I said that you will voluntarily second my story, and so you will. I think there are only two people on this continent who know the true story of why you left Denmark and came to America. Both of those men are at this moment here, inside this room."

Major Elholm wilted visibly. "What do you mean?" he croaked.

"Only this, my dear brother. As an ensign of artillery in the Second Regiment of Royal Danes, you had the bad taste to become enamored of the wife of your commanding colonel. You embezzled regimental funds to satisfy her appetite for trinkets, and when the colonel discovered all that you had done, he challenged you to a duel. Again your judgment was poor, and in the ensuing engagement you killed him. The scandal over the entire affair was so great that it became necesary for you to flee from

Copenhagen to America. Here you have built for yourself an enviable and successful new life, but you have taken great pains to keep your notorious past hidden, as it might hurt your political career here."

There was little fight left in the adjutant. "How did you learn all this about me? Why have you gone to so much effort to dig up that which has been buried for so many years?"

Janus was again relaxed and casual. "My reason you already know, as I have taken care to explain it to you. How I came upon your unsavory past is both amusing and ironic. Some years ago, when I was first achieving repute on the field of battle, I returned to Copenhagen to visit my father after the conclusion of an especially exhausting campaign waged for the Swedes. Word swept through the city that I was there, and within twenty-four hours the royal provost marshal, Prince Karl, had placed me under arrest—thinking that I was you.

"I had to expend considerable energy and time to prove that the wrong Elholm had been seized. In the course of establishing my innocence I learned the whole sad story of your misdemeanors. As it is my policy never to waste anything, I determined that someday the incident would repay me. And so it is doing now, most handsomely."

George again removed his glasses and buried his face in his hands. "I love the United States of America," he said in a muffled voice. "I have done everything in my power to live down the errors of my youth and to create for myself a good and useful life. You may not understand why I feel as I do about America, but I—I have lost blood for my adopted land."

Janus stared at him for a moment, then laughed contemptuously. "I was wounded when I served under the Saxon flag, but that does not make me love the Elector more. And the saber gash which I suffered on my arm when I led a Polish cavalry squadron into battle does not endear the King in Warsaw to me. You are too noble, my dear Major. Had you starved as did

Gustavus Elholm and his family, you would not now be hampered by false illusions."

"Gustavus Elholm—of the office of chief postal inspector?"

"The same. You do know of my family, then."

"My father and uncles," replied George with renewed spirit, "were forced to deny for many years that we were in any way related to the infamous Madame Helena Elholm, who eloped to Paris with the terrible old Count of Kronstadt."

"Wise men do not discuss my mother, Major." Janus's composure had deserted him, and his voice shook. "Let us merely say that you will, where necessary, acknowledge me as your brother."

George glared at him. "I have no choice, apparently. Very well, Mr. Elholm. I accept your terms—provided the safety of my adopted land and of the state of Franklin are in no way placed in jeopardy. Should I at any time discover that you are doing harm to either, I will prosecute you to the ultimate degree of which I am capable, regardless of the damage that may be done to my own career as a result of your exposures."

"So be it. And that concludes our business, Major. You are no doubt busy, and I have several errands to perform before joining your little band of militia tomorrow. This has been a most interesting and profitable quarter of an hour." Janus arose, bowed, and hurriedly left the office, carefully closing the door behind him. He could hear Major George Elholm muttering and cursing on the other side of the partition, but he was indifferent to his namesake's anger. He could now travel with impunity throughout Franklin.

And in the meantime he was about to increase his store of military information. As he strolled down the corridor to the courtyard he laughed aloud. A brigadier general of Imperial Spain would become, for a brief time, a mere enlisted man in the ranks of the world's least professional army. A new well of unexpected humor bubbled up in him; for the first time in his career he would be fighting without pay. He wished he could share the joke with

Aranda; the First Minister would, he was sure, appreciate the situation.

As a matter of fact, he would refuse to accept a penny of pay from the Americans, even if they offered him some paltry sum, for that would spoil the jest. Yes, he would wait—until his Spanish divisions struck against the very militiamen with whom he was now going to serve. Then, but not until then, he would extract payment in full.

Chapter VI

High Street in Jonesboro was at best a dismal thoroughfare. Beginning at the north end of town, near the Westlake farm, it meandered along an uncertain course into an increasingly populated district, and when it finally gave promise of turning into a street worthy of the name, it ended abruptly at the edge of a mud flat. However, it was broad enough to allow two teams of oxen to pass each other in safety; and aside from the deep ruts that appeared in the section between old Martha Hempstead's house and the new stables every time it rained, it was the best road in all Franklin.

The legislature and courthouse, which consisted of two sprawling wings connected by a tavern, dominated High Street, and the hitching posts inside the broken picket fence were almost always in use. Another center of activity was the New Flag, an eating and drinking establishment owned by the state's most prominent diplomat, William Cocke. No woman had ever set foot inside the New Flag's doors, and the habitués of the establishment swore that none ever would. It was the one place in town where a man could eat beef or bear steak, roast pig or smoked venison in peace, and although Cocke's ale, beer, and rum were of an inferior grade, the corn whisky which was distilled on the premises was infinitely better than any within a radius of one hundred miles. It was rumored that the liquor's success was due to Cocke's method of aging it in barrels made of wood and carted into town from one of his own farms, but he consistently refused to discuss the formula with anyone.

The Senators' Inn, located only one hundred yards from the official government buildings, was the headquarters of all visiting representatives of the people, and the circuit-riding judges invariably stopped there too. The wealthier merchants, trappers, traders, and the few professional men who came to Jonesboro declared that there was no other hostelry in town worthy of the name, and although they complained about the quality of the inn's food and the cleanliness of the bed linen, they continued to give their patronage to Asa Bennett, who had built the place.

The town's fiercest partisans, of whom there were many, claimed that when Franklin was recognized by her sister states and admitted into the American Confederation, Jonesboro would come into her own. They were justly proud of the recent growth of commerce, and as proof of their contention that Jonesboro would someday be the Philadelphia of the West, they argued that while there had been only one store on High Street a decade ago, there were today three booming marts. At Williamson's, the largest, one could purchase anything from a real glass mirror—at ten shillings—to the newest brand of New York manufactured nails, which cost ha'penny a pound. There was locally ground flour for sale, too, along with bacon, rice, dried beans, and peas. Harvey's, the newest of the stores, was having a notable success with vegetable and grain seed, which the immigrants conscientiously purchased as soon as they saw the posters tacked up beside the front door.

There was certainly no denying that when the militia came to town High Street was lively. Groups of unshaven, hard-eyed men in buckskins or in the remnants of their wartime uniforms roamed up and down the road in twos and threes, looking for excitement. When they could find none they invented their own, and a quartet of pranksters was making passage difficult at a spot not far from Ezra Brewer's barbershop, dentist emporium, and burial parlor. They had dug a barbecue pit in the middle of the street and were roasting a side of baby deer over the low flames. Crowds of the hungry and curious began to gather, and the hosts at the impromptu party, spurred to generosity by the draughts they consumed from a large and battered earthenware jug, loudly invited all passers-by to accept their hospitality.

Despite the carnival atmosphere, Rosalind Walker was low in spirit as she daintily picked her way along the side of High Street to the Senators' Inn. She knew that her father would have told her she was suffering from the impatience of youth, and she supposed the accusation would be justified, but it was heartbreaking, nevertheless, to be forced to wait for an indefinite time before journeying to Nashville. She had been looking forward to the moment when she would actually take the first steps toward the establishment of her seminary, and she realized now that she would be marooned here until the nasty business with the Tiptonites had been concluded.

Equally unpleasant was the prospect that she would have days, perhaps even weeks, to kill in this dreary community before being allowed to move on. All of her books were in the boxes the Dolsons were carrying to Nashville, and she very much doubted that reading matter could be found anywhere in Jonesboro. It would be next to impossible for her to while away the time doing nothing in the tiny, cramped room that Asa Bennett of the Senators' Inn had reluctantly given her.

Two militiamen, long frontier rifles slung over their shoulders, approached her from the opposite direction, and although she had inspired considerable comment from others who had seen her, Rosalind had held her head high and had kept moving. That was plainly going to be impossible now. A low, penetrating whistle from the lips of one of the men was her first warning that trouble was afoot; an instant later the two stopped directly in front of her, blocking her path. She attempted to sweep past them first on one side, then on the other, but they countered each move.

"This here town ain't near so bad as we figgered it was, Dan'l," said one of the soldiers. "Drinkin' places all primed t' give the thirsty their fill o' good sperrets——"

"Right agin, Benny," replied the other. "All we needs now is a pert 'n' friendly little girl t' go gallivantin' with us. I feel lonesome, and what I need is some comp'ny. Know whereat we're like t' find us such a one?"

Rosalind stopped and stood very still, staring first at one, then the other. "You both look old enough to have fought in the war, so I suppose you did," she said. "What was your regiment? And yours?"

Checked by the unusual question, the taller of the two mumbled that he had fought with several regiments but that he had spent most of his service in the 43rd North Carolina Light Infantry. Rosalind smiled sweetly at him.

"I'm sure I've heard of them," she said. "They fought alongside Massachusetts troops many times, I'll wager. Perhaps you heard of the 16th Massachusetts. One of my brothers was a lieutenant in that regiment. He lost both his legs while on duty with the 16th."

Reddening, the taller man turned his head aside and blew his nose violently. His companion swept off the thick stocking cap that had been perched so jauntily on the side of his head and fidgeted first on one foot, then on the other. Twice he tried to speak, but the task was too great for him.

At last the one who had been addressed as Benny spoke. "Ma'am," he muttered, "you've a right t' butt us clear down t'other end o' High Street 'n' back with these here rifles. I reckon me 'n' Dan'l will go have our little drinkin' bout by ourselfs. But I'd like t' kind o' make up for any consairn or rilin' we've mebbe caused you. If anybuddy in this town don't treat you right, you come out t' the milishee camp round about suppertime and just tell me 'n' Dan'l. We'll fix him good, won't we, Dan'l?"

The shorter man nodded violently, then marched past Rosalind without glancing at her again. His companion stood still for a second, then took off down the street too. Trembling slightly, but in full command of herself, Rosalind resumed her walk at an even but slightly increased pace.

She had gone only a few yards when she heard a man shout. His words were unintelligible, but running footsteps sounded on the road, and when he called again there was no mistaking that he was coming after her. In exasperation she began to walk still faster, telling herself that under no circumstances would she forget her dignity and break into a run. Apparently the men of Franklin had seen virtually no women in months, and if her experiences to date were going to be repeated in Nashville, she might be far better off back in Boston, where a lady was safe on the streets.

"Rosalind! Rosalind Walker!"

The man was very close now, and Rosalind stopped short as he called her name. Turning, she saw a tall, wiry young man in his late twenties approaching at a full run. That he was a militiaman was evident by the blue bit of cloth he wore around the upper part of his left arm and by the musket in his right hand. Otherwise he looked like a gentleman, for his neatly pressed woolen suit was well tailored, his shoes and stockings were of good quality, and his three-cornered hat boasted a braided silk piping.

His eyes and hair were dark, and his face, although firm, was not too thin. There was a small scar across the bridge of his nose, and she stared at it uncertainly. Then suddenly she drew a deep breath, exhaled slowly, and smiled.

"It's—it's Harold Jordan—from home—isn't it?"

"Of course! Who did you think I was? I've been chasing you

for almost a quarter of a mile." He shifted his musket to his left hand and held out his right. "You certainly do look wary!"

"I—I didn't quite recognize you, Harold. It's been so long since we've seen each other. And you've changed."

"So have you." Harold Jordan seemed more than a little surprised as he surveyed her with frank pleasure. "You were a pretty enough little girl when I left Boston, but now you've become—— Look here, this is no place to talk."

Rosalind gathered up her skirts. "I was on my way to the Senators' Inn. Are you going in that direction?"

"I am now," he said emphatically, offering her his arm. "Strange that I should see you accidentally like this in Jonesboro. I'd heard from home that you were coming out to Nashville, but I had no idea when you'd be arriving. This is a great bit of luck."

"You live in Nashville, I believe?" Rosalind knew very well that he was making his home in the new community that had been so recently carved from the wilderness of the Cumberland, but she was enjoying the amenities of polite conversation that had been so conspicuously lacking from her life in recent weeks.

"Yes, I do. It's a fine town—and I'm sure you'll like it, Rosalind. I—hum—I'll do everything possible to make things pleasant for you there. Not that I'm anyone important, but I do manage the largest tannery on this side of the mountains. Happen to own a small interest in it, as a matter of fact. So I'm acquainted with most people in town. Do you know where your school will be located—or where you're going to live?"

His interest in her was obviously so sincere that Rosalind beamed. It was the most comfortable of all sensations to be walking with a young man who spoke with the same distinctive twang that marked her own accent, a gentleman who instinctively showed her the deference to which she was accustomed. It would have been easy to imagine herself strolling toward the Boston Common with Harold at this moment had certain obvious differences not been only too apparent. A wild-haired youth of seventeen or eighteen, dressed in ancient rusty black, came whooping and shouting down the center of the street, leading a black bear cub by a thick length of rope. It was evident that the boy was drunk, and it seemed likely that he had given the animal something to drink, too, for the bear staggered from one side of the street to the other in what was a credible imitation of his master. Few people bothered to notice them, however, for a spectacular fight had developed in front of the establishment which proclaimed itself "Jonesboro's Only Boot-Maker."

A militiaman and a bearded individual, who, judging by his dress, was a farmer, were engaged in a fierce rough-and-tumble. The farmer was sitting astride the younger man's chest with both hands clutched around his windpipe, while the militiaman struggled desperately to reach his tormentor's face with his clenched fists. At least twenty people had gathered in a circle around the two men, and no one made any attempt to interfere, although shouts of advice and encouragement were frequent.

Rosalind felt squeamish, but Harold guided her quickly past the thrashing figures. "I know a dozen or more good families who'll be happy to take you in and who won't charge you too high a rent for your room and board," he said rapidly, giving her no chance to look back over her shoulder at the fighting men. "And if you're going to build a schoolhouse for yourself, I think I know just the man to do the job for you."

Rosalind told him she would live with the Dolsons, provided their house was built in time. Otherwise, she said, she would gladly avail herself of his information and help. He listened intently, and if he was walking a trifle closer to her than was necessary, she did not mind.

Busy men were hurrying in and out of the Senators' Inn as Harold and Rosalind approached, and they stopped a few feet short of the entrance. A colonel of militia entered the building, conversing earnestly with a tall, spare individual who wore breeches and a long coat of a style prevalent a decade or more before the War of Independence.

Rosalind looked up directly into Harold's eyes. "I haven't asked you this, but I—I assume you're going with the militia against Colonel Tipton."

"Yes, I am. Like everybody else who fought in the war, I joined the militia right off when I came out here, and of course I volunteered for this little party as soon as I heard about it." His tone was light, almost gay, and he made the expedition sound as harmless as a picnic on the banks of the Charles River back home.

But Rosalind was not to be fooled; she had seen too many men march off to war. "I'll be—watching for your return," she said simply, holding out her hand.

He showed immediate interest. "You'll be in Jonesboro when I come back?"

"Yes, I must wait here until there are enough men to form a convoy."

"It couldn't be better! I'll join that convoy myself, and we'll ride out to Nashville together."

At the same instant they realized that their hands were still clasped, and each hastily withdrew. There was a flash of mutual understanding and sympathy, then Harold doffed his hat and started back in the direction from which they had come. Rosalind watched him for a second before she turned toward the hotel. She felt rather than saw that someone was observing her intently, and instinct told her not to stop walking. In any event, a single, quick glance was sufficient.

Leaning indolently against a hitching post, hands jammed into the pockets of his breeches as he studied her, was Janus Elholm. On his handsome face was the sardonic grin she hated.

Chapter VII

Jogging along midway in the column of cavalry, Harold Jordan seemed outwardly calm, but his mind was in a tumult. He had never been a particularly religious man, but he was beginning to understand the meaning of the biblical statement: "Vengeance is mine, saith the Lord."

Again and again the question hammered at his brain: What would Rosalind Walker think of him if she knew that in reality he was no successful young tannery manager but was a paid agent of the Spaniards who conspired to take possession of the rich American West for themselves? Even the tannery, he thought wryly, was actually no more than a front, a headquarters for the operatives of King Charles who traveled freely and with impunity through Franklin and Kentucky.

Yes, Rosalind no doubt thought of him as highly as she would anyone else from Boston who had come out to the new country to wrest a fortune from the wilderness, and he was determined to do everything in his power to preserve that illusion. But it was going to be difficult, extraordinarily difficult. Had he known four years ago, when he had first taken Spanish dollars, that he would eventually become embroiled to the point where normal human considerations no longer weighed in the balance, and where his life itself was in grave danger, he would have avoided the entanglement as he would a victim of the great pox.

It had been so easy at first. His sole duty for many months had been to sing the praises of Spain—cautiously, of course—whenever the subject arose in conversation. He had felt so smug, so proud of himself then. The pay had been high, and unlike hundreds of other immigrants, he had never been forced to chop a farm out of the forest; to plant crops and work in the fields like some grubbing animal, too tired to think, too tired to enjoy any of the niceties of living, too callous to appreciate the refinements reserved for a man who worked with his brain rather than with his hands.

Everything had been so clear, so sharp, four years ago. The Spaniards, he could see now, had been clever enough to recruit their helpers from the ranks of ambitious, war-weary, and disillusioned veterans. It had mattered little in those days whether Franklin became an American state or a Spanish satrapy. Indeed, he was still indifferent to the problem; it mattered little to him which flag flew over the governor's headquarters in Jonesboro. What did matter was that he was involved in a plot which meant certain death if he was caught, and exile and disgrace—if he was lucky enough to escape—in the event that the latest and most grandiose scheme of the dons should fail.

Only two weeks ago he had been informed that a new general was coming out from Spain and that within a very few months an attack in force would take place against the Franks. It was to be an undisguised, bold military venture, for the powers in Madrid had apparently decided that the Confederation was too weak, too divided to go to war over the annexation by King Charles of one of her remote Western provinces.

Nashville, of course, was to be the first objective of the invading armies, for the land-greedy Spaniards were all too aware that the wealth-producing Cumberland was the choicest plum on the tree. Furthermore, it would be preferable from the standpoint of military strategy to conquer the Cumberland first. From there the legions of Castile and the Floridas, Aragon and Louisiana could most readily choose whether next to move into Kentucky or against the eastern strongholds of the Franks.

And Harold had been given the most hazardous of all pre-attack tasks. He had been ordered to learn the exact strength of the American forces: he was to find out how many men were prepared to come to the defense of John Sevier's realm, how many of these were veterans and how many untried troops. He was to acquire exact information on Frank armaments: the number of their cannon, of their muskets and rifles, of the quantity and quality of their ammunition. And worst of all, he was to steal the defense plans for the region which had been formulated by the state's leaders in secret conclave and which, the Spaniards had learned, reposed in an iron stronghox located in the library of Colonel Jim Robertson, Nashville's founder and leader.

It was this last step at which he balked; although he knew Robertson only slightly, it might be possible to find some pretext to gain admission to the library. Once there, however, he would be unable to act like a common thief, to force the lid of the box, and to make off with a paper on which the safety of the Cumberland depended. The risks, he was convinced, were too great. The militia barracks were conveniently located next door to the Robertson house, and soldiers of high and low rank were always coming in or out of the big home, for Jim Robertson never closed his doors to his fighting men. Furthermore, the colonel was too wise and too shrewd a man not to provide safeguards that would insure the safety of his defense plans.

Justice was swift and merciless and sure in this raw country, and Harold was under no false illusions as to his fate if he were caught. At best, he would be dangling from a tall tree in ten minutes; if he were less fortunate, well—he shuddered. He had seen angry Nashville mobs in action too often.

Yet he was trapped, for if he refused to do the bidding of the

Spaniards, he knew they would not hesitate to kill him. For many days he had been miserable and badly frightened, knowing that his only hope for salvation lay in his ability to outthink, outsmart both sides. And so he had slowly, carefully conceived a plan that was as intricate and brilliant as it was daring.

In a few weeks, he had been told, Baron de Carondelet, Intendant General of the province of Louisiana and chief of all Spanish secret agents in the West, was coming to Nashville in disguise to receive firsthand reports from his men in the area and to see for himself the territory over which he would soon exercise jurisdiction. The baron, Harold recalled from their three brief but memorable meetings, had a master list containing the names of every spy, every agent in Franklin and Kentucky. In giving instructions to Harold, he had referred to the list often, and he was unlikely to travel without it, for it contained scores, perhaps even hundreds, of names.

By some means Harold had determined to gain possession of that list. It would trouble his conscience less, he knew, to steal a paper from Carondelet than from Jim Robertson. And once the document was in his pocket, he would race from Nashville to Jonesboro and would offer the damning evidence to Governor John Sevier.

The governor would take steps at once and would either jail, execute, or drive out every representative of Spain from the state. Harold, then, would be safe. More than that, his act would guarantee that the governor would pardon him for his own activities on behalf of Spain.

It might be possible to avoid the risks of stealing the list of agents by going straight to the governor and simply telling Sevier all that he knew, and he had toyed with the notion but had discarded it. In the first place, he was acquainted with only a few of Spain's men; the dons exercised great care, and each agent came in contact only with the few others in his immediate sphere of activity. Hence if he named the men whom he himself knew to be in Spanish pay, only a small percentage would be arrested, and his danger of assassination would be in no way lessened. Equally important was the knowledge that he could win forgiveness for his own betrayal of Franklin only if his contribution to the future welfare of the state was sufficiently significant.

In the meantime, he thought, he must be patient; until Baron de Carondelet came to Nashville there was nothing he could do to further his scheme. He had joined this expedition in order to have it on the record in his favor when the time came to confront Governor Sevier, but it appeared as though dangerous complications might result unless he exercised extreme care.

He glanced at the man riding beside him on the trail, the foreign volunteer, Janus Elholm. The medallion of Svintillus Rex swayed back and forth as the Dane's horse stepped out across the tall grass, and the sight of that medallion made Harold slightly ill. He had seen three identical ornaments in the past four years, and he knew only too well what they symbolized. Here, without a shadow of doubt, was one of the ringleaders of the Spanish conspiracy, and from the man's military bearing he was a soldier. It was not too difficult to guess that he would be a leader of Spanish legions in the field, that he was one of the small group depending on receiving the information that Harold had been commanded to procure.

Analyzing swiftly, Harold concluded that in all probability Elholm did not know of his own connection with the Spaniards. Certainly he had no intention of revealing that he recognized the medallion. If the Dane should speak to him about the forthcoming campaign of conquest, it would be time enough to open the subject. Until then he would keep his own counsel and leave well enough alone. . . .

An order was shouted from the front of the column, and the horsemen, two by two, broke their mounts into a trot. The long line swept into a little valley where the grass was short and the land was level and smooth. On the far side a line of greenish-

brown fruit trees dotted the landscape, and behind them could be seen a small but sturdy cabin. Wood smoke was rising from an outdoor cooking pit, and three little children half hid themselves in the shadow of the trees as they watched the militiamen ride past. The youngest clutched a doll made from an old sack, and she sucked hard on her thumb as she surveyed the soldiers with wide eyes.

A man, thick-waisted and broad-shouldered, appeared from behind the screen of trees and waved a greeting. In his other hand he held a long-handled ax, and he leaned on it as he shouted something friendly but unintelligible to the troopers who thundered past his little dwelling. He wore no shirt, and the sun glistened on the sweat that covered his bare torso.

Looking at him, Harold felt a twinge of envy. Perhaps the road he had chosen for himself four years ago had not been the right one. Granted there was money in his pocket and that he had suffered few of the discomforts of wilderness living. But this simple farmer had achieved a measure of inner peace and happiness beyond anything Harold had known.

To the eye of an experienced military observer there was no doubt that the men of Franklin were veteran soldiers. Despite their ragged appearance, they rode across hills and through woods with the assurance of fighters who had often tasted battle and who knew what to expect. Janus let his glance rove up and down the long double line, and he was forced to admit that these poorly uniformed, unimpressive-appearing militiamen knew their business.

There was virtually no talking in the ranks, and no one smoked. And most significant to Janus was the way the column had spread out of its own accord, without a single order having been given. Only troops with service in many campaigns did that, and he recalled that even the best of German mercenaries huddled together on the march unless expressly commanded by their officers to move in looser formation. Yes, he admitted to himself, no one was going to succeed in luring this battalion into a trap.

He could not help admiring the manner in which General John Sevier and his aides supervised the march, too. From time to time a small detachment would peel off from the main body and ride ahead or off to the flanks on a scouting trip. Then, shortly before that group reappeared, a second scouting patrol would depart. The Americans seemed to have an extraordinary instinct for timing, and Janus could not understand how it was possible, time after time, for one scouting detachment to leave the battalion just before the return of its predecessor. Wilderness fighters, he eventually concluded, must have developed unusually keen hearing which permitted them to detect the approach of horsemen or foot soldiers more rapidly than could even the most battle-hardened Europeans. And if they could pick out the sound of approaching friends, they would be doubly alert to an enemy.

Somewhat uneasily he wondered whether he could ever catch the Franks off balance with a surprise attack. It was well enough for Aranda to intimate that such a plan would prove inevitably successful, but King Charles's First Minister had never seen these hardy Americans in action. Janus found his own scorn for them disappearing, to be replaced by a reluctant, grudging admiration. Naïve they might be in their outlook on life, but there was certainly no question but that they knew what they were doing in the field, and he was judging them solely from a military standpoint. Politics he would gladly leave to others.

But despite the lack of concern he professed to feel over matters outside his own immediate realm, there was one thing that puzzled and bothered him. Nowhere in his many and varied experiences as a soldier had he encountered anything comparable to the spirit of comradeship that existed among these Americans. Officers and men ate their meals side by side; they laughed and talked together on terms of astonishing equality; and even General Sevier did not hold himself apart from the enlisted men during halts. Yet this lack of barriers in no way reduced the efficiency of the battalion. When a command was given, the men accepted it cheerfully, even willingly.

What a contrast this was to even the least disciplined regiments in the Old World. In the French Army it was not uncommon for officers to beat their men into submission with riding crops and the flats of their swords. And no one looked askance at the practice of the Poles and Russians, who used horsewhips and bayonets to keep their troops in line.

Like every other commander, Janus had often dreamed of heading a unit where the use of force and fear would be unnecessary, and he began to understand why these easygoing militiamen had so decisively beaten the finest armies of the English generals. Perhaps, he thought, there was something to this atmosphere of freedom. In any event, he knew that his own task, when the time came to meet the Americans in battle, was going to prove far more hazardous than he had anticipated. Before he struck a single blow he would have to perfect both his over-all strategy and his battle tactics. To improvise in a fight against men who were at least as competent as those he had led at Warsaw and Milan would be to court disaster.

A cold, driving rain transformed the Watauga River and its tributaries into churning, writhing serpents, and clouds of mist boiled and rolled down from the mountains toward the two-story log house on Sinking Creek. Men of Franklin huddled under the inadequate shelter of trees and held their drenched blankets over their heads in a futile effort to keep partially dry. In the distance foraging parties splashed off in search of food, but on the hill overlooking the log house there was no sign of activity. Occasionally a horse neighed irritably or a man coughed and cursed under his breath. There was no other sound but the incessant drumming of the rain.

Unmindful of the elements, John Sevier stood with his hands plunged deep in the pockets of a faded Continental Army greatcoat and stared moodily at the house below. The fifty or more men inside it were showing no sign of life, but a thin stream of smoke gave evidence that Colonel Tipton and his company were enjoying the luxury of hot soup and a sizzling roast. The general sighed, and two men near him exchanged glances and moved closer to him. One, lean and of medium height, was Colonel Henry Conway, second-in-command of the expedition. The other, a chunky man with long, drooping mustaches, who looked considerably older than his forty years, was Colonel Charles Robertson, brother of the illustrious founder of Nashville.

It was Sevier himself who broke the stillness. "Young Elholm, George's brother, says there were at least a dozen men who slipped through our lines into the house during last night's storm, gentlemen. But"—and he laughed mirthlessly—"that gives Tipton twelve more mouths to feed."

Colonel Conway cleared his throat. "At least they're warm in there, General. And they're eating more than dried beef and parched corn. Man alive, what I'd give right now for a platter of sizzling bear bacon!"

"You wouldn't like it, Henry," Colonel Robertson said, watching Sevier closely. "You—and all the rest of us—are no doubt falling sick of the flux at this moment."

The governor turned to his subcommanders for the first time, and his eyes were twinkling. "Living in peacetimes has made you flabby, gentlemen. I can recall countless occasions during the war when we endured weather far worse than this without complaint or ill effects, and on empty stomachs, too."

"We can stand a bit of discomfort now, if we must," Robertson growled, his neck and face turning a deep red. "But I'm damned if there's any need for it! Please, General, give the order to attack and let us wipe out that nest of vermin down there!"

"They are not vermin, Robertson. They are fellow Americans.

And we must give John Tipton an opportunity to answer my surrender demand before we shed blood."

Charles Robertson wiped his sopping face with a damp sleeve and spat disgustedly. "That last note you sent him was your sixth, General. And he answers them all the same way, by ordering *you* to surrender to the duly constituted authority of North Carolina."

Colonel Conway blew his nose and tried to pull his coat collar higher. "I say what I've been saying for thirty hours and more. Your plan of merely threatening to use force is not enough. We must act—and at once. Tipton is stalling. He's waiting until the whole damned Carolina militia gets here. And you know what'll happen then, General. Our two hundred men, armed with one puny three-inch cannon, aren't going to make much of a dent in General Shelby and his fifteen hundred troops."

All in the little battalion were tired, but there was more than weariness in John Sevier's voice when he at length responded. "Evan Shelby was my commander for three years. We fought together in nine battles, often side by side. He saved my life at Charleston, and I carried him from the field at Yorktown. No, gentlemen. I'll die on North Carolina's gallows before I'll fire at General Shelby or his men."

A brisk figure stamped through the mire to the trio, halted, and executed a salute that was a model of perfection. "Major Elholm at report, General. Our cannon is now trained directly on the house, sir, and the shot is being heated under a canopy of blankets." His voice became supplicating. "Let me fire three or four rounds, sir, and we'll drive the rascals out of their hole. In spite of the rain, a red-hot three-inch ball will start fires a-plenty."

Governor Sevier shook his head, and Major Elholm looked at the two colonels, his eyebrows cocked cynically. Robertson shrugged, swore colorfully under his breath, and sloshed away to inspect the militiamen who were keeping the Tipton house in the sights of their rifles. Colonel Conway's lips moved, but it was several seconds before he could control himself sufficiently to speak calmly about his senior officer.

"The general," he said bitterly, "thinks that Tipton and his bandits are good, honest citizens. They've stolen his property to the tune of some hundreds of gold pounds, and they're only waiting for reinforcements to slaughter us, but he won't let us fight. Jack Sevier, the Nolichucky soldier, doesn't exist any more, George. No, by God—we're being led by a—diplomat like that mush-mouthed John Jay, who agreed to let the Spaniards close the Mississippi—so the coastal ports can enjoy all the dons' trade!"

His angry shot found its mark, and Sevier straightened abruptly. "No man can claim that the interests of Franklin aren't nearest to my heart, Henry. And if any but my oldest friend threw such a lie in my face, I'd call him out for it. But I'm trying to make you understand. Tipton and his followers are not good citizens, as you so facetiously insist. Nevertheless, they *are* citizens, good or bad. And I'll not be a party to the start of a civil war. But perhaps you're right about one thing, Henry. Perhaps I have become a diplomat. What do you think our chances for recognition would be if the Congress in New York heard we were wantonly killing men who have been merely doing their duty as they see it?"

George Elholm forgot the rain and threw his hands toward the sky in a gesture of violent exasperation. "*Schrecklichkeit!*" he shouted. "We must take our risks with that donkey Congress, Jack! The time to attack is now, before General Shelby and his brigade arrives. We——"

The governor interrupted the outburst. "Colonel Conway," he said formally, "be so good as to make the rounds of our outposts, and remind each man that he is not to fire under any provocation unless we are fired upon. In that eventuality, I will myself give the order to return the lead of the—hmmm—enemy."

For an instant it seemed that Colonel Conway would refuse,

but the habit of military obedience was too strong. He saluted methodically, turned, and trudged off up the slope. Sevier watched him go, then put a damp hand on George Elholm's shoulder. A clap of thunder roared directly overhead, followed by a fresh deluge of rain, and the governor was forced to shout in his adjutant's ear.

"There's more at stake here than my little property, George," he fairly screamed. "But I give you my word, if we're fired upon, we'll give as good as we receive, round for round."

Elholm pulled off his tricorne, shook the water from the crown, and replaced it on his head. Now that his fury was spent, he seemed slightly ashamed and more than a little penitent. "I have followed you before, Jack. I shall do so again."

"Thank you." The governor peered off into the fog. "Your brother and that man Jordan are late in reporting from their scouting trip up the Watauga. If Evan Shelby *is* marching on us, I'd like to be informed of it before his bullets crease my scalp."

"Imagine how old Shelby must feel, knowing he's got to fight *you*." George Elholm grinned. "I'll wager that even his colonels are quaking in their Carolina-leather boots. . . . But it's true that my—brother and his companion are overdue."

"Well, call in the foraging parties, George. My bad elbow is twitching again, and from the way it rages, I wouldn't be surprised if we're in for a bad time today."

Here at last was some promise of action, and Major Elholm darted off. A few moments later the sharp echoes of hunting horns cut through the gloom of the sodden countryside, followed by three volleys of rifleshots fired in quick succession. More than fifty muskets blended their voices in the signal, which could be heard at the limits of Washington County, beyond which the foragers had been directed not to roam.

The flurry of noise over, all was quiet again, and the rising waters of the creek gurgled louder than ever. Major Elholm's duties finished for the present, he trudged back to the spot where his commander in chief had returned to his unblinking surveillance of the Tipton house.

"Jack."

"Mmm? What is it, George?"

"Come and warm yourself at the fire we've built for the round shot. You'll be chilled for fair if you stay here."

"If the men can stand up to this weather, so can I."

"If one of the men dies of the flux, it's—well, it's too bad, Jack. But there's only one John Sevier. And if anything happens to you, it will be the end of Franklin. There's no one else who can hold the state together, and you well know it."

Sevier opened his mouth to reply, but at that instant both heard the approach of galloping hoofbeats. Others in the battalion heard the sound, too, and one hundred firing pans clicked open under the shelter of coats and shirts and blankets. The governor stood immovable, but George Elholm quietly removed his loaded pistol from its holster under his coat and jammed the weapon into his outer pocket, where he kept a tight grip on it.

The horsemen drew nearer, and one by one the taut men of the battalion relaxed. As any experienced woodsman could tell, there were only two in the approaching party.

After what seemed like an eternity of waiting the riders came into view as they rounded the crest of the adjacent hill, and the white identification handkerchiefs they wore on their left sleeves were plain to be seen.

"Elholm and Jordan," the major said.

Janus saw the governor, wheeled his horse toward him, and thundered forward. His eyes were glistening with the light of battle, and despite the sorry condition of his clothes he contrived to present a jaunty, almost neat appearance.

Harold Jordan, by contrast, seemed worn out. His arms sagged and bone-weariness was written in every line of his face. There was a long, jagged tear in his left sleeve, and his shirt and breeches clung to him, soggy with water. Yet he refused to wilt in the presence of his commander and sat erect in the saddle. And when Janus leaped to the ground and saluted, he followed more slowly, but with dignity.

Wasting no words, Janus began his report in short, concise sentences. Using his enlarging glass, he had seen a large body of men approaching Dungan's ford several miles away up the Watauga. Utilizing a screen of trees and heavy shore brush as a cover, the two had swum their horses across the river at a narrow point and had stopped to confer. Janus had conceived a daring plan: One of them would ride up slowly, attach himself to the formation at the rear, and learn what he could about it. Because of the rain, Janus had argued, no one would notice that a newcomer had attached himself to the unit.

Each had demanded the privilege of performing the task, and Harold had finally won out because of the simple persuasiveness of his argument. His command of the English language was natural; Janus, on the other hand, spoke the tongue with a noticeable accent and therefore might more quickly draw suspicion on himself.

And so, while Janus had remained in the rear to return alone in case Harold failed to come back, the scheme had been put into operation. Harold had moved ahead and had joined the North Carolinians. Growing increasingly bold, he had ridden up the length of the column, which consisted, by his actual count, of three hundred and eighty-seven men. Neither General Shelby nor any other general officer was present. The commander, to judge by his epaulets, was a colonel, a red-haired man with a smashed nose.

"Peter Parkinson!" Governor Sevier groaned.

Major Elholm gritted his teeth. "Parkinson. He would be in command. That hot-tempered ass."

A heavy weight seemed to have settled on Sevier's shoulders, and he closed his eyes. Neither Elholm said anything, and Harold looked into the distance and tightened his pistol belt. The governor passed a hand over his brow and shook himself.

"This accursed rain," he said softly. "Well, no matter. Blood will flow before the day ends. Major, be good enough to see if all foraging parties have returned. If not, tell my lad to raise our flag to guide them as they come in. We don't want them firing on the wrong side in the heat of battle."

Major Elholm saluted, then hesitated. "May I pump a few rounds of shot into Tipton's house now, sir?"

"You may not," Sevier snapped. "Franklin militia fires only on due provocation. You will carry out your order, sir."

The major executed the most military about-face of which he was capable in the slime, and departed. Janus, who had watched in silent curiosity, gave no indication of his own reactions as he continued to stand at attention before Sevier. He was accustomed to the military discipline of Europe's armies, and he would stand there all day and all night, if necessary, until the general ordered him to go.

Governor Sevier, still irritated, suddenly became conscious of the presence of the two young men he had sent scouting.

"What do you want?" he asked.

Janus's lips curled slightly. "If *mon général* has no more to request of me, he will dismiss me," he hinted.

Sevier chuckled. "Not so fast, lad. You haven't yet told me how you made your escape from the Carolina militia."

"We did not escape. That miserable excuse for an army was so busy trying to keep dry its precious skin that when Jordan dropped back and rejoined me, we returned to Dungan's ford, crossed, and came at once to you. Never have I seen such idiot soldiers."

The governor resented the other's obvious contempt and answered sternly, "They weren't expecting to be spied out, Elholm. Had you fought with those troops through six years of campaigning, as I did, you'd have respect for them."

"Yes, sir. Is that all, sir?"

"No, it is not. Jordan, I want to congratulate you on performing a difficult task with distinction. And you, Elholm, my respects for your ingenuity."

"Thank you, sir." Both saluted and withdrew a few paces.

George Elholm raced up, panting slightly. "All foragers are back, General, except the largest party. The one commanded by your son John."

"Oh? And where did that party go?"

"Toward the Carolina border, General. And I don't like it. If those thirty men are picked up by Parkinson it will go badly for them. Peter the Nincompoop would like nothing better than to take Captain John Sevier, Jr., and his brother James back to Carolina as prisoners. I recommend we send out a rescue group, sir."

Sevier shook his head. "I don't play favorites with my sons, George. You know that."

"Nevertheless, General, the prestige of Franklin is certainly at stake. Our cause will suffer harm if your boys should be captured and dragged off like prize hogs to be exhibited through the hill towns of Carolina. We can't let that happen."

"We also can't spare the men for a rescue mission, George."

"All right, General. I'll admit it would be dangerous. But at least let Elholm and Jordan seek out your sons. These two know the route Parkinson is taking, and they can show your lads and the rest back here by a different path."

Reluctantly John Sevier nodded assent. Janus and Harold were off immediately, and the two who watched them shared the same thought: Twice within the span of a single afternoon these young men had accepted unpleasant, risky assignments without flinching and had executed the first of their tasks brilliantly.

Thirty minutes later the sound of many horsemen was heard, and a trumpet called a challenge in the gathering dusk. A ragged cheer went up from the men besieged in the Tipton house, and a moment later three rifles were fired from behind chinks in the logs. The shots were the opening gauge of battle, but John Sevier still refused to fight. Despite the frantic pleas of his lieutenants, he mounted his horse and rode part way down the hill to a place where he could intercept Colonel Parkinson and his North Carolinians. That he made a perfect target for the Tiptonites in the house never crossed his mind.

And they, strangely, held their fire, either because they feared the stigma that would be attached to them if they shot the man who was the acknowledged leader in the Western lands, or—and this was the more probable—because they knew Sevier's followers would never rest until all of his murderers were in their graves.

The oncoming North Carolina militiamen were within rifle range when their trumpet blared again. The rain was beginning to lessen, but the cold mists seemed to grow thicker. John Sevier sat quietly, resting his long gun on the saddlebows. Plunging his hand into the pocket of his greatcoat, he withdrew the silver whistle which his men had given him after the battle of Kings Mountain, and blew shrilly. His troops grew very still, and the North Carolinians halted abruptly. Their first ranks could be seen dimly now through the fog and the screen of hemlocks and sycamores.

"Parkinson! Peter Parkinson! This is John Sevier of Franklin!" The governor's voice, raised to its loudest, crashed and echoed through the hills. "In the name of humanity and of the Congress of the Confederation, I implore you! Let us settle our dispute by peaceful means. I ask only that those things which are mine be returned to me! I seek the blood of no one! What do you say, Parkinson?"

The drip of rain water from the tree branches could be heard as utter silence reigned. Somewhere in the hills a man coughed and a horse whinnied and stamped. Then a trigger lock clicked, and more than five hundred men took firmer grasps on their weapons. But Sevier remained cool and unruffled.

"Colonel Parkinson!" he shouted again. "Did you hear me? This is Brigadier General John Sevier, governor of Franklin! I promise personal immunity to all who took part in the raid on Mount Pleasant if——"

C-c-r-a-a-a-c-k! A rifle spoke out in the silence, and there was immediate bedlam. No one could tell which side had fired, and no one waited to find out. Deadly pellets of lead began to fly between the two forces.

Dry, pungent puffs of burned powder rose in the air, then settled back on the leaves of the sycamores. The battle was on in earnest, and further parley was impossible. A series of heavy flashes burst from a position near the creek, and four small Carolina cannon barked in unison. Even as Sevier had been talking, then, Colonel Parkinson had unlimbered his artillery. Major George Elholm needed no added invitation to fight, and his three-inch gun sent a red-hot ball crashing through the stout timbers of the Tipton house.

Meanwhile, unmindful of the bullets singing past his ears and over his head, John Sevier turned his horse slowly back up the hill. Not even when an enemy shot plowed through his hat and sent it forward across his eyes did he urge his mount to a faster gait. And he turned neither to right nor left until he had reached safety behind the crest of the slope. Then, when he faced Colonels Conway and Robertson, his eyes were cold.

"I tried, gentlemen. But it would be easier to reason with a madman than with Peter the Nincompoop. He's never forgotten that General Lincoln gave me his regiment when we were chasing Lord Cornwallis, and because of that fancied slight he's condemned good men on both sides to death. Very well, then. Wait until he has charged. We shall repulse him and then counterattack. Colonel Conway, you will take active command, if you please."

Heartsick, Sevier rode a short distance to the rear, where his youngest son joined him, the flag of Franklin flapping bravely but unseen over their heads in the murk. It was all the governor could do to restrain himself when the Carolina militia, whooping wildly, swept up the hill. But he sat in the saddle, rigid as a statue, and no one but his own offspring knew that tears trickled slowly down his immobile features.

Henry Conway was a seasoned Indian fighter; no one was more expert than he in making the enemy come to him and in withholding his fire until the precise second when it would do the most damage. Grimly he watched the North Carolinians creeping closer under cover of an artillery and rifle barrage. He chewed savagely on a blade of grass, then spat it out venomously. If the Carolina gunners had been no better marksmen during the war, it was no wonder they had needed help from their brothers-over-the-mountains to drive out the Lobsters. Peering down the hill, he caught a glimpse of a boy crawling toward the Franks' positions, a boy too young to have fought in the Revolution, and he felt a stab of compassion.

But the feeling vanished when a man a few feet to his right shrieked with pain. It was either kill or be killed, conquer or be conquered. His brain functioned coolly as he watched the men of Carolina inching closer, and closer still. Another minute . . . just a bit longer . . . wait . . . wait . . .

Now!

"Fire at will!" he bellowed, and the hill came alive. The Carolinians wavered under the blazing heat of the Franks' guns, and their line broke. The mountain men were firing and firing again, as fast as they could reload, and the Carolina infantrymen staggered back to comparative safety.

Major Elholm hurried to his commander in chief after quickly conferring with each unit leader in turn. There was an occasional shot now from the Tipton house, but elsewhere the field was momentarily quiet, and Elholm's voice boomed loudly.

"Sir," he said, "we've lost six men in the exchange. And Colonel Robertson estimates that there must be twenty Carolina bodies on the hill."

"That's enough. More than enough." No one had ever heard Sevier speak with such resignation. "Have my sons returned?"

"No, Jack. There's no sign of them as yet."

"Mmm. It doesn't matter. They'll know how to find their way home."

"Home?" George Elholm was unable to repress his alarm.

"Yes. Give the order to retreat. We'll pull back to Jonesboro. I hope I'll live to be a very old man, George, and I can't spend the next forty years arguing with my conscience over this night's work."

George Elholm blinked and swallowed hard. "But your silver service and tea set, Jack—the things Kate loves. And your good furniture. And——"

Sevier smiled wearily, and his eyes were bleary. "They're no more than things, George. Things that men buy with money. My Maker has been kind to me, and I have enough to replace that which has been stolen. Silver and beds and rugs are a poor substitute for human lives, for American lives, George. Be good enough to order the retreat, if you please."

The foraging party under Captain John Sevier, Jr., had ranged far into the hills, and it was near midnight before a remarkably spruce Janus Elholm and a tired but dogged Harold Jordan found the group. Each of the thirty was carrying bundles of food behind him on his saddle, and one hardy trooper had trussed a live baby pig and was carrying it across his pommel. Janus conferred rapidly with the young captain, who, like all the Seviers, bore a strong resemblance to the governor. There was an immediate meeting of minds, and the two agreed that it would be best to take a long route back to the camp in the hills above Sinking Creek.

Captain Sevier strung his men out in single file, with himself in the lead and Janus riding directly behind him. Young Sevier had grown up in this wild country, and with uncanny instinct he found trails and even footpaths which would have been invisible to anyone unfamiliar with the territory. But despite his skill, dawn was breaking before the little band heard the rushing waters of Sinking Creek. There was no sound of conflict, and two ivory-billed woodpeckers chattered their greeting to the new day without interruption.

The sun was rising as the party approached the ring of hills around John Tipton's house. There was scarcely a breath of wind, and a thick cloud of smoke rose almost straight into the air from the fireplace in the recalcitrant colonel's little fortress. Captain Sevier signaled for the column to halt and motioned to Janus to join him.

"What do you think, Captain?" Aside from deep circles under his eyes, Janus still looked fresh.

"Johnny to my friends."

"Thank you. Johnny. How do you reflect on this? My view is that there is too much quiet."

"That's my opinion, too, Janus. Pa—the general—is a great believer in drawn attacks. But there's nary a sign of life anywhere." Captain Sevier was uneasy and showed it.

"Is it possible there has been a withdrawal?" Janus's eyes narrowed, then he smiled suddenly. "No. Not possible," he answered himself. "It is repeated by even the little children that General Sevier only attacks."

"When I was little," young Sevier said with a ghost of a smile, "Pa used to tell me never to step into a bear pit without first making sure there was no bear in it. Jim!" he called over his shoulder softly to his younger brother. "Ride up here and take command of the column. Mister Elholm and I are going on ahead to sniff out some bears."

Cautiously the captain walked his horse up a small hill, and

Janus fell in beside him, envying the officer's noiseless grace. Janus's stallion was light-footed but would require months of rigorous training before he could step out as silently as the captain's gelding.

Halting on the near side of the crest, young Sevier dismounted and crouched low as he moved to the summit. Emulating him, Janus felt slightly ridiculous, though he could see the wisdom of taking no unnecessary chances. Together they stared at the house and the creek beyond, but saw no sign of activity. Then Janus looked toward the hill where the Franks had made their camp, and a fluttering object high in the air caught the tail of his eye.

"Observe, Johnny!" he said triumphantly. "The flag of your state."

Captain Sevier peered at the proud circle of fourteen stars. "Uh-huh," he said, expelling a deep breath, "that's ours. It's the flag Kate, my stepmother, made for Pa last winter, all right. No two ways about it. So I reckon our folks are still tarrying hereabouts."

He stood upright, making no further attempt to conceal himself, and waved to his brother. In a few moments the entire group was riding toward the Franklin flag. Despite their fatigue, the men chatted in low tones, buoyed by the prospect of a meal and a few hours' sleep. But the lack of activity in the camp of the Franks bothered Janus, who hoped dubiously that the crude Americans knew enough to throw out a protecting chain of sentry outposts when fighting a battle. The complacency of the Sevier brothers decided him against mentioning his fears, but he drew a loaded pistol from his belt and cocked it.

As the leading riders came up the slope of the hill which Governor Sevier had used for his headquarters it became apparent that something was radically wrong. Before the captain or Janus had a chance to warn the foragers, however, a single rifleshot shattered the morning calm and a rough, jeering voice bellowed a command.

"Up with yer hands, ye Franklin bastards!"

Janus's pistol raised in a flash toward the hemlock tree from which the voice came, but a second shot rang out, and the gun went spinning from his hand.

"None o' yer tricks now! We got ye covered, every last, blasted one o' ye."

A whistle shrilled, and seventy or more men stepped from behind trees on all sides of the hill. All pointed loaded rifles and muskets at the Franklin foragers, who sat in helpless confusion as their captors closed in on them.

Janus looked at his useless pistol lying on the ground and raged inwardly. That he who had been decorated for his efforts in the siege of Breslau and promoted by a prince for gallantry in the Riga campaign should be captured by peasants wearing homespun leggings and long buckskin shirts was humiliating beyond endurance. He jerked forward savagely in the saddle and found himself looking straight into the muzzle of the enemy leader's rifle.

"Easy there, bucko. Ye'd not want me t' blast that purty blond scalp off'n ye now, would ye?"

A dawning suspicion grew in Janus. Surely this burly rascal was the same who had led the brigands against Rosalind Walker and her friends, the Dolsons. He deliberately slumped back against the leather and made his eyes blank. It wouldn't go well with him if the men had caught a glimpse of him that day and could recognize him.

Half a dozen Tiptonites, accompanied by two lieutenants wearing the faded uniforms of the North Carolina militia, carefully worked their way up the line of Franks. Each of Sevier's followers was relieved of his powder and ammunition but was permitted to keep his weapons, for no white man living in this sparsely settled land would permanently deprive another of his means of defending himself and his family from the terrors of the wilderness.

"Officers o' this flea-bitten comp'ny, come up here," the Tipton leader yelled. "Lively, mind!"

James Sevier joined his brother, and they sat coldly erect on their mounts, looking straight ahead. The Tiptonite recognized them and chuckled obscenely.

"Wal, now! Sevier's brats, or do my pore old eyes do me wrong? My! Ain't the colonel goin' t' be glad t' see the both o' ye, and ain't he goin' t' give ye a right warm greetin'! Ye, there!" A grimy finger pointed suddenly at Janus. "Mebbe ye're no officer, but ye're a mite too frisky t' leave loose, so we'll take ye with us t' Colonel Tipton's little social gatherin' too." His beady eyes swept the ranks of the Franklin contingent and lingered on Harold Jordan. He leered and showed his rotting gums. "Wal, if this ain't a mornin' full o' s'prises. Another gentleman back there, tryin' t' hide his flabby carcass under his hoss's belly. All dressed up in fancy britches that come from Philadelphy, and carryin' a blanket the likes o' which I ain't set eyes on since b'fore the war. My! Join the social, Mister Fancy Britches."

Harold, his face slowly draining of color, was led to the front of the line and placed inside the circle of guards forming around the Sevier brothers and Janus. The remainder of the Franklin men glanced at each other out of the corners of their eyes, but none dared move so long as Tipton muskets were trained on them. The leader ordered the Seviers, Janus, and Harold taken down to the house on the creek, and sped them on their way with a vicious blow on the flanks of Janus's stallion. Then he turned to the now leaderless group from Jonesboro.

"Go back t' yer damn guv'nor 'n' tell him t' keep his fat arse out o' Wash'ton County hereafter—or we'll give him what we're goin' t' give his brats. Now git, ye filthy mountain goats. If ye ain't out o' my sight in one minute, ye'll get yer tails full o' lead."

The Franks, smarting under his insults but unable to avenge themselves, had no choice but to turn and spur their horses toward the west and home. And if any had been wavering in his loyalty to John Sevier and the state of Franklin, the last crumb of doubt was now swept away. After the twenty-eight told their story, no partisan of North Carolina, and particularly no follower of John Tipton, would be safe anywhere in the West—provided any Carolina partisans would still be living after General Sevier returned to set his sons free. . . .

A long-legged messenger sped ahead of the four captives and their guards to the log house, where Colonel John Tipton and his guest, Colonel Peter Parkinson of North Carolina, were at breakfast. Parkinson, a lanky red-haired man with sad blue eyes, who boasted that he never wore a suit of clothes longer than six months, pushed away a platter of eggs and bear bacon and frowned at the intruder who was dirtying the floor of the house with his muddy boots. His own militiamen were better trained, and he looked to his host to dress down the man who had so unceremoniously interrupted their meal.

John Tipton continued to eat, however, and acknowledged the presence of his follower by no more than a slight lift of a shaggy gray eyebrow. In his fifties, he looked considerably older, and his once handsome face was deeply lined. His near-white hair was long and tangled, and he had neglected either to comb it or to club it. His hands were rough and gnarled, and his doeskin jacket and speckled green stock seemed too large for him, which indeed they were. He continued to shovel eggs into his mouth with the haste of a man who expected each meal to be his last.

When he heard that the two eldest sons of his hated enemy, John Sevier, had been taken prisoner, he at last lifted his head and fixed his watery brown eyes on Colonel Parkinson. A stranger who might have wondered at the disintegration of what had once so obviously been a man of power and stature, would wonder no longer after seeing those eyes. The whites were bloodshot and yellowed, and the pupils were barely able to focus. As the energetic and forthright members of the Tipton family were only too well aware, the head of the clan drank heavily and constantly.

He shoved back his chair so vehemently that it toppled over, threw his napkin to the floor, and half ran, half hopped to the courtyard, leaving Colonel Parkinson to follow him. At the appearance of their leader, the men clustered in front of the door fell back, leaving a clear space between Tipton and the four captives, still astride their horses.

Tipton marched up to young John Sevier and took the reins in his bent fingers. "Welcome to my hall, Mr. Sevier," he said, cackling slightly. "And what are your thoughts this bright morning?"

"Thank you for inquiring, Colonel," Captain Sevier replied evenly. "Since you ask, I've been occupied with two thoughts. The first is a desire to express my gratitude and that of my companions for your—ah—hospitality. The second is more personal. When I return to Mount Pleasant I shall thrash my youngest brother so he cannot sit at table for a month. That will be my method of impressing on him the foolhardiness and stupidity of leaving behind a flag that should accompany the soldiery it represents."

John Tipton sneered. "You assume your pa and his Franklin lice are still alive. How do you know my boys and me didn't kill every last one of them?"

Captain John Sevier looked down from his horse and didn't bother to answer in words. Instead he guffawed, and his merriment was unfeigned.

Infuriated, Tipton danced up and down. "You talk about going home, do you?" he shouted. "By creck, what makes you think you're *ever* going home?" He turned to his followers and waved his shrunken arms. "Take these rebel hounds back of the house and give them a taste of North Carolina justice. Hang them!"

The adherents of Carolina "justice" whooped lustily and led the four shocked prisoners to the orchard behind the house. Colonel Parkinson, who had watched in silence, turned deathly white and laid a hand on John Tipton's arm. "I say, Tipton," he murmured, "you—can't hang them, you know. There's been no trial, and besides, they've committed no hanging offense."

Tipton brushed off the offending hand and glared through glassy eyes. "I'm chief judge of Washington County," he said, drawing himself to his full height. "And I condemn them to death. We'll hold a formal court session after we've buried them."

"But what have they done to deserve——"

"They're rebels against the state, that's what. They've taken part in an insurrection against the sovereign commonwealth of North Carolina. And if your stomach is too soft, Parkinson, you needn't watch. But don't interfere. By creck, I represent the law here!"

By the time Colonel Tipton reached the orchard, eager hands had fashioned nooses of stout hemp and had tied them around the necks of the Sevier brothers, Janus, and Harold. The plan of execution was simple: the ropes would be thrown over high branches of the fruit trees and secured; the Franks' horses would be kicked out from under them, and the four condemned men would be left dangling.

Neither Janus nor his companions offered any resistance, but young John Sevier was choked with rage, and his brother muttered to himself. Half a dozen self-appointed hangmen shouted orders simultaneously, and the brigand who had effected the capture of the victims bustled about self-importantly and got in everyone's way. But it didn't matter, for there was such an uproar that no man could hear his closest neighbor. Someone had dragged a large keg of cooling ale from the creek, two earthenware jugs of rum had been produced from nowhere, and the majority of the dispensers of Carolina justice were getting themselves quickly and roundly drunk.

A man in his late thirties, dressed in the uniform of a major of North Carolina militia, appeared from the house and stood unnoticed, surveying the bedlam from the back porch. Tall and husky, he bore a strong resemblance to Colonel Tipton, but his dark eyes were alert and his hair was neatly brushed. He took in the scene before him, and without a second's hesitation picked a bull whip from its stand at the side of the porch and strode resolutely into the center of the milling mob.

"Stop! You drunken idiots, I command you to stop!"

He was forced to repeat his order several times before the crowd fell silent. Meanwhile, without waiting to be obeyed, he drew a skinning knife from his belt, cut the bonds that secured each of the Franks' hands, and then began to tug down the rope that was to be used for the execution of John Sevier, Jr. The men watched him in surly resignation.

"Good morning, Captain. Sorry I slept overly long today." The newcomer spoke with a trace of humor.

"Major Tipton, your servant, Sir." Captain Sevier was remarkably calm. "My relief that you slept no longer is boundless, sir."

Colonel John Tipton, his face purpling, scurried forward, shaking his fists. "Eb, by creck, what in tarnation do you think you're doing?"

The major took his time answering, and when he did, he spoke for the benefit of the entire assemblage. "I might ask you the same question, Pa," he said in cold distaste. "But the answer, I'm afraid, is obvious. I told you no good would come of raiding General Sevier's farm. Yes, and now you would have added murder to robbery if I hadn't stopped this—this wanton, criminal act."

"You're stopping nothing, Eb. I'm your senior officer, and this is my property. You don't own it yet, by creck, and while it's mine, I'll give the orders here."

His son held his ground. "You're not on duty with the militia, Pa. I am. And I'm commander for Washington County. Anyone who doubts me is welcome to look at my commission, signed by the Speaker and the Secretary of the North Carolina House of

145

Commons. I forbid you to go on with this mockery. What's more I don't want General Sevier gunning for *me* to even the count for the death of *his* sons. This is a big country, and we've got to learn to live together in peace and compose our differences, or we'll all perish. The militia is dismissed—ride back to your homes, men. As for those of you who are here unofficially, I'll be glad to argue the merits of this matter with you individually."

Slowly, with painstaking care, he uncoiled the bull whip and began to swing it, casually at first, then with growing momentum. The men remained quiet, and those on the edge of the crowd began to slip away. Those nearest the iron-tipped thongs of the whip backed off and, deciding they had chores elsewhere, hurried from the orchard. Only a relieved Colonel Parkinson remained, along with the brigand who had started the trouble and a livid Colonel Tipton.

The major wound up his whip again with the same slow care and smiled at young Sevier. "A speedy ride home to you, Johnny," he said. "You too, Jim. For plain reasons, I don't advise you to tarry hereabouts. Tell your pa that even though we hold different views I hope we can thrash out our troubles over a jar of ale someday."

Colonel Tipton was making unintelligible noises in his throat, but his loyal helper seemed to understand him and, pulling a long horse pistol from inside his frayed and soiled shirt, he leveled it straight at Harold Jordan's head.

"Mebbe ye're lettin' the Sevier whelps go free, Eb Tipton," he snarled, "but I'll take care o' the other two my way. These Franklin bastards are goin' t' learn oncet 'n' for all who runs this mountain country."

Janus leaned forward slightly and whispered something to his horse. The stallion reacted immediately, rearing and then plunging down at the startled and terrified brigand. He threw himself out of the path of pawing hoofs, and his pistol went off, but the bullet cut harmlessly through the treetops. Snorting, the stallion started for the fallen man, but Janus patted his neck and clucked soothingly, and the beast quieted instantly.

"Come on! Let's go home!" Captain John Sevier called. "Let's get out of here before somebody is hurt!"

He started around the path that led past the front of the house toward the hills, and his three companions were close behind. Looking over his shoulder, Janus saw the brigand scrambling to his feet. Colonel Tipton, his pent-up rage exploding at last, was screaming at his son, who, completely unmoved, watched the Sevierites depart.

Chapter VIII

Never had the Franklin immigrants seen a land so lush, so bounteous as the Cumberland Valley and its gently sloping plateau. A dazzling blue-green carpet of thick, luxurious grass stretched over the rich black soil in every direction as far as the eye could see. Trees broke the regularity of the rolling landscape, trees of every description. There were giant pines and stately oaks, hardy gnarled hickories and graceful sycamores and hemlocks, and in the settled districts were fruit trees in abundance—wild peach, apple, plum, and pear.

The sun shone as brightly on the pioneers from New England and Ireland and Switzerland as it did back home during the kind months of May and June, and the winds from the south were soft and sweet. Their caravan rolled past the occasional farms, where a brief decade before there had been nothing but wilderness, and their eyes glistened as they saw the abundance of the produce. Farm-wise, they took in every detail of the tall stalks of corn, the thick, spreading cabbages, the glistening bean shoots, the sturdy potato plants. And as they drank in the sight of sleek brown cattle and fat, woolly sheep they knew that those who had boasted of the Cumberland as a modern Garden of Eden had in no wise exaggerated.

Carts drawn by horses, by oxen, by nervous donkeys, and even by calm, tireless men moved slowly in a compact body across the ever-broadening trail that Jim Robertson had chopped and plowed through a blazing land of plenty to found the town of Nashville. Children strayed from the dirt road to pick juicy gooseberries, blackberries, and raspberries from endless rows of thickets, but they were soon hauled back into the column by their watchful elders.

No one, in fact, was permitted to wander far from the trail, and the guides who led the caravan warned repeatedly that, despite the presence of all the good things necessary to sustain man, there were countless unseen dangers waiting to cut off the pilgrim from the promise of never-ending plenty. In the thick patches of woods were packs of wolves and foxes, and, in the hillier regions, there were fierce bobcats. But the worst hazards of all were men, tough brown-skinned men who had been pushed westward by the settlers of the Watauga, savages who stubbornly claimed this paradise as their own.

Sevier and Robertson had exchanged peace wampum with the Creeks and Chickasaws, but the Cherokees were a different breed, and this was Cherokee country. Despite the ceaseless efforts of the noble lord known variously as Corn Tassel and the Tassel to keep his warriors quiet, raids on small settlements and isolated farms by marauder Cherokee bands were common, and travelers who scorned the protection of caravans often disappeared, never to be seen again.

Trappers and traders, the oldest white inhabitants of the valley, swore that the Spaniards were responsible for the burnings and scalpings and lootings; the Indians, they insisted, would be docile enough were it not for the dons' generosity in doling out new-model flintlocks and jugs of whiskey. But the newcomers were not yet concerned with the causes of unrest; for the moment the possibility of sudden death merely added spice to the taste of a new life in a new world.

And so, free of care as they rode or walked, they sang lustily with the loud, sure voices of youth. For they were all young, most in their twenties, some still in their late teens, only a few scattered stalwarts among them admitting to the ripe maturity of thirty-five years. Their voices drowned the song of the robin and the thrush and the meadowlark as men and women alike called out a challenge to the world they had come to conquer:

> "For a shilling an acre,
> We'll take up our stand,
> Oh, rie-dum dum-diddle
> De-dee.
> Pay a shilling an acre
> To own our land,
> Oh, rie-dum dum-diddle
> De-dee.
> We've beaten the Lobster,
> The world now is ours,
> Oh, rie-dum dum-diddle
> De-dee.
> We'll roam where'er we will,
> Build our home upon a hill,
> Oh, rie-dum, oh raw-dum, oh faw-dum
> De-dee."

Riding near the head of the column with the single men who were unencumbered with family or baggage trains, Rosalind Walker found herself singing as loudly as the rest. There was something catchy about the tune, something contagious about the rollicking chorus of rie-dum dum-diddle de-dee. But Harold Jordan, taking his turn in the advance guard, was not singing, nor had he indeed shown much inclination to smile at any time since his return from the expedition to the house of Colonel Tipton—except when he was with Rosalind. He sat subdued and quiet now, hunched over in the saddle as his eyes expertly but gloomily scanned the trail for any telltale signs that Cherokee braves were abroad.

Rosalind was suffering from no sense of depression, however. Her cheeks were flushed, her eyes sparkled, and she rode easily and comfortably, swaying slightly now and then as her mare picked a dainty way across the ruts and holes of the worn path. The only discomforting note was that Janus Elholm was traveling to Nashville with a guide and was at this moment only a short distance ahead of the caravan. She said to herself that she had no desire to see his arrogant, handsome face again. But Nashville was still a full day's journey away, and the sun was warm, the air sweet, and the earth friendly.

> "Oh, rie-dum dum-diddle
> De-dee."

The young man nearest Rosalind howled out his sheer exultation in a powerful baritone, not a whit embarrassed by his total inability to carry a tune. Smiling to herself, she examined him covertly and concluded that she had never before seen a human being who radiated such rugged good health.

Scarcely twenty-one years of age, the young man carried himself with such an air of authority that even the guides listened to his counsel, and when he took upon himself the burden of assigning guards and foraging parties, no one disputed his leadership. Something other than his appearance was responsible for the common acceptance of his captaincy of the group, for his looks were far from impressive. He was gawky and lanky; his bones seemed too big for the thin layer of flesh that surrounded them. His cheekbones were as high as an Indian's, his forehead was both high and broad, and his long, ill-kempt hair was tied carelessly in back with an eelskin. He carried a long frontier rifle, and across his back was slung a battered Continental Army musket. His deerskin leggings were frayed, and his leather shirt was faded and patched. But his eyes, when he returned Rosalind's glance, were warm, intelligent, and self-assured, and his full-lipped grin seemed to split his lean face in two.

"By Jupiter and Moses, ma'am, it's a grand country and a grand day and a grand time to be alive!"

His enthusiasm was infectious, and Rosalind found herself answering with greater gusto than she had intended. "Yes, it's wonderful. I think this is the most beautiful land in all the world!"

"That it is, ma'am. And it's ours. America's. From here to the Western sea—it's ours."

It was strange that this seedy frontiersman should have caught the germ of Alexander Hamilton's dream, and Rosalind was still more intrigued by him. "I'd think there's plenty of land right here for all the world to settle on," she laughed. "Don't you agree, Mr.——"

"Jackson, ma'am. Andrew Jackson from South Carolina way. Sure, it's acres a-plenty for us. But not for the folks who'll come after us. They'll sweep past our new farms and cities like we over-ran the redcoats' earthworks."

Rosalind blinked. "Did you say 'we,' Mr. Jackson? Surely you were too young to have fought in the war."

Young Jackson's whole mood changed instantly, and his thick eyebrows contracted until they formed a single line. "I fought the bast—— Beg your pardon, ma'am. I fought when I was thirteen, and I've a scar on my arm for the rest of my days as a medal for it. Every time it rains and my arm pains me, I'm reminded of those English rascals, and by Jupiter and Moses, I'll pay them back someday, with interest compounded!"

Taken aback by Jackson's fierce declamation and fiercer scowl, Rosalind tried to soothe him. "And now you've come to the Cumberland to buy a farm, I suppose. I hear that Governor Sevier is selling lots to veterans for only sixpence an acre."

The horseman was properly mollified, and his mercurial temper softened. "Maybe I'll pick up a little land, but I'm a lawyer by profession, ma'am. I passed the bar in Jonesboro only last Thursday. They charged me two bearskins and a dozen fox pelts for my license. Didn't have any skins, so I had to go out and shoot 'em. Those judges were sure surprised when I came back so soon with a fee. By Jupiter and Moses, I showed 'em!" He chuckled and managed to look so boyish that it was impossible to believe that here rode a veteran of the war and a full-fledged attorney at law.

Leaning toward Rosalind, Jackson spoke again in what for him was a confidential tone. "You look like a lady of quality, ma'am," he bellowed. "Nashville won't be easy on folks like you, and you may need a helper sometime. Any time your larder runs low and you have a hankering for bear steak, or any time you run afoul of the law and want a fellow who'll swap Latin with the best of them, just you holler for A. Jackson, ma'am."

A small but powerful stream cascaded and erupted through a narrow gorge and provided cold, clear drinking water for the immigrants. Women busied themselves around half a score of fires, and the pleasant odors of stewing meat and carrots and potatoes blended with the more pungent fumes of wood smoke. Three of the men carried buckets of water to the horses and mules, and the others lazed in the bright, warm sun. Young Jackson had spread a large handkerchief over his face and was sprawled on the grass, sleeping soundly, his restless energies at last in repose. A thin-faced couple from Pennsylvania stood in the shadows behind their wagon, arguing softly but bitterly. Occasionally one or the other would raise an angry shout, then look around guiltily. Again their voices would drop to a low murmur.

Two earnest men with serious faces were discussing the benefits of settling in Nashville; meanwhile their wives, unconcerned by considerations of the future, stolidly continued their preparations of food. Even the two lookouts who had been posted on high ground here relaxed. One had dropped his musket to the ground, where it lay within easy reach, and the other sat with his knees drawn up to his chin, half dozing. In short, the convoy had stopped for midday dinner.

Rosalind Walker and Harold Jordan sat on a slope a short distance removed from the busy immigrants. Rosalind's skirts were carefully spread, and she absently braided two long strands of orchard grass as Harold, at her feet, looked at her with eyes that revealed far more than he intended.

After a few moments he tried to take her hand, but she eluded him. He paused, wetted his lips, and the humor left his eyes. "May I say something to you? May I give you warning?"

She studied him for an instant. "I don't know I'll want to hear what you wish to say. But as I'm none too sure of what that will be, I guess I'd better listen."

He sat up and moved closer to her. "I'm not a very good or a very nice person, Roz. Someday I hope to—to be able to tell you a long and a none too pretty story. However, I have no intention of doing so until—well, until many matters are resolved. But this much I want to say now—my intentions toward you are—are far from frivolous. Now, if you'd care to find some excuse to help Mrs. Bobbins dish up that stew, I'll understand and will stand aside."

Rosalind did not move. She stared for a long, quiet moment at the hills that surrounded the little cupped valley in which the immigrants had stopped to dine, then she turned suddenly, and there was color in her cheeks and she looked squarely at Harold. "I beg you, Harold, do not be impatient. I am going to Nashville because I have a real and honest desire to teach school there. I intend to allow nothing to interfere with the fulfillment of that wish."

He showed his relief. "I can promise you that I will be the last to interfere with that," he murmured.

A low, insistent whine sounded overhead, and Rosalind looked around in blank bewilderment. But Harold reacted differently; he was on his feet instantly, and so was every other man. The Pennsylvanian who had been arguing with his wife forgot her and leaped for his musket; young Andrew Jackson was awake in a second and was racing for the front line of horses and carts; the two who had been placidly discussing the merits of Nashville fell instantly silent and reached for their firearms and the two lookouts were lying on their stomachs in the tall grass, peering up at the ring of hills. The children who had been playing scurried to the sides of their mothers as if by some prearranged signal. And the food cooking in the big pots was forgotten.

"That was a bullet, Roz. A rifle bullet." Harold poured a charge of powder into his pistol even as he spoke quietly. "It may be a lone shot fired by some trapper by accident, but I think not. Seems to me it's Cherokees. And we're in a bad spot for an attack."

A second shot cut through the still air, then a third. The animals shifted restlessly, and suddenly a horse emitted a thin, high shriek of terror and sank to its knees.

The men of the convoy knew what they were doing. Those who had been charged with the care of the animals moved quietly and efficiently to place them behind a screen of wagons and carts. The others half ran, half crawled toward the outer perimeter of the little encampment, where they formed a rough semicircle facing out toward the hills. Young Jackson, scowling fiercely, crept up to two or three and whispered something to them. Each in turn nodded, and in a few moments the small band was making its way cautiously toward the far side of the camp, where they spread out as they crouched in the grass. Their intention, obviously, was to provide cover from the rear.

Harold remained standing, and his eyes never wavered from a small clump of trees at the top of a hill. "Here, Roz," he said, not looking at her. He tossed his second pistol and his powder horn to her. "Fill the pan with powder for me. You know how?"

"Yes." She was wasting no words either.

"Those shots may have been directed at us. We're separated here from the rest of the convoy and we make a fine target. I'll fire both pistols and then we'll make a dash for the carts. The smoke will cover us. Ready?"

He hardly waited for her breathless "Yes." The pistols spoke almost in unison, and with that they turned and ran for their lives to the shelter of the nearest wagon. Before she knew it she had reached temporary safety and was lying face down behind a cart.

Someone apparently gave a general order to fire, and ten or more of the settlers' guns spoke simultaneously. The Cherokees accepted the challenge, and the air was suddenly filled with the ominous hum of flying bullets.

She had no opportunity to thank Harold, however, for no sooner had he seen her fling herself behind the wheels of one of the largest of the wagons than he raced off to the spot where he had left his pack and musket. He picked up his gun in a single, swooping motion, barely slackening his pace, and in a few seconds he had joined the other men in the semicircular defense line.

Rosalind was able to see virtually nothing else as she peered out through the wheels of the wagon. Puffs of smoke from the crests of the hills and the sharp cr-r-a-c-k of rifle fire assured her that the Cherokees were there in considerable number, but she failed to catch even a single glimpse of one of the enemy. It was plain to her, though, that other, more experienced eyes were sharper than her own, for occasionally one of the men would shout in triumph and would point a grimy, powder-scarred finger toward the hills.

The majority of the women, Rosalind noted, were unable to watch the progress of the fight. Most of them huddled together on the ground, and some covered their eyes and ears with shawls or skirts. But there was no sign of panic or hysterics from anyone. A little girl sobbed quietly in her mother's arms beneath the small cart that contained the sum total of the family's worldly goods, but even the weeping child showed no sign of frenzy. The immigrants had known the risks they were taking when they began their journey, and they didn't flinch now.

Among the men there was even a spirit of rough humor. They called encouragement to each other above the piercing rattle of muskets and rifles, and occasionally someone guffawed over a crude joke. Young Jackson and his companions on the far side of the perimeter seemed to be having an almost hilarious time as they kept up a steady stream of spirited conversation.

Only one woman was taking an active part in the battle; big, rawboned Mrs. Bobbins had taken her place in the line directly behind her husband. Between them they had two muskets, and as soon as he fired one she handed him the other, which she had quickly cleaned, loaded, and primed. No words passed between them, and no words were necessary.

It seemed to Rosalind that the battle had gone on interminably, when suddenly it ended. There was a final flurry of rifleshots from the hills, then the pounding of horses' hoofs as the Indians rode hurriedly away.

Only when she had crawled out from under the cart and once again stood in the sunlight, brushing off her skirt, did she realize that the entire flurry had lasted for no more than a quarter of an hour. And childishly, almost pettishly, she felt cheated; at no time had she caught so much as a glimpse of a Cherokee attacker.

The men began to relax, each in his own way. One or two sat in the grass and held their faces in the palms of their hands. Several laughed and pounded each other on the back. And the Pennsylvanian who had been arguing with his wife before the fight took a long draught from a small but heavy earthenware container that reposed in his hip pocket. Then he wiped his mouth with his sleeve, and with a new look of determination went off in search of his spouse to continue what he manifestly considered to be the more important battle.

Ed Bobbins stood up and wiped his fingers on the sides of his breeches. "Reckon we beat 'em off, Ma," he said.

Mrs. Bobbins nodded shortly, never one to waste words on the obvious.

"You take the big musket back t' the cart, Ma," her husband directed. "I'm keepin' the little one fer a spell. And get that dinner goin' agin. If'n it's spoilt I'll tan you good. I got me a real hearty appetite fer vittles."

He motioned to two other men and started to drift off, but a look from his wife stopped him. "Where you headin' now, Ed?" she asked. "Do you good t' set 'n' rest afore we eat."

"Got some things to do." His companions were already strolling toward the hills, and he was plainly restless.

"What sorts o' things?" Mrs. Bobbins stood with her feet planted firmly on the grass, the heavy musket tucked under her arm.

"Skelps, Bess. Good Cherokee skelps. Must be a big mess of 'em up there. But those buzzards racin' ahead o' me are goin' t' get 'em all less'n you stop your jabberin' 'n' leave me be."

Without another word he turned on his heel and strode off. Mrs. Bobbins shrugged, smiled a tight, secret smile at the ways of men, and hurried toward her fire and stewpot. It would be necessary, she reflected, to add a little water to the contents of the pot, but with any luck there would be nothing scorched, and that would be truly fortunate. Above all else, Mrs. Bobbins hated serving burned or spoiled dishes, especially when she had invited company to a meal.

Even the Choctaw guide, who knew every trail, every ridge in the Cumberland, had difficulty in keeping his swift pony ahead of Janus Elholm's stallion. There was a drive, a determination in Janus that would not be denied, and he rode at a sustained pace that the Choctaw had never before seen in a white man.

They had been eating their noon meal, chewing peacefully on

the thin strips of buffalo steak the guide had roasted, when they heard the sounds of a battle in the distance. Janus had been on his feet instantly, his food forgotten, as he had demanded that they ride to the aid of the convoy. And even now, though the sound of shooting had long since ceased, he was no less insistent.

Crouching low but at ease in the saddle, he reflected that it might have been wiser had he traveled with the convoy in the first place. But he had wanted to compare the terrain with certain maps he carried under his shirt, and he had known that he would be making innumerable notes for future military reference. So it had been necessary, he had told himself, to remain apart from the curious, talkative men and women who would observe and wonder and ask questions.

But now he was not so sure. If Rosalind Walker had been killed in an Indian raid—and his guide had assured him that probably there had been a Cherokee attack on the convoy—he would feel that he had in some way been responsible, that had he been near her no harm could have come to her.

Skirting around the edge of a huge dead tree root, he told himself that he was actually losing no time by riding to join the convoy. If all were well, he could make off again at once and would have wasted only an hour or two at the most, for he would arrive in Nashville sometime tomorrow in any event. If he learned that something unpleasant had happened to Rosalind, however, he was uncertain as to what course of action to take. Retaliation against the Cherokees was out of the question, for the tribe was a carefully cultivated Spanish ally, and he would soon be using the very braves who had conducted this raid as scouts and outriders and guides.

If the girl had been taken prisoner, he felt that he might use his prestige as a general of Spain to persuade the savages to set her free, but in so doing he would be taking a terrible risk: Rosalind might learn who he really was, and that knowledge in the hands of just one person could force him to leave the Cumberland prematurely. There was still too much for him to learn in this part of the world before he departed for New Spain, and he could take no undue chances that might place his great mission in jeopardy.

His purpose, then, in riding back to the convoy was merely to reassure himself that Rosalind was safe. And as the knowledge of this fact grew in him, his irritation with himself increased too. It was galling to be forced to admit that he cared what happened to any woman. And that this particular female should have so caught his interest was inexplicable.

She was lovely, to be sure. But beautiful women were certainly no novelty to him, and he had known girls in Paris and Vienna and Budapest who were equally attractive. He had always demanded sophistication, and here was a girl who was painfully naïve. He had invariably been aroused only by those who had enjoyed a certain amount of experience, and here was someone who was woefully lacking even in a knowledge of her own beauty and its power. He tried to compare her with Francisca de Guzman and smiled wryly. There was a demanding, provocative quality in Francisca that Rosalind Walker would and could never achieve.

What infuriated him most was the knowledge that Rosalind would have nothing to do with him. Perhaps, he decided, it was her rejection of him that had drawn him to her. There were few women indeed who had spurned him, and the very novelty of this experience gave it piquancy.

No doubt Harold Jordan was with her, and Janus did not doubt Jordan's ability to look after her. Although he did not like the American, they had shared danger together, and he had to admit that Jordan was both courageous and forthright.

The odor of wood fires drifted through the trees, and in the distance Janus could hear the stamping and snorting of horses. Calling a curt order to his Choctaw guide, he pulled down his stallion to a walk. Feeling faintly foolish, he thought that the very least he could do was to make a dignified entrance; he would appear asinine indeed if he rode into the camping grounds at a canter, brandishing firearms.

A man stepped from behind a tree, a long rifle in his hands, and gestured curtly for Janus and the Indian to halt. Glowering for a moment, he then broke into a smile. "How do, Mr. Elholm," he said. "Got lonesome 'n' decided t' come 'n' have a bite o' dinner with us, did ye?"

Janus recognized him as one of the militiamen who had been taken prisoner and then set free in the final incident of the Tipton battle. "I heard shooting and came to see if I could be of help. I trust there have been no difficulties?"

"Naw." The man grinned, displaying a row of small, yellow teeth. "We was findin' the trip a might dreary, so some o' them goddamn Cherokees obliged us by livenin' up the mornin' for us. But we took care of 'em right proper. Ride on into camp if ye like, Mr. Elholm. The folks'll be glad t' see ye. But leave yer Injun friend set out here with me, if ye don't object. Some o' the women might be kind o' skittery if they set eyes on one o' these critters that smears hisself with paint."

The Choctaw undertood English better than either of the white men realized, for he dismounted from his pony at once, glided to a flat rock, and sat down upon it, his features immobile, revealing nothing. Janus nodded to the militiaman and slowly walked his horse forward. Breaking through the trees into a clearing of tall grass, he saw that he was at the top of a gentle incline and that a small valley was cupped directly below him.

He blinked in surprise at the sight that greeted his eyes. The immigrants were seated in small groups, calmly eating their dinner. Here and there someone laughed quietly, and nowhere was there any sign of strain or tension. Allowing his gaze to wander quickly from one party to another, Janus saw that a small, rather wiry man was wearing his left arm in an improvised sling. And another of the settlers moved rather stiffly, for a clumsy bandage was wound around his neck and left shoulder. There were no other visible signs that a battle had been fought.

The rifles and muskets of all were within easy reach, however, and Janus saw that two sentries were posted on the hills directly opposite him. He noted, too, that scalp locks were hanging from the belts of three or four men in the valley. There *had* been a vicious fight, then, though one would never have known it from the air of serenity that prevailed in the little valley. These new-comers to the wilderness were already hardened to a life of in-security and danger; they accepted a Cherokee attack with the same aplomb and grace that they would take the good things of life that came their way.

Shaking his head, Janus felt a reluctant admiration for these incredible men and women. Nowhere in Europe had he en-countered a people so willing to endure hardships for the sake of a dream.

Such thoughts served no useful purpose, he reminded himself sternly, and he forced himself to look squarely at Rosalind Walker for the first time. He had seen her as soon as he had broken through the fringe of trees, of course, but had not glanced at her again. Now he saw that she and Harold Jordan were sit-ting close to each other, much closer than was necessary, and that they were sharing a meal from the same steaming bowl. Two other people were seated around the same small fire, a gaunt, bony woman and a heavy-set man who sported a row of scalps at his waist. But Rosalind and Harold seemed absorbed in each other.

Although several of the immigrants had no doubt seen him, Rosalind was unaware of his presence on the hillside, and Janus felt an urgent desire to be gone before she learned that he was there. He wheeled his stallion about and plunged back through the trees. He would insist that his Choctaw guide make greater speed than ever before during the remainder of the journey.

He felt humiliated and was enraged at himself for having been so soft. But the lesson was a good one; never again would he allow sentiment to stand in the way of the mission that would bring him all he had ever really wanted.

There was no church edifice in Nashville yet, but three hundred people, almost one fourth of the total population of the town, were gathered on the broad lawn behind Donelson's store, facing the river. Only a few yards away was the inner wall of the original stockade, built by the first settlers who had accompanied the Robertsons and Donelsons to the town that had mushroomed so fast in eight brief years that it had become the hub of the Cumberland and had recently been vested with the dignity of a county seat.

Among those who trampled the grass were a handful of loafers and curiosity seekers, but the vast majority were serious people who too seldom had the opportunity to hear a minister of God preach the Gospel, and who as a result had looked forward to this day with extraordinary anticipation. There were plain women with gray homespun shawls thrown over their shoulders, brawny farmers and settlers who wore broad-brimmed hats and carried their ever-present rifles with unconscious dignity. There were a few eager young couples standing hand in hand, patently disinterested in the sermon and waiting only until the services ended so they could approach the pulpit and pay the required sum of four beaver skins for a marriage ceremony. There were parents, too, holding infants in rough linsey-woolsey blankets, awaiting the long-discussed moment when their offspring would be baptized with a few drops of Cumberland River water.

Standing near the rear of the throng, Rosalind and Harold had to crane their necks to see the crude pulpit which had been thrown together out of hastily sawed logs. Despite the solemnity of the crowd, Rosalind was thrilled—and impatient. On her arrival in town she had learned that the Reverend Houston was away visiting smaller settlements down-river but that he would return on the Sabbath to preach his first sermon in Nashville since May.

There had been plenty to occupy her in setting to rights the one-story addition which the Dolsons had built onto their hastily constructed cabin. But her scouring and polishing had only made her more restless. She knew that if the Reverend Houston refused to accept her she would be forced to return in utter defeat to Boston.

It took an effort to wrench her thoughts from the brink of pessimism on which they teetered, and she tried to concentrate on the Reverend Houston and his sermon, but it was difficult. That deep voice had been thundering from the pulpit for almost three hours now, and Rosalind wasn't the only one who yawned and stamped cramps out of aching feet. For the hundredth time she stared at the minister and tried to guess how he would react to her. But his appearance gave no clue.

He was dressed in a broadcloth suit of stout black wool, common to clergymen everywhere, and around his neck he wore a small, plain silver cross suspended from a thin chain. But there the similarity to others of his profession ended abruptly. His feet were clad in the ungainly, heavily oiled rawhide boots that were universal among rivermen throughout the West. On his head was perched a thick deerskin hat with a broad, floppy brim to keep off the sun, and from the crown arouse an incongruous faded green feather, as weather-beaten as the headgear itself. Most unusual of all was his belt of rawhide, from which hung two pistols, each carefully secured in an open-topped rawhide holster. His long, meticulously combed hair was gray, but his trimmed beard still showed patches of a deep brown. And no one who had ever heard him preach could deny the power of his voice. Now, after almost one hundred and eighty continuous minutes of exercise, it was still strong and vibrant.

" '. . . Behold, there came up the champion (the Philistine of

Gath, Goliath by name) . . . And all the men of Israel, when they saw the man, fled from him, and were sore afraid. . . . And David said to Saul, Let no man's heart fail because of him; thy servant will go and fight with this Philistine. . . . David said moreover, The Lord that delivered me out of the paw of the lion, and out of the paw of the bear, he will deliver me out of the hand of this Philistine!' "

A vulgar laugh rang out only a few feet from Rosalind and Harold, and they looked in the direction of the noise, as did a score of others. Two ruffians were weaving unsteadily through the throng, their arms around each other's shoulders. Out of respect to the Reverend Houston, all three of Nashville's taverns had closed their doors for the day, but the intruders had found a cache of liquor somewhere, and from their every move it was their plain intent to break up the religious gathering. They laughed again, more loudly, and this time the Reverend Houston heard them.

Marking his place in his heavy leather-bound Bible, he closed it and placed it on the rough pulpit. "Friends and fellow Christians," he said above the sudden murmurs, "there's a lesson for us all in the faith of the noble shepherd boy David. All the rest of the Israelites were scared. Scared purple. But not David. No, sir! He had faith in the Almighty God. The living God. The same God who watches over you and me today."

His right hand whipped the nearer pistol from its holster, and with deceptive speed he raised it, cocked it with a practiced thumb, and fired. The fur hat of the taller ruffian was lifted neatly from his head and fell to the ground. Those who examined it later found a hole through the crown only a half inch from the scalp line.

"You all know what David did," the Reverend Houston continued calmly, slipping the gun back into its holster. "He killed Goliath, and he saved the field for the Israelites."

The two ruffians, considerably sobered, sneaked away quietly and with astonishing speed. Neither made any attempt to retrieve the fallen hat. There was a faint flurry of conversation among the newer arrivals to the Cumberland, but those familiar with the Reverend Houston's technique for keeping order at his services paid no attention to the departure of the scoundrels. Rosalind, accustomed to the dignity and formality of Boston churches, was both horrified and spellbound by the minister's method, and it was several minutes before her mind again focused on what he was saying.

"Here in this glorious land where you want for nothing," the silvery voice went on, "you are in a position much akin to that of the Israelites. Your rich domain is threatened from the south by the thieving Papists of Spain and from the north by the rascal mock Papists of England. All that stands between you and destruction is your faith in the Lord God, my fellow Christians. Stumble into the gutters of sin and you will be devoured as Jonah was by the sea mammal. But David escaped that terrible fate—and so can you." If his biblical metaphors had become slightly confused, the Reverend Houston was unaware of it. He was plunging now to the climax of his oration, and perspiration poured down his sun-dried cheeks and made his plain white stock a sodden rag.

"When last I visited Nashville," he cried, "there were but two taverns here and no more than four houses of iniquity. Today I find three taverns and more dens of sin than a man of God can rightly count. And in your own homes I've found men and women and even little children playing games of chance. Well, by the living God, you'll stop your gaming and your fornication and your drunken debauches or my name isn't Houston. You'll turn back to the Good Book, and you'll send your sons to school so they will learn to read it too. The day is coming, friends, the day is almost upon us at this moment, when force won't suffice. To save yourselves and your new homes, you'll be required to bend your knees and pray to the Holy Lord God Almighty for salvation. Yes, sir—and He'll require me to pray, too, and to lay down my pistols. Those guns of yours and mine will be no more effective in stopping the hordes of Philistines who'll march down on us than a bucket can scoop up the flood tides of the sea. Repent, you miserable sinners—and pray! Down on your knees, every mother's son and every mother's daughter of you—and pray! Pray for forgiveness! Pray for deliverance! Pray for succor! Pray for salvation! Pray, I tell you—pray!"

So compelling was the minister's exhortation that rational, skeptical men who fed and clothed and protected their families with their rifles threw their weapons from them and fell to their knees. Soon the entire congregation was kneeling on the dark blue-green grass, and Rosalind, after a moment's hesitation, joined them. Her concept of how to worship God differed from that of the Reverent Houston, but she had no desire to be conspicuous. To her relief, the minister began to speak the Lord's Prayer, and she joined wholeheartedly with those around her in repeating the familiar phrases.

The prayer meeting was over, and people were eager to return to their homes, where a Sunday roast or a barbecued pheasant or grouse awaited them. Bidding Harold to wait, Rosalind wriggled through the crowds ahead of the prospective brides and grooms and soon found herself at the foot of the pulpit, where the Reverend Houston was carefully wrapping his Bible in a large square of cloth. He was even more impressive at close quarters than at a distance, and when he fixed his flashing eyes on her she felt unaccountably shy. Stammering slightly as she introduced herself, she handed him the letter she had received before leaving Boston, the contract which she had thought to be equally binding upon herself and upon the state of Franklin.

Grunting, the Reverend Houston finished reading the document, jammed it into a pocket of his loose-fitting coat, and glowered down at her, his eyes brighter than ever.

" 'Arma virumque cano, Troiae qui primus ab oris,' " he thundered.

Rosalind conquered a sudden desire to giggle. This was going to be considerably easier than she had dared to hope. " 'Italiam, fato profugus, Lavinaque venit,' " she responded promptly.

The Reverend Houston was so astonished he could only blink. Taking a clean handkerchief from his pocket, he blew his nose vigorously and then glanced again at Rosalind, a new respect dawning in his eyes. "So you are familiar with the *Aeneid*. Very unusual. Most young women in our day have never heard of Virgil. Even my own daughters-in-law were in ignorance until I enlightened them."

Smiling for the first time, Rosalind said nothing. But she felt sure of herself, and he responded to her confidence.

"You know your English letters, Mistress Walker? Your arithmetic is free from blemish? You have a sufficient knowledge of music, weaving, and cookery to conduct yourself with dignity and honor in the instruction of young females?" The questions were hurled at her in a sudden torrent.

Still smiling, Rosalind raised her chin. "I taught for a year at Mistress Baker's Academy in Boston, a most proper institution, and I shall gladly submit to any examination you care to have me undergo, Mr. Houston." She had almost called him "Dr." Houston, after the New England fashion, but realized just in time that he had probably not received a Doctor of Divinity degree at the time of his ordination.

"I judge people by what I see in them, not by rote," was his surprising answer. " 'For the word of God is quick, and powerful, and sharper than any twoedged sword, piercing even to the dividing asunder of soul and spirit, and of the joints and marrow, and is a discerner of the thoughts and intents of the heart.' I have confidence in you. No examination will be necessary. You have the quarters in which to conduct your seminary?"

"Yes. I was told you would expect me to provide quarters, so

I have made inquiry. There is an empty house at the edge of town, on the river. The man who built it died and left it to the town. Colonel Robertson says I may use it."

"Very well, then. If you fail, you'll disgrace Jack Sevier, who vouches for you. And you'll place me in a most embarrassing position, too, for I shall make the needful arrangements with Colonel Robertson. Your license will cost you five beaver pelts, which we require of the headmasters of our boys' schools too. And you'll need an attorney to draw up the papers for you. Good day, Mistress Walker."

His Bible under his arm, his pistols slapping against his legs as he walked, the Reverend Samuel Houston plunged into the crowd of young people and parents. Rosalind took a series of quick breaths. It had happened so quickly, so smoothly, that she was unable to believe her ordeal was finished. She would have her school now and could stay on in Franklin indefinitely.

Slightly dazed, she wandered across the lawn in search of Harold and saw that he had gone across the road for their horses. Three young men, the last of the crowd that had gathered to hear the Reverend Houston, were standing nearby, deep in conversation. The lean figure of one of them was familiar, and Rosalind called to him impulsively.

"Mr. Jackson!"

He hurried to her, his long legs devouring the space between them. "Hello, ma'am. How are you?"

"Never better in all my days, Mr. Jackson!" Rosalind glowed with happiness. "I've been granted permission to open my seminary, Mr. Jackson, and if you will help me, I have a commission for you as attorney. There are licensing papers to be drawn up, the Reverend Houston said, and——"

"I'm familiar with the licensing of schools, ma'am. How heavy a fee do you plan to charge your pupils?"

Jackson's tongue was brusque, and Rosalind felt accountably chilled. "Why—why, only as much as their parents can afford to pay, sir. Enough to pay my salary and the expenses incurred by the state. I have no intention of becoming rich from the teaching of girls who have as much right to an education as I myself had!" Two red spots burned at Rosalind's cheekbones, and her lips thinned. She would have turned away from the rude South Carolinian, but he leaped around and blocked her path.

"Ma'am," he said earnestly, "it will be my greatest pleasure to represent you, at no cost to yourself or to Franklin. By Jupiter and Moses, I'll do more than scribble the papers for you. I'll bring you back those pelts myself. So don't be offended, ma'am. You see, I had to find out where you stood. I have views of my own about schooling. The little I know I had to teach myself. I had no money for schoolmasters. But if we're to have the right to the pursuit of happiness, like Mr. Jefferson said, then every boy and girl in this land should have the privilege of reading and writing."

Chapter IX

More than double the population of Nashville was gathered in the large, cleared area of the banks of the river, and their sustained, happy laughter would have made a disinterested observer think that twice as many people again were convened there. The chief merrymakers, of course, were the children, for Nashville held a jamboree only twice a year, and the younger generation was making every minute count. The smallest cavorted and wriggled and shouted for the sheer joy of shouting. Those a few years older played violent games with balls made of tightly wound strands of yarn which had been soaked in salted water. And the adolescents, freed for one day from the watchful, hovering eyes of parents, wandered two by two along the edge of the Cumberland, shyly holding hands and discovering for the first time the mystical joy and pain of growing up.

Fortunately, the weather was fine. There was a crisp, cool nip in the air, and the branches of trees bobbed and waved in a steady but gentle breeze. But the sun shone brightly, and only an occasional fat white cloud crossed its path and momentarily deprived the people of the Cumberland of its warmth.

A flock of geese swooped overhead, and the men at the jamboree watched them with bright, keen eyes. Trigger fingers tightened, then relaxed again. No one was going to frighten the children or upset the women with the noise of firearms. Other geese would be moving south on other days, but this was a special day, a day apart.

Never before had so many attended a jamboree, and even the leaders of the community, those who were responsible for its growth and well-being, were surprised. Whole families had traveled great distances, some as far as fifty miles across rutted roads, along deer paths, and, where necessary, through the tangled wilderness of the deep woods, in order to spend jamboree time with each other.

For the men the day provided sound excuse for heavy drinking, yet very few were drunk. The time for that would come later in the day when the shadows lengthened across the field. A handful indulged themselves even now, of course. New Englanders brought out precious hordes of aged rum; Pennsylvanians produced ales and beers that had been brewed with loving skill for just this occasion; Virginians proudly offered the brandies they had themselves distilled.

The women, as always, were busy. They had toiled for days preparing their most succulent dishes, dressing themselves and their children in the best their patient, nimble fingers could contrive. Their labors would not end today until the last hungry mouth had been filled, the last wooden platter and long knife washed clean in the waters of the Cumberland.

Some of the men, at the request of their wives, had dug barbecue pits in one corner of the field, and sides of beef and venison, bear and buffalo were cooking slowly over hickory flames. There were whole baby suckling pigs turning slowly on spits, too, and here and there the delicate odors of roasting lamb sharpened the appetites of the older boys who were charged with the responsibility of barbecuing the meat.

Rosalind Walker strolled slowly across the field, her hand resting lightly on Harold Jordan's arm. Rarely in her life had she been as happy as she was at this moment. After only two months in Nashville she had established a place for herself in the community, and she was proud of the respect and admiration in the eyes of her pupils as they curtsied to her.

Her pleasure was in no small measure due to the visit the Reverend Sam Houston had paid her only two days ago. He had arrived unannounced at the schoolhouse and had stood, silent and glowering, through the final hour of the afternoon's classes. Then, when her twenty-seven pupils had departed with more haste than usual, he had glared harshly at Rosalind for so long that she had felt weak in the knees. Then the Reverend Sam, his expression unchanged and unchanging, had grasped her hand and had shaken it so hard that her knuckles still felt sore when she wriggled her fingers.

"Miss Walker," he had boomed, "I'm pleased with you. Jack Sevier and Jim Robertson are pleased with you. You're doing the Lord's work here, helping Him tend His flock, and you've justified the trust we've placed in you. And I'm honor-bound to tell you something that'll swell your head so big your hair will feel tight on your scalp.

"Being as you're a woman, you'll doubtless remind me of this someday when we have cross words. But that can't be helped. The truth is, Miss Walker, you've stirred up a hive of wasps, and the masters of the boys' schools are so jealous of you that I'm forced to spend a goodly part of my time quoting Scripture to them so they'll rid themselves of their sinful thoughts. There's only one boys' school in the state with an enrollment larger than yours, Miss Walker. Think of it—only one! And there are so many girls who are demanding the right to a schooling now that Jack Sevier and I can't enjoy a day's peace any more. If you continue this way, we'll have to hire an assistant for you and set up a branch of the seminary in Jonesboro next year."

Yes, Rosalind thought, she had a right to be happy. In all honesty, she was forced to admit that more than her work was responsible, and her grip on Harold's arm tightened. He had been so attentive, so solicitous, so unsparingly generous that she was increasingly sure he was the right man for her. Yet when he had asked her to marry him, she had begged for time.

She had learned yesterday that Janus Elholm was back in Nashville after a prolonged trip into Kentucky and that he would be present at the jamboree. She was disgusted with herself for being weak enough to feel any interest in Janus, but that interest was making it difficult for her to decide about Harold. Without being consciously aware that she was doing so, she kept searching for Janus in the good-natured crowds that filled the jamboree playground.

Meantime there was much to delight an Easterner who was attending her first jamboree. Harold guided her toward a place where a hilarious group had gathered for the purpose of throwing horseshoes at stakes while blindfolded. As most of those taking part in the sport had already consumed considerable quantities of hard liquor, the blindfolds were unnecessary, but they added to the merriment.

Rosalind did not see the horseshoe pitchers, for no sooner was she standing near the circle than she noticed Janus Elholm on the far side of the crowd. Aside from the medallion that hung from his neck, he was indistinguishable in dress from many of the men present, for he wore a shirt and trousers of bleached buckskin that showed evidence of his wearying trip. Yet he was the most conspicuous man in the crowd, chiefly because of his companion. Rosalind could barely restrain a gasp when she saw that he stood with an arm tightly encircling the waist of the notorious half-caste girl, Llandu McGuire.

No decent woman in Nashville ever spoke to Llandu, and no man would risk being caught exchanging greetings with her in broad daylight. The daughter of a Choctaw squaw and a wild Irish trapper, Llandu lived in a small house near the river's edge. All Nashville knew that Llandu was unstinting in her affections, provided a man could pay her price. That many wished to pay it was understandable, for there was no denying her appeal. Her hair was a light brown, and her eyes, unexpectedly, were a deep greenish-blue. Otherwise she looked like a full-blooded Choctaw, from the straight cut of her nose to her dark skin. No man could look at the supple waist, the full pointed breasts, and the firm, shapely thighs which revealed themselves under her dress, without appreciation.

She was more than a little drunk at the moment, and her husky laugh was louder than usual as she parted her full lips and smiled intimately into Janus's eyes.

If Janus was aware of the presence of Rosalind he gave no indication of it and seemed completely absorbed in Llandu. He was apparently telling her some joke as he leaned down and whispered in her ear. For all the attention they were paying to anyone else, they might as well have been alone somewhere on the riverbank.

Seeing them together, Rosalind thought there was a primitive quality in Janus that matched the savagery of Llandu. His face was tanned a deep shade of reddish-brown after his travels, and he had lost a little weight. But still he didn't look her way.

In spite of herself Rosalind couldn't keep from flushing with annoyance. In an instant Harold was bending over her. "Is something troubling you, Roz?"

"Yes. Let's go elsewhere, please."

Later that afternoon Janus Elholm stood by himself, his thumbs hooked into his belt as he idly watched a pair of stalwart frontier boys wrestling half seriously and half in fun. In reality the jamboree bored him. Llandu McGuire had been a disappointment, and he had discarded her quickly. Although she had offered more excitement than anyone else in the town, he had soon come to the conclusion that she was not even in the same class with camp followers he had known in Europe.

Although his work in Franklin and Kentucky was virtually finished, he had received a message from Baron de Carondelet, asking him to remain in Nashville for another two weeks to await the arrival of the baron himself, who was planning an incognito trip into American territory. Frowning, he drew a small silver snuffbox from a pocket of his rough buckskin shirt. How he would spend his time during the next fourteen days was a problem he did not care to contemplate. He could, of course, go directly to New Orleans, for he was not under the baron's orders, but as this Flemish noble who had risen to such a lofty pinnacle in the hierarchy of New Spain was the man who would provide him with troops, he deemed it the wiser and more diplomatic course to do as he had been bid.

On his long journey through the interminable forests from Louisville in Kentucky to Nashville he had thought that he might once again seek the company of Rosalind Walker, but after seeing her today he had changed his mind. It was plain that she and Harold Jordan had arrived at some sort of understanding, and every time he had noticed them they had been walking arm in arm, shoulder to shoulder. Jordan, he thought, was welcome to her. No woman but Francisca de Guzman had ever meant anything to him, and Francisca was important only because he would, through the peculiarities of Spanish law, acquire her title when he married her. . . .

Chapter X

After weeks of waiting, the decisive day had come. Harold Jordan knew that as he rode toward the Dolson house to meet Rosalind and take her to the Blue Grass Inn for a festive dinner. Baron de Carondelet had arrived in Nashville twenty-four hours ago, and this was the afternoon that Harold was going to put his long-planned scheme into operation, break free of Spanish domination, rid himself of fear, and walk once again as a free man.

If only his nerve did not falter, there was every chance of success. Last night, when he and the baron had met at the tannery and had talked for hours, he had again seen the list of agents which Carondelet carried. Harold had scrutinized it carefully across the candlelit office, peering at it without seeming to do so, and had realized more than ever before that, if he could steal it, here was the most damning of all evidence to present to John Sevier, the one irrefutable proof of Spanish duplicity that would force counteraction and drive the dons and their paid servants from Franklin, for on the document was the Great Seal of Imperial Spain. Only once before had Harold seen the seal, but he could not forget it: in Latin was printed a creed of the Spanish Kings, and in one corner was a blob of green sealing wax into which was cut a crown and from which hung two short ribbons, one of yellow, the other of black.

How fortunate it was, he reflected, that men everywhere felt a need to affix their symbols of official authority to the papers that were important to them. When he handed the list of spies to Sevier, the governor would be unable to doubt its authenticity and would undoubtedly act at once with all of his accustomed crisp vigor, and the plotters would be banished.

Leaving the road in order to give clearance to an oxcart, Harold slowed his horse and tightened his belt a notch. He wished there were someone other than Sevier to whom he could present the document, for Jonesboro was so far away. But there was no one else in Franklin with the authority to move with the speed and dispatch that were so typical of Nolichucky Jack.

Jim Robertson, Harold knew, was a patriot and a leader, but he was somewhat naïve and slow to act until he was sure that a given course of action was the right one. If the Spanish list were placed in his hands, he would assuredly send it on to Sevier, but he would ponder the matter for several days, and by that time Harold would be dead.

It was right, then, to leave the original plan unaltered; Sevier was the man to whom he must go. And Harold had no doubt of his own ability to follow the laboriously detailed scheme he had concocted. It should not be too difficult, under the right circumstances, to gain possession of the list of spies. Nor should his escape from Nashville and his flight to Jonesboro be too difficult, either—under the right circumstances.

Under the right circumstances. How that phrase kept running through his brain. He had not anticipated that the Spaniards would send a delegation of traders to Nashville offering financial enticements to Franklin, or that they would hold a fandango, a lavish party, in order to bedazzle the Franks.

He hoped that the spirit of fandango would prevail at the Blue Grass Inn today, for it would make his own work much easier. But he was afraid that Nashville was too tired for another celebration so soon, and that if the pre-party atmosphere at the inn was lethargic and dull, the baron would be more alert to what he was doing, the baron's men quicker to follow him, capture him, and kill him.

Well, the time for worry was past. He could only hope now that the inn would be crowded with people arriving for the fandango and that the then inevitable merriment and confusion would aid him. When he had first laid his plans he had not counted on a fandango, and whether it would help or hinder him was beyond his power to determine.

He knew he must concentrate now, step by step, on the immediate problems at hand. The house of the Dolson family came into view beyond a clump of trees, and in a few moments he would be with Rosalind. Then his grim, desperate game would begin. Though he longed to confess everything to her, he knew he could not until his scheme had succeeded.

He had carefully rehearsed what he was going to say to her; he would tell her that it would be necessary for him to excuse himself from the table in the taproom of the inn for a few minutes; when he returned, he and Rosalind would leave the place at once; he would then bid her farewell and depart on a journey that would keep him away from Nashville for a period lasting anywhere from a few days to many weeks. He would explain nothing to her, but would ask her to trust him and would promise to give her a full account on his return.

Success in this dangerous mission was essential. On it depended his future, his freedom from the Spaniards, his release from the ever-present fear of death. And so he could not, he would not, fail. The rewards would be too great. It would be so wonderful, so peaceful, to live a long life with Rosalind.

An unusually large crowd filled the public room of the Blue Grass Inn, and a roar of lighthearted chatter made conversation almost impossible, yet no one in the throng cared, and only shouted the louder at his dinner companions. Merchants in staid woolens and their wives in spruce taffeta brushed against farmers wearing buckskins and countrywomen in shapeless linsey-woolsey, but today the people of Nashville were one in spirit, for they were enjoying a holiday of the most unexpected sort.

Without prior warning, a delegation of Spaniards from New Orleans had arrived in the town to sound out the possibilities of opening negotiations which might lead to the resumption of trade. There were many who questioned the motives of the commission, but almost no one in the community objected to the lavish display of hospitality which the representatives of the dons had promised for the following evening. They had no sooner arrived in Nashville than they had announced their intention of taking over the inn completely for a night, and they indicated that anyone who came to their fandango, as they called it, would be served with all the food he could eat and all the liquor he could drink.

Word had spread rapidly through the Cumberland, and despite the universal low regard for the Spaniards and their intentions, folk from all over the county were beginning to arrive for the festivities and the free refreshments. Unlike the jamboree, at which one could play and frolic, the fandango promised to be an elegant affair, and Nashville was unfamiliar with elegance. But the people of Nashville liked novelty, were intrigued by it. Those most liberally supplied with funds were taking rooms at the inn, and even the poorer elements elbowed their way into the public room for a glimpse of those who would be their hosts at what gave every indication of being an affair unique in the annals of the frontier. To all intents the Spanish delegation was headed by military men, and three high-ranking officers in black and yellow sat with a large group of guests at a long table in the center of the hall. A colonel was carving a roast pig, his associates were pouring wine into goblets for the thirsty Americans, and an atmosphere of good fellowship and conviviality seemed to prevail.

But two men sitting at an inconspicuous small table tucked

away in a far corner of the room looked on the scene of gaiety with somber eyes. One was Janus Elholm and the other was a newcomer to Nashville, a man even taller than the Dane, thin but wiry, with a large black patch over one eye. He was dressed in a suit of unrelieved rusty black, and his limp, dark hair was clubbed behind in a queue. He might have been anywhere from thirty to forty-five years of age. There were two points of similarity between Janus and his guest that might have been noted by those at the nearest table had they paid any attention to the quiet pair; both spoke with strong foreign accents, and each wore a large silver medallion of unusual design, Janus on his dagger chain around the neck, the other on a heavy, plain watch fob that dangled from his waistcoat.

"You will spend a goodly number of King Charles's beautifully minted dollars at your fandango, Mr. Winkleman," Janus remarked gloomily. He had been instructed to address the man here as "Mr. Winkleman." "I have learned a little something about Americans, my friend. They will take all you can give them, but they will not change their views on the cause that is dear to both of us."

Winkleman smiled unpleasantly. "I am well acquainted with the views of these loud children. They will accept us and our views only when we fill this land with prisons and jailers and garrisons," he remarked sourly.

"Then, if you will pardon the impertinence, why do you squander the money? You do not bear the reputation of a man who is overly free with funds."

The black patch was turned toward Janus, and he could not read his visitor's expression. "I have had appointments of importance in this remote corner of the earth. Men like"—he dropped his voice—"Colonel Wilkinson of Kentucky, who finds it difficult to come to New Orleans, must nevertheless be interviewed. So I must create a diversion for these simple peasants. They are so occupied with the little gallantries of my colonels—

your colonels, in truth, Mr. Elholm—that they do not note my presence in their midst, nor do they recognize me. The cloth that covers my eye is merely an added precaution, of course, but I cannot be too careful. I would be murdered instantly if it were known I was here."

There was a trace of fear in Winkleman's voice, and Janus grinned broadly, frankly enjoying the other's discomfort. The man was a member of that exclusive clan, the nobility of the Old World, and Janus could not conceal from himself the undeniable fact that he was envious. But all he said was, "Your name and your record of treatment of Americans has preceded you here, Mr. Winkleman. I first heard of your dungeons the very day I arrived in Franklin, and I have since anticipated this meeting."

Janus's irony was not lost on the man. "It is greatly to be pitied, then, that our present association must be so short. But as I told you, Don Esteban requests your presence in New Orleans to examine the levies newly recruited. And before you sail down the river a most important conference awaits you."

"I understand perfectly." Janus found his dislike for the tall official growing. "I travel by night, this night, to Chickasaw Bluffs on the Mississippi River. Tomorrow night I am to meet there with those who would lead a military revolt in these provinces. Then a boat awaits me. I will meet you at the appointed spot and we will, with good luck and a lack of American interference, travel safely together to Louisiana."

Winkleman's face twisted in the grimace that was his smile. "My pilot is the most experienced on the river. Don Esteban expects us in eight days, and we will not disappoint him."

"Indeed, sir. Indeed. But why do I not wait here and accompany you? We could make the overland trip to Chickasaw Bluffs together, too." Janus was not anxious to spend any more time than was absolutely necessary in the man's company, but the common code of politeness dictated that he make the offer.

To his infinite relief, the visitor declined. "Your meeting with the dissatisfied American militia leaders cannot wait. Even now they risk discovery. Also, it is best that we travel through Franklin separately. Should the Franks discover my identity, they will certainly murder me, and anyone with me will suffer also. And Don Diego has too few men of ability here. We——" Breaking off sharply, Winkleman stared across the room. "The young woman across the room—who is she?"

Janus did not bother to look up. "You mean the lady with the young American, Jordan. She is an American, of course. A person of some personal substance and background. Why do you ask?"

Struck by Janus's firm tone, the guest ignored his question and asked one of his own. "You have an interest in her and have perhaps——"

"I have not."

"Very strange. She shows an uncommon curiosity in us—or perhaps it is only in you. I wonder if Jordan has revealed anything to her regarding our affiliation."

Janus shifted in his chair and faced his visitor. The sun was setting, and it was growing difficult for Janus to see the man's face. Candles had not yet been lit in the room, and the first shadows of twilight were soft and deceptive. "How would Jordan be in a position to know anything about us?" he demanded.

Winkleman laughed unpleasantly. "Jordan, like all men, has a weakness. He has been placed in a position which is uncomfortable for him but useful to me." There was both disgust and secret amusement in his voice, but he was prevented from saying more by the appearance of the slatternly daughter of the house, who set smoking wooden platters of grouse broiled over hickory, the justly famed delicacy of the inn, before the two men.

Janus attacked the fowl and small roasted potatoes with his usual gusto, and as he washed down the food with cooled ale he said, "I hold Jordan in no high regard, but I do not estimate him too lightly either. I trust your hold on him is sufficiently strong to guarantee that he jumps high when your whip sings out."

The guest disjointed his bird expertly before answering. "I do not make mistakes," he replied loftily, then glowered. "Now where do you suppose Jordan is going?"

Harold had arisen from his chair and, looking neither to the right nor to the left, was making his way slowly out of the room. Janus shrugged and dismissed the handsome American from his mind. Rosalind Walker was continuing to eat her dinner. She was nearly halfway through the main course when Harold returned with perspiration streaming down his face. He threaded his way across the room in great haste, and when he reached his table he muttered something to Rosalind. She stood up at once, and her companion removed her cloak from a wall peg and flung it over her shoulders. A moment later they were gone.

Janus tried without success to catch Rosalind's eye as she left, and he felt chagrined and slightly foolish at his failure. He, who was never sentimental, was disappointed because a girl who despised him had not seen fit to give him a smile of farewell.

Winkleman, who was finishing a second tankard, was showing signs of restlessness, and Janus suggested that they share a blueberry pie. His guest shook his head impatiently. "I thank you, no, Mr. Elholm. My time here is too short to be wasted on unnecessary pleasures of the palate. I suggest that we retire to my quarters here and say our farewells. If you wish, I shall gladly trade some of your American pounds and shillings for good Spanish dollars."

Janus thanked him and agreed to exchange some of his money, saying that something yet remained of the amount supplied by Don Diego Gardoqui. That he still had in his possession a little over six hundred dollars in Spanish gold of the sum that the First Minister had given him in Madrid was his own affair, and he intended to tell no one of the cache.

As they mounted the steps built on the outside of the inn, Janus felt a pang of uneasiness. He never liked to be abroad without weapons, and he had nothing with him but his little silver dagger. His sword was in his visitor's room, and so was the belt with his pistols. And in the bottom of one of his holsters, carefully concealed, was his copy of his precious agreement with Don Pedro de Bolea Aranda. He had wanted to come armed to dinner, but Winkleman had urged him to leave his guns and sword behind in order to be less conspicuous, and as he had shed his own weapons, Janus had been forced to do likewise.

They reached the second floor and entered the corridor, then turned left to the guest's suite. The nearer door opened at the first touch, and Janus frowned. Surely they had not come away an hour before without turning the lock and pocketing the key! Hurrying into the room, the two men glanced around rapidly, then looked hard at each other. Packing boxes, clothing, cartons of food, and bedclothes were scattered everywhere; it was only too obvious that the apartment had been ransacked.

Janus saw his belt and pistols in a corner and strode to them. He hastily removed first one pistol from its holster, then the other, and plunged his hand inside. There was a tense moment of silence, then he shouted in loud relief. *"Gott sei Dank!* My land-grant claim from the First Minister is still here. It is safe!"

The visitor scarcely heard, for he was systematically going through his own belongings and was shuffling through a sheaf of papers in a box with a broken lock. Again and again he examined each document carefully, then a terrible oath escaped his lips.

"Something has been stolen from you, Baron?" In the privacy of the small room it was safe to use proper titles, and Janus was enjoying the other's discomfort.

"Yes. An official paper of great value, Señor General Elholm. Someone has robbed me of the list of officers and agents of Spain who are at present in the United States. And if I were you, I would not laugh—for your name heads the list."

Thoroughly unconcerned, Janus waved a hand airily. "It matters but little," he said. "Suppose your list falls into the hands of the American authorities? I will be gone from Franklin before they can apprehend me."

The baron scowled, and his dark face grew blacker. But he did not reply, and instead raced to the door of the adjoining room. "Miguelo!" he roared.

After a brief wait the door opened and a barrel-chested man with a short, thick neck and extraordinarily long arms lumbered slowly in. "Sí, Señor Baron?"

"Who has entered this room since the Señor General and I retired to dine? Think carefully, Miguelo, for it appears that you have been asleep, and I consider it likely that it will be necessary to have you flayed."

Miguelo blinked his heavy-lidded eyes. "None has been here, Señor Baron, except Señor Jordan. I have kept a very good watch, as I always do, Señor Baron, and——"

Janus tried not to laugh. "Jordan was here, Miguelo? He came into this room?"

"Sí, Señor General." The servant regarded him blankly. "And we both followed your instructions perfectly. Señor Jordan explained to me that Your Excellencies wished a certain paper but had lost your keys to the strongboxes. So with my own hands I broke for him the locks." He spread out his thick, stubby fingers and regarded them with childlike pride.

The baron muttered something fierce and unintelligible under his breath and gnawed nervously on his lower lip. But his tension was lost on Miguelo, who happily and heedlessly continued his recital. "Then I stood in the hall and kept a fine watch for Señor Jordan while he obeyed your orders and removed the papers from this miserable pesthole of an inn. I even offered to assist Señor Jordan in the saddling of his horse, but he informed me that would not be necessary, so I returned to my watch in the other room. Have I done something wrong, Señor Baron? As always, I serve you truly and faithfully, and I——"

"Pig!" spat the baron. "Did you see in which direction Jordan rode?"

Miguelo nodded his heavy head. "Sí, Señor Baron. I happened

to be observing the life of this anthill of a town from the window, for although it was growing dark outside and I could not see easily, I had little else to occupy me. Señor Jordan came into the plaza with a lady and parted with her there. The lady rode that way—along the river. I was tempted to follow her, but my duty to the Señor Baron comes before all, so I did not take to myself this great chance for intimacy with so lovely a creature. And Señor Jordan rode that way—to the east. He followed the chief road, to be sure, for there is no other."

The baron had heard enough. "Take two men with you, Miguelo, and ride through the gap until you reach the short cut to Robertson's Trail. There you will wait for Jordan, who will certainly appear in due time, for he is undoubtedly hoping to reach General Sevier in Jonesboro. Bring him back here. But do not harm him, for I desire his health to be excellent when I begin to question him. Under no circumstances allow him to rid himself of any papers or other documents——"

Smiling amiably, Janus interrupted. "Do you think he is so stupid as to take your list with him, Baron? Surely he knows he will be followed and at most carries on his person a hastily made copy, while the original remains secreted somewhere in Nashville."

The baron glanced at his colleague without emotion. "Your analysis is possibly correct, Señor General Elholm. However, once Jordan is in my hands, I will not only recover any copies he has—but will assuredly force him to reveal the location of my master list. Of this you may be sure, Señor General—there will be no slips. The list was prepared on the official parchment of Don Esteban Miró and bears the Great Seal of His Majesty. If it should fall into the hands of Mr. John Jay, the Americans would have sufficient cause to break off diplomatic relations with Spain."

Janus began to strap on his pistols, shrugged, and murmured, "I wish you the best of luck, Baron."

"Luck, Señor General? Like you, I have learned to trust no one but myself. When Jordan is returned I intend to teach him some of the more delicate refinements of my unique profession. And you may rest at ease that he will gladly tell me all that is now locked away in his heart."

Disgusted at the obvious relish with which the baron casually planned torture, Janus nodded abruptly. Every man to his own trade, he thought, happy that he himself fought in the open. And, fortunately, this problem was none of his affair. "Good hunting, Baron," he said. "We will celebrate your success in either Natchez or New Orleans, whichever of those cities promises the more splendid opportunities."

He shook hands quickly, bowed, and raced out into the twilight gloom of the corridor. Harold Jordan and the baron's missing document were already out of his mind; he was concentrating on the immediate job ahead—his important conference with the dissident American military leaders of the West.

Chapter XI

In the flickering glare of a single candle the face of Baron de Carondelet was bathed in malevolence as he paced up and down the length of the small bedroom at the Blue Grass Inn. He had removed the black patch from his eye, and his stock was loose, his shirt rumpled and soiled. Seldom had he been so agitated; rarely had he allowed his emotions to show so clearly.

"It is impossible for a man to disappear!" he said in a low, strangled voice. "It is impossible even in this wild country for a man to vanish from the earth. Jordan is somewhere between this town and Jonesboro, and he must be found!"

"He will be found, Baron. Calm yourself. Here, try a sip of our good Kentucky whiskey. I always carry some with me for use in times of stress, and I'm sure you'll find it has a most soothing effect." Colonel James Wilkinson leaned back in the room's single wooden chair, completely at ease. His handsome features were smooth and calm, and he seemed in no way concerned by the catastrophe that had so upset the Intendant of Louisiana. Not a lock of his carefully brushed hair was out of place, and as he smoked a long pipe his fingers curved lovingly around the intricately carved bowl.

The baron stopped short and glared at the man who was regarded as one of America's first citizens of the West. "You fail to understand your own danger, my dear Colonel," he snarled. "Your name is prominent on the list that Jordan has stolen from me. If it falls into the hands of your authorities, you will be shot as a traitor to your country."

Wilkinson laughed with genuine amusement. "Your estimate of me is too low, Carondelet," he said. "Even if Jordan were to take the list to General Washington himself, I can promise you that the general would have him whipped off the estate at Mount Vernon. But I have assured you before, and I do so again—Jordan will not escape."

"The reasons for your confidence are beyond my comprehension," the baron snapped, resuming his restless pacing. "My men have failed. Although they followed my instructions and took the short cut to Robertson's Trail, they used no portion of the meager intelligence they possess, and they returned here to report that they could not find him. And each moment that we talk, precious time is being lost. Jordan is riding closer to Sevier and Jay with a document that could destroy all we have labored for three years and more to achieve."

Colonel Wilkinson carefully poured a measure of golden-brown corn whiskey from a small jug into a glass. "Here," he said, "drink this. And listen to me. Jordan has no choice but to follow Jim Robertson's Trail until he reaches Cranny-cross. If he gets there before you find him, I'll grant that you may lose him, for he can then take several possible routes to Jonesboro—and beyond through the Gap. But Jordan doesn't know this region as I do. And even if he rides all night—which is almost impossible in Cherokee country—he won't reach Cranny-cross before seven or eight o'clock tomorrow morning."

Baron de Carondelet was giving the Kentuckian his full attention now and, throwing off the whiskey in a single swallow, he sat on the edge of the bed, his eyes glittering as he leaned forward. "You imply, Colonel," he asked tensely, "that there is a method by which my people could arrive at this Cranny-cross before Jordan does so?"

"It's no implication, my friend. I tell it to you flatly. Jordan has been out here only a few years. I myself could ride to Cranny-cross with ease between now and dawn, for I know paths through the forests that cut off many miles."

Carondelet stood up again. "Surely you are not proposing that you head a searching party, Colonel. If you should be recognized by Americans who know you, and if they should suspect that you—— No! You are too valuable to Spain, Colonel Wilkinson."

Crossing his legs with care in order not to wrinkle his breeches, Wilkinson puffed lazily on his pipe. "In addition to your flattering reasons, Baron, I can't possibly join the chase for Jordan because I have an important engagement tomorrow night. As you know, I am to meet General Janus Elholm at Chickasaw Bluffs."

"Then——"

Once more Wilkinson laughed, and this time a series of complex emotions showed in his face. "I have taken the liberty," he said slowly and distinctly, "of sending your men off to Cranny-cross. They left more than an hour ago in the company of my best Cherokee guide. They will undoubtedly arrive there in sufficient time to enjoy a short sleep before Jordan approaches."

Black anger flared in Carondelet's eyes. "I am deeply grateful for your foresight, Colonel, and I in no wise object because you have given orders to my men. But I consider your behavior in this past hour unpardonable. Why have you allowed me to worry unnecessarily? Why did you not tell me your plan at once—and save me the despair and frustration I have suffered?"

The colonel did not stir. "You are a strong man and an impatient one, Baron," he said quietly. "At times you are too strong and too impatient. I feel the need now and again to remind you that Franklin and Kentucky are my territory. When they are a part of New Spain, I shall govern them, I and no one else. Once in a while I feel obliged to remind you that without me you can achieve nothing here. I am indispensable to the cause of Spain, if Spain wishes to conquer the American West. Do I make myself clear?"

"Eminently so." Baron de Cardonelet was in command of himself again. Although he might not forget the trick that had been played on him, he was not one to waste time or emotion when it served no useful end. "You feel, then, that we must compose ourselves and be patient until we learn whether your theory is correct."

"It is. There's no doubt in my mind that Jordan is at this minute on the trail and that he will ride to Cranny-cross." Wilkinson smiled loftily.

"While I admire your faith in your own convictions, Colonel, I have had more experience than you with men who would betray our cause and our King." The baron gripped a bedpost with long, bony fingers. "And I consider it to be a strong possibility that Jordan has not taken the list with him. The pattern followed by such fools leads me to believe that he has merely gone to warn the Franklin governor or the officials of the Congress in New York that such a list exists. He would not be so stupid as to take it with him, for if he should be captured, his entire scheme would collapse."

For the first time Colonel Wilkinson abandoned his air of faint boredom. "It's true that you must spend the greater part of your time dealing with men of Jordan's sort, Baron. What do you think he has done with the paper?"

It was Carondelet's turn to adopt a lordly and contemptuous air, and the temptation was too great to resist. "To me," he said, "the workings of Jordan's mind are simple, for he is simple. The list in all probability is here in Nashville."

"Oh?"

"Manifestly, my dear Colonel, I cannot rely completely on the correctness of this belief, for even I can be mistaken. Jordan must be caught and brought back to me, if for no other reason than because he knows too much, has seen too much, and would now betray us to the Americans. In the meantime, however, I must take no chances."

It was Wilkinson's turn to lean forward. "You talk in riddles, Baron."

Carondelet's lips parted slightly in a thin, tight smile. "Colonel Wilkinson," he said, "you are a soldier and a · 'itical strategist. On the other hand, I am one who must permit no 'ips, no errors of judgment, no mistakes in action. My task is that f the guardian who must watch over everyone else. Hence in this situation I must ask myself what I would do if I were Jordan. And the answer comes to me that I would give the list of agents to someone I could trust."

Colonel Wilkinson was about to remark that the baron's mind was so devious that he suspected subtleties and complications where none existed. However, he refrained, and his even white teeth clamped down on the stem of his pipe. Although fear was as foreign to him as was conscience, he was nevertheless glad that he and the Flemish noble were not in opposite camps. Carondelet would be the most vicious and merciless of foes.

"What person can Jordan trust?" the baron continued. "Naturally it is the young woman he hopes to marry to whom he turns. I do not pretend to know how much he has or has not told her. But I think—at least I fear—that he has given the list of agents to her for safekeeping."

"And you intend to demand that she return it to you, Baron?"

"Hardly that. I would be revealing too much about myself and our mission. I said to you a few moments ago that it is my duty to avoid all risks, all chances. And so I must deal with this particular situation. I intend to do so."

Wilkinson felt uncomfortable. There was an undercurrent in the baron's voice that disturbed him, an anticipatory relish that made his skin crawl. "I'm an American, Baron," he said, "and although I know you are implying something, I don't understand your delicacies."

Carondelet stood up, and there was a hard gleam in his eyes. "When I left New Orleans I considered it wise to bring with me a number of my Cherokees of the Watumbi, who know Franklin. They have spent their time idling in the forests while I have conducted my business here, and they have grown fat and lazy. I do not like indolence, so I am pleased to find an activity that will occupy their time."

Wilkinson lost his composure and jumped to his feet. "See here, Carondelet," he said, "I won't permit you to harm an innocent girl merely because you suspect——"

"Permit, my dear Colonel? You overstep your authority. I owe my allegiance to King Charles and to none else. I do that which I deem necessary to protect his interests, to further his cause, to carry out his desires. The life of an unimportant individual is as nothing when I think of the stakes for which we play. Under the present circumstances, Colonel—circumstances which are not of my choosing, but of Jordan's—I know the course I must follow, and I shall not hesitate."

Four small ravines, steep and strewn with rock, joined to make the gully that the earliest settlers in Franklin had come to call Cranny-cross. During the rainy seasons the area was covered with a sea of grass and tangled weeds, and even the most inexperienced travelers quickly learned to ride around the lip of the gully, for to take the shorter route and cut across the center was a guarantee that the unfortunate victim would be bitten and stung by swarms of flies, gnats, mosquitoes, and ants.

Dismal and unappetizing as it was, Cranny-cross nevertheless was a spot never to be forgotten by the men and women of the West. To those plodding in the direction of Nashville and of the Mississippi River beyond, it was the last jumping-off place. Where there had been four roads, only Robertson's Trail now stretched ahead, inviting them into the wilderness. To those who found the harsh and primitive conditions of frontier living too strong for their taste, Cranny-cross was a welcoming beacon as they fled back to the softer civilization they had previously known. The mere sight of those four paths spreading out toward the east was a reminder to them of all they had left behind, of all to which they were now of their own free will returning.

Harold Jordan felt a measure of the relief familiar to those who had failed to come to terms with the wilderness. Tired but determined not to stop, he rested his horse for a few moments on a hilltop and peered through the murky gloom of false dawn at the gully. Although his head ached and the muscles of his back and legs were sore, his mind continued to work clearly as he tried to evaluate his situation. He had made far better time than he had dared to hope, and his horse had not been pushed too hard. His pursuers—and he knew that Carondelet had undoubtedly set out after him—must be far to the rear, provided they had followed Robertson's Trail as he had done.

But there were other ways to approach Cranny-cross, he knew. When Colonel Jim Robertson rode to Jonesboro, he rarely remained on the path that he himself had hacked through the forests, but disappeared into the maze of trees and arrived at the junction point more quickly than those who used the road that had been marked for them. And the Indians, Harold realized, scorned the trail, too, for their almost unerring sense of direction never failed them in the forests.

It was reasonable to assume, then, that men who knew the countryside might at this very minute be waiting for him to ride into a trap. Perhaps, he thought, he was being overly cautious, but this was no time for needless risks. His right hand stole inside his shirt, and for the thousandth time he felt the heavy parchment of Carondelet's list of spies. Once more he felt strengthened in the knowledge that he had succeeded in the most difficult part of his dangerous task. All that remained now was to maneuver more cleverly than his ruthless enemy.

The sun, he reasoned, would rise in about an hour, and

although he was afraid of losing himself in the trackless wood-lands, he could use the sun as his guide. If he turned off into the forest now, he would avoid passing through Cranny-cross. He would ride due south for a short time, then would halt and wait for daybreak. The principal road to Jonesboro was laid out in a straight line heading east, and when the sun came up he would get his bearings from it, would ride toward it, and thus find his way to the road.

He was wasting a certain amount of precious time by not dash-ing through Cranny-cross, and he was taking the deliberate chance of losing his way in the wilderness, for he was well aware of his limitations and knew himself to be no woodsman. But viewed dispassionately, it was the lesser risk, and he decided to take it. Without further ado he turned his horse toward the south and rode away from Cranny-cross.

Miguelo sat glumly on a hard, flat rock and listened disgustedly to the whispered conversation of his two Spanish comrades in arms, wishing fervently that he could shut out the sound of their voices. This was no time for them to wonder whether it was more pleasurable to sleep on a bed piled high with three feather mat-tresses than on one with only two. Miguelo was tired, too, and wanted to be elsewhere than at this miserable pin point of no-where called Cranny-cross.

But the Señor Baron, through the American Colonel Wilkin-son, had given them a task to perform, and the word of the Señor Baron was the only law Miguelo knew. It would indeed be a luxury to curl up on a fine, soft bed, to rest one's head on plump pillows covered with smooth, silken casings, but a man did what he was told, and only after obeying orders was he free to pursue his own happiness.

A jug of strong, harsh brandy rested beside Miguelo's foot, and he reached for it absently, tilted it to his thick lips, and drank deeply. Wiping his mouth with the back of his hand, he relaxed slightly as he felt the fiery warmth of the liquor spread through his middle. The Señor Baron would be very angry if he ever learned that Miguelo had been drinking so early in the day. But, Miguelo told himself philosophically, he was not breaking the promise that the Señor Baron had extracted from him last month. He had sworn that he would never again drink brandy during daylight hours. And the sun had not yet appeared; in fact, it was still very dark. Furthermore, it might be many hours before Señor Jordan came riding down the trail, and meantime it was damp and chilly. The brandy made a man feel comfortable, and it helped to pass the time. Again Miguelo raised the jug, but he felt someone watching him and hastily put it down again.

The grave, steady eyes fastened on him were, he knew, those of the accursed Cherokee guide. All savages made Miguelo nervous, and this one particularly disturbed him. The man sat only five feet from him but was so silent, so motionless, that he seemed to disappear into the tree against which he leaned. And although the good padre of St. Teresa's in New Orleans often said that the red men were like all others and that they possessed no evil spirits or powers of magic, Miguelo was not so sure. He half believed that the Cherokee did have the power to make himself invisible.

His eyes watered as he stared first at the Indian, then at the tree, and he blinked angrily. When he returned to Nashville he would tell the Señor Baron that never again would he go off on a mission with two stupid, chattering magpies and a Cherokee so stealthy that a man's flesh was made to crawl.

Suddenly he caught his breath and his heart pounded. The pig of a Cherokee had thrown himself to the ground and was lying with one ear pressed against the earth. This was too much, and Miguelo had no intention of permitting such conduct. He would handle the savage as the Señor Baron would do.

"Stand up, Señor Cherokee," he boomed pompously. "This is improper! I will not permit you to sleep at this time! I insist that you rouse yourself, Señor Cherokee, and——"

"Hsst!" The Indian's whisper cut through the air, and he gestured sharply for silence.

Bewildered and somewhat hurt at the curt denial of his authority, Miguelo watched the Cherokee blankly. It seemed as though the savage was not sleeping after all. On the contrary, he appeared to be tense and strained as he crouched low, the shell of his ear barely touching the ground. The other two Spaniards eyed him curiously, and one muttered a coarse jest under his breath.

At that instant the Indian leaped to his feet and pointed toward the south. "Man," he said. "Man riding on horse."

Miguelo felt a surge of triumphant excitement, but he had no intention of moving until he was sure of the ground on which he would step. "Is it not possible, Señor Cherokee, that you have heard one of your own people riding in the forest? Recall to mind, if you will, that the wise Señor Colonel Wilkinson informed us that Señor Jordan would not approach until a late hour. And if we give chase, Señor Jordan could then ride through this pesthole of a bog unmolested and undetected."

A quick flicker of disgust flashed across the face of the Cherokee. "Man in wood not of Watumbi," he grunted. "Watumbi brave use small horse. Pony. Watumbi brave like wolf in wood. No can hear. This man in wood make great noise."

Miguelo wished fervently that the Señor Baron could be here to tell him what to do. If it were truly Jordan who was making off through the forest, he would disappear if not pursued immediately. But if the man whom the Cherokee had heard turned out to be someone other than Jordan, they might lose their prey while chasing a phantom.

The Indian solved the vexing problem. Leaping onto the back of his pony, he gestured at Miguelo. "You go. Me go. Other men stay."

That was the solution, of course, and Miguelo understood it without too much difficulty. Hurrying to his horse, he tried to recapture the dignity befitting the leader of an expedition, the man on whose shoulders rested the future of New Spain. "Felipo," he commanded sternly, "you and 'Tonio will remain here and will keep watch for Señor Jordan. Should he appear on the trail, you will make him your prisoner, but you will not harm him. The Señor Baron wishes him returned alive, and in health sufficiently good that he will be able to answer all such questions that the Señor Baron may wish to ask him. Fail in this and you will regret it, for I, Miguelo, will crush your heads together like two soft melons. You know that I have the strength to make good my boast, so while I am gone you will do your duty and you will tremble in fear of my wrath."

Satisfied that he was re-established in the eyes of his colleagues as a man of stature, Miguelo ducked his head low to avoid a thick tree branch and went crashing off into the forest after the Cherokee. The Indian rode swiftly, surely, and Miguelo had to strain every nerve to keep pace with him. But he did not mind, for he no longer needed to think. Now he was required only to act, and the saliva ran freely in his mouth. Years ago he had hunted boar in the woods of his native Granada, and the old thrill of the chase came back to him, almost overwhelmed him. This time the quarry was a two-footed animal, and the excitement was greater than any he had ever known. Digging his heels into the horse's flanks, he spurred forward.

Rosalind had been scrubbing the walls and parlor floor of the three-room schoolhouse since her return shortly after dusk, and now, two hours later, she could barely lift up her arms and her knees were sore. But she fought against exhaustion and continued to scour the pine boards until they gleamed white. It was good to work like this while trying to sort out her thoughts; it was easier to think when her body was tired.

A shingle over the door, bearing the word "Seminary," flapped in the wind, but the sound failed to comfort her; tonight there was little warmth in the contemplation of that piece of painted board. Only this morning she had been so pleased at the prospect of importing a harpsichord in the spring; Andy Jackson, who insisted on managing the business affairs of the school for her, had told her that by spring she would have enough grain and hard goods in the schoolhouse, paid as tuition by the pupils, to bring what would be Nashville's first genuine harpsichord over the mountains.

But now she was filled with confusion, and a series of unanswered questions danced through her mind. She wondered why she had turned to Harold so impulsively after seeing Janus Elholm with the dreadful half-caste girl, why Harold had been so mysterious, and why he had behaved so strangely. She came to the conclusion that it was only because of Harold and his behavior that she felt uneasy, and once she had decided this, she felt unaccountably relieved.

The floor finished at last, Rosalind rose slowly to her feet and wriggled her shoulders to ease the muscles in the back of her neck. Lost in thought, she glanced around the room without seeing the bear rug (an idea she had borrowed from Major George Elholm), the two barrels that had been converted into chairs, nor the long benches and pine table which her pupils used.

An unexpected pounding at the door startled her, and with a dismayed look at her coarse work dress and thick apron, she tried to smooth her hair as she hastened to answer the summons. Her relief was infinite when she saw Nat Dolson, accompanied by his three sons, on the threshold.

"Hello, Nat," she said. "I'm just finished working here, and if you'll wait a moment I'll ride home with you for supper."

Nat remained silent; his face was grave, and despite the snap in the air, perspiration rolled down his forehead. The boys were not cavorting or fighting, either, but stood in a row like three solemn miniatures of their father. Rosalind caught her breath.

"What is it, Nat? Min——"

"Um. Her time has come."

She flew from the door. "I'll get my cloak, Nat. I won't be a minute!"

"Wait, Roz. There ain't no need for you at the cabin. There's a passel o' womenfolk there now, a-crowding the place somethin' fierce. I brung the boys over here, hopin' mebbe you'd keep 'em right here at the school for the night. There ain't no room for 'em in the cabin, and they keep a-gettin' in evvybody's way."

Rosalind paused, then waved her guests into the neat room. "Of course I'll keep them here—if that's what you want me to do, Nat. But I—I'd like to be with Min."

It was plain that he had expected such opposition, and he shook his head. "Them as is with Min has had young o' their own. They know better'n a maiden lady what t' do, if you'll be a-forgivin' me for bein' so direct-like. But we are a-needin' t' get these hell-cubs out o' the way, Roz. So I'm much obliged t' you. There's beddin' a-plenty here—and, well, it's best for all. Here—I brung you your supper and your night clothes too."

Afraid of further argument, Nat sidled toward the door. But to his surprise, Rosalind's opposition disappeared, and she nodded cheerfully. "I'm happy to help in whatever way I can, Nat. I only hope I'll know how to manage boys. Girls are more my specialty."

Nat glowered at his sons. "You hear what Miz Roz says, boys. Act right pert and mind her, now! Carl, I'm a-holdin' you respons'ble for your brothers, 'n' I'll skin you if there's any abusin' o' Miz Roz's kindness. Nathan'l, you try t' act real growed up, and no a-takin' o' more'n your share o' what's in the stewpot. Billy, you been a-pleadin' and a-beggin' for a knife. I ain't let you have it b'cause you been too little. Now's your chance t' show how big you be. No cryin' 'n' whimperin' t'night, 'n' when you come home in the mornin', we'll have a little talk again 'bout that there knife."

"Yes, Pa." Three small heads bobbed soberly in unison. All were more than a little frightened; their mother's muffled howls of pain had shaken them badly as they had ridden off with Nat.

Further complicating their emotions, the two older boys in particular were anxious to show off before Rosalind, who, they were convinced, was the loveliest lady they had ever seen.

Rosalind hurried to a cupboard beside the fireplace. "Can I give you a drink before you go back, Nat? The folks who had this place left a little rum here somewhere, or there's a dram of whiskey if you'd prefer it." She began to fumble on the spacious shelves.

Nat stopped her, his voice huskier than he realized. "I thank you kindly, Roz, but my insides are a-shakin' like calf's-foot jelly right now, and a drink'd sit right bad. I ain't a-goin' t' drink till after the baby's come, and then I'm a-aimin' t' finish off a jug o' gennywine grape brandy I got buried under our plum tree. . . . Roz, girl, I ain't one t' go makin' fancy speeches, but I sure do appreciate this here that you're a-doin'. Not many girls your age and looks'd set out on the edge o' nowheres like this for a night. Oh, I reckon it's safe enough—you 'n' the boys'll be pertection for each other. But anyways, me 'n' Min, we been a-meanin' t' tell you—from now on we ain't a-goin' t' take that money you been payin' us for rent."

Rosalind tried to speak, but the words caught in her throat. "Shecks," Nat said, "that ain't nothin'. You're a friend, ain't you?" He twisted his hat in his hands. "If the new one's a girl, we're a-plannin' t' name her Ros'lind. We hope you got no objections," he said, and was gone.

Chapter XII

"Wake up, Miz Roz! Please, Miz Roz—wake up!"

It was several minutes before the frantic whispers of little Nathaniel Dolson aroused Rosalind to consciousness. After making up a bed in the parlor for the three children and fixing a spare feather mattress—old but usable—for herself in the unfamiliar surroundings of what had once been the bedroom of the house, sleep had been elusive. She would have enjoyed another hour or two of slumber now, for she could see that dawn had only broken a short time before.

Then she became aware of the facial expression of the second of the Dolson boys and was instantly awake. Nathaniel's normally ruddy cheeks were white, and his eyes were wide with fear. Before she could speak, a grubby little hand clamped over her mouth, and the boy bent down and put his lips close to her ear.

"There's Cherokees outside the house, Miz Roz," he whispered, unable to control the quaver in his voice. "Five of 'em. Carl has your rifle. He's in the parlor, watchin' 'em, 'n' he told me t' come in here 'n' wake you. Billy is scairt. I'm kinda scairt too."

Springing from bed, Rosalind drew on the flowered silk dressing robe that always seemed so out of place in this raw country and hurried to the window. Stooping slightly because of the sloping roof, she peered toward the fringe of sycamore trees to the west, beside the riverbank. Five horses were tethered among the trees, and her heart contracted in fright. Nathaniel was telling the truth; the animals were of the small, sure-footed strain bred by the Cherokees.

"There ain't been a Cherokee attack hereabouts for quite a spell, Miz Roz." The child was close behind her. "I dunno why they've come a-gallivantin' around here now. Carl says the militia is a-gettin' ready t' drink heavy at the Spanish party t'night 'stead o' bein' ready t' fight. And them dirty old critters knows it, so mebbe that's why."

A numbing fear made it virtually impossible for Rosalind to think. She had heard too many stories of burnings and scalpings, lootings and killings, not to know that the Cherokees would show no mercy either to the three children or to her. Never had she felt so helpless, so alone.

"Miz Roz, ain't we a-goin' t' help Carl 'n' Billy?"

The child's plaintive voice brought her to her senses, and she knew that above all she must not show panic. "In just a minute, Nathaniel," she said in what she hoped was an even tone. "I—I'm looking to see if I can discover where the Cherokees are out there."

"Do you see any?" The boy was trembling violently.

"I'm—I'm not sure. Stand very quietly, Nathaniel, and don't say anything."

"Yes'm."

Rosalind scanned the trees carefully. For a moment she thought she saw human figures everywhere, and then she knew for certain that at least one man was lurking behind the sycamores. The faint shadow that appeared, vanished, and partially showed itself again was unmistakable. She wanted to cry out a warning, but Carl Dolson in the parlor saw that elusive shadow too. Calm and self-reliant for his almost twelve years, he fired, and the thunder of the rifle broke the eerie silence.

There was a yelp of pain, and a Cherokee brave emerged from the shadows, clutching his left shoulder. He wore a white man's buckskin leggings and breeches, but the upper part of his body was bare and was smeared with the green and white paint affected by the warriors of his nation when bent upon mischief. But the clear colors of the dye were obscured now by the blood that gushed from his wound, and he screamed curses at the defenders of the house. Rosalind understood not one word of his tirade, but his meaning was painfully clear—he was calling upon his gods to help him avenge his injury.

Rosalind ran to the parlor, with Nathaniel close after her. Carl was still at the window, gazing intently at the enraged savage while reloading the rifle as rapidly as his clumsy young fingers could manage. He greeted the schoolmistress without turning around, and struggled manfully to keep his voice pitched low.

"I hit one o' the bastards, Miz Roz," he said.

Rosalind, wasting no time, poured charges of powder into the pistols she snatched from the cupboard beside the fireplace, pistols Harold had bought and placed there when she had first taken over the schoolhouse. "I know, Carl. I saw. Where are the—the others? I counted five horses."

"Can't rightly say, ma'am. But I figger they're a-hidin' in the same patch o' woods. There's less open space from there t' the house than from any other side, and it 'pears t' me they'll make a rush on us from there. You got two pistols? Good. You 'n' me'll use 'em. Don't give one t' Nathan'l. He's near as much a baby as Billy, and he'd do himself hurt."

Rosalind suddenly remembered the two younger children. Nathaniel was standing only a few feet from her, his eyes fastened on her, and Billy was crouched in the doorway of the bedroom. Tears were streaking silently down his chubby face, and a dry sob racked his small body. Rosalind ached to take him in her arms and comfort him, but there was no time now for either sympathy or love. At any moment the Cherokees might make their concerted attack on the house.

"Nathaniel," she said softly, "you go into the bedroom with Billy and look after him. And don't be afraid, either of you. Carl and I won't let any harm come to you."

Out of the corner of her eye she saw Nathaniel join Billy, and the two little boys huddled together behind the partially opened door.

She moved toward the window, and Carl motioned her to the wall on its far side. "Stay back o' cover, Miz Roz. Don't let 'em see you, or them filthy damn brutes will take a shot at you."

The wounded Cherokee had disappeared again into the protecting gloom of the sycamores, and Rosalind stared at the first row of trees so hard that tears came to her eyes. There was no further sign of activity from the savages, and she leaned against the wall, suddenly weary.

"We've only to hold out a little longer, Carl," she said at last. "Someone will have heard your shot, and help will soon be on its way to us."

The boy didn't turn his head. "Who's the closest neighbor, ma'am?" he asked.

"Thaddeus Bixby. He's about a quarter of a mile from here." Rosalind couldn't make up her mind whether Carl's self-possession was real or feigned.

"Pa says old Bixby is slower'n cold molasses, Miz Roz. And even if he does round up some fellers right fast, it'll be maybe half an hour b'fore any help gets here. By then I reckon we'll all be scalped."

Rosalind tried to sound equally unconcerned. "They won't scalp *us*," she managed. "We'll hold them off. The one you shot isn't going to be much help to his friends, and we'll take care of the others, one by one."

"It ain't right for a lady t' be a-workin' and teachin' way out here alone," was the youth's unexpected reply. "Like Pa says, you can git yourself in a passel o' trouble. I reckon them filthy damn brutes knowed there was a woman here all by herself. Ha! They got a s-prise a-comin'. They wasn't countin' on me a-bein' here!"

Rosalind was unable to reply, for at that instant a tall brave stepped out in the cleared area, waving derisively. Rosalind's finger closed automatically and convulsively on the trigger of the pistol. The pistol jumped slightly in her hand, and through the haze of acrid smoke she saw that she had missed. But the Cherokee had obviously not expected to be fired on so soon and stood very still for a moment, astonishment clearly written on his dark face. Then he wheeled and raced headlong back into the brush.

Swallowing hard, Rosalind tried to overcome a sensation of uneasiness. Before she had time to probe her feeling, however, something tugged at her dressing gown, and her heart missed a beat. Looking down wildly, she saw little Billy, who was simultaneously trying to tell her something and burying his face in her skirts. But so great was his terror that, although his lips moved, no sound came forth.

"What is it, Billy?" She could not conceal her own fear.

The child tried again to speak and, failing, he pointed with a small finger toward the bedroom. Carl, who had watched the pantomime, would have gone into the other room, but Rosalind stopped him. "No, Carl. You keep watch here. I'll go."

Trying to prepare herself for anything, Rosalind ran toward the bedroom. She glimpsed Nathaniel cringing against the far wall, and then, as she burst into the room, she saw something else.

While she and Carl had been firing without success at the posturing Cherokee, his companions had not been idle, and Rosalind saw that she had been tricked by a diversion.

A Cherokee had stealthily dug a hole under the outside wall of the cabin and was coming up through the dirt floor of the bedroom. His head and neck were already inside the room, and the tops of his shoulders could be seen. In another minute he would be in a position to pull his body through and could jump to his feet.

Throwing the useless, unloaded pistol from her, Rosalind fled into the parlor, her eyes searching for a weapon. Luck came to her aid when she saw a small, sharp ax half concealed in a pile of kindling. Snatching up the hatchet, she flew back into the bedroom.

The Cherokee warrior had made rapid progress in the brief time she had been gone, and she could now see a long green smear carefully painted midway between his shoulder blades. She saw more: in his right hand he carried a long, thin knife; and in a few seconds he would be on his feet.

Rosalind lifted the ax high into the air and concentrated on the smudge of green. Then she closed her eyes and struck with a force born of sheer desperation.

Billy and Nathaniel ran sobbing into the parlor, and Rosalind staggered after them, dry-eyed. She was afraid she was going to be sick and was positive she would faint. But she did neither. She felt overwhelmed with the enormity of her deed. With her own hands she had killed a man. . . .

Carl, his composure gone, was pulling frantically at her arm. "Miz Roz," he screamed, looking suddenly very young and inadequate, "three of them filthy damn brutes are up on the roof. They're a-climbin' t' the top—'n' then they're a-goin' t' set fire t' the house. It's what they always do. Bobby Cook's folks was raided oncet by Cherokees, 'n' he told me—only I forgot. Please, Miz Roz—what'll we do? This house will be a-burnin' up in a minute—and they'll take us 'n' skin the hair off'n our heads when we come a-runnin' out! What'll we do, Miz Roz?"

Nat Dolson's three sons waited for her answer. Rosalind pressed the heels of her hands against her temples and tried to shut out the thumping of those sinister, scurrying figures on the roof. And suddenly an idea took shape in her mind, an idea so daring, so unusual, that it never occurred to her to wonder whether it was practical.

"Carl," she said crisply as she started toward the bedroom, "come with me. Hurry! I want you to help me drag the mattress in here."

The boy might have resisted such a strange request under more normal circumstances, but he trotted obediently after Rosalind and helped her carry into the parlor the huge mound of ancient, brittle feathers sewn into a cambric sheet. Neither looked at the bloody corpse of the Cherokee warrior, the ax handle rising from his back.

Billy and Nathaniel had not moved, and they gaped as Rosalind hauled and tugged the mattress close to the fireplace. Her face was flushed, and when she spoke, there was a new ring of authority in her voice. "One of you give me a knife. Quickly!"

Nathaniel immediately produced the small hunting knife that his father had given him two weeks before, the knife that had caused so much family jealousy and controversy. Rosalind seized it and began cutting open the mattress.

"All right, boys!" she cried. "Start throwing feathers on the fire. As many as you can load into your arms. But be very careful you don't set the room on fire, or yourselves! Now hurry, boys! Hurry!"

The youngsters needed no further bidding, and in a few seconds flames were leaping high in the hearth. A few fluttering, burning feathers drifted into the room, where Billy and Nathaniel gleefully allowed them to fall to the floor, then smothered them. But even that handful of truant torches gave off fumes so nauseous that Rosalind and the boys were soon choking.

Meanwhile a thick, heavy column of black smoke rose through the chimney as Rosalind, aided by Carl, continued to throw piles of feathers onto the flames. How long they were so occupied they never knew, but within a short time the effects of the tactic were plain to hear and see.

There was a series of scraping noises on the roof, then three almost simultaneous muffled crashes as the remaining Cherokees threw themselves to the ground, then ran, gagging and coughing toward their horses. All three followed a wild zigzag course as they ran, and it was only long afterward that Rosalind realized they had undoubtedly been temporarily blinded by the strong poisonous fumes of the burning feathers.

The savages made no attempt at concealment as they reached their mounts, drew the inert body of their wounded companion from the underbrush, threw him across the back of one of the horses, and rode off into the woods.

Rosalind and the two smaller boys stood motionless at the window, watching the Indians flee. Carl, however, quickly regained his air of adolescent bravado and picked up the rifle. He aimed it at the slowest of the retreating figures and would have fired had Rosalind not reached out and gently taken the gun from him.

"No, Miz Roz! Leave me shoot him! I c'n hit him easy!" There was real pain as well as wounded juvenile dignity in the plaintive cry.

"We'll have no more killing today, Carl. See—they'll be gone in a moment. We—we're safe!" Rosalind spoke faintly, each word an effort.

The sound of the Cherokees' swift horses faded away in the forest, and it was Billy who broke the long silence in the frame house. "I'm hungry, Miz Roz," he said casually. "We a-goin' to eat breakfast purty soon?"

Rosalind barely heard the question. The boys were alive and safe, and so was she. For the moment nothing else mattered, and she sank to a bench, put her face in her hands, and began to cry softly.

The last fragments of feathers were catching fire and sending their oily smoke through the chimney. An ivory-billed woodpecker in a nearby tree chattered merrily. And in the distance a horn sounded long and clear. It was the call to arms of the Frank in militia, and Nat Dolson's sons heard it. For the first time that morning they smiled.

Carl drew himself up self-importantly. "Men," he said, "we got guests a-comin'. Billy, you go start a fresh fire in the kitchen hearth and take care you don't hurt yourself or set fire t' your good britches. Nathan'l, you dig out some corn meal from the sem'nary lunch supply and set it t' boilin' in the kettle. Soldiers are always hungry. O' course they ain't as hungry as us, but they ain't been a-fightin' Cherokees afore breakfast, neither. Step out smart-like now! We got t' show 'em how us Dolson men act after we win a battle with them filthy damn brutes."

Chapter XIII

A parakeet cried persistently in a far-off treetop, his mournful wail blending with the damp, heavy dusk. To Rosalind, sitting at the tiny dressing table in her room at the Dolson house, the evening was as unreal as the day had been. She had felt neither pleasure nor excitement at the acclaim heaped on her for her courageous stand against the Cherokees early in the day, and now, as the shadows of twilight lengthened, she felt lonely and unaccountably sad. Dusk was always the most difficult time of day.

It was going to be a dull evening tonight; of that she was sure. But she could not disappoint Nat Dolson, who had asked her to accompany him to the Spaniards' fandango on the lawn of the Blue Grass Inn. Harold, she knew, would not object, and as Mrs. Dolson could not leave the house so soon after the birth of her baby daughter, it was only fair to Nat to help him celebrate. But she was tired and couldn't help wishing for a long night of sleep.

Slowly she turned to her little metal mirror and began to dust rice powder on her face. Looking at her reflection, she suddenly realized that the dress she wore was the same gown in which Janus Elholm had first seen her.

A timid knock sounded in the background, and when Rosalind

called out an invitation to enter, the ill-fitting door creaked slowly open on its leather hinges. Min Dolson, gawky and plain and slightly wan, stood hesitantly on the threshold.

"Might ye be wantin' my help in dressin', Roz? I'm still a mite clumsier'n I ought to be, but I thought mebbe ye'd be needin' a bow tied or sech-like, and a house full o' menfolks is no help when a body wants to perk up."

Rosalind smiled at her friend. "I wish you were going tonight, Min," she said. "You'd enjoy the party far more than I."

"My lands! An old woman like me? Young'uns like you are the ones that need to have a jolly time!"

Shaking her head, Rosalind stood and patted Min on the arm. "Nat would prefer to have you with him, Min. And you have no right to call yourself old. You're one of the most handsome women in Nashville—and don't you forget it."

Min grimaced. "Talk like that don't fool me none. I'm just plain apple jelly. All the same, I do wish I was goin' to the party. I've never b'fore seen Spanish gentry, and the evenin' ought to be right gay. I—I hope it ain't wrong for Nat to be goin'. He has a rightful call to be whoopin' and hollerin' some over the new baby, but I can't help wonderin' if it's wicked to take Spanish food and drink."

Rosalind laughed with less conviction than she felt. "I see no reason to refuse their venison and their buffalo steaks and their wine."

Surveying the younger woman for a moment, Min paused before replying. "My lands," she said without envy, "what I'd have give for your face and your figure when I was your age." Then she added abruptly, "Nat say: the dons are up to no good. All this throwin' around o' gold and laughin' and back-slappin' in their fancy uniforms ain't right or natural. And the way they hang around the county house, tellin' everybody who'll listen that they'll open up the Mississippi to our trade if we'll act more friendly. Humph! Like Nat says, it ain't grand parties over t' the inn that matter. If the King o' Spain wants to be so all-fired friendly, why don't he go ahead and just open up the river? The hard money we'd get for Nat's comin' wheat crop—that's what'd make us feel cozy to them foreigners."

Rosalind drew a comb through her golden hair, then expertly wound a curl around a dampened finger. "I'm sure they'll win no one over, if that's what worries you, Min. Folks here have too much good sense. Oh, they'll eat and drink Spanish provisions, but they'll go home afterward and laugh."

"Well, you have more good sense'n me, so if you say it's all right, I reckon it is. . . . Roz, when is Harold comin' home, and when are you two gettin' married?"

Harold had requested Rosalind not to divulge even the very little she knew about his journey, and she tried hard to comply with his wishes. "I expect he'll be home—soon," she said vaguely. "I—I'm anxious to be married as quickly as possible, Min. Harold is a—a wonderful person, and he has a—vast number of fine qualities——"

"Fine qualities?" Min sniffed indignantly. "My land, ain't that just like a Boston lady, talkin' about 'fine qualities' instead o' how much she loves her man." She tugged at the too short sleeves of her rough dressing robe. "I got to nurse little Ros'lind," she muttered curtly, afraid she had said too much. "Seein' as how you're all ready to leave, I'll tell Nat to get a move on. He's only come in from the fields a short spell ago, and he's been waitin' for a kettle o' water to boil so's he c'n take a bath, but I'll see if I can't get him to hurry. It ain't proper for a gentleman to keep a lady waitin'."

The Dolson parlor was hot and stuffy, and it was pleasanter for Rosalind to stand outside near the front door. Breathing in the cold, clear night air, she was happy to have this brief moment alone. A half-moon made the night friendly, and when it disappeared behind a bank of clouds Rosalind shivered slightly and drew her light wool cape more snugly around her shoulders. Somewhere inside the house the three Dolson boys were scuffling, but she could hear no other sound.

Then suddenly the stillness of the night was broken. A group of horsemen approached down the road at a full canter, and as they drew near Rosalind stepped back until her shoulders were pressed against the rough pine logs of the cabin. Almost before she realized it, the men swept into full view.

In the lead was a Cherokee Indian, his face and torso smeared with the hideous green paint that brought such horrible memories to her mind. Behind him were clustered four other riders, and to her amazement Harold was in the center of the group.

Startled, she could only stare. Harold looked neither to the right nor the left, but sat straight in the saddle, his eyes fixed on something—or on nothing. Rosalind opened her mouth to call to him, but before she could speak the little cavalcade had thundered past.

Blinking in bewilderment, she found herself running down the road before she quite knew what she was doing. She was aware of only one thing: Harold was mixed up in some very strange activity, and she had a right to dig to the bottom of the mystery.

The horsemen remained in sight until she passed the Cook cabin, where little Ruth, the family's new arrival, was crying lustily. Then the riders disappeared in a fog of dust. However, she could still hear the clatter of their horses' hoofs.

Feeling faintly ridiculous but determined to press on, Rosalind increased her pace. Her heavy silk skirts rustled about her legs, and her feet felt uncomfortable in their thin-soled sandals. She was sure that one ankle strap had come loose, but now was no time to tighten it.

A group of revelers, three men and a woman, came toward her

from the opposite direction, their arms over each other's shoulders as they sang happily and off key:

> *"We'll have johnnycakes for our supper,*
> *And wash them down with rye;*
> *Till one johnnycake or another*
> *Floats in the bye-and-bye!"*

The party was obviously made up of townspeople who had been guests of the Spanish delegation at the Blue Grass Inn, had drunk their fill quickly, and were now bent upon spreading their glow of good cheer to the less fortunate citizens who had stayed at home. Rosalind wanted neither to be accosted by them nor to become involved with them, and she slipped into the shadow of some hemlocks until they passed.

> *"We'll have johnnycakes for our supper,*
> *And wash them down with rye . . ."*

The voices faded away into the night, and Rosalind picked up her skirts and ran. Out of habit, she moved toward the center of town. A light was showing in a second-story window of the Davidson County courthouse, and through the open square beyond she could see a blaze of candles in the Blue Grass Inn. A subdued murmur that grew as she drew nearer came from the inn, too, and she stopped in sudden dismay. She could no longer hear the hoofbeats.

She started back in the direction from which she had come, then stopped, perplexed, and stamped her foot in vexation.

"Had a lovers' spat with your young man, Miss Rosalind?" A heavy male voice broke the silence, so close to Rosalind that she jumped.

"Oh, good evening Mr. Eaton. Mrs. Eaton." On the path immediately to her left Rosalind saw the parents of one of her pupils.

"That's a mighty pretty dress, Miss Rosalind." The older

woman addressed her with only the slightest tinge of envy.

"Thank you."

"We saw that Jordan fellow of yours making tracks for the tannery just now." Eaton laughed. "From the way he was hurrying, you sure must have blistered him plenty. He even had some of his lads with him for protection. Just shows you. All this time our little Priscilla has been telling us what a quiet, mild one you are!"

His wife tugged at his sleeve. "Hold your big tongue, Matthew Eaton," she said dryly. "Simply because you menfolks have all balked like ornery steers at going to the party doesn't mean a woman wants to sit home and mope. We have too few chances to parade our finery in Nashville, say I, and we're glad of the chance to step out when the occasion affords. Don't you agree, Miss Rosalind?"

"Indeed I do, Mrs. Eaton." So Harold had gone to the tannery! Filled with a restless desire to follow him at once, Rosalind moved away and was soon walking toward the river.

The little tannery, located on the river's edge in order to utilize the plentiful water supply for its curing and processing pits, was a rambling one-story building, or rather a connecting series of tiny cabins, sheds, drying vaults, and storehouses. Rectangular in general shape, the whole resembled a miniature blockhouse, with some of the structures inside the perimeter partially hidden from view. A tiny pin point of light showed from one of these inner buildings now, but there was no other sign of life anywhere.

The blackness of the night and the absolute silence made Rosalind's flesh creep, and she instinctively stopped behind a large oak and tried to focus her vision on the outer wall of the tannery. She neither saw nor heard anything and stepped again into the open with greater confidence.

A shadow against one of the nearer buildings stirred faintly, and Rosalind's heart missed a beat. A man in buckskins was leaning against a tannery wall. He moved again, and something glinted. Unable to move and afraid to breathe, she saw that his back was partly turned toward her and that he was indolently cleaning his fingernails with a long hunting knife of the type used to skin the larger animals brought into the tannery. She knew both Harold's helper and his apprentice, but she was unable to recognize this man.

She turned away on tiptoe, but once she regained the friendly protection of the trees her courage rose again, and she decided to skirt around to the far side of the tannery. If she was careful, no one would discover her presence.

A way to enter the tannery presented itself to her simply, and it was much easier than she had imagined. Whoever had let the drop-bolt into place on the door of the little hut nearest the river had been careless, and the door itself stood ajar. A small but substantial keelboat was moored to the tiny dock Harold had built, and water slapped placidly at its sides. There was no one in the boat, and no guard stood watch here. Rosalind waited for several minutes, carefully scanning every inch of the tannery wall and the ground surrounding it. There was no movement anywhere, and no sound save the idle swish of water and the drumming of her own heart in her ears. Finally she took a deep breath and drew her cape more closely around her. Then she lifted her skirts high and sprinted for the door. A second later she was inside the tannery.

A peculiarly musty odor at once assailed her nostrils, and as her eyes became accustomed to the gloom she decided that she was probably in the soaking room. Trying to orient herself, she moved through the covered passageway into the next chamber.

Here the smell was sharper, and she hastily drew a handkerchief from her cloak pocket and held it over her mouth to stifle her coughing. She needed no further guide to tell her where she was now. Although she had visited the tannery only once, the acrid stench told her that the lime pit was located here. Holding her breath, she walked the few feet to the next small shed. Here the door was closed, but when she barely touched it, it swung open freely. An instant later something soft hit her full in the face. She jumped back, and only the greatest exertion of will power prevented her from screaming.

Nothing more happened, and Rosalind opened her eyes and slowly lowered the hands she had raised automatically to shield her head. Enough light filtered into the shed from a small window to enable her finally to make out the object which she had struck. It was a large deerskin which hung from the rafters. The small chamber contained five or six other skins hanging from the ceiling or stretched between poles stuck in the ground. She picked her way through the maze with difficulty, stumbling twice as she tried to keep her full skirt from becoming entangled. Then she stopped short, for she heard the sound of male voices in the next room beyond. She recognized Harold's voice, and suddenly she realized where she was. The next room was his office. Peeking cautiously from behind a deerskin, she saw that the warped door stood partly open. Harold and a man facing him were both wearing their greatcoats and hats. The visitor was an unusually tall and ugly man, and Rosalind recognized him instantly as the stranger who had been dining with Janus Elholm at the inn yesterday.

Despite the chilly night air, Harold Jordan was sweating heavily. On one side of him sat the Baron de Carondelet, and on the other, holding a cocked pistol, was Colonel Sola, commander of a regiment of professional troops from Spain and the ostensible head of the trade mission to Franklin. Although both men glared at him coldly, Harold tried desperately to maintain an air of composure.

"There's nothing to discuss, gentlemen," he said in what he hoped was a steady voice. "I gambled. And I've lost my gamble. At one time I wanted to work for you. But I changed my mind."

The baron's eyes never left Harold's face, and when he spoke his voice was harsh and uncompromising. "In our work, my dear Jordan, it is impossible for a man to change his mind. When you committed yourself to us you did so for all of your life—or until such time as I might choose to release you. The choice is therefore mine, not yours."

Colonel Sola tightened his grip on the pistol and cleared his throat. "Whatever your intentions may have been in stealing so valuable a document from the baron, you were ill advised, Jordan," he said in a high, rasping voice, "very ill advised."

"And now you have aroused my curiosity, Jordan." Carondelet leaned forward in the hard chair. "Had you successfully evaded my men, what was your intention? What were you planning to do with my valuable list?"

"You can go plumb to hell, Carondelet!" Harold was beginning to show the strain. "I won't work for you, and I'll tell you nothing."

Colonel Sola studied the pistol and pointed it at Harold's head. "It is my opinion," he said curtly, "that we waste our time with Señor Jordan, Baron. If it is permitted, I will dispose of him at once."

Baron de Carondelet smiled impersonally. "Colonel Sola," he replied, "I must remind you that while you are outwardly the chieftain of this friendly mission to our dear American friends it is in actuality I who command. And I say it will be perhaps unnecessary to kill our good companion Jordan. Our good companion Jordan is a sensible man, hence he wishes to remain alive. Further, he enjoys the finely minted Spanish dollars which are so regularly supplied to him. Think of his position, dear Colonel Sola. Don Esteban pays him a salary to manage this tannery and has even permitted him to acquire a small interest in the business so that he may share in the profits. Nowhere else can he earn so much in return for so little work."

Harold felt himself losing his temper, but he was past caring.

"Take your damned tannery, Carondelet!" he growled. "To hell with it, and to hell with you. I want a little peace. I'm tired of living under your damned, constant threats."

The colonel again raised his pistol, but Carondelet held up a restraining hand. "Please, my dear Sola," he murmured, "you will permit me to conduct the necessary negotiations. Now, Jordan, I give you one final chance—one final choice. Either you will return to work for me, or I shall be forced to give you into the hands of my friends, the Cherokees. As their prisoner, you will have time to reflect and may eventually find it possible to change your mind."

Breathing hard, Harold tried to swallow but could not. Carondelet, he thought, justly deserved the reputation of being the most viciously ruthless man in all of North America. Life as a prisoner of the Cherokees was no life; indeed, it was an absolute promise of slow death by torture. And the baron knew that, although Harold was prepared to die here and now, his spirit and his will to resist would crumple if he fell into the hands of the Cherokees. Nevertheless, there was no turning back.

"Carondelet," he said proudly, "I prefer to be given over to the Cherokees. I will not under any circumstances work for you again."

Before either of his captors could move, Harold heard a long, shuddering gasp that came from somewhere outside the room. The others heard it, too, and Colonel Sola hurried to the door. "Miguelo! Alfonso!" he called. *"Venga usted acá!"*

Running footsteps approached from a distance. Meantime Sola stepped out into the passageway, sword in hand; a second later he shouted in amazement and triumph. Then Rosalind Walker moved into the open, walking boldly and with as much dignity as the circumstances permitted.

Baron de Carondelet, pistol in hand, was near the door of the little room, and when he saw Rosalind his black eyebrows shot up and his dark face lighted in amusement and surprise. But he

221

stopped short and whirled around as Harold cried: "Oh, my God! Rosalind!"

Harold sprang at the baron, but Carondelet was ready for him. He had already shifted his hold on the pistol from the butt to the barrel, and he brought the handle crashing down on Harold's head. Stopping short, Harold stood motionless for a second, then fell unconscious to the floor.

Rosalind would have leaped to his side, but the baron, moving with speed and agility, blocked her path. "Well, señorita," he said, his eyes glittering, "we meet at last. I have much desired to make the acquaintance of a lady who kills one of my brave Cherokees and sends four others fleeing for their lives. But I regret that you have come here, convenient though the occasion is for me. If you were familiar with the barracks game of rolling dice, you would know the old saying that it is never wise to push one's luck too far."

Saying nothing, Rosalind glared into the malevolent face and thought that nowhere had she seen a human being who so completely embodied a spirit of evil.

"You do not care to engage in the high art of conversation with me, señorita? I feel sure that a visit with my Cherokee friends will loosen your tongue." He looked sharply over her shoulder. "Alfonso!" he called. "Throw Jordan into the boat. We leave at once. Colonel Sola, you will of course remain to observe the amenities with the incomparable citizens of Nashville. Miguelo! You will attend our lovely guest, who has overheard too much."

Rosalind's arms were suddenly pinned behind her. She tried to scream, but at that instant a heavy, rough cloth was thrown over her head and face, almost smothering her. She tried to kick out with her legs, but strong hands closed over her ankles. Resistance was useless, but she continued to fight until ropes were pulled taut around her wrists and legs. The hemp bit into her flesh, and she moaned. There was little air under the hood, and she gasped for breath; then, mercifully, she fainted.

She had no recollection of being unceremoniously hoisted to a brawny shoulder or of being carried to the keelboat. It was a long time before she came to, and longer still before the cloth was removed from her head. By then Nashville had been left far behind to the east.

Chapter XIV

A dozen or more campfires winked brightly at Chickasaw Bluffs, but in the forests beyond the trading post and Indian village it was dark and quiet. Janus, trying to make himself comfortable on the damp, hard ground, sat with his back propped against the trunk of a huge oak and peered with narrowed, somewhat bleary eyes at Colonel James Wilkinson. The Dane was both weary and discouraged; his talks with other Franks and Kentuckians in the past twenty-four hours had produced no more than bombast, misplaced enthusiasm, and a display of complete misunderstanding of current and future problems.

But Wilkinson was unquestionably of a breed different from the weak visionaries and zealots. The more he said, the more convinced Janus became that here was a leader of ability and strength. His instant grasp of the most intricate military plans confirmed his stature as a soldier in Janus's eyes, and his crisp approach to the complex and delicate affairs of the administration of conquered lands was a welcome relief to one who had wasted hours listening to wild, impractical talk from power-hungry glory seekers. Wilkinson sat cross-legged on the hard ground now, as at ease as an Indian, and as erect. He exuded an air of self-confidence and strength that matched Janus's own.

"General Elholm," the colonel said, "I don't envy you the job that the dons have cut out for you. You're going to have one hell of a time subduing the Franks. They're tough, they're clever fighters, and they're loyal almost to a man to Jack Sevier. They know and love this country as they do their own womenfolk, and they'll fight like starved grizzlies to protect their land."

Janus smiled cynically. "I gather that you have no admiration for our companions of last night and today, colonel, and that you have no confidence in their ability to make my task easier."

Jim Wilkinson picked up a small twig and crushed it between thumb and forefinger. "That's how they'll hold up when the going becomes hard," he replied, throwing the stick from him in disgust. "Not one of them is worth a ha'penny of the money Don Esteban Miró has squandered on them in return for empty promises. But there's no need for me to tell you this. I think you saw for yourself that they aren't worth a round of bullets or a horn of powder."

"I do not rely on them," Janus said bluntly. "So let us not waste what remains of our time together in discussing them. Our joint concern is the Kentucky district."

"I've promised Don Esteban that I'll deliver Kentucky without a fight, and I make you that same promise, General Elholm. I'm not vain and I have neither respect nor regard for public acclaim. So you'll understand that I'm not bragging when I say that I'm as popular as any man in Kentucky. There are thousands who'll follow wherever I lead them. So after you've reduced Franklin—and I reveal that I'm throwing in my lot with Spain—my whole district will do the same. I know the Kentuckian, General Elholm. He values his personal independence above everything else, and he hates authority. Virginia, under whom we now live, has not yet seen fit to grant us independent statehood. The Congress of the Confederation has imposed set after set of inane orders and regulations on us, and we don't like them. Our people are ripe for revolt. And when they hear that Spain will grant

225

them complete autonomy, they'll flock to the banner of the dons
—behind me." He smoothed his silver hair and smiled.

"And when they find themselves living under the most strict
and uncompromising regime west of Imperial Russia, Colonel,
what then?"

Wilkinson shrugged carelessly. "It will be too late to protest,
won't it, General Elholm? You'll have two or three of your regiments stationed in Kentucky—under my direct command, of
course—and they'll preserve order. There's not much a disorgan-
ized and disillusioned people can do against trained troops armed
with muskets."

"May I ask a personal question, Colonel Wilkinson?" Janus
was on dangerous ground and spoke softly. "Why is it that you,
who hold such a position of esteem in the hearts of your countrymen, should enlist in the cause of your nation's enemy?"

Shifting his position slightly, Wilkinson allowed his upper lip
to curl. "My motives are the same as yours, General. I want gold
—piles of gold. And I want Kentucky and Franklin to be mine—
to do with as I see fit. I reckon I could be governor of Kentucky
if the Congress ever grants us statehood, but I'd be responsible to
a House of Commons for everything I did. And I'll be roasted on
a forked hickory spear over a low fire if I want to be paid a measly
salary of eight hundred beaver pelts and a few deerskins a year.
I want hard money I can feel with my fingers. I like the feel of
gold."

"I see. It is necessary for a man in my position to know such
things. Thank you for your explanation, and I beg that you take
no offense at my curiosity."

"None intended, none taken." Although Wilkinson's face was
as immobile as that of a Cherokee, his tone was cordial.

Only one major issue remained, and Janus was anxious to
bring the talk to an end. "You'll examine the plans I've given you,
of course. They indicate what I shall expect in the way of military support from you when my divisions move through Franklin

into Kentucky. It is understood between us, of course, that such a move may never become necessary. However, study them at your leisure, and if you have any changes to suggest, we can realign our strategy when you come to New Orleans."

The briskness of command was in Janus's tone, and Jim Wilkinson responded to it respectfully but without compromise. "Yes, sir," he said. "I'll read your operational plans with a heap of interest. But I reckon I won't have any changes to suggest. And that's because I'm positive the war won't reach Kentucky. My boys can save their lead for forest game—and when I'm King Charles's deputy for Kentucky and Franklin, the Crown will confiscate half of what they shoot. Um. I must remember when I'm in New Orleans to ask old Don Esteban what share the royal governor can take for himself."

The colonel stood and brushed off the seat of his breeches carefully. Though junior in rank to Janus, he was making it plain that he and he alone was taking full responsibility for Kentucky, and that even a general of the armies of Spain would enter the province only on his sufferance. Looking at him, Janus was well aware that Wilkinson himself possessed the very qualities of fierce independence of spirit which he intended to exploit.

Janus arose and held out his hand. Although he had no lofty scruples, he always had been contemptuous of traitors. But in spite of himself he felt a reluctant admiration for Wilkinson. "I look forward to our meeting in New Orleans, Colonel," he said.

"Thanks, General Elholm. I'll enjoy it too. Now, can I give you any help in finding your boat? These woods can fool a man who doesn't know his way around in them."

Even if Janus had not spent many weeks in the forests of Kentucky and Franklin, he would have refused. But he tried to sound gracious and hoped that Wilkinson would catch the implication that not only Kentuckians could be self-sufficient and independent. "I have already marked my meeting place with the baron. And I assure you, it will not be a difficult task to find it for one who made his way across the Polish marshes without a map and without food or water. You need never fear for the safety of Janus Elholm. When it rains, I always find a stout roof under which to keep dry."

"As you will, General. Good-by."

They shook hands again, and Wilkinson moved silently toward the shadows of the forest. Janus began to make his way stiff-legged down the slope toward the river. Looking over his shoulder, he caught a final glimpse of the Kentuckian, and he shook his head. Once again he wished he had the knack of these tough frontiersmen in mastering the techniques of foot travel in the wilderness.

Wilkinson waved a final farewell, and Janus returned the salute, thinking that here at least was one American who fitted a European's concept of attitudes and values. Francisca de Guzman would approve of a man like that. It was strange, he mused, how little he had thought of Francisca lately. The blond American girl had crowded her out of his mind.

He could not help hoping that Rosalind had not been an accomplice of Harold Jordan's in the theft of the baron's document. Carondelet would certainly show no mercy to anyone who posed a threat to Spain, and while Jordan deserved whatever was done to him, it was unpleasant in the extreme to think of what would happen to a lovely and innocent girl who fell into the baron's hands.

Directly below now was the Mississippi River, broad and swift and forbidding in the dark. Janus could hear the water hissing and bubbling along the banks as it swept downstream, and he instinctively slowed his footsteps. It would be easy to miss the baron's boatmen and rafts on such a night, and he began to pick his way carefully along the muddy shore. Nevertheless, he stumbled over a partly concealed tree root, stepped heavily into a patch of mud, and almost fell headlong. Only his agile footwork saved him, and he cursed violently as he righted himself.

At last his efforts were rewarded by the dim outline of a clumsy raft riding at anchor close to the shore. Near it must be the remainder of the baron's makeshift fleet. The nearest raft sat low in the water now, with bales of beaver and deerskins piled amidships, for the fleet traveled in the guise of trading boats. Janus grinned as he saw a tent pitched aft on top of the logs. It was on the verge of collapse and swayed dizzily as the raft bobbed up and down.

Halting, he whistled three times as per the prearranged signal. There was a long pause, and he was about to reach for a pistol when someone on the raft repeated his signal.

"Carlo?" Janus's voice was low, but it carried across the intervening distance.

Again there was a pause, then a gruff reply. "*Sí, señor.* Come aboard."

Janus was wet and muddy as he scrambled onto the raft, and he felt out of sorts. "The Señor Baron and his party are not here as yet?"

"No, señor." The gruff voice was somewhere behind him.

Janus walked across the logs and peered out through the dark night toward the other rafts. They were extraordinarily difficult to see, and he blinked hard as he tried to focus his eyes. Although the boats had been berthed close together, there was no sign of the other vessels. Disturbed, he was about to turn and demand an explanation, when strong hands seized him by the throat and pulled him backward. As he fell, his head struck the logs of the raft with a crash.

Groggy and helpless, he could feel his pistols and sword being removed from his person but was utterly unable to resist. A moment later his assailants moved away from him, and he could hear a muttered rumble of conversation. Gradually his head cleared, and he noticed that the clouds were rolling away and the night was growing somewhat brighter. Gathering his strength, he hoisted himself to a sitting position on the hard, bobbing deck of the raft.

Watching him silently were two men. Both were clad in faded, greasy buckskins from which most of the fringe had fallen away, and both wore circular fur hats; they were clean-shaven, and even in the dim light Janus could see that their long hair was clubbed at the nape of their necks. No further examination was needed to convince him that they were Americans—and frontiersmen.

The smaller of the two, a thin man with large ears, looked at Janus with cold indifference.

His companion was a man of great height and bulk, with square shoulders and a thick bull neck that reminded Janus of Malachi Stevens, a frontiersman well known for his skill in the art of rough-and-tumble and a militiaman with whom Janus had served in the Tipton expedition. In his big hands he lightly held a long frontier rifle, which was pointed directly at Janus, and he began to move slowly across the raft toward the Dane. Despite his size, the man was quick on his feet.

"Fooled ye, didn't we, Spaniard?" The voice was the same as that which had responded, "Sí, señor," when Janus had approached the raft.

"I am no Spaniard," Janus answered cautiously, holding himself very still as he fought to regain his equilibrium.

"We don't like Spanish bastards hereabouts, do we, Clem?" The man spoke to his companion, ignoring Janus's reply.

"Sure as hell don't, Bill." The second man's voice was high-pitched and raspy.

"We scairt them other ones good and proper." Bill addressed himself now to Janus. "They was scairt so bad they went scuttlin' off down the river in them other rafts. Me and Clem figgered mebbe them Spaniards got careless-like and left some o' their bastards b'hind. Then sure as shootin'—along ye come."

The picture of what had happened began to clarify itself for Janus. Apparently Baron de Carondelet and his party had appeared at the appointed site and been chased off by these frontiersmen, leaving Janus in an untenable spot.

He had faced death sufficiently often to judge the intentions of an enemy, and these Americans, he knew, were killers who would snuff out his life with as few qualms as he would dispose of them. His brain began to race, but he was careful to present a façade both unafraid and unflustered. "You misjudge me, monsieur," he said. "I have already informed you that I am not a Spaniard."

The shorter man spat into the river. "Ye lie in yer ugly teeth," he snarled. "We listened t' them Papist bastards holdin' a little powwow afore we let 'em know we was hidin' on shore. Uh-huh, and we larned a thing or two from 'em. Mostly we larned they *was* Spaniards, exceptin' the Cherokees they had with 'em, and a Cherokee stinks near as bad."

"Have you ever seen a man of Spain with hair the color of mine, monsieur? Even in this bad light you can see it. Observe." A desperate edge was creeping into Janus's voice despite his attempts at self-control.

The larger of the men took a step closer. "I never seen a white wolf, but that don't mean there ain't any," he said shortly.

"You condemn me before you hear me."

"We're listenin'." The big hunter grunted.

"I am the brother of Major George Elholm, adjutant general of your state of Franklin," Janus began, biting off the words sharply. "I was setting out on a mission of the greatest secrecy on behalf of my brother and of His Excellency, Governor Sevier. I am not permitted to reveal to you the nature of the assignment. I will only say that by driving or frightening away the Spaniards who were here—and I do not deny that they were Spaniards, mind you—you have placed in jeopardy a plan of the utmost importance to the United States."

"He talks right fancy, don't he, Bill?" Clem grinned, but his tone was humorless.

Bill's face was inscrutable. "Ye want us t' take ye down t' N'Orleans or somewheres, I reckon. Ye'd be right pert about it if we was t' ride ye where them Spaniards was goin' t' lug ye."

Janus felt he was gaining. "I would be greatly in your debt, monsieur. You would be performing a service of patriotism."

"And ye'd pay us, o' course."

"Handsomely. You may name your own price."

Bill suddenly scowled. "Buffalo manure," he said. "Ye be no kin t' George Elholm. And if ye're no Spaniard, ye're still cahootin' with 'em, so it's all the same. I seen rogue coyotes runnin' with a wolf pack. Seen it with my own two eyes. And we're seein' it again right now. Me and Clem here, we thought mebbe ye'd want ter tell us what ye was doin' snoopin' around Chickasaw Bluffs. But even a Philadelphy tenderfoot could see ye ain't got a honest bone in yer body. So we'll waste no more time tongue-clackin'. Where do ye want yer bullet, mister—in the head or in the heart?"

There was a long, tense pause, and then Janus laughed. To one who did not know him, it was a sound of pure, unfeigned merriment. "So this is the justice of America—the justice of which all Europe has heard and stands in awe. It is as well that I die. I should have known that the tales I have heard were no more than a myth."

"What in hell you spewin' about now, mister?" Bill was both suspicious and confused.

On sure ground at last, Janus was quick to press his advantage. "It is your privilege to disbelieve the truth when it is told to you. But never did I think that an American would disarm a man through a trick—and kill him as one would a beast. But I begin to understand. In my final moments on this earth I am granted the boon of enlightenment. The trapper of the American wilderness has within him a great fear. He cannot meet an adversary on equal terms."

Blinking in amazement, Bill stared at the Dane. "Ye mean ye think I'm scairt o' ye? Me?"

"To be sure." Janus was coldly weighing the odds against him.

If he could maneuver Bill into a position between himself and Clem, he might have a chance to dispose of them one by one.

"Ye pulin', pukin' little snot, I'll fight ye any goddamn way ye like, no holds barred. It'll save me a round o' lead. And ammunition bein' so scarce-like, ye'll be doin' me a favor. How do ye want ter die? Rassle? Sluggin' match? Free-for-all?"

Feeling that he was truly master of the situation now, Janus pushed his luck. "The only weapon you have left on my person is my poniard," he said softly. "If you should happen to possess a similar——"

"Hell, yes! I got me a knife that's skinned the carcasses o' varmints that stink a heap less than ye do." Bill threw his long rifle onto a pile of beaver skins, and from inside his oily buckskin shirt he drew a heavy, slightly curved blade.

Janus immediately pulled his dagger from its scabbard, and as his fingers closed around the handle he felt a sense of infinite relief. It was going to require all of his wit and strength to win a knife fight from a man bigger and just as agile as himself, but he felt for the first time that he was now in a position to hold his own. However, there was one aspect of the coming duel that remained to be settled. "What of your friend there?" he asked, letting scorn creep into his voice. "He will join you against me, no doubt. It is to be expected that Americans consider it fair and proper for two men to fight against one."

A low, deep growl escaped from Bill's lips. "Clem ain't goin' ter budge agin ye. Ye hear me, Clem? Sit ye down at the helm o' this here mis'ble craft. And no mind what happens, don't go using yer rifle. I aim t' have the pleasure o' killin' this timber rat all by my lonesome."

Clem nodded, obediently dropped to his haunches, and pushed his rifle away. A gleam of sardonic satisfaction shone in his small eyes, and it was evident that he was looking forward to a bloodletting. It was seldom a man was given an opportunity for such pure enjoyment, and if this Spaniard—or whoever he was—knew anything about the Silent Country, he would have heard of Bill, who had never been bested in a trial of strength.

"Are you ready, monsieur?" Out of the corner of his eye Janus was gauging the distance to the edge of the raft. With any luck, he might be able to bring the fight to a quick end: a sudden rush might throw the frontiersman off balance, and steady footwork on rough, slippery logs might tumble him overboard.

"I be ready." The pleasure of imminent combat was in Bill's voice, and he crouched low, his knife held high above his head.

The two adversaries began to circle warily around the raft, and Janus remained close to the bales of skins. If the idea had occurred to him to shove the enemy into the water, the same notion might have crossed the mind of the canny American. Drowning, he had been told, was a good way to die, but he had no intention of sampling its pleasures.

Without warning Bill sprang forward, and his knife blade flashed as it swept down in a swift, vicious arc. Barely in time, Janus side-stepped, almost losing his balance as his left foot caught momentarily in the crevice between two heavy logs. He heard the steel rip through the fabric of his sleeve, and grimaced.

Bill thought that Janus's retreat presaged victory, and with a smile of triumph he again leaped. But this time Janus anticipated the attack, and without moving his feet he twisted his body out of the way, then struck with his poniard. The blade connected with solid flesh, and Bill grunted. Although the wound was painful, it was superficial, and only a small, spreading crimson blotch on the greasy buckskin shirt indicated that any damage had been done.

Janus shook his head angrily. Another inch or two to the right, and the fight would have been over by now. He was not accustomed to missing at close quarters, and he wondered if a lack of practice had deprived him of his skill. No, it was these accursed logs, combined with the shifting current of the river, that made it virtually impossible for a man to judge a blow correctly.

The American bared his white teeth and advanced. His knife was poised, and with lightning-like rapidity his free hand shot forward. His heavy fingers closed around Janus's wrist, immobilizing the Dane's poniard. The frontiersman suddenly threw his right leg behind Janus and pushed with all his might.

Caught off guard by the unorthodox trick, Janus crashed to the deck of the raft, flat on his back, with Bill on top of him. Again and again the American's knife jabbed downward, while Janus twisted from side to side, squirming out of the path of that merciless blade.

Never before had he engaged in hand-to-hand combat with an opponent so impersonally ruthless, so determined to kill. There was neither rancor nor rage in Bill's attitude; his approach was that of a competent butcher who wanted to finish off a none too pleasant task as efficiently and as quickly as possible.

In a supreme effort Janus managed to free his left hand from the heavy knee that pressed it onto the logs of the deck, and reaching up wildly, he caught hold of Bill's knife wrist. But his fingers were cramped, and the American pulled his arm clear. Before the knife could descend again, however, Janus once more caught hold of the wrist, and this time he did not let go. For the moment at least, the fight was equalized—each man had stayed the power of the other's dagger. However, Bill was still on top, and he had no intention of giving Janus a breathing spell.

Janus slackened his grip on Bill's wrist, then shot his arm around that brawny neck, pulling with every ounce of his strength. Simultaneously he lifted his legs and torso as high into the air as he could, heaving violently.

Bill, who had obviously thought that the enemy was weakening, was taken by surprise, and before he could recover he found himself catapulting over Janus's head. He sprawled face down on the rough logs, momentarily stunned.

Janus was in no condition to utilize this change in fortune, though. Lifting himself groggily to his feet, he stood on shaky legs and gulped in precious draughts of air. What finally galvanized him into action was the sight of Bill lifting himself to his hands and knees. Janus's head cleared, and he threw himself headlong at the American, his poniard raised for the finishing blow.

Some instinct beyond reason prompted the frontiersman to twist partially out of the way, and even in his foggy condition he retained enough cunning to lift his own knife and bury it in the hard flesh that swept down on him.

Thus it was that both men drew blood at the same time. Janus's dagger cut deep into Bill's thigh, and the American's blade penetrated two inches or more into the attacker's shoulder. Janus grunted with pain as he felt the warm blood spurt. He could not tell how effective his own strike had been, for Bill clamped his big teeth together and made no sound.

However, in twoscore military engagements, Janus had learned to gauge the moment when his enemies lost control of their reason and allowed themselves to be guided by animal passion. Whatever success he had enjoyed had resulted from the fact that he had always kept his head when others had lost theirs. Now he felt rather than saw that Bill was no longer a rational, cool fighting man, and he knew that the moment of ultimate decision was at hand.

Ignoring the raging pain in his left shoulder, he hauled himself to his feet and began to circle warily. Bill also dragged himself to a standing position and glared wildly from side to side. Carefully and slowly, Janus maneuvered until Bill stood between him and Clem, who watched in awed silence.

The Dane twisted the handle of his poniard until it felt snug and secure in his fingers. Then he rushed toward his opponent, raising his arm high. A second later he struck with full force and fury.

This time there was no missing the target. Bill lifted his own knife for the death blow, but he was too slow, and Janus plunged his five inches of steel into the frontiersman's heart. Bill died instantly, without making a sound.

But Janus's work was not yet finished. He had to dispose of Clem, who was fresh while he himself was weary. He drew his poniard from the inert body and half leaped, half slid across the few feet of intervening space to the tiller, where Clem still sat spellbound, not quite able to grasp the fundamental fact that the fight was over and that his companion was dead.

Janus pressed the point of his dagger against Clem's throat and kicked the American's long rifle overboard. "The time has arrived, monsieur," he panted, "for a brief discussion between us. What have you done with my pistols?"

Clem stared at the Dane stupidly. "Ye kilt Bill," he muttered semi-intelligibly. "Ye kilt the best friend I ever had."

"My pistols," Janus replied, emphasizing his firmness by pricking the frontiersman's skin.

"Over there—in the tent."

"Very well. I shall get them. And you shall continue to sit right here until I return. If you make one false move I shall kill you with my knife."

Clem gave no sign that he had heard the threat, but he continued to sit as one mesmerized while Janus retrieved his weapons. Only moments later, when he found himself staring into the muzzle of a graceful French dueling pistol, did the import of the situation dawn on the frontiersman.

"Monsieur," Janus said softly, "it is time for you and me to part company. Listen to me carefully. I shall cut the ropes that hold this boat to the trees on the shore. We shall rapidly drift out into the stream, and I shall attempt to steer the accursed craft with this foul tiller. When we have traveled a short distance you will jump overboard. Are you able to swim?"

"Yes."

"Good. Then you will not drown. You will have a chance to reach shore and to save your life."

237

"What—what about Bill?" Clem's skin was drawn taut across his face, and beads of sweat dotted his forehead.

"We shall dispose of your friend—like this." Janus rolled the body with his foot to the far end of the raft and nudged it over the side. There was almost no sound as Bill disappeared.

Clem sobbed and his body shook, but Janus ignored him. The battle for survival was not yet over, he thought as he sawed with his poniard at the thick rope. He would have to navigate the ungainly raft alone until he reached Spanish territory and could hire a pilot to take him the rest of the distance to New Orleans. But he had no doubt of his ability to accomplish what was necessary; he would succeed because his alternative was death.

Chapter XV

Fifteen hundred or more citizens of New Orleans lined the dirt walks on the sides of the Place d'Armes, and every home and shopwindow was crowded with onlookers. On the south side of the square the aristocracy of the city was gathered in coaches and sedan chairs, but the faces of the elect wore the same expression of eager but contained curiosity as those of the humblest bayou fisherman or back-country settler. It wasn't every day that the capital of New Spain enjoyed the spectacle of a military parade and review.

Even the most blasé were impressed by the erect figure mounted on a black stallion to the right of the governor, and far more attention was directed toward him than to the troops, for whom the good citizens felt the friendly contempt that comes with too great familiarity. That the new general was a ferocious warrior could not be doubted by the throngs who saw him sitting in careless splendor on the great steed, and his reputation was magnified tenfold as the onlookers repeated and embroidered tales of his exploits, many of which bore a stronger resemblance to early-morning wineshop visits than to the truth.

Janus was keenly aware that he was the center of interest, but he was not enjoying himself. His uniform of black and red and yellow, with its gold epaulets and braid, was both dashing and handsome, but it was hot almost beyond endurance, and he was forced to exercise great self-control in refraining from squirming as rivulets of perspiration streamed down his back under the thick wool jacket. His neck itched as the high, stiff collar rubbed against it, and he wondered for the hundredth time whether the imitation diamonds in the center of each of his epaulets would tarnish in the withering sunlight. Only the Spanish, he told himself cynically, would require their generals to wear diamonds as a part of their insignia.

Two companies of provincial infantry marched into the square, and he raised his sword in an automatic salute. Studying them keenly, he concluded that these men were capable of virtually nothing beyond taking part in parades. It was true that they carried impressive muskets of the latest design and make, and equally true that few uniforms anywhere could match their plumed hats and their broad multicolored sashes. But there was an air about them that the competent professional soldier immediately recognized as one of inferiority. Baron de Carondelet had explained in detail last night that every male resident of the province under forty years of age was required to serve in the militia and that a penalty of twenty lashes was imposed on those who failed to answer the call to part-time conscription. Janus had argued that troops always fought more effectively and with greater fervor when the reasons for their recruitment were explained to them, but the baron had replied disdainfully that no incentive was the equal of fear of the whip.

For a moment Janus envied John Sevier of Franklin. There was a leader who knew to the last man the value and temper of his militia and who could count on them to function under the most trying and exasperating of conditions. But it was serving no good end to dwell on the gloomy side of the picture.

The regiments from Spain gave promise of being all that he

had secretly dared to hope, and after his careful inspection early this morning he knew that few shock troops anywhere were in a class with the reinforced battalion of silent, efficient Basque mountain men who had come to the New World in search of adventure and loot.

Janus also reflected that the soldiery of Don Alfonso Galvez, governor of the Floridas, provided him with another tough, balanced, and rounded cadre. Approximately twelve hundred such trained fighters were stationed at Pensacola, and they all would be made available for the campaign.

Janus felt a peremptory tap on his shoulder and swallowed a feeling of annoyance before he turned his head toward the governor. Don Esteban Miró, senior representative of His Majesty in New Spain, had demonstrated again and again in the brief span of two days that he was incapable of harboring an intelligent, constructive, or serious thought. Carefully arrayed in his most gorgeous uniform, he sat now on a mild and elderly bay mare. The gold threads of his ornate collar had turned a dark, musty yellow as he had sweated through the band. Like so many others, he had learned that it was next to impossible to wear a dress wig in New Orleans for any length of time.

His mild eyes flickered over the seemingly endless rows of marching men, and he glanced more than once toward the carriages on the opposite side of the Place d'Armes. He was bored beyond measure by the review on which the new general had insisted, and he longed for the cool patio of his mansion and the comfort of a loose dressing robe.

Watching him, Janus was unable to resist comparing him with John Sevier of Franklin. One had risen to his position of preeminence through wealth and family influence; the other governed because his own qualities of leadership had carried him to the top. Perhaps there was something to be said for the American system after all.

241

The thought disturbed Janus, and he turned his attention back to the troops. It was a soldier's place, he reminded himself severely, to concentrate on military affairs and on nothing else.

It was two o'clock in the morning, and the *palacio* of Don Esteban Miró was exceptionally quiet. Here and there a footman drowsily extinguished a taper, and blinds were closed to shut out the bright moonlight. A carriage rumbled on the cobblestones of the courtyard as the last of His Excellency's guests departed. In the kitchens the exhausted chefs banked their fires and stumbled off to bed, and in the cellar the chief wine steward poured himself a long drink of Canary wine before locking the liquor vaults for another night.

Yawning, Janus made his way slowly down a dark corridor to the suite he occupied in the governor's mansion. A bit of tallow from his flickering candle dropped onto the back of his hand, and he wished he had not been so hasty in refusing the services of a footman to guide him to his bedchamber. In his mouth was the stale taste of brandy, and he felt sluggish as well as bored. Don Esteban's idea of an evening's entertainment was, to say the least, unique. But Janus wanted no part in debauchery, and it was some satisfaction to know that even the highest-ranking of the Spanish colonels who had been present tonight had refrained from taking part in the festivities when they had seen disgust and revulsion written on their general's face.

The door of Janus's small sitting room was open a crack, but when he entered, the air inside was stale. Annoyed, he shut the door, put down the candle, then walked to the blinds and pushed them open. A breeze swept through the chamber, and he breathed deeply. Spaniards, he thought crossly, were afraid of fresh air. He picked up the candle again and walked to the door of his bedroom. When he opened it, the same musty odor assailed his nostrils. Then suddenly he forgot about ventilation and was glad he had worn his sword with his dress uniform tonight. His right hand moved quickly to the hilt; a man was sitting on the edge of the bed.

"Enter, Señor General. I have been waiting for you." The harsh voice was that of Baron Hector de Carondelet.

Something was manifestly very wrong, and Janus quickly transferred the candle to his left hand. Showing no outward sign of fear, he advanced steadily into the room and put the candle down on a small table by the window.

"I missed you at supper and at His Excellency's little party afterward," he said casually. "We were told you were occupied by affairs of state, so you'll pardon my surprise. My last expectation was to find you hiding in my room."

There was a brief silence, and Janus could hear the baron breathing hard. As he turned and looked at him directly, he noticed for the first time that Carondelet held a cocked pistol in his right hand and that his sword was lying naked across his lap. By no stretch of the imagination was this a friendly visit, then.

"Come no closer, Elholm. We will hold together a little discussion from the positions in which we now find ourselves."

"Well?" Janus was trying to find some reason for this menacing intrusion but could not.

"You have been a lucky man, Elholm. Your luck has now changed. And lest you try to escape or do me bodily injury, let me warn you that men in my employ are stationed in the outer corridor and on the lawn outside these windows. If they see you, they will shoot to kill."

"Don Esteban is unaware of this visit?" Janus was still searching for a clue.

"The ancient goat knows nothing, my unfortunate companion. Plainly you are at a loss to understand why I am here, but I shall explain—in order that we may mutually benefit."

"Please do. And please stop pointing that pistol at me, Baron. I find it difficult to concentrate with a loaded gun leveled at my head."

243

Carondelet laughed unpleasantly and placed the pistol carefully on the bed, within easy reach. "We will hold our little talk in an atmosphere of civilized amity? That pleases me immensely, Señor Elholm."

Janus made no effort to stir but stood poised and wary, waiting to hear what the baron wished to say, and ready for any quick move.

"Early this evening," the baron continued, "a galleon arrived from Spain, bearing on board the Deputy Grand Constable Don Luis Martinez. On his person he carried a warrant for your arrest, also a revocation of your commission as brigadier general in the armies of His Majesty. Both of these papers are here in my pocket, and you may examine them before our interview is ended in order to convince yourself of the truth of what I say."

He paused to let the words sink in, but Janus had no intention of appearing shocked, dismayed, or upset, despite the fact that the ground was suddenly cut out from under him. "What cause does the warrant give for an arrest—and on what authority was it issued?" he demanded boldly.

"You are charged with murder, señor—and the lovely Marquesa Francisca de Guzman, the most beautiful woman in Spain, has been arrested as your accomplice. The authority you question is that of the First Minister of Imperial Spain, who has done you the great honor of signing the warrant himself."

Janus shook his head to clear it. "But why should Aranda charge me——"

"Ah. I have not yet told you all. There has been a change of government in Madrid, so Don Luis Martinez tells me. Don Luis is a gentleman of becoming craft and guile. Rather than alarm you and give you an opportunity to run away, he summoned me to the galleon to inform me of your sad fall from grace. But I digress. Aranda is no longer in power. His enemies have persuaded the King that he is too old to be useful, and he has been forced to retire to his estates. The new First Minister is Don José

Moñino y Redondo, the Conde de Florida Blanca. However, I hasten to assure you, señor, that your land-acquisition agreement with his predecessor remains in force, for Aranda signed it as an official, not as an individual.

"But I go too fast and must speak first of other matters. The dearly beloved nephew of Florida Blanca, the young marquis, was found outside Madrid, murdered, on the very evening on which you left the city, señor. How your guilt has been proved I do not know. How Francisca de Guzman was associated in the enterprise I cannot even guess, but as the new First Minister had often expressed his fear that his impetuous nephew might marry her, it is not too difficult to conjecture that he has found the opportunity convenient to be rid of one whom he hated."

Remembering the still body of the Marqués de Florida Blanca on the side of the Madrid road, Janus was sure no real proof could be established that he had been connected in any way with the young noble's death. A protest that they had dueled fairly would be useless without witnesses, and a complete claim of innocence would be an utter waste of time. Spanish justice was notoriously lax, corrupt, and inefficient, and the interest being shown by the new First Minister was a guarantee of speedy conviction and execution, regardless of the circumstances of the case.

"You contemplate, señor, and you find your position is not to be envied. Aha! How very sad—and how true. But think, if you will, of the poor Marquesa de Guzman, who already languishes in chains in the great city prison of Madrid. Her future is to be pitied. The First Minister will most certainly confiscate her property and add it to the already extensive holdings of the family of Florida Blanca, and she herself will live out her days in jail."

Although he deeply regretted the loss of the Guzman title, Janus could feel no sympathy for Francisca herself. "I sincerely hope the jailers will not too greatly mar her beauty, but at the moment I am concentrating on my own neck."

"To be sure. How relieved you will be to learn that you are

quite safe, señor—provided certain conditions are met." Caron
delet leered suggestively and tapped a booted foot on the floor. "
have already told the deputy grand constable that you and I hac
some weeks ago completed the arrangement I am about to sug
gest to you. It is this.

"A month past, it is presumed, you signed over to me you
land-grant claim for one million or more acres. You will, I fee
sure, affix your signature and appropriate date to the paper now.

The baron's scheme was coming into focus now, but Janu
wanted to force him to spell it out. "Why would I do such
stupid thing?" he inquired with deliberate brusqueness.

"In order to save your life—and to put to some practical us
that which has no other value for you. Should you be returned t
Spain you will surely be put to death—and the land grant wil
revert to the Crown. But a properly dated signature on the docu
ment will give you your freedom. I shall be more explicit. I shal
place you under arrest, and Don Alfonso Galvez will personall
take command of the expedition against the Americans. We
guarded by my troopers, we shall start to ride toward the harbor—
and Don Luis's galleon. But as we pass through the narrow
crowded streets of the city an unfortunate happening will trar
spire. The dangerous prisoner Elholm will escape. And in orde
that the deputy grand constable may not implicate me, two of m
brave men will lose their lives when the prisoner shoots his pat.
to freedom."

No leader was as contemptible to Janus as the man who place
no value on the lives of his followers, and it was only with an ex
traordinary effort that he concealed his thorough disgust for th
calculating Intendant of Louisiana. "You would sacrifice two c
your troopers for this purpose, Baron?"

Carondelet shrugged. "It is a small price to pay for what wi
be one of the largest landholdings in all of North America."

"I see. And what guarantee do you give me that once I hav
signed over my interest in the property to you I will not be kille

: once? It would be a most convenient method of preventing me
om telling the deputy grand constable about our little bargain
-and it would be so very easy for you to claim that you had shot
₁e as I *tried* to escape."

The baron laughed humorlessly. "I knew you would think of
₁at phase of the matter, of course. And the only possible guar-
ntee I can give to you, my former comrade in arms, is the word
f one gentleman to another. You will accept my terms, Señor El-
olm, because you have no choice but to accept them. Do not
₁ink you can fool me or manipulate me to your advantage.
Iarold Jordan was stupid enough to think he could be more
lever than Hector de Carondelet, but he has learned better."

Janus forced a smile to his lips. "Harold Jordan? Why do you
₁ention him at this particular time?"

"Because I am generous. You have several times asked me how
disposed of him. And you have hinted broadly—very broadly—
₁ your attempts to learn what may have happened to the attractive
merican girl, Jordan's good friend, in whom you have shown
₁ch a marked interest. Until now I have avoided giving answer
₁ your inquiries. Now, because it suits my purposes, I will tell
ɔu. Both are my prisoners. They are being held by a band of my
Iherokees at a village known as Bogalusa, not too many miles to
₁e north on the Pearl River."

"And why do you tell me this, Carondelet?" The definite
nowledge that Rosalind Walker was the baron's captive in-
₁riated Janus, but he continued to think rationally.

"As I indicated, I am generous. If you agree to my terms, I
₁all make you a free gift. I shall sign an order to Lieutenant
₁rez, the commandant at Bogalusa, directing him to deliver the
irl into your hands. After you make your escape you may go to
₁r and take her with you. Jordan will not trouble you, for he
·ill remain a prisoner, and you may be sure that his life will not
₁ a long one."

"I see. Your generosity overwhelms me, Carondelet."

Satisfied, the baron leaned back on the bed and smirked "Then we understand each other at last. What is your answe Señor Elholm?"

Janus stood very still, apparently giving the proposal his mo serious consideration. In actuality he was tensing, then relaxin his muscles preparatory to a violent movement. Calling upo every fiber and nerve to do his instant bidding, he leaped acros the room, picked up the baron's pistol, and dropped it into water jug that stood uncovered on a small table. Then, in almo the same motion, he drew his sword and took a dueling stance.

"The terms of your offer are too tenuous, dear Baron. Far to tenuous. I prefer to feed the now worthless land agreement to th crows—and to protect my skin and my life in my own way. Stan up! Although it would give me great satisfaction to kill you as yo sit there, I prefer to give you the opportunity to defend yoursel Stand, I say!"

His face twisting in silent rage, Baron de Carondelet haule himself upright and took a firm grip of the handle of his swor "You are a worse fool than I had imagined, Elholm," he hisse "You have lost your last chance for survival. I shall disarm you— and put into practice my justly famed methods of persuasion t induce you to sign over the land grant to me. Then it will giv me pleasure to introduce you to the slow death which I invente three years ago and which is even now being installed in ever prison in Spain."

"No, Carondelet, I have other plans for my future."

"Ass! Were I unable to best one with twice your skill swordsmanship, what would prevent me from crying out for hel and thus rousing all of Don Esteban's household as well as m own men?"

"Your greed, you Flemish miser. Your lust for gold. Call fo help and you know it will be too late to cajole or force me int signing over Aranda's land grant."

They were cautiously circling the room now, and Janus picke

up a chair with one hand and threw it out of the way and onto the bed. The light from the candle caught their white, intent faces and cast great shadows on the walls behind them.

First one sword, then the other darted out as the opponents warily tested each other's dexterity. Neither wanted to open an attack prematurely; each was on guard against a sudden assault. Janus's wrist was the stronger, but the baron held a slight edge in speed and maneuverability.

"Elholm?"

"Yes, you Flemish dolt."

"Do you know I have killed a baker's dozen and more who have dared to cross their swords with mine?"

"How interesting. I long ago stopped counting the number of my unfortunate victims."

Janus was beginning to enjoy himself. Seldom in a career in which his sword had been used to provide food and shelter had he been able to afford the luxury of a duel with a man he hated. The thought spurred him into a sudden burst of activity, and he slashed at the baron's head, his sword whistling as it cut through the air.

The renegade noble brought up his own steel barely in time to fend off the vicious blow, and although he managed in part to deflect the stroke, a slight cut appeared on the side of his high brow, directly above his left temple.

Janus grinned and disengaged. "First blood, you Flemish jester. We have an old saying in Copenhagen—perhaps you have heard it. 'He who first causes red to appear will win the day.' A most excellent proverb, don't you agree?"

The baron said nothing, but darted slightly to the right and jabbed forward toward Janus's heart. Parrying, Janus danced out of reach and raised his sword to his forehead in a mocking salute.

"Is that your best, Baron? Is that the swordplay at which all of Europe has trembled? Come, now. Surely you can do better."

Goaded beyond endurance by the scoffing voice, Baron de

249

Carondelet lost both his temper and his caution and began to lay about wildly with his sword. Beating at thin air, he muttered a stream of oaths as he advanced across the room.

Ducking, weaving, and keeping a healthy distance between himself and the baron's unpredictable blade, Janus chuckled, then threw back his head and roared aloud. "Permit me to suggest a new occupation for you, Flemish clown," he said. "When the Spaniards tire of your nonsense, take yourself to the court of Prince Ludwig of Styria. He always has room for another idiot jester, and you need only present yourself to be accepted."

The effect of the gibe was the opposite of what Janus had anticipated. Carondelet stopped short and shook himself hard, his eyes cleared, and his breathing became quiet and normal. He continued to attack, however, and lunged at his opponent, this time with the consummate deftness of an experienced duelist. Feeling the difference at once, Janus quickly brought his own sword into play and parried the blow.

But the baron was not to be denied now and pressed his advantage repeatedly. Steel sounded against steel as strike after strike was attempted and repulsed. Janus had no time to joke and found himself fully occupied in keeping the point of his enemy's ever-active sword from his face, his neck, and his chest.

A thin film of sweat appeared on Janus's brow, and a trickle of salty water ran down his cheeks and soaked his collar. He realized vaguely that he should not have indulged himself and wasted opportunity by insulting the baron; the net result had been to arouse the man to a dangerous pitch of cold fury. But there was no time for regrets—he was still on the defensive, and unless he could force a change of pace it was inevitable that Carondelet's sword would sooner or later find its target.

It was no easy matter to change over to an attack against an opponent as determined as the Flemish nobleman. However, the conviction grew in Janus that the baron was not trying to kill him but merely to put him out of combat. Of course! A dead man would be unable to sign over a land grant, but one who was merely incapacitated and helpless could easily be beaten into doing so.

Thus he saw that the fundamental advantage was his. Unlike Carondelet, his own aim was to end the duel by causing the death of the enemy, and if he allowed himself to gamble, he might be enabled to reverse the trend. Without stopping to weigh the consequences of failure, he halted his retreat across the room, parried a lunge with a neat riposte, then plunged forward, his blade aimed straight at the baron's heart.

So unorthodox and abrupt was the maneuver that Carondelet was taken off balance, and none but the expert he was could have deflected the vicious thrust. But the tide was turned, and Janus remained on the offensive. Into each cut of the blade he poured all of the vigor and strength of a climactic blow. Few swordplayers, regardless of their skill or courage, could have long remained unscathed under the impact of such a withering assault. It was to the baron's credit that he neither wilted nor became panicky. But he was too experienced a fighting man not to realize that his time had come.

The Dane's moment of triumph came with unexpected suddenness. His blade penetrated the baron's tightly held guard, and the point disappeared beneath the collarbone.

But Hector de Carondelet would not be denied a final theatrical gesture. He raised his sword high over his head, and although the flourish caused him to cough violently, he completed the prescribed salute for the finish of a fencing match.

"May your soul join mine in eternal hell, Elholm," he whispered, "and may you rot forever in the purgatory reserved for those who are friendless and alone."

A trickle of deep red blood ran from a corner of his mouth, and he slumped to the floor, dead.

Janus permitted himself no pause for breath, no moment of elation. He thrust the still wet sword into the scabbard at his side, picked up Carondelet's cloak and old-fashioned black plumed hat from the bed, and donned them. Then, after rolling the baron's lifeless body into a place of hiding under the bed, he hurriedly unlocked a clothes cupboard and removed his ammunition and pistols.

Jamming the guns into his belt, he pulled the collar of the cape high around his face, walked through the sitting room, opened the door, and stepped into the corridor. It was dark, and he began to move rapidly but without panic toward the staircase that led to the first floor—and the front entrance. He stiffened slightly as he saw a man's shadow, then a second shadow near the end of the hall. However, he did not hesitate, and as he approached he felt the two figures straighten.

"Señor Baron." The two men saluted meticulously.

Janus murmured something unintelligible in the back of his throat and, looking neither to the right nor the left, he started down the stairs which were lighted by candelabra in the hall below. He sensed that he was being watched, but did not allow himself to falter. Another of Carondelet's men and a very sleepy servant were standing directly inside the polished oak panels at the entrance, and Janus brushed past them without a glance. They sprang to open the massive doors for him, and he paused only long enough to tap his foot imperiously, then plunged into the night.

Several horses were standing patiently in the courtyard, reins looped over hitching posts. Only a single guard was on duty here, and the Dane ignored him as he swiftly examined the animals. A sleek gray gelding seemed the best of the lot, and without hesitation he strode to the animal, untied the reins, and leaped into the saddle.

Baron de Carondelet's man started forward, a question on his lips, but Janus gave him no opportunity to ask it. He slapped the horse's withers with the palm of his hand and the beast leaped forward, hoofs clattering on the cobbles.

A moment later rider and animal were on the deserted streets of New Orleans, traveling north. Never once did Janus look back. The worst of his immediate perils was past, and with each passing second he was moving closer to safety—and to the village where Rosalind Walker was imprisoned.

Chapter XVI

It was easy—even for one unfamiliar with the territory—to ride along the banks of the Pearl River, knowing that Bogalusa was, after a long and difficult trip, only a few hours' journey away. It was more difficult to contemplate that if Baron de Carondelet had been lying, Rosalind Walker would not be found in the village, and it might be impossible to learn her whereabouts. It was hardest of all for Janus to realize and to admit to himself that he had fled from New Orleans without his money belt, that his reserves of Spanish gold remained in Don Esteban Miró's palace, and that he possessed nothing but the clothes he wore, his weapons, and his wits. He was as poverty-stricken as he had been on the day he had ridden into Madrid so many months before, when his grandiose schemes had been so full of promise. Neither a noble title nor wealth awaited him now.

Strangely, it didn't seem to matter too much. Perhaps he was too tired after two days and two nights of travel through wild swamps and lonely forests. Perhaps the task that remained before him, that of freeing Rosalind Walker from the Spaniards and Cherokees who held her prisoner, weighed too heavily on his mind. Strangely enough, he never asked himself why Rosalind's safety was suddenly so important to him. The decision to rescue her at all costs had been made quickly and almost instinctively.

It was all too clear what he would do—what it would be necessary for him to do after he returned the girl to her own people. It was essential that a man eat to ease the pangs of hunger that gnawed at his stomach. Hence he would go to John Sevier and offer his services to the Americans in the coming trial of strength with Don Alfonso Galvez and his Spanish regiments. The Franks could use an officer of experience, especially one who knew so much about the enemy and his intentions.

Lieutenant Jerez, chief of the garrison in the miserable collection of mud-and-straw huts known as Bogalusa, was deeply impressed, despite his inner struggle. Granted that the uniform of the Señor General Elholm was torn and dirty. Granted that the Señor General carried no letter from Baron de Carondelet and therefore had no right to interview the female prisoner. But there was no denying the authenticity of the identity of the blond man with the firm jaw and the cold blue eyes. Lieutenant Jerez had seen him last week in the *palacio* of His Excellency Don Esteban Miró for a fleeting instant and had been deeply regretful ever since that the baron had sent him back to this filthy Indian village. Now that the leader of the forces of New Spain was actually here, Lieutenant Jerez intended to do everything in his power to ingratiate himself with the new commander in chief.

But the Jerez family had a reputation for caution that had been passed down from one generation to the next, and the sole surviving member of the house could not forget his heritage. Baron de Carondelet had given him specific instructions regarding the handling of the American girl; to cross the will of the baron was a guarantee of demotion and disgrace. Lieutenant Jerez had no desire to learn the intimate secrets of the torture chambers in the underground vaults of Carondelet's headquarters.

Realizing that he was even now disobeying the baron's orders, he paced indecisively in front of the hut in which the female prisoner was held. He wanted to approach closer in order to eaves-drop, but the Señor General had deliberately thrown aside the deerskin flap that covered the entrance and stood just inside so he could observe Lieutenant Jerez's every move.

If possible, the lieutenant would have sent one of his Cherokees to the rear of the hut to hear what the general and the lovely American captive had to say to each other, but none of the brutes spoke English, so such a move would not only be a waste of time but might arouse the Señor General's ire.

It was difficult enough, Lieutenant Jerez reflected somberly, to have directly disobeyed the unequivocal commands of the baron. But he had been placed in the terrible position of defying either the Intendant of Louisiana or a brigadier general of Spain.

Again he looked toward the hut where the beautiful señorita was imprisoned, and then hastily averted his glance. Although the Señor General was speaking earnestly to the woman, his eyes never left Lieutenant Jerez's face. Biting hard on the *cigarro*, the lieutenant contrived to appear bland and unconcerned. As a cap-tain he would undoubtedly be transferred to a better post, perhaps even to New Orleans itself. How the women there would admire his double epaulets! And how he would enjoy the increased salary and the prestige that would go with higher rank!

Beyond all else, Rosalind was aware of her slovenly, filthy appearance. Her dress, the same she had worn the night she had so foolishly blundered into the tannery at Nashville, was ripped and dirty. Her hair had not been combed for days, and on her smudged, bare feet were long red welts that gave eloquent testi-mony to her suffering at the hands of the Cherokee women who had daily amused themselves at her expense. There were similar marks on her back and on her hands, but she was able to conceal these from Janus Elholm.

That the Dane was offering her a chance to escape was too much for her to believe. He was as unscrupulous, as wicked, as heartless as Baron de Carondelet, and she considered him at least partly responsible for her present plight. She knew that such an attitude was both unfair and irrational, but her shame at having him see her in such a sorry condition was overwhelming, and she felt a need for self-justification.

"Mademoiselle," Janus said, wanting to look at her but continuing to watch the swarthy officer who paced up and down outside, "if you value your life, listen to me—and believe me. We are both in great danger. I am here to help you, but I cannot unless you will let me."

Rosalind said with anger in her voice: "I'm no more afraid of you than I am of those horrible Cherokees. I've already been sufficiently degraded, and I prefer their sort of torture to yours. So please leave me alone."

"You seem to hold me responsible for your presence here," he replied, carefully keeping his voice pitched low. "That is not true. There is no time now to convince you of this. I only urge you to listen to me carefully, and you will gain your freedom. If you do not, we will both lose our lives."

"Go away, I tell you!" A flush appeared on Rosalind's cheeks, and Janus, glancing at her quickly, thought she looked exceptionally pretty despite the dirt on her face and the condition of her clothes.

He waited deliberately until Lieutenant Jerez spun on his heel to walk in the opposite direction, and then turned to Rosalind. Raising a hand, he slapped her expertly across the side of her face. Although the blow was not hard, it was totally unexpected, and Rosalind gasped. But she neither flinched nor pulled away, and Janus, once again warily watching the Spanish officer outside, felt that she truly did not fear him.

"In time to come," he said huskily, his deepest instincts stirred, "you will understand why it was necessary for me to strike you. Now you will listen. I am no longer in the employ of Spain. If I am apprehended I will be killed instantly or returned to Madrid and there sentenced to death on the rack. Two days ago I fought a duel with the Intendant of Louisiana, Baron de Carondelet, and he is no longer alive. Therefore, I must flee with you from this village and from the domain of Spain.

"If you remain here, the Cherokees will in time break your mind and your body. Hence in my opinion there is no choice for you, but I cannot spend more time urging you to come with me. If you wish to go, you must say so now, immediately."

Rosalind breathed deeply and stood very straight. "Look at me," she commanded.

Janus deliberately turned away from Lieutenant Jerez and stared straight into her eyes. Rosalind found herself unable to think rationally, but every instinct told her that he was not lying. She felt an urge to trust him, and her blind, unreasoning desire to be at his side swept away every other consideration.

"All right," she said. "I'll go with you."

There was no change in his expression, but as he again returned his gaze to Lieutenant Jerez his eyes narrowed. "So be it," he murmured. "Say nothing while I deal with that stupid Spaniard."

Nodding, Rosalind was about to agree, but suddenly changed her mind. "Please, Janus—Mr. Elholm—wait."

He frowned. "If we make good our escape, there will be more than sufficient time to converse later, mademoiselle," he said tartly.

"I—I can't leave without Harold. He's being held prisoner here, too, and——"

An unreasonable flame of rage enveloped Janus. "My own skin is more important to me than that of your lover."

She shook back her blond curls and stamped her foot. "I can't run off and leave him here to rot. I can't."

There was a long pause, and at last he sighed quietly. "Very well, mademoiselle. I shall endeavor to secure the release of Jordan too. Do you know where he is at this moment?"

"They—they've kept him in a hut directly behind this one. I haven't seen him, not even once in all this time, but I—I've heard him when they've—hurt him."

"Very well, mademoiselle," he said with considerable annoyance. Then suddenly his voice became crisp and practical. "You are familiar with the use of firearms?"

"Yes."

"Good. In a moment or two the lieutenant out there will turn his back to us for an instant. When he does, I will throw one of my pistols to the mat. Pick it up when he turns his back again and hide it in your dress. Fire it only if necessary. In the event that our attempt to escape should fail, have no hesitation in—using it on yourself."

"I—I understand." Rosalind was barely able to whisper the words. A second later the pistol landed with a soft thud on the pallet. Rosalind watched for her opportunity, retrieved the pistol, examined it quickly, and hid it behind her. At last she was convinced of Janus's sincerity; by handing her the loaded weapon he had given her the power to kill him here and now if she chose to do so.

"Jerez! Come here!" Janus shouted.

The lieutenant approached the hut with alacrity, stopped at the entrance, and saluted with an elaborate flourish. "Yes, Señor General?"

Janus was stern but not unfriendly. "Jerez," he said crisply, "I have decided to take with me to New Orleans the two American prisoners. You will have three fresh horses saddled, and you will bring the man Jordan to me at once."

Lieutenant Jerez began to sweat. "Señor General, I—uh——"

"You hesitate, Jerez? When I give an order I expect it to be obeyed!"

His face pale, the lieutenant began to squirm. "I—I am not permitted to release the prisoners, Señor General. I—even if His Excellency Don Esteban were to make such a request of me, I could not comply with it. Those are my instructions from the Señor Baron de Carondelet, and I dare not disobey him. Please, Señor General, understand and sympathize with my delicate position. It is my last desire on this earth to earn your displeasure, but——"

Janus tapped his left foot haughtily, and his right hand crept to his belt and his remaining pistol. "Who is your second-in-command?" he demanded.

"Sergeant Fiola, sir. He and I are the only white subjects of His Majesty stationed here at the present. But please, Señor General—do not remove me from my command. Do not replace me. I am only a poor soldier who does his duty. And I swear that I will serve you with the same loyalty, the same fidelity——"

"Call the sergeant for me. At once." Janus glowered at him fiercely.

Lieutenant Jerez sagged perceptibly. He would write a long report to the Señor Baron, but the best he could possibly expect in return was a mild vindication and transfer to another remote wilderness outpost. He had made an enemy of the general, and his hopes for promotion were permanently dashed. He turned slowly and cupped his hands. "Sergeant Fiola!" he wailed. "Come here at once. The Señor General wishes to see you!"

No sooner were the words out of his mouth than the butt of a French dueling pistol crashed with great force on the back of Lieutenant Jerez's head, and he dropped unconscious to the dirt floor. Janus wasted no time and instantly dragged the inert body into the farthest corner of the hut. He picked up one end of the pallet to throw over the body of his victim and noted with gratification that Rosalind sprang to help him. She was, he saw, dry-eyed and unemotional. Not many women, he thought, would respond so well in an emergency.

"Remain constantly at my left side," he said quickly, "and pretend that you are much afraid of me." He hurried to the open doorway and stepped into the sunlight with Rosalind beside him. Their timing was perfect, for Sergeant Fiola, a fat, slovenly man, was approaching at a run.

At the sight of an officer of such exalted rank Fiola slowed to what he hoped was a dignified walk. He intended to approach and salute, but discovered to his surprise that the general, accompanied by the woman prisoner, was moving toward him. Uncertain of what to do, he stopped short, executed a precise salute, and stood at rigid attention.

Janus sauntered to within three feet of him and smiled. "Fiola," he said in a kindly tone, "I am sending Lieutenant Jerez elsewhere on a mission of some importance. Therefore, you are in temporary command of this post. Execute your duties properly and I promise you a full month of leave in New Orleans."

"Yes, Señor General, sir. Thank you, Señor General, sir."

"Have three of your best horses saddled and brought to me here," Janus directed. "And send someone at once for the male prisoner, Jordan." One did not explain one's reasons to a mere non-commissioned officer.

"Yes, sir. I will have all done as the Señor General directs." In his excitement Fiola forgot to salute as he bustled off, calling out a series of commands in broken but adequate Cherokee.

Several braves, naked to the waist and without the smears of paint they usually wore in the presence of whites, hurried from a large hut and walked with long, silent strides to a corral at the far end of the village. They ignored Rosalind, who was no longer a curiosity, but they stared with interest at Janus. Neither animosity nor respect was reflected in their faces, and Janus tried to return their looks with the same imperturbable calm, but it was he who glanced away first.

The afternoon sun was waning, and he estimated that twilight was less than an hour distant; that was all to the good. His gaze swept across the collection of mud huts and he tried, as he had done on his arrival, to imprint every physical detail of the little community in his mind. There were five main buildings, each a large hut in which groups of people lived. Four were apparently used by whole families, and the fifth was the dwelling place of the fighting men, who ate and slept apart from the others. If trouble should develop, the danger spot would be the hut of the braves. Smaller structures of mud and straw were scattered here and there, and it was in two of these, set apart from the rest of the village by approximately fifteen yards of open space, that the prisoners were kept.

While Janus wanted to ride directly into the forests with Rosalind and Harold, he knew that such a move would simply arouse the suspicions of the Cherokees, if not of Sergeant Fiola. It would be necessary, therefore, to parade the two Americans through the center of the village to the riverbank, where they would turn south in the direction of New Orleans. After they were out of sight of Bogalusa, they would swim their horses across the Pearl and would then proceed north on the far bank.

In short, concise sentences Janus told Rosalind his plan, and she nodded almost imperceptibly. She remained poised, ready for any emergency, and he again felt a surge of admiration for her.

Footsteps sounded on the hard dirt behind them, and Janus turned to see Sergeant Fiola strutting toward him. Behind the Spaniard were two Cherokee braves leading a man who was scarcely able to walk. It was something of a shock to recognize the filthy, emaciated creature as Harold Jordan. His hair was long and matted, his once handsome suit was in rags, and beneath the dirt caked on his face he was wan and sickly. His eyes darted first to Rosalind and he tried to smile. Then he saw Janus and his head jerked back.

"Elholm!" he cried in a weak voice. "You lousy bast——"

Sergeant Fiola barked a command in Cherokee that drowned the remainder of Harold's epithet. One of the braves stepped behind the American and kicked him viciously in the small of the back. Harold fell headlong and sprawled in the dust, his arms outstretched. Rosalind ran to him, knelt at his side, and began to whisper to him soothingly. One of the braves would have hauled her off, but Janus gestured him away.

"Tell your Cherokee," he said curtly to Sergeant Fiola, "that the girl may minister to him. She is his woman." He felt a stab of something close to pain as he said the words. Pretending to comfort Harold, Rosalind, he could see, was apprising Harold of the true situation.

Two tall braves approached from the opposite end of the village, leading three horses. Janus was relieved to see that saddles of good Spanish leather had been secured to the mounts; rapid travel for Rosalind and for a weakened Harold would have been virtually impossible had the Indians equipped the animals with only the usual Cherokee saddle, which consisted of a thin blanket folded and then secured with leather thongs.

"Get up, Jordan," Janus commanded in English. "We are expected in New Orleans, and I don't intend to waste my time."

Harold struggled painfully to his feet and looked straight at Janus. A faint trace of a grin appeared on his cracked lips and his left eye fluttered in the suggestion of a wink.

"Place the woman on the brown mare," Janus commanded. "The man will take the smaller gelding." He moved to the largest and strongest of the three horses and swung himself into the saddle. Then he turned back to the sergeant and made his final pronouncement as a brigadier general of Spain. "Fiola," he said, "Lieutenant Jerez will return soon. Very soon. You will then proceed to New Orleans for a holiday of one month. The necessary papers pertaining to your leave will be ready for you at the headquarters of the 12th Aragon Regiment, which I use for purposes of personal administration. I am proud of you, Fiola. Spain is proud of you." He drew his pistol with a flourish and waved it at Rosalind and Harold. "Keep ahead of me, you two," he directed, secretly hoping that the thought would not occur to the sergeant that under no conceivable circumstances would a general ride alone for two days and nights through the wilderness with a brace of prisoners.

The little cavalcade started off slowly through the village, with Rosalind in the lead, Harold directly behind her, and Janus some paces to the rear. If trouble developed now, the Dane thought, he could at the very least fight a delaying action and give the others a chance to get away.

One hundred or more Indians crowded in the doorways of the large huts and stood outside in the dust to watch the three whites depart. A few children cackled and jeered at the captives who were being taken away, and the squaws grimaced unpleasantly, making no effort to hide their hatred. But the men of the Cherokee village were blank-faced and unmoving, and not even in their black eyes was there any visible sign of emotion.

Sergeant Fiola stood at salute, holding a rusty, ancient dress sword stiffly in front of his nose and chin. Janus waved to him, then nodded a grave farewell to the Cherokees. A moment later the three riders reached the scrub pines that lined the riverbank, and the village and its inhabitants disappeared from view. This was too easy, Janus told himself—far too easy.

"Not so fast, mademoiselle," he called. "Jordan, if you feel sufficiently strong, take the lead and let Mademoiselle ride between us. About two thousand feet ahead the river turns sharply to the right. When we reach that place we will cross to the other shore. Remain as quiet as possible."

Harold spurred ahead, and Rosalind allowed him to pass her on the narrow trail. Within a few minutes the little party reached the bend in the river, and the crossing of the shallow stream was accomplished without incident. As Janus pushed his horse up the embankment on the eastern side, he found the two Americans waiting for him.

"Our worst ordeal lies ahead," he told them. "If Fiola and the savages have not yet found the unconscious body of Lieutenant Jerez, they will soon discover him. It is possible that Jerez may already be awake, in which case I blame myself for being soft-hearted. It would have been better had I killed him. In any case, I consider it likely—more than likely—that the Cherokees will soon set out in pursuit of us. And if we are caught we will be murdered at once."

"You—you don't think we can get away, then?" Harold was plainly showing the results of his many days of starvation and torture.

"We've got to escape. Here is my plan—we will strike inland for a distance of perhaps half a mile, then we will ride north. Toward Franklin. We must, I fear, ride all night. I am sorry, mademoiselle, if the prospect of enduring such fatigue distresses you, but we have no choice. It is either ride on—or perish."

Rosalind spoke for the first time. "I'll do whatever you think we need to do, Janus," she said simply.

"Good. We will break our own trail through the wood. It is vital that we do not pass close to Bogalusa as we move north. At dawn, if all is well, we will again ride to the Pearl and will follow it north. Jordan, how is your sense of direction in the forests?"

Harold hesitated for an instant. "Not too good, Elholm," he admitted at last. "Even in these scrub pines I'm afraid I'd get lost."

"Very well. Then I will take the lead. Stay close behind me in the darkness, and speak only when absolutely necessary. Remember that our danger is great until we leave Bogalusa far behind." Without further ado, Janus walked his horse into the tangled underbrush.

For almost thirty minutes the trio rode in silence. The night had settled down, and save for the occasional faint noise of an animal scurrying off through the woods, Janus and the two Americans heard no sound but the hoofbeats of their own horses. Then a short time after they once more turned toward the north, they heard a rifleshot, followed by two more in quick succession.

Janus halted immediately, his eyes grave. "Our deception is

discovered," he called softly over his shoulder. "They search for us, and from their shots I judge that they mistakenly think they have found us. It will not take a long time for them to learn their error. I warn you that the odds against us are great. We are no match for a band of Cherokee braves in country which they know and which we do not."

Harold exhaled noisily. "You're right, Elholm," he said, his voice unexpectedly clear and strong. "The three of us will never make it."

"What alternative do you suggest?"

Inching his horse closer, Harold paused before replying. "You and Roz deserve your chance more than I do, Elholm. The only way for two of us to get away is for the third to act as a decoy and make a great deal of noise. I elect myself for the job. Maybe I'll break clear, too, and maybe I won't—but your chances will be a damn sight better."

Rosalind found it difficult to speak. "No, Harold," she begged. "I—appreciate what you're offering to do, and I know you mean it for me, but I can't let you——"

Janus broke in gruffly: "You can't, Jordan. We'll all escape together—or be caught and killed together."

By way of answer Harold dug his heels into the horse's flanks, and the animal crashed loudly through the undergrowth, heading south once more. "We'll do this *my* way!" he cried shrilly. "Take care of her, Elholm. Good-by, Roz! Good-by—and God bless you!"

Chapter XVII

They sat side by side before a small, bright fire a few yards from a running stream, eating ravenously and saying little. Janus sliced a slab of broiled, smoking meat, speared it with his poniard, and handed the knife to Rosalind. Ignoring the dripping juice, she ate around the edges, seemingly absorbed in the task. Janus watched her as he consumed his portion with his bare fingers and thought that she looked extraordinarily beautiful.

"The first thing I'm going to do when we find a town," Rosalind remarked dreamily, "is to buy a respectable dress. They'll have to trust me for payment, of course. I'll have no money until I'm back in Nashville and can send it to them."

Janus regarded her solemnly, but his eyes twinkled. "There is something amiss with the gown you now wear?"

"It's so torn and filthy that it—it's hardly a dress any more."

"In my opinion it sets off your loveliness to perfection." Finishing the last of the meat, he licked his fingers and edged closer.

Rosalind moved away quietly. "Have you ever tasted bear steak before?"

"Never." He inched closer still. "Nor would I have believed that bear could be found so far to the south." His right arm tried to circle her waist, but she twisted away and jumped to her feet.

"Mr. Elholm," she said defiantly, "I am very grateful to you for your great courage in saving me from bondage. I am especially in your debt for your attempt to rescue Harold too. May he be—more safe at this moment than I am! I have hoped with all my heart that you now intended to see me safely back to the United States and that, as a gentleman, you would insure to the best of your ability that I remain unmolested—by anyone.

"If this is your intent, I thank you again. But if your purpose is to seduce me, to make me your mistress, then I prefer that you kill me here and now."

Although startled by the intensity of her outburst, Janus was in no wise dismayed. "I cannot see myself shooting you with one of the few bullets that remain to provide protection and food for us in our travels. And before you make another impassioned little speech, let me only say that it had never occurred to me that you find me repugnant."

"What makes you think I do?" Her fury had chilled into an air of icy remoteness.

"Every word you have uttered, mademoiselle."

"I'm afraid you know nothing of women, sir."

"I?" In spite of her seriousness, he laughed again.

"You, sir." Rosalind remained uncompromising and firm. "Your encounters with trollops and camp followers and—and fashionable tarts have equipped you with a lesser wisdom than you think you possess. I shall say it in a different way. You must obviously know very little about ladies, Mr. Elholm."

The grin disappeared from his mouth, and he stared at her hard. "I have at no time forgotten that you are a lady, mademoiselle. You have given me no opportunity to dismiss the fact from my mind. However, you need have no further fears. I will not force my attentions upon you."

"Thank you . . . Janus." She softened immediately.

The Dane did not respond to her change of mood but remained cold. "Lest you delude yourself and believe your power to be greater than it is, permit me to enlighten you. Before us there stretches a journey of hundreds of miles. The searching parties of my former colleague may at any moment stumble upon our trail. There are swarms of savages and untold natural hazards between ourselves and the safety of what you Americans call your civilization. Our sole hope for survival, considering that neither of us knows much about wilderness travel, lies in the continued and uninterrupted amity of our relationship. Therefore, rather than jeopardize your life or my own, I freely promise you that your honor will be safe in my keeping."

Rosalind was about to respond, when he twisted on his heel and returned to the fire. Picking up his poniard from the ground, he deftly fished a chunk of sizzling meat from the coals and, resuming his squatting position, began to eat it. His back was turned squarely toward her.

Although more of the steak awaited her, Rosalind had no appetite. In a way she could not analyze, the victory had been Janus's, not hers. Feeling very lonely, she wandered a short distance into the wild brush. Under no circumstances did she want Janus to know that she was crying.

Governor Sevier and Colonel Jim Robertson exchanged long glances and nodded. Incredible though Harold Jordan's story was, they both believed that he was telling the truth. His gaunt appearance, the deep lines in his face, and the suffering in his eyes were in themselves sufficient indications that he was not lying.

Harold hitched forward in his chair, the most comfortable in Robertson's big Nashville house, and dug a fist into his knee. "I still can't believe my good luck," he said. "They almost caught me four times, and four times I managed to get away. Without knowing where I was headed, I reached the Mississippi River—and didn't even know it was the Mississippi. That's where the fur traders from Chickasaw Bluffs found me—and almost murdered me, thinking I was a Spaniard. I had the devil's own time convincing them that I was a Frank and that I had no intention of telling the Spanish river patrols they were sneaking contraband into our territory. They finally believed me, as you see, and brought me north."

John Sevier made a small notation on a sheet of paper with a stubby quill pen and frowned. "And you don't know what became of Miss Walker or Elholm?"

"No, sir." Harold's face contorted. "I saw nothing more of them after I rode off from them near Bogalusa. I wish——"

"So do I." Jim Robertson was emphatic. "That devil Elholm could tell us a heap more about the Spaniards' military plans than you've done. You say you have no idea how large a force they intend to employ or when the attack is scheduled to take place?"

"No, Colonel. I've told you everything I know. I'm pretty positive they'll move north sometime this spring. I gathered that impression pretty definitely from Baron de Carondelet when he was here in Nashville. But I can't name any specific dates."

"You've given us a good bit of information, Jordan, so you needn't feel too bad about the things you *can't* tell us." Sevier tapped the pen lightly on the edge of the small desk at which he was sitting. "We'll put all the men you've named as Spanish agents under arrest, and we'll question them. You understand, of course, that we may have to set some of them free again. It's merely your word against theirs."

"I know that, General Sevier." Harold clenched his fist. "I keep wishing I had that full list of the baron's. Then you could clean out every last spy in the state."

"As we don't have it, we'll do the best we can with what you've told us." Colonel Robertson stretched his long, thin legs. "Maybe one of the men you've named can give us more precise military information."

Sevier stood up, walked to the window, and stared with unseeing eyes at a row of hickory trees on the Robertson lawn. "Jim," he said softly, "I've had a notion cross my mind, and I reckon the same thought has occurred to you. If young Elholm was really a key man in Spanish planning, they must be as panicky as a flock of wild geese when you flush 'em out. Provided they haven't caught him, the dons must be mighty scared right now. Imagine how I'd feel if I knew *you* were running down to New Orleans!"

Robertson's thin, straight lips twisted in a smile. "I reckon I wouldn't get my proper sleep for a few nights," he declared. "Sure, Jack. If old Miró and Galvez haven't found Elholm, they know they've got to attack soon—mighty damned soon—or not at all. They can't take the chance that he'll come to us and try to sell us the whole portfolio of their strategy."

"Exactly." The governor began to pace up and down the length of the room. "And that means we've got to be ready for war—at any time."

"Mmm. We are ready." Robertson stood up too. "In the same hour that I sent a messenger asking you to come to Nashville as fast as you could, I ordered a full company of scouts off to our border with Louisiana. They're to report back to me in a hurry if they see anything suspicious. Anything at all."

Sevier stopped abruptly and hooked his thumbs into his worn rawhide belt. "We'll need to put the militia on the alert too. But we've got to do it without alarming every last man and woman in Franklin. Or letting the Spaniards' agents know that we're preparing. That's going to take a bit of plain and fancy doing."

Immersed in their problems, the two men had apparently forgotten Harold, who tried to remain inconspicuous. He kept silent, aware that his own future remained to be settled, but unwilling to intrude himself when greater issues were being discussed. But John Sevier surprised him.

"Jordan," he said suddenly, "we've left you sitting up in a tree like a mountain cat that's been chased by a pack of dogs, and that isn't very fair. What'll we do with you?"

Harold found himself unable to speak for several seconds. "I—I'll accept any punishment you think is fitting, sir," he said at last.

Once again the older men exchanged looks, and Sevier cleared his throat lightly. "What would you say, Jordan, if we offered you a post in the militia?" he asked.

"Please don't mock me, sir." Harold choked with emotion. "I'd give anything for a chance to fight those Spanish bastards."

"You have it." There was a note of finality in Sevier's voice.

"I—I don't know how to thank you, General. I give you my solemn word, I won't let you down again. Not you, and not Franklin."

"I know that. It's why we're wiping out the past."

Governor Sevier dropped a hand on Harold's shoulder. "You aren't going to have an easy time in these next weeks, son," he said. "First of all, I don't think Nashville is a safe place for you. If the dons learn you've returned, they'll send after you again. So I propose that you ride down to the Nolichucky, and we'll swear you into the militia company there. I'll stake my life on the loyalty of every last one of those lads. You'll be secure with them, and you'll have a real chance to redeem yourself when the fighting starts."

Overcome, Harold bobbed his head in agreement. After his treachery he had not expected complete exoneration; after all he had suffered at the hands of the Spaniards and Cherokees, he had not anticipated this sudden release from fear of them. He lifted his head and for the first time looked into John Sevier's eyes. "There's—there's just one thing, sir," he said. "I keep hoping—that is—there's always the chance——"

"Of course." Few people had ever seen Sevier so gentle. "If we receive any word about Rosalind Walker, or if she should reappear, you'll be notified at once. I give you my hand on it."

Chapter XVIII

"My lands, Roz! Stop that fidgetin' or ye'll have me plumb wore out!" Min Dolson stamped hard on the foot pedal of her loom to emphasize her words, and tugged so hard at the thread that the linen strand snapped. "Now see what ye've made me do! All this fussin' and stewin' and carryin' on—where does it get ye?"

Rosalind looked slowly around the crude, comfortable Dolson living room and thought that it represented home. It was unbearable that she should be at her ease while Janus was made to suffer. "It isn't right that they keep him locked up in jail, Min!" she cried. "He came back here to help, not to connive against us. And he brought me home, didn't he? He saved me from the worst——"

Min ran a new line of linen through her loom with expert speed and adjusted her spools. "Ye've had a letter from down Nolichucky way from your Harold, haven't ye? Well, ye ought to be thinkin' o' him instead o' that wuthless, good-for-nothin' — Ah, land sakes! It ain't my place to go pokin' my nose where it don't belong! But I'll tell ye this much. I can't say as I c'n rightly blame Gin'ral Sevier nor Colonel Robertson for takin' no chances, and ye wouldn't either if ye wasn't so soft in the head over that Elholm critter. Suppose ye was the gov'nor, and along

comes a foreigner who done awful things to yer country and
even showed ye a slip of paper that says he's goin' to own every
last smidgin o' the land that American folks is livin' on. Ye'd up
and throw him in jail too!"

"Maybe I would, Min—for a time." Rosalind made a supreme
effort to curb her agitation. "But after I became convinced that
the man was sincere and was honestly trying to help, I'd accept
him and not keep him cooped up in a cell."

"Could be the gov'nor ain't convinced yet."

Rosalind arose and shook out her skirts. "Janus Elholm saved
me from slavery and he saved my life. So even if I didn't have a
—high personal regard for him, I'd be a dreadful person if I failed
to do what I could. I'm going down to the courthouse right now
and speak to Governor Sevier."

"Ain't he turned ye away now, three days in a row?"

"Well, yes. But Andy Jackson has promised to make an appointment for me, and I'm sure the governor will listen to him."

"Lands, that Jackson boy! I declare he eats blazin' logs o'
kindlin' for breakfast every mornin', he has that much fire sparkin'
in him. O' course he believes all this wild talk that an army o'
Spaniards is skulkin' up on us, but me 'n' Nat has come t' know
Andy right well, and I tell ye plain that he's achin' 'n' itchin' so
bad for a shootin' fight that he'd as lief start a war hisself."

"You'll believe Janus all right, all of you—when it's too late,"
Rosalind said acidly. "But let me tell you something, Min. If no
one else will ride out against the Spaniards, Andy will. And he
won't go alone. Because I'll ride with him!"

A crowd of farmers, trappers, homesteaders, and stray Creek
Indians lounged in the sunshine outside the two-story Davidson
County courthouse. An enterprising huckster was selling roasted
corn and mugs of lukewarm ginger beer to those interested in
spending a ha'penny, and two of the women from river-front

houses strolled along the edge of the dirt path, swinging their hips carelessly.

Men smoked their pipes placidly and exchanged an occasional idle remark. Then they settled back again, rousing themselves only when another militia leader rode up to the front of the building, threw his reins to a stableboy, and disappeared inside. For two full days there had been a steady stream of traffic in and out of the courthouse, and the citizens of Nashville had speculated on what was happening until they tired of the sport. Sooner or later they would be told news of a momentous nature, but in the meantime no one was enlightening them, and the prominent men of the state were maintaining a tight-lipped silence.

It was true that last night at the Blue Grass there was almost a leak. Speaker of the House William Cocke had liberally sampled his favorite potion of raw corn liquor washed down with draughts of ale and had become expansive. But when his drinking companions had gingerly opened the subject of the incessant round of conferences taking place he had snorted and had taken himself off to bed in silent, somewhat drunken dignity.

A new diversion was apparently in store this morning, and the hangers-on lifted their heads to gape as Rosalind Walker rode into the square and dismounted with the delicate grace that the town had come to expect of her. There was an immediate buzz of comment as the men followed her with their eyes. The prostitutes from the river taverns seemed incensed, however, and deliberately turned their backs. But the men's eyes were fastened on Rosalind, and they failed to note the rudeness of the women.

"Thar she be."

"Um-hum. Right fancy filly with a right pert figger. How'd ye like to go travelin' through the Louisiana with her, Phil?"

"I reckon it'd give me somethin' t' r'member 'n' ponder on while I cooled my arse in prison, that's for sure."

"Ken ye my wife's sister, Annabel? She heard it straight from Mistress White, the greengrocer's mother, that yon wench was neither slave nor prisoner in Donland, but of her own will entered into a fancy house in New Orleans, that nest o' sin, and has come home again, brazen as ye please, with her purse bulgin' and heavy with the gold o' harlotry."

Rosalind walked with her head high, looking neither to right nor left. She heard the low murmur, and her imagination did the rest. Although her flesh crawled at what they must be whispering about her, she knew she could not cringe or run away. It was inevitable that Nashville should gossip after her long journey with Janus through the wilderness.

A youthful figure bounded down the steps and catapulted toward her, his long, unruly mane of hair flying in the breeze. "I've been watching for you, ma'am," Andrew Jackson shouted with his customary exuberance. "Come indoors—and brace yourself."

Rosalind stopped him at the entrance. "There's bad news Andy. What is it?"

"Step in and I'll tell you more than you'll want to hear. But I'll say nothing out here where the ears of loafers stretch like a strip of wet leather in tanning brine."

Hurrying into the cool, dark corridor, Rosalind turned and stood erect. "Well, Andy? Don't be kind and don't be tactful I want to know the very worst, quickly."

"Here it is, then. Jack Sevier sent three men south, and they ran smack into the advance guard of what seems to be a powerful Spanish and Indian force heading in our direction. Thaddeus Hatcher was killed, but Jeff Wyatt and his brother fought their way clear and returned."

"But that proves Janus has been telling the truth!" Rosalind was radiant, a crushing weight lifted from her shoulders.

"By Jupiter and Moses, ma'am, wait until I've finished. He's told the truth and so has Harold Jordan. But the drooling apes of the governor's council are in a right ugly mood, I can tell you The militia is being summoned—and meantime your Danish friend has been sentenced to twenty years in prison for conspiring with the enemy. Yes, and they've added ten years more for good measure on the charge that he had a hand in your abduction."

Aghast, Rosalind could scarcely believe her ears. "But that's insane gibberish, Andy!"

Jackson stroked his long chin. "Aye, that it is. As your attorney I tried to plead with them, but I was told to shut my trap or be denied my place in the columns that will march against the dons." His eyes begged silently for understanding and forgiveness.

"But that's preposterous, Andy!" Rosalind was rapidly losing her temper.

"By Jupiter and Moses, so it is, ma'am. We fought a war against the English to guarantee every man the right to a fair trial and the right to have his say, but some of these high-and-mighty Franks have forgotten what it feels like to wear a buckskin shirt, they enjoy the feel of that fine linen against their skin so much. Someday us younger men are going to get ourselves elected to the Commons, and we'll change all that. But meantime I don't see what can be done for Elholm. Thanks to him and to Jordan, we have time to mobilize, but there's consarned little Elholm will get out of it."

Rosalind began to stride down the hall, and Jackson had to lope along at her side. "Where is the meeting taking place, Andy?"

"In the chamber of the circuit-rider judge, down at the end of the corridor. But you can't go in there, ma'am."

Not replying, she increased her pace, and the stubborn set of her jaw indicated trouble ahead. Turning a bend in the hall, she saw two sentries posted outside a closed door. That, she swiftly concluded, was where Governor Sevier and his lieutenants were closeted. She marched straight for the room, ignoring the gaping of the two militiamen and shaking off the detaining hand of Andrew Jackson.

"Please, ma'am. You'll only boil them up, and they'll throw you out. You won't help Mr. Elholm—or yourself, either. And if those two boys with the muskets there get rough, you could get yourself hurt."

"Let them dare to stop me!" Her cheeks flushed and her eyes aflame, Rosalind stepped defiantly between the astonished militiamen. Quailing under the impact of righteous feminine wrath, they made no attempt to halt her as she picked up her skirts with one hand, threw open the door with the other, and swept into the chambers. When Andrew Jackson would have followed her, however, they recovered quickly, slammed the door shut, and barred his path with their muskets. They could cope with a mere man but were relieved beyond measure to leave the lady to their peers within. Neither of them envied the first gentlemen of Franklin at that moment. . . .

To Rosalind's chagrin, the room was empty save for a single man who was sitting at a large table, writing industriously. The door on the far side was open, and she could see the members of the council beyond it, chatting in small groups and smoking.

"Good day, Major Elholm." Rosalind spoke civilly, but her disdain was apparent.

The governor's adjutant looked up, startled, then jumped to his feet. "Mistress Walker. Your servant, ma'am. If you have business before the governor and his council, I'll have to ask you to wait. We have taken a brief recess."

"I'll wait." She made no attempt to sit, but stood erect, tapping a slippered foot.

After a discreet silence Major George Elholm coughed and blinked at her through his glasses. "Is there anything I can do for you, Mistress Walker?"

"You, sir, should be ashamed of yourself. That you could treat your own brother so abominably is beyond——"

"I have no brother, Mistress Walker. As I informed the governor and the houses of the legislature several days ago, the man called Janus Elholm is in no way related to me. Through a—sense of personal weakness I permitted him to make such a claim. But as I warned him, when his interests clashed with those of my country, I exposed his deception."

Rosalind bit her lip. "Then I presume, sir, that you have a lesser interest in seeing justice done than any of the others here. Revenge must be very pleasing to you."

He stiffened, but his voice remained low and quiet. "I fail to understand your allegation, ma'am."

"I don't think you do. You'll happily let Janus rot in a foul prison for years, even though he shouldn't be there. You'll——"

"Oh, that." He grinned and patted her on the shoulder with no trace of condescension. "If you've come to make another plea to the governor to release your friend from our jail, you may save yourself the breath and the time. Master Elholm is already a free man and has been for some hours."

Her knees gave way, and she sank to a hard bench. "You have no right to jest with me, sir," she stammered.

"I am not joking, Mistress Walker. My namesake requested an appearance before the council. And as several captains as well as a number of senators wished to question him, his application was granted. He was here immediately after breakfast."

She wanted to laugh and cry, but she did neither of these things and instead sat very still and managed to look even more beautiful than usual. "If you please, Major," she said at last in a very small voice, "how did Janus persuade the council—to reverse the sentence? What did he——"

Again Major Elholm smiled. "You know the young man better than I, Mistress Walker. It should be unnecessary for me to tell you that his persuasive powers are—hmmm—considerable. When he had finished speaking to us, Governor Sevier called for a vote, which was almost unanimous in Master Elholm's favor."

"Oh. And he—he's now left Nashville, I suppose?" She stared hard at the dirty, roughhewn floor boards.

"No, ma'am. He's still here." George regarded her with quiet compassion. "His release from prison was conditional, and he has an obligation to perform for the state before he goes off."

She forced her eyes to meet his. "But he's—he's going back to Europe eventually, I suppose."

"He hasn't confided his plans to me, Mistress Walker. But I would guess that he'll tell you about them himself."

She drew herself to her feet and tried hard to master her pride. "Thank you very much, Major. But we both know that isn't so. If Janus has been free since early morning, he would have—come to me by now if that had been his intention."

Rosalind twisted away and strode rapidly toward the entrance through which she had come. It was all too clear that she was crying. Watching her go, George sighed and wished he were ten or fifteen years younger. There were times when a bachelor's life lost its savor for him, and never had the taste of his single state been more flat or insipid.

As the call to militiamen spread through the county, a crowd of considerable consequence began to gather in front of the courthouse, and by the time the first platoons were formed, the square in front of the building was thick with onlookers, most of them women and children. There were few men too old to serve against the approaching enemy, and the handful of middle-aged citizens whom Colonel Robertson had ordered to remain and maintain order at home sulked because they were not permitted to accompany their younger brothers.

There was considerable speculation as to the location of the secret rendezvous point with battalions from other counties, and some of the women loudly proclaimed their intention of following their husbands and spending one last night with them. But the scheme was squelched before it could gather momentum: someone had told John Sevier what was afoot, and a proclamation was read in the open square forbidding any but duly qualified and sworn members of the militia to travel on the roads and paths leading south and west.

Janus, wearing old buckskin trousers and shirt, a fur hat, and soft Indian shoes, which George Elholm had loaned to him, stood in the shadows of a huge chestnut tree on the courthouse lawn, buckling on his sword and watching the crowds. His lips were twisted in a familiar, cynical smile as he thought that no European army would permit a mere enlisted man to carry a sword. Here such rules were unknown; every man provided his own weapons, and he brought to the campaign any instrument of destruction that might be utilized in killing a potential foe.

But one significant development encouraged Janus. Despite his lowly status, his knowledge of Spanish tactics and his experiences were not going to be wasted, and he had been assigned to no militia company. Instead he had been ordered to serve alongside John Sevier's orderly, and presumably the commander of the American expedition would call upon him for advice when necessary. Hence the prospects of the campaign were not as dismal as he had first feared they would be.

Amid a roll of drums and a fanfare of trumpets two platoons of infantrymen marched raggedly out of the courthouse square and swung down the road leading south. Several small boys cheered shrilly, but most of the women remained silent. No one knew better than they the enormity of the issues at stake. If their men were defeated, nothing would save them and their homes from the Spanish invader, and only a formal declaration of war against Madrid by the feeble Congress of the Confederation would give them a faint hope that the land would someday be reconquered and restored to American sovereignty. Looking at the rows of intent, solemn faces, Janus stirred uneasily. This was a phase of warfare with which he had never concerned himself, and it was uncomfortable in the extreme to contemplate a campaign from any point of view other than that of pitting brain and brawn against an enemy equally determined to use skill and strength in pursuit of victory.

A glimpse of blond hair in the rear of the crowd drove all thoughts but one from Janus's mind, and he elbowed his way through the throng until he reached Rosalind Walker's side. "Good afternoon, mademoiselle." He tried to draw her away from the people who hemmed them in on every side.

Min Dolson, whom he had not noticed, placed herself directly in front of Rosalind, her hands on her hips. "Mr. Elholm," she said flatly, "you caused Roz enough misery already. Why don't ye act like a gent'man 'n' leave her be?"

Peering over her shoulder, he tried to speak directly to Rosalind. "I have displeased you, mademoiselle?"

"Leave her be, I say!" The strident note in Min's voice was beginning to attract the attention of the crowd.

Rosalind stepped in front of her friend and gently but very firmly pushed Min aside. "I'll handle this myself. Mr. Elholm, you have your freedom again——"

"Indeed I have." He made a futile attempt to catch her hand, which she snatched away. "And I have been waiting here for you. I was not permitted to leave the courthouse square, but I was in hopes you would come here, and so you have." He drank in every detail of her appearance, from the light blue scarf that partly concealed, partly revealed her waves of golden hair to the frilly lace piping on her pink linen gown.

She spoke too softly for those nearby to hear. But even the most casual bystander was aware of her dignity and pride. "You will no doubt be riding for Philadelphia or New York in the immediate future, Mr. Elholm. I am sure you want to return as rapidly as possible to Europe and to—to your own kind."

"I am riding against the Spanish."

Rosalind's lips parted, and she blinked. "You, sir?"

"I, mademoiselle."

There was a considerable thaw in Rosalind's demeanor, and she began to twist one end of her neck scarf with her thumb and forefinger. "Which regiment will you command, Janus?"

"None, mademoiselle. I have been enlisted as a private soldier in the militia of Nashville."

She shook her head. "This doesn't sound like you, Janus. Why have you done it? Why?"

"If I were to tell you that I have gained an appreciation of the American concept of freedom, that I believe it worth a man's life to fight for that concept, you would laugh at me."

"I'm not laughing." Rosalind leaned toward him, but he drew back.

"That was not my sole reason." For an instant he seemed at a loss for words, then his familiar, cynical smile flashed. "I am told that the company from the Nolichucky will ride through Nashville sometime late today."

"Yes, I've heard about it." She was not looking at him now, but stared at a curving limb of a dead tree.

"You will see Jordan, of course?"

"Of course."

Janus tried to be casual but succeeded only in sounding curt. "In the event that you take up residence in Nashville after you are married," he said, "I trust that you will allow me to call upon you someday—to call upon you both. You see, I intend to return here, and it is only proper that I be permitted to pay my respects to Jordan and to—his wife."

He reached out unexpectedly, snatched her scarf, and jammed it into the deep pocket of his leather shirt. Then he stepped forward, kissed her lightly, and promptly started off toward the center of the courthouse square. Rosalind leaned back weakly against the trunk of the tree and watched him as his figure merged with those of the scores of other men in buckskin. Not once did he look back.

Chapter XIX

For four days and the better part of four nights the long, thin column sliced a path through forests and uninhabited valleys, across hills and plateaus and rivers, until at last it came to a halt beside the placid banks of a body of water to be known in later times as Lake Wilson. Here the weary foot soldiers washed their clothes and swam, joked and stole whiskey and rum from each other, grumbled about their tasteless rations of jerked meat and dried corn—but ate every morsel of food they could snatch.

Meanwhile their leaders studied maps, held endless rounds of conferences, and patiently counted noses and rifles as reinforcements arrived from every part of the state of Franklin. Day by day, hour by hour, the newcomers appeared at the rendezvous place; there were organized companies of militiamen from the Holston and Nolichucky, small bands of farmers from the rich lands of the central plateau, and silent, sharp-eyed lone woodsmen from the Western frontier. Word of the impending disaster had spread over mountains and rivers with the speed of a brush fire blazing in the dry season, and the Franks responded to a man.

Seventy-two hours after the main body had pitched camp beside the lake, Colonel Jim Robertson announced jubilantly to his brother officers that the command now comprised more than sixteen hundred men. Even those least concerned with facts and figures, like Lieutenant Andrew Jackson, were impressed. Rarely during the late bitter struggle for the nation's freedom had the West mustered a force of such size.

Elation was universal throughout the encampment as word was passed that, despite the continued absence of an overdue cavalry patrol from the eastern mountains, the march against the Spaniards would be resumed in full strength at dawn. Everyone dined heartily, and the younger men threw caution to the balmy winds and greedily drank their last reserves of strong spirits. One squad from the Cumberland became gloriously and noisily drunk on a raw mash of partially distilled potatoes and corn, while nearby in a furious dice game men gambled their homes, their livestock, and their furniture with cheerful abandon.

Squatting on the ground as he brewed a tin of tea over a small fire, Janus Elholm watched the festivities with misgivings. It was quite possible that the Franks could give a respectable account of themselves if sober and held in check. Drunk and undisciplined as they were, the odds were now against them. Feeling the soles of his feet gingerly through his soft moccasins, he wondered if he could ever develop the stamina these Americans displayed on the march. He had to admit that they could cover more territory at a faster pace than any army he had ever seen.

The prevailing opinion among the lieutenants, ensigns, and warrant officers of the army was that Colonel Jim Robertson was too old to be second-in-command of the expedition. They whispered to each other that his younger brother, Charles, also a senior colonel, was better fitted for a post entailing so much responsibility. Not even the fearless firebrands among the junior contingent like Calvin MacGinley or Andy Jackson dared to express such views aloud, however, for Colonel Jim was sensitive about his age, and his pleasant demeanor had been known to erupt into a volcano of fiery intensity when he became sufficiently aroused.

But even Jim Robertson himself was ready to admit tonight that he was growing old. The army had been on the march again for five days, and he was openly and admittedly tired. It was scant comfort to look at the faces of his brother, of John Sevier, Henry Conway, and George Elholm, and to read there the undeniable fact that they were bone-weary too. War had become less of an adventure, less of a lark to the leaders of the West in the years since they had helped send the redcoats packing.

Colonel Jim smothered a yawn and tapped with the point of a hunting knife at a spot on the map spread out before him. "George," he said, coughing slightly, "move that damned candle a mite closer, and take care the tallow grease doesn't burn the map. Now then, gentlemen, gather round me again. Our position is approximately right here—about fifteen miles into Spanish territory. Those who wish may claim we're still on American soil, but I maintain we're carrying the war to the enemy, and we'll force him to fight in New Spain."

General Sevier diplomatically moved the knife an inch to the right. "I think this will define our position a bit better, Jim. We're closer to the Mississippi here."

"True," Colonel Conway chimed in. "My scouts say that the river is only a quarter of a mile distant."

"I reckon it at half a mile," Jim Robertson replied, and no one dared argue with him. He who had blazed every major trail in central and western Franklin was manifestly a more expert judge of forest distances than some young whippersnapper who had spent no more than five or ten years exploring wild woodlands.

"We'll reconnoiter personally in the morning, Jim." Sevier was quietly soothing. "I'd like to mosey around anyway so's to pick our own battle site."

"Think we'll have time in the morning?" Colonel Robertson knew he was being needlessly surly, but he was too tired to care.

"How do we know the dons won't be on us shortly after sunup?"

"We can do no more than believe the reports of our own advance scouts, Colonel Robertson." Henry Conway was showing the strain of recent days too. "The estimates of three of my best men are identical: the Spanish Army won't reach the point opposite us until midafternoon."

"Unless they learn we're lying in wait for them."

"Thunderation, sir! That's the gamble we've got to take. Or maybe you're not satisfied with the way I've handled my scouts. If so, you can always remove me from my command at your discretion, sir!" Colonel Conway's face was a bright red, and his voice had become brittle and sharp.

John Sevier spread his hands across the map and leaned on them. "No one is being removed from any command so long as this army is mine. I have full confidence in every one of you. But let me remind you, gentlemen, that unless we begin rowing the skiff in the same direction, she'll sink. Let me also recall to you that the strategy this army will employ is mine and mine alone. I take full responsibility for its success or failure."

Jim Robertson felt suddenly sheepish. "Hell, Jack—we all agreed with you that it's smart to let the don come up to us—and to attack him from the forest."

"Sure," said Henry Conway in the same conciliatory tone. "There's no sounder plan than to hit him when he least expects it —and to make him fight with his back to the river."

Charles Robertson carefully knocked the dead ashes from the bowl of his pipe as he spoke for the first time. "George," he asked in a slow drawl, "can we trust that turncoat namesake of yours?"

"Damned if I know, Charley. Why?"

"Well, it looks to me like maybe we're sticking our necks way out in the open, waiting for a tomahawk to chop them off. We're basing our whole scheme of action on the word of a Spanish traitor who swears the enemy has three thousand men. Suppose old Galvez is marching with five thousand. Then what do we do?"

There was an uncomfortable silence, and one by one the officers looked to their general for an answer. John Sevier smiled and said: "If young Elholm is being honest with us, we're outnumbered only two to one by the Spaniards, and we can clean the living daylights out of them by hitting them from three sides and making them think we're a bigger outfit than we are. On the other hand, if our Danish friend is a party to an extraordinarily clever plot against us, we might find ourselves wiped out. In that case our children will grow up bobbing their heads every time a dandy from Madrid walks by. And our wives—well, I'll put it to you this way. If Janus Elholm is foxing us, I'll plug him through the back of his head with my last bullet.

"But I don't think he's lying. So we'll go right on figuring that there are three thousand in the Spanish column and not plan on double that number."

Colonel Conway stood up and shuffled his boots in the dirt. "I tried to send my scouts in closer for a more accurate estimate of enemy strength, General. But you heard the reports. Galvez has thrown a net of Indians around his whole force, and we can't penetrate them without giving ourselves away."

Sevier leaned back and wiped his hands on the sides of his trousers. "You've done all you could, Henry," he said quietly. "All of us have. I've never run into General Galvez before, but a couple of you have met him, and from your accounts he's an able commander, even if he's a bit old-fashioned and stuffy. But there's a bright side to everything. I'll put it to you this way. I'm mighty glad we have young Master Elholm where we can keep a watch on him—instead of pounding our heads on rocks trying to guess what he'd be planning against us in *his* fancy tent upstream yonder if he were still on the other side."

There was a general laugh, which died abruptly as Lieutenant James Sevier stepped into the tent and saluted smartly. His father looked up, very much annoyed. "Blast and damnation, Son, I told you we weren't to be disturbed."

The youth did not flinch. "Yes, sir. I know your instructions, sir. But there's an officer outside who asks to see you."

"Any officer who wants to interrupt a staff conference should be broken. Who is the upstart, and which of our regiments is he——"

"He's not one of ours, sir. It's—it's Major Eb Tipton, and he's arrived with one hundred and fifty or more mounted and armed men, Pa—I mean General."

Colonel Jim Robertson growled in rage and, drawing his pistol from his belt, he slapped it down on the map. "If those pestiferous Tiptons think they can annoy us with their fool private wars when we have the fight of our lives on our hands, I aim to take a few minutes of breathing spell and scalp every last one of them, just like I would a redskin who got in my way."

The others nodded assent, but John Sevier was curiously gentle. "Tell Eb Tipton to come in, Son," he said. "I'm always happy to see a neighbor, 'specially when we're both traveling in a far country."

Jim Sevier ducked through the flap, and a moment later Major Tipton entered, bending low as he passed through the opening. He straightened, trying to hide his embarrassment as he executed the most formal of salutes.

"Evening, Eb," John Sevier said conversationally. "You're a mighty long way from home. I hope you haven't brought a posse all these miles to put me under arrest on some tom-fool charge or other."

"No, sir." Eb Tipton's voice was hoarse and tired. "I've got a posse with me, right enough—one hundred and sixty-three of us, me included. But we're out looking for Spaniards this time, Jack. I heard a rumor you knew where the don hunting was pretty good this season, and I thought maybe you could lead us to a few pelts."

The silence was thick, and Jim Robertson coughed. "Eb," he said, "many's the time I warmed your seat so's you had to eat your supper from the mantel, and I'll do it again if you talk riddles at us. Tell us straight—have you come to join us?"

"That's right, Uncle Jim. First squadron of North Carolina cavalry militia at your service, gentlemen." A weary grin creased the major's lean face.

"How about that hog-headed old man of yours, Eb? He'd rather see Spaniards on the Holston than let the Franks live there in peace." Charles Robertson remained unconvinced.

Eb Tipton held his temper in check. "Pa is sorry he couldn't come with me, Uncle Charley, but his gout is bothering him something fierce. Doc Sneeders was aiming to bleed him the morning we left. But he sent a message. He said, 'Tell Noli-chucky Jack to nail three of the greasy bastards for me. If he don't, I'll guarantee the whole county votes agin him when he runs for governor of North Carolina.'"

Colonel Jim Robertson was the first to reach young Tipton's side and to wring his hand, but the others were not far behind. A truce in the long-standing feud between Franklin and her parent state in the face of great danger was not an everyday oc-currence, and Charles Robertson produced a flask of applejack from his hip pocket and passed it around. General Sevier re-mained in the shadows, glad that the dim light hid the tears that welled in his eyes. He waited until he was master of himself be-fore he spoke.

"Eb," he said softly, "when this business is finished, we'll all go home and be real neighbors. I call on these officers of mine to bear witness to a promise I want to make right now, through you, to your father. Tell him that the Franks want to bury the black wampum and live side by side with him in peace from this night forward. Your lads and ours are going to lose some blood to-gether, and I reckon there's no closer bond than that. You tell old John this is the finest gift he could deed us, and we'll do what we can to return the favor." He laughed in a deliberate, self-con-scious attempt to break the mood of sentiment. "I heard him say last year that he thought the name of Franklin was a real damn-fool name for a self-respecting state. Well, we'll make him happy and change the name for him. We'll call it Holston or Tennessee —or maybe we'll even call it Tipton!"

The others chuckled, and the flask of applejack again made the rounds. Then Colonel Jim Robertson remembered his duty. "Major Elholm," he said, "be good enough to assign the new battalion to a bivouac area. Then you and Major Tipton come back here for a final briefing. And in the name of a Cherokee chief's pinfeathers, shake a leg! Maybe you youngsters want to stay awake all night just before a battle, but I need my sleep."

George Elholm and Eb Tipton started toward the tent flap, but the North Carolinian turned back. "I plumb near forgot," he said. "Special courier from New York was on his way to see you, Jack, but we had all the good horses with us, so he couldn't travel past Big Bend. He asked me to give you a letter, and I said I would."

General Sevier took the proffered document, murmured his thanks—and then raised his eyebrows as he saw the imprint on the blob of sealing wax. It was the crest of the Congress of the Confederation, and the mere fact that the Government of the United States had seen fit in writing to recognize the existence of Franklin made the document an important one. Not more than twice before during Sevier's long term of office had he received official communications from New York. The others clustered around the tent opening, giving him room as he flipped open the paper and read intently. Conversation ebbed away as the officers watched him for some clue, but their leader remained as blank and uncommunicative as the proverbial wooden-faced Choctaws.

"Jim," said the general with an air so casual that no one was fooled, "do you reckon these youngsters would all clear out of here for a spell and let a couple of old men chew a slab of bacon rind by their lonesome?"

The hint was sufficiently broad to send the officers scurrying out into the night. No sooner were Sevier and Robertson alone than the general began to pace up and down. "Ever meet John Jay?" he inquired bitterly. "Has a long lock of hair that'd make it mighty easy to scalp him. And I'd sure like to hang his pelt from the veranda of my house. Jay and all the other corn-meal-mouthed cowards who are supposed to be heading our American government. I tell you plain, Jim—if that new Constitution isn't ratified by all the states soon, we won't have any country left for those puling capons to lead to wrack and ruin."

Colonel Robertson laid a restraining hand on his superior's shoulder. "The last time I saw you really riled up was when that liaison officer from Connecticut—what was his name?—said the redcoats were better than mountain men, soldier for soldier. And when you wanted to hit him I tamped you down. Well, Jack, I can't do much tamping right now, not unless I know what's causing the fire."

Sevier glared savagely and jammed his hands into his trouser pockets with such force that the side seams were in dire peril of bursting. "Some big-mouth," he said acidly, "went riding off to New York after our first council meeting—and told the Congress that a Spanish attack on us was imminent."

"Probably Freddie Howard," replied Robertson sagely. "I didn't see him after that first session when young Jordan made his way home and told us his story."

"Howard or whoever, Jim. Doesn't much matter. The fat is simmering on the fire for fair now. Jackass John Jay and the whole kit and caboodle of the Foreign Affairs Committee of the Congress are chewing off their fingernails, scared near to death that we're going to get them mixed up in a war with Spain."

"Is that what the letter says?"

"That isn't half. It's from Jay, of course. Just listen to this, Jim: 'By virtue of the authority vested in me by the Congress, you and your militia, your paid troops, your volunteers, and your auxiliary services are hereby and herewith expressly forbidden to take to the field in a campaign, expedition, or sally that will bring you into open armed conflict with the accredited representatives in North America of Charles IV of Spain.' How do you like that, old friend? Our homes, our families—our very liberty—are at stake, and we're forbidden to protect ourselves!"

Jim Robertson laughed silently. "New York and Philadelphia and Boston are a long ride from the frontier, Jack," he said quietly. "Put you or me in the place of those Easterners. Here we are, just getting over a bad war, when along come the crazy wild men of the West, threatening to involve us in another—maybe a bigger fight. We might react the same as Jay and the others have done. Let me see that letter."

Without waiting for a reply, he picked it up from the corner where the general had thrown it, and patiently smoothed it out. The wrinkles at the corners of his eyes grew deeper, and he again laughed to himself, his sense of fatigue utterly banished.

"What's so funny, Jim?"

"Seems I had me an idea a minute or so ago, Jack. And it looks like I'm not the only one. Did you read this paragraph at the finish?"

"I reckon so. Which one do you mean?"

"Where he says he hopes you'll understand the delicacy of the international position he's trying to maintain. Then comes this: 'To you, dear Governor Sevier, my warmest greetings. Colonel Hamilton of New York joins me in extending his personal felicitations, and requests me to assure you of his confidence that you will find an appropriate path to safety through the labyrinth of your difficulties.'"

John Sevier stopped short, and his evil mood evaporated. "I'll be damned! Curse me for a nitwitted sop! I thought Alex Hamilton was trying to soften the blow, but he's throwing us a gemcracker of a suggestion."

"And poor old John Jay was too much of a dullard to see it. There's the real joke, Jack. Can't you see Hamilton dictating the words? You know the way he does it—like he's making a speech.

And there sits Johnny-come-lately Jay, writing it down like a faithful clerk."

The general shook his head ruefully. "Can't say as I'm any smarter than Mr. Jay. I was too busy buzzing like a hornet myself to get a whiff of that hidden flower scent."

Jim Robertson grinned, scratched his ear, and sat down on the ground, where he crossed his legs Indian-fashion. Still fingering the communication from Jay, he folded it carefully and then slipped it into a pile of papers that reposed in a pouch. "Ever skin a polecat cross-grain, Jack?" he asked amiably.

"Umm. Cross-grain, long-grain, backside, belly side. Lots of ways."

"That's what I thought."

"Colonel Robertson, you lumbago-ridden, rheumatic-bent grandpa, I'm glad you were strong enough to hobble along on this little Indian hunt."

The colonel's eyes twinkled merrily. "Never in all my life found anything to beat all like a good, tight little war against redskins, General Sevier—you hotheaded, wet-behind-the-ears young milksop, you!"

Franklin's first citizen pulled a pipe from his pocket and began to fill it with long shreds of tobacco. "What brand of Indians would you say we're going to fight tomorrow, Colonel?"

"Cherokees, I reckon."

"Ummm. Must be Cherokees. Remember to make a note of that in our report to Mr. John Jay and the almighty Congress of the Confederation, the all-wise body that won't admit Franklin exists but presumes to give us orders when it suits their convenience."

"Easy now, General. We were talking about Cherokees."

"So we were, Colonel. Our battle plan for tomorrow remains as is, of course. We'll march at dawn against the Cherokees— three thousand of them, and not one last blasted Spaniard in the whole shebang."

A fine mist made the ground soggy and dampened the spirits of all but the most ardent warriors as the sergeants awakened their men in the hour before dawn. Scouts returning from night patrols brought back the gloomy word that the waters of the Mississippi were boiling and churning, a sure sign that the day would be foul. An order from headquarters forbidding the lighting of fires caused considerable grumbling, but the army ate large quantities of cold breakfast and took extra precautions to keep powder and ammunition dry.

Shortly after a muddy, gray dawn word was passed that the army was to convene in a field on the edge of the forest, and junior officers hustled their commands to the appointed place. General Sevier, looking as though he had enjoyed a long night's rest in a goose-feather bed, addressed the men briefly. They were, he informed them, going into battle against the Cherokee nation. Few understood the subtleties of his remarks, and the vast majority roared their approval of Nolichucky Jack's unquenchable sense of humor. They sobered down a moment later when, according to his custom, the commander outlined his plan for the day.

The army would be divided into three groups, he said. The frontier scouts and a battalion of infantry from the west would take up positions deep in the woods on the north flank, with both units under the command of Colonel Conway. On the south flank, lined up along the riverbank, would be Colonel Charles Robertson's regiment of tough mountain men. Theirs would be the unenviable task of stopping an enemy break-through at any cost. Major George Elholm and his small artillery battery would back up the regiment. In the center was to be the main body, under the personal command of the general and Colonel Jim Robertson.

All three groups, the general explained, would attack at a given signal. Until then absolute silence was to be maintained, both on the march and after the men took up their assigned posi-

295

tions. If the strategy was successful, he said, the foe would be unaware of the presence of an American force until attacked. Then, if the Franks pressed forward with sufficient vigor, it might be possible to cut the larger body of the enemy into smaller pieces and to dispose of these one by one.

No sooner was his address concluded than the rain began to fall in torrents, and the companies formed their lines in ankle-deep slime.

The Nolichucky company enjoyed considerable sport at the expense of Harold Jordan, who, because of his Boston accent, was accused of being a foreigner. But he gave as good as he received, for he knew that the men of the Nolichucky accepted him as one of their number. He was going to fight side by side with honest men who held no grudges against him for his past indiscretion, and he was at peace with himself—more content than he had been in many months.

Ensigns counted noses and tried to hide their undisguised nervousness. Lieutenants raced up and down the ranks, checking on last-minute details with their sergeants and corporals. Captains stood at the heads of their companies and sent messengers ahead to inquire why the lines had not started to move. Of senior officers there was no sign; battalion and regimental commanders were nowhere to be seen.

Then, amid hushed murmurs, General Sevier and Colonel Jim Robertson conducted a whirlwind review of the army, and the mystery of the absent colonels and majors was solved. All of them trotted and splashed through the mud at the heels of the commander in chief and his deputy. Jack Sevier said nothing as he inspected each company, platoon, and squad, but the men knew how he felt and were satisfied. He had worn the same look of eager confidence on the eve of the immortal battle of Kings Mountain, and there were enough veterans of that affair present to remember—and to catch the germ of his present optimism.

But the elements remained indifferent to the drama about to be enacted at the unimpressive site some four hundred or more miles from the delta of the Mississippi River, and a strong west wind joined forces with the driving rain to insure that the army suffered every possible discomfort. The men pulled their collars higher and hunched their shoulders, but colonels and privates, majors and corporals were equally wet and chilled.

Only the two eldest men in the gathering of Franks and North Carolinians seemed appreciative of the weather. Finishing their inspection, General Sevier and Colonel Jim Robertson mounted their horses and took their places at the head of the army. The general nodded to his standard-bearers, and three pennants dipped toward the ground. A split second later the army swung into motion and the silent columns streamed into the woods.

The general blinked involuntarily as a large drop of water fell from a high tree branch and splashed in his eye. He chuckled and leaned toward his old friend. "Grand day, Jim," he said softly.

"Lovely, Jack. Lovely. I've never seen better."

"We could march a brigade of Hessians through brushwood on a day like this, and those Cherokees from Madrid would never hear us."

Colonel Robertson frowned and wiped a trickle of rain water from his chin. "Hope they don't think it's too bad a day for travel. Our boys are raring for scalps today, and they'll be mighty disappointed if they're forced to sit in a downpour without any customers for their knives."

"Don't worry that tired old head of yours, Jim. One of Mel Tyler's scouts was keeping watch from a hill out of sentry range, and he brought back word that the Span—the Cherokees began to break camp almost three hours ago. There'll be a fight for sure today, Jim. But if this rain doesn't let up by noontime, I'll be sorry we haven't petitioned the U. S. Navy for three frigates and an armed brigantine!"

Chapter XX

Corn Tassel, most respected of sages of the tribes west of tne mountains, had long been urging his brethren to make their peace with the white men who streamed through the passes and down the valleys in ever-increasing numbers, and all save the Cherokees had listened and heeded his word. Son of Fiery Plume was happy that he was a Cherokee, happy that the headmen of his village had decided to throw in their lot with the Spaniards who gave them rifles and bolts of cloth and whiskey. He would be a rich man before this gloomy, rainy day ended, Son of Fiery Plume reflected as he streaked through the soggy forest to the command post of the Spanish general, Don Alfonso Galvez.

For day after dull, weary day, Son of Fiery Plume and the other young men of his nation had scouted in advance of the army that slowly made its way north along the banks of the Mother of All Rivers, and until this morning the adventure had been profitless. Now, however, he had something of vital interest to report and would be rewarded beyond his most cherished dreams. He would be taken before the great general himself and would be permitted to kiss the hem of the cape of the Spanish chief, a man so powerful that he not only commanded a huge army but ruled the Floridas and received the homage of many tribes.

The don would bid Son of Fiery Plume to rise and would greet him like a brother, for all the warriors of the Cherokees and all the fighting men of Spain to witness and to marvel. Thereafter Son of Fiery Plume would be a man set apart. On the floor of his house would be thick pelts of beaver and fox. In his war chest would repose a variety of weapons more vast, more imposing than those of any other brave in the valley. And waiting to serve him at any hour of the day or night would be three or four of the most comely, most obedient squaws in all the world.

Son of Fiery Plume rejoiced as he saw a fierce Spanish officer riding toward him at the head of a troop of cavalry. Bowing low with mock humility, Son of Fiery Plume took hold of the white gentleman's reins.

"Oh, noble lord," he cried, "I, Son of Fiery Plume, lay claim to the reward offered by your great King Beyond the Seas and by his general, Don Alfonso the Incomparable. I shall take possession and hold as my own the cloth of many colors, the long rifle and musket, the short gun that fits into the loincloth of a man, the sharp blade with the point like that of a needle. I, Son of Fiery Plume, have found the enemy, lying in wait for this army. I have found the Americans, who hide now in the shadows of the trees, beneath the brush, behind the thick, spreading roots. Take me to your chief that I may receive my reward. Then I will lead you to the place of ambush."

As Janus Elholm peered through the leafy concealment toward the narrow clearing along the riverbank he remembered that Don Alfonso Galvez was too wise a tactician, despite his advanced years, to advertise the presence of his army in the wilderness. Yet a full battalion of Spanish foot troops was marching out of the woods in parade formation. Four abreast they came, their muskets resting on their shoulders, their gait stiff and formal. Most incongruous of all was the presence of eight boys in double file at the head of the column, beating their drums in unison. No army had taken to the field in so flamboyant a manner in more than a quarter of a century, and Janus strongly suspected a trick.

But neither General Sevier nor Colonel Jim Robertson appeared concerned, and although Janus was minded to tell them of his fears, he refrained. Sevier was grinning softly as he crouched behind the trunk of a giant oak, obviously convinced that his strategy was working and that the Spaniards were moving into the trap he had set for them. Colonel Robertson seemed equally unconcerned and whistled to himself under his breath as he loaded the two pistols he would soon fire, one after the other. That was to be the signal for the army of Franklin to swoop down on the unsuspecting foe. The fight gave promise of being too easy, Janus told himself.

Furthermore, every Spanish plan of battle Janus had seen had been drawn up with the tough battalion of Basques in the forefront. Instead, the men who were at this moment making such perfect targets of themselves were a mixed group of Catalonian infantry, militiamen from New Spain, and marines. Something was decidedly amiss, and Janus came to a quick decision. He would speak to Jack Sevier.

Crawling painfully to the heavy tree, he plucked at Sevier's sleeve. "General," he said without preamble, "it is my belief that the Spaniard knows we are here."

The American commander eyed him shrewdly. "What makes you think so, Elholm?"

"My view is compounded of too many factors to explain quickly, sir. But I implore you to bring together again the three elements of your army and to withdraw a safe distance into the woods. Should that which I suspect be true, Don Alfonso will do to us what we have intended to do to him. He will cut each section of our force into small bits at his leisure."

Before Sevier could reply, the entire forest seemed to erupt in a blaze of rifle fire. From every side came the steady pounding of muskets, and in the distance could be heard the deep, crunching

beat of cannon. The Spaniards along the riverbank were not surprised, however, and immediately threw themselves to the
ground and began to fire into the forest too. The army of Franklin was completely surrounded by a force almost double its
strength, and only a miracle could save it from total annihilation.

But General Sevier lost neither his nerve nor his composure.
"Colonel Robertson," he bellowed above the din of fire, "take the
main body and try to join hands with Conway. He has only two
battalions, and he'll be wiped out sure if we don't reinforce him.
Meantime I'll send word to Charley to try to make his way along
the river to us. There seems to be just the one battalion of enemy
holding him back down there, and with any luck he can blast
them out of the way."

Colonel Robertson darted off with an agility that seemed impossible in one of his advanced years. General Sevier watched
him for a second, then turned to Janus. "Elholm," he shouted,
"come with me—and don't stray from my side. Yes, and the next
time you smell out a Spanish trick, speak out—fast! Let's go, boy.
We have a day's work ahead of us."

Had the Spaniards succeeded in their initial attack, or had the
momentum of their drive carried them through the American
lines, the battle would have been ended immediately. But
Charles Robertson's battalions refused to panic and held their
ground. Major George Elholm recovered from his surprise with
astonishing speed, too, and in less than five minutes' time his
small guns were pumping shells into the enemy ranks. One other
factor favored the outnumbered men of Franklin—the battle was
being fought principally in the forests, where the great bulk of
Spanish cavalry was of little value.

Nevertheless, the carnage was heavy, and only the almost
superhuman efforts of Colonel Charles Robertson prevented a
rout—and subsequent collapse. Hastily forming a defense, he organized his units in lines three deep, and when the Spaniards ad-

vanced, his militiamen held their positions. His exposed flank was in danger of buckling under the impact of the enemy assault, but an anonymous sergeant from the Cumberland poured a steady stream of rifle fire and invective at the foe, and so inspired his company that the attack was thrown back.

A small group led by Lieutenant Jackson of Nashville broke out from behind the cover of the trees and started after the retreating Spaniards, but they shortly ran into fire from the principal body of enemy regiments and were forced to withdraw. This brazen, unorthodox maneuver so astonished the dons, however, that Robertson was enabled to pull back in good order. Fortunately, it was no feat of consequence to overrun the sacrificial mixed battalion at the riverbank, and the men from Louisiana quickly surrendered, as did the royal marines. Only the Castilian infantry continued to fight, and those who refused to quit the field were either slaughtered or were forced into the river, where they drowned.

Thus it was that the main body under General Sevier and the principal secondary force under Colonel Charles Robertson became one again. Dozens of volunteer hands pushed Major George Elholm's small cannon forward, too, and the army, despite its losses, remained a fighting force.

It was another matter, though, to make contact with the men of Colonel Henry Conway. The Spaniards had mistakenly assumed that here was the pivotal point of the American position, and wave after wave of infantrymen struck at the beleaguered mountain men. It was blind good luck, in a sense, that the frontiersmen were those against whom the heaviest attack was taking place, for they were best able to absorb punishment. Woodsmen who had stalked and had been stalked in numerous encounters in the Silent Country calmly reloaded their long rifles, wriggled deeper into the thick grass, and fired again at the enemy who was advancing on them in a seemingly endless stream.

Someone had to give way eventually, but the mountain men

were determined not to budge, and so accurate was the collective aim of these buckskin-clad marksmen that the Spaniards lost their appetite for the assault. The front row of militiamen from New Orleans slowed and then broke, and the professional soldiers who backed them up were unable to stem the tide that surged without warning to the rear. This gave Colonel Conway the opportunity for which he and his men had battled so valiantly, and they, too, retreated, taking their wounded and their dead with them.

After forty-five minutes of the most vicious fighting, then, the three parts of the army of Franklin were reunited—at a cost of one hundred killed and almost double that number wounded. At best the situation for the high command was grave; for the Americans found themselves in the selfsame tight box in which they had hoped to trap the Spaniards. A force equipped with superior fire power had them penned up in a restricted area where their ability to maneuver was limited by the presence of trees and where possible retreat was partially blocked by the Mississippi River.

The commanders of the army held a brief conference in a mossy glade while company leaders hastily formed the troops into a hollow square facing the open fields. Colonel Henry Conway wiped his forehead with the back of his sleeve and tightened his belt a notch. "I'm not worried about our lads fighting on until they drop," he muttered. "What bothers me is what will happen afterward. Once we've been eliminated, there'll be nothing but empty land between the dons and our towns and farms. Maybe the Kentucky settlers will take to the field in time."

John Sevier slapped his hand on his thigh. "You can forget any illusions you may have, gentlemen. The Kentucks won't save our families. Not one of their companies has taken to the field, and not one of them will—that is, if what young Elholm assures me is true. And I'm afraid he's an excellent prophet. He says there are traitors in high places in the Kentuck militia, and it looks like he's right. Boone and Shelby would have come to our aid long before this—if they weren't beset by troubles too great to handle."

Chewing on a long stalk of grass, Colonel Jim Robertson shook his head impatiently. "Never mind the Kentucks and their traitors. What'll *we* do *now?*"

There was no reply to his query, and several of the colonels and majors shifted uneasily. Without exception they had faced death many times, but their concern was not for themselves in their present predicament. If they failed to drive the Spaniards south, their wives and children would be easy prey for the legions now massing in the fields for a decisive blow. Unable to find a way out of the dilemma, they looked to their general for salvation. In war and in politics Nolichucky Jack Sevier had led them to victory when defeat had loomed up before them, and their unswerving concerted belief in his ability to save them now was the one positive, cohesive factor in their favor.

The general knew what they were thinking, and the awful responsibility weighed heavily on him. Drawing apart from the others, he walked a short distance down an old deer path and paused at a limestone rock that rose six or seven feet from the edge of a grassy ravine. He gazed at the stone for several minutes, then turned resolutely and strode back to his officers. He stopped short, and they waited for him to speak.

"Gentlemen," General Sevier said softly, "we're in for a mighty hard time. If young Elholm was out there commanding the Spaniards, he'd hit us right off as soon as he could. And that would be the end of us. But I don't think old Galvez is that smart. His basic thinking is defensive, not offensive. We all know of the forts he's built in Pensacola. Very well. We've hurt him this morning, and he's going to take a few hours to lick his wounds—or I miss my guess pretty badly. That gives us a little time.

"And we'll take advantage of that time. Put every man to work.

We'll throw up the stoutest breastworks we can dig. Yes, and I want every officer to do twice as much as his troops. That includes you, gentlemen. And me. We're going to erect a high, deep breastworks. And when the don attacks, we'll hold. We'll take all the punishment he can inflict on us, and then we'll strike back.

"Remember this, gentlemen: our situation is far from hopeless. We have the protection of the forest, and despite the rain our visibility is better than that of the enemy. He can't see us in these woods, and he doesn't know what we're doing. He's in the dark, but we aren't. We know the odds against us, and I say to you that if we face them with courage and resolution, we have a chance of carrying the day. Chance, did I say? We must win, gentlemen. There is no alternative. None whatsoever."

"That's him over there."

A grimy forefinger pointed at Janus, and a weary, dirt-smeared figure hurried toward him. But the Dane did not bother to look up. Stripped to the waist, with his torso wet with perspiration, he was using an old bayonet as a pick, digging it again and again into the ground. He had stopped thinking and was working with such concentrated fury and speed that two militiamen were kept busy scooping up the loose earth with their bare hands and piling it on the rapidly growing breastworks.

"You Janus Elholm?" The voice of the newcomer was flat and unemotional.

"Um." Janus nodded his head but did not break the rhythm of his savage downward bayonet thrusts.

"Man wants to see you."

"Tell him I have no time." The point of the bayonet struck a rock, and Janus moved a few inches to the right.

"It's one of the wounded, bub. He wants to see you. Name is Jordan."

Janus straightened and wiped the sweat from his eyes with the back of his forearm. "All right," he said shortly. "Gilly, you take the bayonet. I shall be back in a moment." He turned to the new arrival. "Where is Jordan?"

"This way." The man started off through the underbrush toward a particularly heavy clump of trees. "His comp'ny was with Conway. They was hurt pretty bad."

"And Jordan?"

"You'll see for yourself, mister. I hope you got a strong stomach. It ain't very pretty where them wounded are."

They walked for several moments in silence, then the man stopped. "He's right in there. You can't miss him."

Janus pushed through a tangle of weeds, skirted around four tall trees, and walked into a different world. High branches formed a natural protective covering over a small, mossy glen. In this miniature amphitheater were lying fifty or more casualties of the morning's encounter. The majority were quiet, enduring their pain in silence. Here and there someone moaned or grunted, but the only sign of activity came from a surgeon and two perspiring assistants, who conversed in low tones as they moved from one prostrate figure to the next. A few of the wounded men were half sitting, half reclining, and one burly frontiersman who wore a heavy, bloody bandage around his head was methodically chewing on a large wad of tobacco despite the obvious effort that such exertion cost him.

It was even darker in the shaded glen than in the other parts of the forest, and it was several minutes before Janus, wandering slowly past rows of the wounded, found the man he was seeking. Harold was lying flat on his back, one hand pillowed under his head. The front of his linen shirt was smeared with a crust of brown, dried blood, and to his left leg was strapped a crude splint of green wood. His face was waxen and ivory pale, and his half-closed eyes were glazed. He lay very still, making no sound.

Janus knelt beside him. "Well, Jordan," he said quietly. "They tried to put you out of the fight, eh?"

Harold opened his eyes and focused them with an effort. "Elholm," he whispered.

"We'll soon have you out of here." Janus was too familiar with war not to know the truth about the wounded man, but he felt at a loss for words.

"No." Harold shook his head feebly, and on his face was stamped the certain knowledge that he was dying. "Roz," he muttered. "Roz . . ."

A lump formed in Janus's throat. "I'll see her for you," he said, forcing the words through clenched teeth. "I'll tell her—whatever you wish."

"Roz," Harold said loudly, his voice suddenly clear and penetrating. "She's yours. Not mine. Roz—I——" He raised his head an inch or two, then slumped back and was motionless.

Janus studied him silently for an instant, then reached out gently and with thumb and forefinger closed Harold's eyes.

Wishing fervently for a drink, the Dane stood up and walked slowly out of the glen. His head was slumped low, and his clenched fists were jammed into the pockets of his buckskin trousers. He failed to notice that the rain was stopping and that here and there a bird was beginning to whistle cheerfully, unmindful of the coming slaughter that man was planning and preparing for his fellow man. The thought that Harold Jordan was dead and that Rosalind was now free ran through his mind again and again, but there was no sense of elation or even of release. The wistful longing, the terrible loneliness that had been the last expression in Harold's eyes would remain with him to the end of his days.

A heavy hand clapped on Janus's bare shoulder. "I been lookin' fer ye. I heard tell ye jined up with us'ns."

The Dane raised his head and saw the powerful frame and grinning face of Malachi Stevens. In spite of his inner turmoil, he smiled. "Stevens," he said, "I'm glad to see you."

"I been lookin' fer ye. I been in free-fer-alls with a heap o' men, and I know a fighter when I see one. B'twixt us, ye and me c'n lick all livin' hell out o' them damn foreigners."

Inexplicably Janus felt his spirits lift. To Malachi Stevens he himself was no alien. "It is good," he replied slowly, "for a man to go into battle with a partner in whom he has confidence. Between us, you and I will drive the damned foreigners into the sea."

It was late afternoon when the Spanish artillery opened a concentrated barrage on the forest position of the Americans. The sun had come out for an hour or more and had then disappeared again behind thick banks of heavy, scudding clouds. Meantime the American injured had found time to bind their wounds, and the dead had been buried. The need to hold, regardless of cost, had been carefully explained to every militiaman, and all had long since taken up positions behind breastworks and trees.

Only the cavalry remained in the clear and lined up along the bank of the Mississippi. If all else failed, the horsemen would be expected to make a final, desperate stand there. George Elholm's small three-pounders were emplaced along the shore, too, but the guns were not manned. General Sevier had reasoned that the cannon would be of little value in the close combat that would develop, and might cause more casualties among the Franks than in the ranks of the Spaniards. So the artillerymen had picked up the rifles of fallen comrades and had joined the infantrymen, with instructions to fall back to the river and their cannon only if the situation called for such a move.

The majority of Spanish iron balls whistled and screamed overhead, and Janus, hugging a thick tree trunk, reflected happily that the aim of Spanish cannoneers was notoriously bad. It had been little better, as he remembered, in Italy two seasons ago. But at that time he had watched the dons' handiwork from behind the thick, protecting stone wall of a duke's castle. . . .

For almost thirty minutes the Spaniards poured iron balls over the American position, with the majority of the potentially destructive missiles falling harmlessly into the Mississippi. No one stirred within the forest itself, and Don Alfonso must have believed that the enemy was properly softened for the final attack, for no sooner was the barrage lifted than the Basque battalion trotted into the open and headed for the American lines. Behind them came Castilians and Louisiana militiamen in long, orderly rows.

Acting under strict orders, the Franks held their fire, ignoring the bullets that whistled over their heads. General Sevier, who had been cannily awaiting the appropriate moment, at last blew a single blast on a high-pitched, shrill whistle. The Basque assault troops were at that second no more than fifteen yards from the breastworks.

Sevier's men responded to his command at once, and the forest came alive. Rifles, muskets, and pistols sounded simultaneously, and the Basque line wavered, then halted. There was no diminution of the deadly American fire as militiamen reloaded their weapons with a skill and speed born of the knowledge that on their accuracy depended the lives of their loved ones.

Slowly the Basques began to retreat, but even under pressure they did not waver. However, the Louisiana and Castilian infantrymen who had been advancing on their heels were forced to move back, too, and these units lacked the stamina and strength of the tough shock troops. One company broke ranks, then another, and a stampede born of panic was under way. Professional soldiers and raw conscript militiamen from New Orleans raced side by side to escape from the woods where death awaited them.

General Sevier gave the order to counterattack, and the North Carolina cavalry of Major Eb Tipton rode into the clear and gave chase to the retreating Spaniards. While this small force managed to inflict considerable damage on the enemy, it was insufficiently large to turn the tide of battle permanently in favor of the Americans, and by the time the Franks had climbed over their breastworks and formed into compact lines, the frantic efforts of Don Alfonso's colonels to bring order out of chaos were beginning to show results.

The Basque battalion and the Castilians were re-forming into squares, and the legion of Don Alfonso was once more becoming a cohesive fighting unit. The American infantry, led by a wild-eyed Henry Conway, broke into the open fields just in time to face a new wall of Spaniards.

Janus, trotting beside Malachi Stevens at Colonel Conway's heels, took in the situation in a single, swift glance. The enemy still outnumbered the Franks, and if the counterassault was halted by Don Alfonso's musketmen, it would be a fairly simple tactic for the Spaniards to renew their attack and to annihilate their foes. Therefore, the don must be allowed no time to complete the regrouping of his battalion.

But Colonel Conway understood none of this as he halted, blinking in surprise. A moment ago he had been under the impression that he had been pursuing a scattered foe; now he was confronted by massed rows of black-and-yellow uniforms. The men from the Holston and the Cumberland and the Nolichucky slowed their pace, too, and Janus saw that in a few moments the American opportunity to win the field would be utterly, devastatingly lost.

Wasting not one instant, Janus brandished his sword high over his head. "Come on, you—you Yankee bastards!" he shouted over his shoulder, and headed straight for the new Spanish line. A bellow of triumph sounded directly behind him, and out of the corner of his eye Janus saw Malachi Stevens, his face red and his long hair flying, sprinting in the same direction.

First a scattering of individuals, then squads, and finally complete companies took up the cry and ran across the grassy plain that separated the two forces. The new Spanish line, not yet

olid, began to buckle under the attack, for the Americans fired
s they ran. But Don Alfonso was not one to flinch, and he sent
is cavalry hurtling into the melee.

Where there had been two distinct, separate forces only seconds
efore, there was now a snarled and twisted arena of individual
ombat. Men of both armies fired until their ammunition was
one; then they fought with their knives, rifle butts, and—lacking
eapons—bare fists.

Janus had long since exhausted his supply of bullets and was
acking and cutting with his long sword whenever and wherever
e saw a Spanish uniform. A sudden sense of imminent disaster
ade him look around, and he saw four Spaniards bearing down
pon him. He turned and set himself for their charge, and as he
id so a shout of harsh glee sounded in his ear.

"We c'n take fifty o' them dandies!" Malachi Stevens's face
as a study in almost maniacal delight as he brandished his long
fle over his head as though it were a light club. Grasping it by
e muzzle and swinging it in a wide arc, he advanced toward the
emy quartet.

Janus kept out of reach of the heavy oak rifle butt and, circling
arily, approached the Spaniards from the side, jabbing and
inting with his sword. "I'll take these two, Mal!" he called.
The others are yours!"

While the Castilians fought valiantly with their bayonets, they
ould not cope with the Dane's darting blade or with Stevens's
urderous rifle butt. The most aggressive of the Spaniards was
e first to go down under the impact of the double assault; then
vo others fell almost at the same instant. The remaining
astilian quickly lost his lust for combat and fled, and although
nus or Stevens might have pursued him, they made no attempt
catch him but merely looked at each other and laughed.

The incident was typical of what was taking place all over the
eld, for the aroused and inspired militiamen of John Sevier bean to drive their enemies before them like so many cattle. For

the last time that day the conscripts from New Orleans took t
their heels and fled, and the Basques and Catalonians, believin
that their cause was lost, followed.

The growing darkness made it impossible for the Franks t
chase the vanishing foe across open, rolling country dotted wit
patches of wood, and the regimental officers called their troops t
a halt. Watching the fleeing Spaniards disappear, every son c
Franklin knew that although the battle had not ended in
definite military victory it had accomplished its primary purpose
the power of Spain had been broken and her legions had bee
halted; the American frontier was safe.

Malachi Stevens pumped Janus's hand and spat in the dire
tion of the prostrate body of a Castilian lance corporal. "Com
next jamboree time," he said, "ye 'n' me are goin' t' have us
free-fer-all. Yes, sir—'n' if ye practice right good b'twixt now '
then, damn if mebbe ye won't beat the tarnation out o' me. . .
How about a drink o' whiskey? I know where I c'n get one if
sartain sergeant ain't been kilt."

"Save a portion of the drink for me," Janus yawned. "I'll
around to collect it later. Although I have often done foolis
things in my life, I hope I am never so foolish as to risk my nec
against a champion—a real champion—from Franklin." Shakin
hands again, he wandered off toward the trees.

Colonel Jim Robertson nursed a wound in his shoulder an
a bad bruise on his right leg as he limped painfully toward h
general. "Jack, you rascal," he called, "you've done it! You'
whipped the dons!"

"I?" replied Sevier. "I've done nothing. I'm a lucky begga
Jim, and so are you. We've won because our lads fought as
never knew they could, every last one of them." He looked aroun
the littered field, and his voice softened. "Bronson over ther
and the Keene brothers. Bill Cocke's nephew—what's his nam
—and that big storekeeper from Jonesboro who always tries
sell you a short measure of wheat flour. Your brother and E

Tipton—and my own sons. Yes, and that wild Dane who led our last charge at exactly the right moment."

Suddenly he pointed and began to laugh hoarsely. Propped up against the rotted stump of a tree was Janus Elholm. His legs were sprawled out before him, and his head drooped so low it almost touched his knees. His sword was at his side, and his empty pistols were still jammed into his belt. But he was unaware of the admiration being bestowed on him by the expedition's commanders, for he was sound asleep.

The army of Franklin broke up after it reached the big bend of the Tennessee River east of Chickasaw Bluffs. The Holston men were anxious to hurry home for their spring planting, while the frontiersmen preferred to linger in the wild, untamed forests, where game was now plentiful. General Sevier headed straight for his plantation on the Nolichucky, and most of the other leaders traveled their separate paths.

But the Nashville contingent continued to march together, and by common consent they slowed their pace to that of Colonel Jim Robertson, who knew he was tired but could not bring himself to say so. Had the three bedraggled companies exerted themselves, they might have arrived home on Friday night, but it was Sunday noon before the spire of the Davidson County courthouse came into sight.

Warriors who had previously sped through the town at a faster clip had brought the good news of victory, and Nashville was waiting for her sons. A church bell began to peal, and someone set off a string of firecrackers on the roof of the Blue Grass Inn. But there was no triumphal procession into the center of town, for the soldiers shed their military status and became husbands and fathers again; one by one they left the column and hurried down familiar roads to their homes.

Janus plodded along methodically, wearily, in the thinning ranks, and the courthouse loomed directly ahead when he suddenly shook himself and dropped out of line. He turned left, then right, and walked with an ever-slower step, not thinking and not daring to think.

At last he saw the roof and chimney of the Dolson house through a curtain of trees. He wanted to stop but could not, and a moment later the house itself came into view. There, standing in the doorway, was Rosalind. She was dressed in yellow, and in her hair she wore a sprig of fresh spring flowers. He could see that there were tears in her eyes.

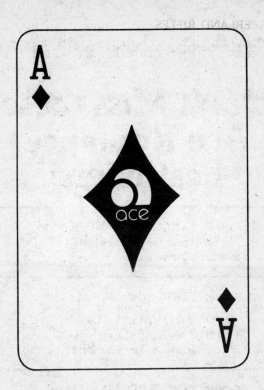

There are a lot more
where this one came from!

ORDER your FREE catalog of ACE paperbacks here. We have hundreds of inexpensive
books where this one came from priced from
75¢ to $2.50. Now you can read all the books
you have always wanted to at tremendous
savings. Order your *free* catalog of ACE
paperbacks now.

Don't Miss these Ace Romance Bestsellers!

———— **#75157 SAVAGE SURRENDER** $1.95
The million-copy bestseller by Natasha Peters,
author of Dangerous Obsession.

———— **#29802 GOLD MOUNTAIN** $1.95

———— **#88965 WILD VALLEY** $1.95
Two vivid and exciting novels by
Phoenix Island author, Charlotte Paul.

———— **#80040 TENDER TORMENT** $1.95
A sweeping romantic saga in the
Dangerous Obsession tradition.

Available wherever paperbacks are sold or use this coupon.

D.E. STEVENSON ROMANCES

"Finding a re-issued novel by D. E. Stevenson is like coming upon a Tiffany lamp in Woolworth's. It is not 'nostalgia'; it is the real thing."

—THE NEW YORK TIMES
BOOK REVIEW

ENTER THE WORLD OF D. E. STEVENSON IN THESE DELIGHTFUL ROMANTIC NOVELS:

AMBERWELL
THE BAKER'S DAUGHTER
BEL LAMINGTON
THE BLUE SAPPHIRE
CELIA'S HOUSE
THE ENCHANTED ISLE
FLETCHERS END
GERALD AND ELIZABETH
GREEN MONEY
THE HOUSE ON THE CLIFF
KATE HARDY
LISTENING VALLEY
THE MUSGRAVES
SPRING MAGIC
SUMMERHILLS
THE TALL STRANGER

IMPROVE YOUR HOME AND GARDEN WITH THESE HELPFUL GUIDES FROM CHARTER BOOKS

HEALTH AND BEAUTY—ADVICE FROM THE EXPERTS